Praise for Jack Whyte

"Whyte's descriptions, astonishingly vivid, of this ancient and mystical era ring true, as do his characters. Whyte shows why Camulod was such a wonder, demonstrating time and again how persistence, knowledge, and empathy can help push back the darkness of ignorance to build a shining future—a lesson that has not lost its value for being centuries old and shrouded in the mists of myth and magic."
—*Publishers Weekly*

Praise for *Uther*, the newest book in Jack Whyte's acclaimed series, The Camulod Chronicles

"As readers follow the rise of Uther from grandson of the king of the Britons to king himself, they are drawn into a world of battle and lust, where the former leaves little time for the latter. As Whyte waves off the fog of fantasy and legend surrounding the Arthurian story, he renders characters and events real and plausible."
—*Booklist*

"Jack Whyte's Camulod Chronicles are a stunning interpretation of the Arthurian legend. . . . A powerful love story with compelling characters."
—*Romantic Times* (4 stars)

Praise for *The Skystone*, Book One of The Camulod Chronicles

"It's taken 1,500 years to work through, but now we have the Arthurian legend the way the noncoms saw it: tough and gritty and compelling."
—Tom Shippey, former professor of English Language and Medieval English Literature, University of Leeds

"Strong characters and fastidious attention to detail make this a good choice for most libraries and a sure draw for fans of the Arthurian cycle." —*Library Journal*

"It's one of the most interesting historical novels that I've ever read and I've read plenty." —Marion Zimmer Bradley

"An interesting (and largely plausible) historical foundation from which the Arthurian legend might have risen . . . A rousing historical adventure, full of hand-to-hand combat, hidden treasures, and last-minute escapes, a refreshing change from the many quasi-historical, politically correct Arthurians out there." —*Locus*

"Richly detailed history . . . Whyte's finely wrought background make the tale more dazzling than any fantastic setting possibly could." —*Hackensack Record*

THE SINGING SWORD

THE CAMULOD CHRONICLES

JACK WHYTE

A Tom Doherty Associates Book
New York

THE SINGING SWORD

Copyright © 1996 by Jack Whyte

This book is printed on acid-free paper.

Map by Ellisa Mitchell

A Forge Book
Published by Tom Doherty Associates, LLC
175 Fifth Avenue
New York, NY 10010

www.tor.com

Forge® is a registered trademark of Tom Doherty Associates, LLC.

Library of Congress Cataloging-in-Publication Data

Whyte, Jack.
    The singing sword / Jack Whyte.
        p. cm.—(The Camulod chronicles ; bk. 2)
    "A Tom Doherty Associates book."
    ISBN 0-312-85292-4 (hc)
    ISBN 0-765-30458-9 (pbk)
    1. Great Britain—History—Roman period, 55 B.C.–449 A.D.—Fiction.
    2. Romans—Great Britain—Fiction. I. Title. II. Series: Whyte, Jack. Camulod chroni-
cles ; bk. 2

PR9199.3.W4589 S56 1996
813'.54—dc20   96-19966
                                                      CIP

Printed in the United States of America

0 9 8

For Beverley . . .
my personal Jean Armour

INTRODUCTION

THE SINGING SWORD is a work of fiction, but the historical background against which the action of the story takes place is very real, and the major political events occurred as described herein. As we approach the turn of a new century, few of us understand much of what went on at the birth of the twentieth. The story of *The Singing Sword* is set at the turn of the fifth century—fifteen hundred years ago—and most people have no idea at all what life could have been like in those days.

Some circumstances, occurrences, words and expressions in the narrative will be unfamiliar to modern readers. As the author, I could have changed or "modernized" all of these, but I have opted often to retain them in the interest of authenticity. Measurements, for example, were not as precise then as ours are now: seconds and minutes, inches and yards, were unknown to the Romans. They spoke in terms of heartbeats and moments, handspans and paces. A Roman mile was a thousand (*mille*) paces long, slightly less than a modern kilometre.

For the convenience of modern readers with little knowledge of life as it was at the turn of the fifth century, I have added, at the rear of the book, a section dealing with the Roman Empire, its armies, the early Christians, and the names of the people in this story, including a guide to pronunciation of the classical equivalents of John and Jane Doe. A map of Roman Britain appears on page 11.

THE LEGEND OF THE SKYSTONE

Out of the night sky there will fall a stone
That hides a maiden born of murky deeps,
A maid whose fire-fed, female mysteries
Shall give life to a lambent, gleaming blade,
A blazing, shining sword whose potency
Breeds warriors. More than that,
This weapon will contain a woman's wiles
And draw dire deeds of men; shall name an age;
Shall crown a king, called of a mountain clan
Who dream of being spawned from dragon's seed;
Fell, forceful men, heroic, proud and strong,
With greatness in their souls.
This king, this monarch, mighty beyond ken,
Fashioned of glory, singing a song of swords,
Misting with magic madness mortal men,
Shall sire a legend, yet leave none to lead
His host to triumph after he be lost.
But death shall ne'er demean his destiny who,
Dying not, shall ever live and wait to be recalled.

PLACE NAMES

The land the Romans called Britain was only the land we know today as England. Scotland, Ireland and Wales were separate and known respectively as Caledonia, Hibernia and Cambria. They were not recognized as part of the province of Britain.

The ancient towns of Roman Britain are still there, but they all have English names now. What follows is a guide to phonetic pronunciation of Roman place names, with their modern equivalents.

Londinium	[Lon-dinny-um]	London
Verulamium	[Verr-you-lame-eeyum]	St. Albans
Alchester		
Glevum	[Glev-vum]	Gloucester
Aquae Sulis	[Ack-way Soo-liss]	Bath
Lindinis	[Linn-dinnis]	Ilchester
Sorviodunum	[Sorr-vee-yode-inum]	Old Sarum
Venta Belgarum	[Venta Bell-gah-rum]	Winchester
Noviomagus	[Novvy-oh-maggus]	Chichester
Durnovaria	[Durr-no-varr-eya]	Dorchester
Isca Dumnoniorum	[Isska Dumb-nonny-orum]	Exeter
The Colony		
Camulodunum	[Ca-moo-loadin-um]	Colchester
Lindum	[Lin-dum]	Lincoln
Eboracum	[Eh-borra-cum]	York
Mamucium	[Mah-moochy-um]	Manchester
Dolaucothi	[Doh-loh-cothee]	Welsh Gold Mines
Durovernum	[Doo-rove-err-num]	Canterbury
Regulbium	[Re-goolby-um]	Reculver
Rutupiae	[Roo-too-pee-ay]	Richborough
Dubris	[Doo-briss]	Dover
Lemanis	[Leh-mann-iss]	Lympne
Anderita	[An-der-reeta]	Pevensey

THE
SINGING
SWORD

PROLOGUE: 387 A.D.

THE TRIBUNE RECOGNIZED the first signs from more than a mile away, just as the road dropped down from the ridge to enter the trees: a whirlpool of hawks and carrion-eaters, spiralling above the treetops of the forest ahead of him. With a harsh command to his centurion to pick up the pace of his men, the officer kicked his horse forward, uncaring that he was leaving his infantry escort far behind. The swirling birds meant death; their numbers meant that they were above a clearing in the forest; and their continuing flight meant that they were afraid to land. Probably because of wolves, he guessed. The tribune lowered the face-protector of his helmet to guard himself from whipping twigs and took his horse into the trees at a full gallop, sensing that all danger of ambush or opposition was long gone.

He heard wolves fighting among themselves while he was still far distant from them, and he kicked his horse to even greater speed, shouting at the top of his voice and making the maximum possible noise to distract them from their grisly feast. He had little doubt about what they were eating.

As he burst into the clearing, the wolves crowded together, bellies low to the ground, snarling and slavering as they faced the newcomer. He put his horse at them without hesitation, drawing his short-sword and slashing at them, his horse using its hooves in its own battle. The snarling fury of the pack quickly became a crescendo of yelps of pain and fear as horse and rider laid about them, and soon one, and then all of the lean, grey scavengers broke off the fight and fled to the protection of the bushes that surrounded the clearing.

When they had gone, out of sight among the bushes and safely beyond his reach, the tribune looked around at the scene he had ridden into. The clearing was dominated by one massive, ancient oak tree that had an arrangement of ropes and pulleys strung across one of its huge branches. One of these ropes reached to a ring fastened to a heavy stake that had been driven deep into the ground. The condition of the ground around the stake—the grass trodden flat and dead and scattered haphazardly with piles of human excrement—showed that someone had been confined there for many days. The bodies of three men, one of them absolutely naked, sprawled on the dusty, blood-spattered ground. Flies swarmed everywhere, attracted, like the birds and the wolves, by the smell of sun-warmed blood. The two clothed bodies had both been badly bitten about the face by the wolves, particularly

15

the younger of the two, a blond man whose neck and throat had been slashed by a sword almost deeply enough to decapitate him.

The naked man lay face down, his left arm extended and ripped open on the underside, close to the shoulder, where one of the wolves had been chewing at it. There was another clear set of tooth-marks on the body's right thigh, although the bite had not been ripped away. The only blood visible on this corpse was pooled beneath it.

Incongruously, a rolled parchment scroll lay pinned beneath the out-stretched arm of the naked body, and the tribune idly wondered what it contained. He threw his leg over his horse's neck and slid easily to the ground, where he collected the scroll, carefully making sure no blood touched it. That done, he rolled the corpse easily onto its back and gazed at the massive, eloquently fatal stab wound in the centre of its chest, just below the peak of the rib-cage. He snorted through his nostrils, then prised open the seal on the rolled parchment and began to read, whispering the words to himself to clarify the sense of them as he deciphered the densely packed characters. After the first few sentences, he stiffened and lifted his eyes to look at the dead man at his feet, then squatted, picked up the corpse's wrist and felt for a pulse. There was none. He dropped the hand, stood erect again and contin-ued to read.

The sound of his men approaching at a dead run brought the tribune's head up. As they broke from the tree-lined path and drew up in two ranks facing him, he ordered them to spread out and chase away the wolves hiding in the undergrowth, offering a silver *denarius* for any wolf killed. The soldiers scattered enthusiastically to the chase, their centurion with them. The tribune watched them until they were out of sight, then returned to his interrupted reading, his lips once again moving almost soundlessly as he worked his way through the document. When he reached the end, he made a clicking sound with his tongue, glanced again at the naked corpse and then read through the entire scroll a second time, scanning the words more quickly this time, his face expressionless until he reached the end again, when his brow creased in a slight frown. He folded the scroll carefully several times, creasing the edges sharply to reduce the bulk of the packet thus formed, and tucked it securely beneath his cuirass. By the time his men returned to the clearing, he had remounted his horse and was deep in thought.

From the corner of his eye he saw the centurion approach him and asked what he wanted.

The centurion nodded towards the naked corpse, a look of uncertainty on his face. "What d'you want us to do, sir? With the bodies?" He cleared his throat nervously. "Is it him, sir? The Procurator?"

The tribune took his time in answering, but when he did speak, he pitched his voice so that the men standing silently at attention could all hear him.

"Am I in debt to anyone for bounty on those wolves?"

Several of the men shook their heads along with their centurion. The wolves had all escaped. The tribune looked all around the clearing, tacitly inviting his men to do the same.

"I have no idea, at this stage, what happened here," he said next, "although any man with a brain could probably make an accurate assessment simply by looking around him. The man with no clothes obviously escaped from bondage beneath the big tree, there. You can see the scabs on his wrists, and the ropes and tackle they bound him with, and the trampled area where he was confined. You can also see from the piles of human dung, whoever these other people were, they showed him no humanity. It seems evident that he loosed himself—broke free, somehow—snatched a sword and managed to kill two of his captors before being killed himself. Whoever these abductors of his were, they allowed themselves to grow fatally careless."

"Your pardon, Tribune!" The centurion, whose gaze had drifted to the naked corpse, was frowning and now moved quickly to kneel by the body. Narrow-eyed, he slipped his fingers underneath the chin, pressing gently with finger and thumb beneath the points of the jaw where, against all reasonable expectation, he discovered a very faint but quite regular pulse. The man was alive. The wide-eyed centurion informed the tribune, who frowned as he heard the words.

"Alive? He can't be! Are you sure?" He swung towards his troops and pointed at two of them. "You two, use your spears and tents to make a litter, quickly!"

As the soldiers scrambled to their work, he turned back to the centurion.

"I shall answer your impertinent question this time, simply to discourage any others. It is not for such as you to be curious about diplomatic matters, Centurion, but I suppose, under the circumstance, it is understandable enough. The answer is no. We were called out to search for the Procurator of South Britain, but these abductors were apparently as stupid as they were careless. This man is not the missing Procurator. He is not Claudius Seneca— doesn't even resemble him, apart from the broken nose. I look more like Claudius Seneca than this man does, which is only natural, I suppose, since Claudius Seneca is my father's brother. Mistaken identity. Stupid, as I said. They took the wrong man."

He turned back to where the two soldiers were constructing a serviceable stretcher. "I don't know who he is, but I want you to take the utmost care of this man. Carry him gently, one man to each arm of the litter, and I'll flog any man who bumps him. He deserves to live, if only because of the fight he put up." He looked at the rest of his men, silently gauging their response to his words. Apart from the sullenness caused by his threat, their expressions were disinterested. They had accepted his assertion completely and without curiosity.

"All right, then," he snapped. "Let's get this man to a military sick bay as quickly as we can. But I want these other two bodies brought in, too, for identification. Let's move!"

By the time the litter was ready for the injured man and the procession had set out on its journey back to the barracks at Aquae Sulis, the spa town the local Celts called Bath, no one in the party even remembered that the Tribune had been reading a parchment when they'd reached the clearing.

BOOK ONE

COLONISTS

I

A BROKEN SHUTTER banged somewhere. I could hear it clearly over the howling wind and the hissing roar of the driven rain. It was almost dark. I could barely make out the shapes of the two men flattened against the wall on either side of the door of the one-room stone hut across the narrow street from me. To my left, two more men flanked the door of the hut I was leaning against, and there were twelve more men similarly placed at the other six buildings that lined the narrow street. My reserve of thirty-four men was split into two groups, one at either end of the village.

At forty-eight, I was *far* too old for this kind of nonsense.

I stood with my shoulders pressed against the wall, my sodden tunic clammy cold against my back. I raised my hand in a useless attempt to clear streaming rain-water from my eyes, and my waterlogged cape was a dead weight dragging at my arm. I cursed quietly.

A dim yellow glow appeared as somebody lit a lamp in the hut across the way, and then a quavering, moaning scream rose above the wind. I gave the signal—one blast on my horn—and my men went in, bursting through the doors, their swords and daggers drawn. House-cleaning can be brutal, dirty work.

I looked down at the dead man at my feet. The rain had washed most of the blood away, but he still looked dreadful. I guessed an axe had killed him. His open eyes were glazed in the fading light.

One of my men reappeared, silhouetted against the light in the doorway opposite me, wiping his sword on a rag. He leaned out into the street, and though I heard nothing, I saw him tense and open his mouth in a shout. Then he was running up the narrow street. I cursed my age and my bad leg and thrust myself away from the wall, forcing myself into a lumbering run, only now aware of the fight going on in the street about thirty paces from me. The weight of my cloak was awful. I fumbled at the clasp and felt the burden fall away, and then I was in the middle of the fight.

I remember little of the tussle itself, but with me, that is a far from unusual state of affairs. Images are all that remain in my memory: a bare neck with a prominent Adam's apple, and then blood spouting as I jerk my sword point out of it—no memory of the stab; the feeling of a living body under my feet and then my braced arm, up to the wrist in mud because my crippled leg has let me down again and I've fallen; the crotch of a man whose sheepskin-wrapped legs are criss-crossed with cloth bindings, and my blade again, taking away his manhood; and a face, wide-mouthed and staring-eyed, and hands with no strength clutching at my sword, trying to pull it out of their owner's breast. All this I recall in silence. There is no noise, no screaming—no sound of any kind.

When it was over, I was badly winded, puffing for breath like an old man. I leaned over, hands on my knees, and hung my head, sobbing to clear my chest.

"Commander Varrus? Are you all right?"

I knew the voice; it belonged to young Kyril, one of my lieutenants. I nodded my head as clearly as I could in that position and he left me, moving on to check the others. Gradually I became aware of my hands, gripping my knees. Neither held a weapon. I had no sword, and no memory of dropping it. I blinked my eyes clear of rainwater and saw, by the darkness of blood on my right wrist and hand, that I was wounded. I straightened up, feeling no pain, and touched my right hand with my left. My hand responded, but strangely. My whole arm felt numb. I moved my left hand up along my arm, and I felt the cut—just above the elbow, and bleeding fast. My stomach lurched and I puked—my normal reaction after a battle, and one that usually left me feeling better. But this time, as I straightened up from retching, it seemed to me I saw a light, somewhere ahead of me, spinning in the strangest fashion and coming towards me at a roaring speed. And that was all I saw.

They picked me up out of the mud in the roadway and carried me to one of the huts, and I was out of my mind for more than a week.

My wound, on its own, was not too serious, although there is no such thing as a dismissible battle wound. Some whoreson had swiped me with an axe that had no edge. The weight alone had dug what little edge the thing had into the flesh and had broken my upper arm in what the medics call a twig-fracture. At my age, it's a wonder the whole bone didn't shatter. At least, that's what I thought then. Now I know that I was only mellowing into my prime in those days. But I bled a lot, they told me later: a sullen, angry bleeding that worried them because it would not stop. And on top of that, I'd caught pneumonia from the soaking. For a while my men thought they were going to lose me.

I still remember the corpse that lay at my feet that night. If the axe that hit me had been as sharp as the one that hit him, I would not be telling this story today. Of course, much of the story would not have happened.

My name is Gaius Publius Varrus, and I am an ironsmith and a weapons-maker. I was born and raised in Colchester, in East Britain close to Londinium, the imperial administrative centre of the Province of Britain, and it was to Colchester I returned to reopen my grandfather's smithy after I was crippled in an ambush during the Invasion of 367 and invalided out of the legions.

During my years as a soldier, I had met Caius Britannicus, a wealthy nobleman, a patrician Roman of ancient lineage. He first came into my life as a young tribune who saved my skin, then later as a Commanding Officer whose life I saved, and he finally ended up as a Roman senator, a proconsul

of Rome and my brother-in-law and dearest friend. My friendship with Britannicus, however, had made his enemies my enemies, particularly one family,
the wealthy and powerful imperial bankers, the Senecas, who had feuded
bloodily and bitterly with the Britannicus family for generations.

That adopted enmity brought me to violent, personal confrontation with
Claudius, the youngest of the six Seneca brothers. We fought, and I scarred
him for life. After that, I had to remove myself and my affairs permanently—
and hurriedly—out of the way of Claudius Seneca's wrath. I travelled west
to the rich farmlands below the spa town of Aquae Sulis to live at Caius's
villa.

On my arrival there, my whole life changed. I met and married Luceiia
Britannicus, and she showed me where to find something I had been dreaming
about for most of my life: a stone made of extraordinary metal, which I called
the skystone. I smelted the stone and, from the metal it contained, sculpted
a crude statue of Coventina, the Celtic goddess of water, to commemorate
the struggle I had had to salvage the stone from the bottom of a lake. I called
it my Lady of the Lake. My main intent was to preserve the metal in dignity,
rather than leave it to rust as a plain, raw ingot until I should find a purpose
for it. Someday, I knew, I would make a sword from that same metal, but I
wasn't ready yet.

Someday, too, we would have need of that sword—and hundreds like it,
if Caius's ideas about the disintegration of the Empire ever came to pass.
He believed the Empire was dying rapidly. He was convinced that someday
soon—in the foreseeable future—the legions would be withdrawn from Britain to defend the Motherland against invasion. When that happened, we,
the people of Britain, would be left alone and defenseless, with nothing to
rely on but our own strengths.

I remember that when I first heard Caius voice this idea, it struck me as
being too ludicrous for words. The single greatest truth in the world was that
Rome was eternal! It could never fall. But as the years went by, the signs
Caius had warned of, every one of them, began to come thick and fast, so
that I finally came to believe that the Empire, like the fabric of most things
ancient, was grown thin and rotten.

Armed thereafter with the zeal of all new converts, I threw myself whole-
heartedly into Caius's plans to fortify and defend the beautiful villa properties
on which he and his friends lived. I worked as hard as any man, and harder
than most, to hasten the building of a stone-walled fort on top of the ancient
Celtic hill fort behind the Villa Britannicus and to make weapons and armour
for the young men, the trainee soldiers of our private little Colony.

We knew from the outset, of course, that everything we were doing was
illegal. It was treasonous to build a private fortress and to train a private
army, and discovery of what we were about could bring death and ruin on
all of us, women and children included. In all things military, and in all
aspects of life governing the provisioning of soldiers to protect and serve the
rule of law and the established order, every able-bodied man and boy within

the Empire owed his primary, dedicated allegiance to the Emperor alone. The Emperor's will and rights were paramount. No private citizen could withhold his services from the legions, nor could any man or any group, no matter how endowed with wealth or station, maintain a private, armed force within the Empire's bounds. We knew all that, and we ignored it, for we knew also that the Empire was dying, and we knew the Emperor was not one man but three, and sometimes four. Most of all, however, we knew our lives, our own survival as a people, depended on our preparations for the chaos that would come. And so we toiled to build our fortress, and we trained and armed our men.

It was the search for iron for new weapons that had led us out of the Colony, and into the confrontation in which I was wounded.

I opened my eyes eventually in a small, smelly hut and realized that for some time I had been hearing a skylark singing, although I had not been listening to it. I lay there on my back for a few heartbeats, feeling bleary-eyed and *itchy*; my whole body itched, including my face. I raised my hand to scratch my chin and passed out from the pain.

I could not have been unconscious for more than a few moments. The bird was still singing when I opened my eyes again, the room was unchanged. I still itched, and my arm was on fire. God, it hurt!

I tried to remember what had happened on that dismal wintry day.

We had been up and on the road in driving rain well before dawn. It had rained all night long and the dawn took a long time to arrive through the slate-grey skies. We had eaten a breakfast of dried meat, dried corn and dried peas on the move, hunched and miserable under the lashing downpour.

I was riding my grey stallion, Germanicus, named after an ancestral cousin of Caius Britannicus. I had chosen the name deliberately, pointing out to Caius that if he could ride my back mercilessly and whip me into carrying out his every whim, then I would do the like to his cousin. Six of my men were mounted, too; their job was to herd the horses we had collected on our journey. The remainder marched like the infantry they were, slogging through puddles with long-suffering sighs and muttered curses. We had six four-wheeled wagons in our train, three loaded with iron ingots from the Weald, two filled with salt boiled from the sea and compressed into blocks, and one commissary wagon.

We were far from home, and had been on the road for four weeks. We had left our Colony, close by the Mendip Hills, and headed east until we hit the road running north to Aquae Sulis. From that point on we had travelled all the way to our present location on the solid, paved roads built by Caesar's legions. Twelve miles south of Aquae Sulis, we had swung around to the south-east again and passed through Sorviodunum and Venta Belgarum, stopping outside both towns without entering. From Venta we swung directly south to Noviomagus, taking less than two days to make this last leg of our outward journey.

Our passage attracted much attention. This was the first time that we had come this way, and most of the people we met on the road took us for regular troops. One night long ago, by a fire at Stonehenge, Caius Britannicus had said that he might change the colour of our uniforms. He had said it in jest, but the Celts who were his audience did not know that. They believed him, and their king, Ullic, in particular, became serious about it and gave us his regal permission, no less, to use the red dye that was reserved for his use alone among his people. It had become a matter of diplomacy to humour him, and now the soldiers of our colony wore a royal red that troubled me by its resemblance to the crimson of the Imperial Household Troops. A few of the people we encountered on that trip knew better, of course, and that caused me great concern. But we experienced no trouble along the way. Who would start trouble with a hundred well-armed, disciplined men?

We had arranged to meet a merchant called Statius in Noviomagus. This fellow had made a name for himself by living up to his own boast that he could supply anything to anyone at any time in any place, if the price was right. We had contacted him through Bishop Alaric and agreed to pay him in gold for all the iron ingots he could supply by mid-November—one gold *aurus* for every hundred pounds of ingot iron he could supply, if he delivered it to Noviomagus. This was more than twenty times the going rate. In *his* eyes, it was the deal of a lifetime. From *our* viewpoint, we were stealing his iron. We had no use for gold in our Colony and iron was becoming harder and harder to find anywhere, since the Hibernians, too ignorant to know that there is no gold in iron ore pits, had shut down the Cambrian mines with their raiding. To the Hibernian Scots, it seemed logical that since gold was dug from the Cambrian mines in Dolaucothi, then every other hole in the ground of Cambria should have gold in it, too.

I was disappointed that Statius had only had five cartloads of iron with him. We loaded that onto three of my big wagons. On the way to the meeting I had dreamed of loading all five wagons and buying a few more of his to carry the rest of the haul. When we met, over a mug of ale in a tavern in Noviomagus, he told me that he had scraped the foundries of the entire eastern part of the country to accumulate the three thousand pounds of iron he had brought with him. When he saw the bag of gold I paid him from, however, his eyes almost fell out of his head and he suddenly became convinced that he could probably find as much again, and perhaps even more, given time.

"How much more time?" I asked him. He did some rapid calculation and we agreed to meet again in June. Feeding his greed, I told him my wagons could easily carry a thousand pounds each. For every hundred pounds, therefore, over five thousand pounds, I would pay double if he would throw in the carts and horses. We shook hands on the deal, and when we parted the following day, Statius was a happy merchant, firmly convinced that he had found the biggest fools in the Empire.

On the way home, we kept to the south coast road in order to avoid the towns we had passed earlier. It almost doubled our journey, but I had sound reasons for the circuitous route, the main one being that I wished to attract no attention to the richness of the train we were escorting. On the way, we picked up our two wagonloads of salt and passed by Durnovaria in the dark hours before dawn, trying to make no noise and attract no attention. Just beyond that town, the road runs along the seashore for several miles. There are no other towns out that way except Isca in the far west, and the road was seldom travelled, even that long ago—a truth attested to by the amount of grass and weeds growing between the cobblestones.

We travelled slowly. The wagons were fully loaded and we had managed to acquire a fair-sized herd of horses of all descriptions. Most of them we had bought along the way; gold is a powerful persuader. Others we had found, and many of these were wild.

At one point, where the road ran very close to the sea, the horses took it into their heads to stop and graze. In trying to get them moving again, one of my men panicked them and they scattered. With difficulty we rounded them up, and then one of them, a big black gelding, the finest horse in the bunch, decided to show us his heels and headed off at full gallop for the west. Three of us chased him. The going was dangerous because of the wetness of the grass, and we were a long way from the road, which had swung north, by the time we finally ran him down.

I tied a halter around his head and handed the rope to Bassus, the young soldier who had ended up with me. We were just turning back to the road when I heard a shout, seemingly cut off in mid-breath. We froze, both of us listening for more. There was only silence, broken by the sound of waves on the pebbled beach a hundred paces away and the whisper of the rain, which had lessened, in the leaves around us. We were in a grassy hollow, surrounded by hawthorn bushes. I turned to look at young Bassus.

"Where did that come from?"

He shook his head uncertainly. "It sounded as though it came from over there." He pointed towards the beach.

"Where's the young fellow who came with us?" I had just noticed that he was nowhere in sight. "What's his name? Anicius. What happened to him?"

Bassus shrugged. "He was behind me to my left last time I saw him."

I tried to tell myself that he had only fallen from his horse, but even to me it sounded like a lie. "Tie up the horses and follow me," I whispered, suddenly aware of a need for silence. "And don't make any noise!"

I climbed out of the hollow and began to head cautiously towards the beach. The ground was rough and stony beneath the turf, and I cursed my limp for forcing me to move more slowly and more awkwardly than I wanted to. My palms were sweating, which is my mind's way of letting me know that it does not feel good about something. I glanced backwards and saw young Bassus following me, coming fast. I signalled to him to slow down.

There was a flash of brown to my right. Anicius's horse. It had begun to graze. I headed towards it, moving very slowly now, and then I heard noises off to my left: a grunt, and the rattle of metal.

They were down in a hollow like the one we had been in when we heard the shout. Anicius's body lay sprawled on the grass, its head, still in its helmet, about five paces away; there was a surprised expression on its face. The whoreson crouched above him was working fast, stripping the corpse. There was bright-red blood all over the grass between the boy's head and his body.

I fumbled at my belt for my skystone dagger, thinking to throw it at the assassin's back, but there was a hissing sound close by my ear and then that unmistakable *thunk*! of an arrow hitting a human torso. Bright-yellow feathers gleamed between his shoulders and he arched his back, reaching behind him, almost gripping them before he fell face down across young Anicius, an agonized moan the only sound he made.

"Well done, lad," I said, and stepped down carefully to where the bodies lay, my feet slipping on the wet grass. As I stood above them, I heard Bassus retching behind me. Probably his first killing, I thought, and his first sight of violent death. I knew how he felt.

I bent down and hauled the killer away from Anicius, turning him over as I did so. He was big. A round shield and a bloody axe lay a short distance away. The shield was covered with scrollwork. Celtic. But not from Britain. At least, not from this part of Britain, for I knew my Celtic design. I went and picked it up, holding it in both hands. Bassus came down to join me.

"Who is he, Commander Varrus?"

"I don't know, but you can bet he's not alone. He's not from these parts, judging by his clothes and by his shield. I think he's a Scot."

"From Hibernia? How did he get all the way down here?"

"Same way they get everywhere, son. By boat."

"A galley?" Bassus looked around him as if expecting to see a boat tied up to a bush.

"Aye, and if I'm correct, it won't be far from here. Let's take a look. But watch your step—you'll get no second chance and no mercy from the likes of these." I looked around and pointed ahead to my right. "You go that way, to the west of that headland. I'll take the left. And be careful!"

A short time later—I had lost track of time—a yellow-feathered arrow smacked into the ground ahead of me and frightened me half to death. Bassus was about sixty paces from me, waving excitedly for me to join him. I retrieved his arrow and went to him.

"It's beached below the headland, Commander! I saw three men. One of them almost saw me."

"Are you sure he didn't?" I held out his arrow to him.

"No." A quick headshake. He took his arrow from my hand. "Thanks, Commander. I didn't want to shout."

"Quite. Well, let's take a look, then."

They had drawn their galley up onto the beach below the headland, in the lee of the cliff, where it would be safe both from observers and from the prevailing tides. I counted three guards on my first glance, pulling my head back quickly after getting a glimpse of them and placing them in my mind. My next look was more confident and I bellied as close as I could get to the edge of the cliff, chilled to the bone from the wet grass. There were six of them visible this time, three out of the line of sight of our first view. Six seemed like a reasonable number to guard the boat, which looked as though it would hold about thirty men, fully crewed. But there was one more dead in the hollow behind us, making seven. How many more? I did not have much time, I guessed, before somebody noticed that the dead one was missing.

I crawled backwards and jerked my head in the direction of our horses.

"Let's go, but keep your eyes open. There's room for another two dozen in that boat. God knows where they are, but we could run into any of them at any time."

My head was buzzing as we made our way back to the horses, which were still tethered to the bush where Bassus had left them. How many more men were there down on the beach? Where were the others? How many of my men would I need to be sure of winning a tussle without serious loss? Rats' teeth! One man lost already was too serious! We vaulted onto our horses and took off at the gallop, back to the road, leading Anicius's horse and the black gelding with us.

Our party had stopped to wait for us where the road swung north. Severus, my lieutenant, had obviously given them a break, for they were huddled in small groups, some of them squatting against the sides of the wagons, getting what little shelter they could from the wind and the rain.

It didn't take long, however, for them to realize that something had gone wrong, for they started scrambling to their feet while we were still a good hundred paces from them, and by the time we had reached them they were falling into their ranks, silent and watchful. I was giving orders before my horse stopped moving. Severus and fifty men were left to guard the wagons, alert now to the danger suddenly uncovered, and the other half of the detachment returned with me at the double towards the beach. Bassus stayed behind with the wagons and the horses.

I placed a dozen bowmen along the top of the cliff above the longboat and sent twenty-four men down to the beach to the west of the headland, warning them to go quietly, out of sight of the guards below, and to stay hidden until they heard my signal. The remaining fourteen I sent down on the blind side of the headland to block any escape from that direction. Then, when I judged the time was right, I blew one blast on my horn.

The surprise was complete. Three of the Scots, the three below the cliff, ran along the base of the cliff, out to the point of the headland. An arrow felled one of them before he had gone five paces, but the other two made it all the way to the point, where they were killed by the men I had sent there to cut them off. The three on the boat saw the odds against them, identified us as Romans and threw down their weapons. It was over that quickly.

By the time I had made my own way down to the beach, a slow and slippery progress thanks to my crippled leg and the wetness of the whole world, my men had herded the three prisoners onto the beach and tied them together. I ignored them and went straight to the boat, climbing up the rough ladder that some of my men had put in place against the side.

The boat was strong and sound, bone-dry inside, except for rain wetness. It was no Roman galley, though. In the first place, it was far too small; it was slimmer and lighter, built for speed. The booty the crew had already gathered lay in a heap in the middle, piled around the single mast. There were four casks among the pile. I ordered one of them broken open. It was full of oil. So were the others. We smashed them and fired the boat. It was tinder-dry and flamed like a torch, but oily clouds of black smoke rose high into the air. Watching it billow upwards, I realized too late that it might be seen from a long way away. If the rest of the crew were nearby, they would be coming soon, on the run.

"Right, lads," I called. "Back up to the top! Quick as you can! Tullus, you and your mate there stay here with me. Quickly now, the rest of you! Form two ranks up there and keep your eyes open. We may have company coming."

They were gone, already half-way up the cliff. They were well trained. Tullus and his friend stood waiting for orders, eyeing the three prisoners. I approached the Scots for the first time. They were an ill-looking trio, and they knew I held their lives in my hand. I wondered if earlier, non-Christian commanders had had to contend with conscience when dealing with prisoners, but I knew that was foolish.

If I let these men go, if there was any way I *could* let them go, they would terrorize the coastline for God alone knew how long. There was nothing else they could do. I had burned their boat. They had to stay. And if they stayed, and lived, they might rejoin their comrades. So, I had to keep them as prisoners, or kill them. Just like that. As a Christian, I would be doing murder by killing them. But if I spared them, I would be condoning murder, for they would kill others as surely as they breathed. They were the enemy. Invaders. Pirates. I glanced up at the cliff-top and the decurion in charge of the bowmen was looking straight into my eyes. I turned to Tullus and his friend.

"I've changed my mind. Rejoin the others."

"But—"

"You heard me!"

They walked away, looking back over their shoulders at the three Hibernians. I watched them reach the path on the cliff side and start to climb. I turned back to the prisoners, looking each of them in the eyes. They read my intent in my face, all at the same time, and, tied together as they were, they began to attempt a shambling run along the beach. The sound of arrows hissing and thunking into flesh was very loud. None of them made a sound. They died in silence. Two were still kicking as I cut their throats.

As I climbed slowly back up to the top, I grappled with the problem of what to do about the others. There had to be at least two dozen more men somewhere close by. If they saw the smoke from their burning boat and came running, the problem would solve itself. If they saw my train on the road, on the other hand, they would hide until we left, and then, God help any poor souls living within a few days' march of here. I tried to tell myself that was not my business. But it was. I had made it my business by burning their damned boat. They were trapped here now. They could no longer simply sail home. I cursed the anger that had made me burn the thing before thinking it through. When I had seen that oil spilling from the broken cask, the only thing that occurred to me was that here was the means to stop these animals from sailing on to murder some other poor boy like Anicius for his clothes.

I was panting when I reached the top of the cliff. The decurion in charge of the bowmen was there waiting for me, offering his arm for the last few feet, and I was grateful.

"Well, young fellow," I said after I had gasped my thanks. "We have a problem that's not going to solve itself."

"What's that, Commander Varrus?"

"The others, lad, the others."

"You mean our men on the road?"

I looked at him, amazed that he had not caught my meaning. "No, lad. Not our men. The other marauders. They can't be far away."

"No, Commander. Of course not."

That was slightly better, but the baffled look in his eyes betrayed him. I shook my head.

"Don't humour me, boy! I know, because I looked, and you do *not* know, because you *could* not. That fire the sentries had down on the beach had not been burning long. Hardly any ashes. Which means they must have landed there early this morning. They left seven men to guard the boat, and they took off inland. It's not noon yet. At least, I don't think it is. So, they haven't had time to get too far away. D'you follow me? Am I being logical?"

"Yes, Commander, I understand." He did, too; his eyes had lost that baffled look.

"Good. Walk with me to my horse and help me up. My leg's on fire."

As we walked to my horse I continued talking; I couldn't remember his name and I was racking my brain trying to think of it. Not knowing his own men's names is an unforgivable fault in a commander. Thank God I could call him "lad"!

"As I see it now," I continued, "I've got little option as to what to do: I've left *them* none at all. They can't sail away. So we have to find them and dispose of them, otherwise they'll terrorize this whole damn countryside. By the way, how did you know I'd need to kill those men on the beach?" I looked straight at him as I asked this.

He didn't hesitate. "You said it yourself, Commander. Options. You were committed as soon as you sent Tullus and his brother back up to the top. You were alone. You couldn't set them free, or even try to bring them up with you. That left three options. You were going to kill them yourself, or you were going to leave them there alive, or you were going to call on my men. Any one of the three, you needed us to back you. So we did."

I looked at him again, conscious of a new respect for him. "Simple as that, eh?"

"Yes, Commander." He looked surprised.

I grunted, not wanting him to know that I hadn't really been aware of the danger I had placed myself in by dismissing Tullus and his "friend," who was his brother. I kicked myself mentally for not having noticed any family resemblance.

"Tullus's brother, how old is he?"

"Same age as Tullus, Commander. They're stepbrothers."

I grunted again, and then the decurion's name clicked into my mind.

"Your father, he's married again, too, isn't he?"

He blinked at me in surprise. "Yes, Commander. Last year."

"Aye. He's a good man and he was a fine soldier. Did you know he was my first centurion, when I joined the legions?"

"I know, Commander. He's told me." There was pride in his voice.

We had reached my horse, and he legged me up onto its back.

"Thanks, lad. Now!" I sat there and marshalled my thoughts. "All right, first things first." I turned to the infantry ranked behind me. "I need four of you men to make a litter for young Anicius's body there. One of your tents slung between two spears and one man on each end of each spear. You know how to do it." I swung back to the young decurion in charge of the bowmen. "I'll need your people to remain with them, to act as escort and ensure they get back safely. Don't dawdle, because the hostiles could be anywhere and you won't be really safe until you're back with the train. The rest of these men I'll need back at the road, as quickly as we can get there."

He saluted me and ran off, back to his bowmen. I turned my horse and signalled to the remaining infantry to move out at the double, back to the road. As I did so, the rain, which had almost stopped, returned in blowing, chilling sheets. I kicked Germanicus into a walk and watched my men jogging miserably through the bushes and long grass. God! I was getting old and careless! Here I was with a valuable train of wagons and horses, less than four days from home after four weeks away, and instead of leaving well enough alone, I had acted like a stupid, unthinking boy, burning a boat I had no need to burn and bringing upon myself and my men, some of whom must surely die because of it, the responsibility for finding and killing a mob of crazed Hibernian Scots.

Seeing the senselessness of berating myself after the fact, I asked myself instead what Caius Britannicus would have done under the same circumstances. Would he, could he, have acted differently, solving the problem more efficiently, yet none the less effectively, without endangering his men? The answer to that, I knew, was that Caius would have done just what I had done, except that, being Caius Cornelius Britannicus, he would have thought the entire exercise through, including the implications of his act, before committing either himself or his men. That forethought, his anticipation of the outcome as opposed to my belated realization of it, would have been the only difference in our actions and I accepted the truth of that as being normal. The men of the Cornelian family, one of the Founding Families of Rome, had been bred to accept their aristocratic responsibilities—with everything that those entailed—for more than a millennium, and Caius had been trained to appreciate and exercise command responsibility since his earliest childhood. That training ensured that he brought an analytical eye to bear on everything he did, weighing each decision carefully before acting upon it.

As Legate and general, strategist and tactician, I knew Britannicus would have perceived all I had perceived in this situation through different eyes, detached by his status from the personalized, individual pain of the foot-soldier. He would have considered the general welfare of his command ahead of the need to avenge one young boy.

That task completed, nevertheless, and his responsibilities accounted for and acknowledged, Britannicus the man, the soldier, friend and comrade-in-arms, would have acted as I had done, recognizing the need for Draconian measures, then making his decision swiftly and in full acceptance of whatever consequences might result. That comforting realization brought me back to myself and my circumstances.

Germanicus was ambling at a slow walk and I noticed that I was being left far behind the column, who were still doubling. I kicked him to a canter and had regained the head of the column by the time we reached the road, where Severus and his contingent stood guard around the wagons and the horses.

"Fall in—four ranks!" When they were assembled at attention, I stood them easy and spoke to them.

"Is there anyone here familiar with this part of the country?"

"Aye, Commander!" One of the youngest soldiers raised his clenched fist.

"How well do you know it, lad?"

"I was born close by here, Commander."

"Where, exactly?" I wished the damned rain would stop.

"About six miles from here, Commander. My father worked on a villa in the hills, there." The young man, more accurately a boy, nodded to the low, rolling hills behind me.

"Is there a town nearby?"

"No, Commander. Just a village."

"How far from here?"

The boy frowned and shrugged his shoulders under his soaked cape. "Six, maybe seven miles, Commander."

"How many people?"

He shrugged again, clearly not knowing.

"Come on, lad! How many? Guess! Twenty? Thirty? More?"

"I don't know, Commander. I haven't been there in years. Perhaps thirty or forty."

"All farmers?" He nodded. "Fine," I said. "Thank you. Can you take us there?"

"Yes, Commander." His wide eyes reflected puzzlement.

I looked at the others. "All right, listen closely, all of you." I pointed back towards the beach. "We have just burned a galley on the beach back there. There were seven men guarding it. One of them killed Anicius, who was riding with us. He could not have known there were three of us. Young Bassus here killed *him*, and then we found the galley on the beach, burned it and killed the other six guards. Now!" I paused to let my next words reverberate clearly. "There was room on that boat for thirty men, give or take a few. Seven of them are dead already. That leaves twenty to twenty-five hostile Hibernian Scots roaming around here, somewhere. They could only have arrived this morning. Not enough ashes in their fire for them to have been here yesterday as well." I paused again to let them think about that, before continuing. "These are not friendly people. If they have gone inland, the chances are they'll find this village, if they didn't go directly there in the first place. In this weather, they'll probably stay there for shelter. D'you take my meaning?" They did. I kept talking.

"After they find the ashes of their boat, they are going to be very unhappy. And the Christ save anyone they meet after that. Even if they wanted to go home, they can't. They'll stay here, and they'll burn, they'll rape, and they'll kill, and when they've had their bellies filled with that, they'll stop for a while and march overland and then do it all again. They have to do that, they must. There is no other choice open to them."

My men all looked very sober now, the discomfort of the pouring rain forgotten. I carried on.

"If we can catch them at this village, we may be able to wipe them out before they know what's hit them. They won't be expecting soldiers. These people live on women, children, old men and the occasional farmer. They're nasty animals, and they're brave enough, but they're not used to disciplined opposition and they have no discipline themselves. With surprise, we can sweep them up like a pile of last year's leaves and bury them or burn them." I paused again before going on. "Of course, there is the chance that they may miss the village. Or they may have been here longer than I suspect, and the men on the beach just didn't light a fire. They may be hardier than I take them for. In either event, however, I can't take the chance that they won't come back here while we're on our way to the village, so we will leave half our force here to guard our goods. I want fifty volunteers to come with me to take them in the village."

A hundred men stepped forward. I smiled.

"That's what I thought might happen. Fine! Ranks one and three, men on the left stand fast. Every second man from the left comes with me. Ranks two and four, alternate from men on the left. Wait for it!" They swayed and held still as I continued. "Severus, you will remain in charge of the defences here. We have a three-hour march ahead of us. By the time we conclude our business it will be dark. We'll head back here at first light. You will bury our young friend Anicius, and you will need a camp with a ditch and rampart. Site it carefully."

A groan went up from the men to be left behind. I grinned at them.

"That's enough! The exercise will take your minds off the weather and the fun the rest of us are having, slogging across country through this long, wet grass." I looked around them one last time. "Each man in the strike force to take two days' rations from the commissary wagon. We leave in half an hour. Fall out!"

We came in sight of the hamlet, for that's all it was, late in the afternoon. It was obvious, even from a distance, that I had been right. A few of the buildings burned sullenly in the heavy rain, and from our viewpoint in a copse half a mile away, we could see men moving around. The marauders were still there, sheltering from the foul weather.

I planned our moves carefully and we moved in just as darkness was falling.

And so, here I was, lying on a wood-framed cot and wondering how long I'd been in this place. At least the rain had stopped. I opened my mouth to shout, but nothing came out but a croak, and suddenly I was consumed with thirst—parched like a dry leaf. I thought about trying to stand. I decided to count to ten and then make an attempt to roll onto my left side, holding my arm rigid, in the hope that I could then get my feet under me and sit up.

At ten, I discovered that I was strapped down and couldn't move in any direction. A shadow blocked the sunlight coming through the door, and Severus entered and stood looking down at me.

"Commander. You're awake! How are you feeling?"

"Awful. I itch. What are you doing here? I left you with the wagons."

He smiled down at me. "Well, at least your mind's still functioning, Commander. The wagons are safe. I brought them with me when I came."

"You brought them with you? When you came? I see. Well, then, if you did that, how long have we been here?"

"Nine days, Commander."

"Nine days! God in heaven, man, why?"

"Well, sir, we were afraid to move you."

"Then you should have left me here with a dozen men as escort and sent the others back to the Colony! Have you no damned initiative at all?"

"Yes, Commander. Sometimes."

"Well, then, what in God's name . . . ach!" I realized the futility of what I was saying to him, and changed tack.

"How many did we lose in the fight?"

"Three killed and five wounded. Of those, one died, three are back on duty, and you're the fifth."

"How many Scots?"

"All of them. Twenty-three. We got most of them in the huts, in the first sweep, but there were nine of them who were together in the main hayloft. They were the ones who headed into the street and tried to rally the others. But they were too late. The others were already dead."

"So! No prisoners?"

"None, Commander."

"How many villagers still alive?"

"Most of the women. Some of the men. About twenty-eight, all together, counting women and children. Six men were away from home and came back later."

"How are they off for food?"

"They'll do, Commander. We got here before the hostiles had time to do much other than spread the women."

"And how many men do we have here now?"

"Ten, Commander, counting yourself."

"Ten?" I felt my face showing my shock. "But you said . . . Where are all the others?"

"I sent them on ahead to the Colony, Commander. I didn't want to take the chance of moving you, as I said, so I kept a few good men back to help me look out for you until you were fit enough to be moved."

He let that lie there, and I felt the flush of colour staining my neck and cheeks. I cleared my throat and apologized.

"I'm a fool, Severus, and I'm getting to be an old fool. I should have known you'd do the right thing. Why do I itch so much?"

He was smiling. "Because you're filthy, Commander, and you need a shave."

"God, yes! And a steam and perfumed oils." I tried again to move. My arms were strapped tight to my chest. "Why are both my arms tied down?"

"To stop you from thrashing around. I'll have you released."

"Please do. And then get me onto a cart, and get me back to the Colony. But first, get me some water. Cold for drinking and hot for bathing!"

Two days later, we were home. Whatever it was that had weakened me had done so with absolute success. I was so helpless, so feeble, that I could not even sit propped up in the wagon. The rocking of its ordinary, plodding progress nauseated me, and my muscles, which seemed to have been transformed completely into jelly, permitted me no control over my own balance so that, even when tied into place with a rope, I flopped around like a landed fish, totally at the mercy of the bumps in the road. I was conscious of the folly of my determination to sit upright but I refused to accept it as such, and it was only with very ill grace that I finally accepted that I would have to remain supine for the entire journey back to the Villa Britannicus. From that position, flat on my back on a pile of furs in the wagon bed, I did nothing for the remainder of the journey but watch the clouds that came and went across the sky above me. It was a very real blessing to learn, eventually, that we were finally only a matter of hours, and then moments, away from the villa.

We missed Britannicus and his doctors, who were on their way to find us. They arrived back the following day to find me well on the way to restored humanity—oiled and steamed and massaged and scraped and shiny and relaxing under the pampering of my dear wife, who had betrayed only momentary consternation at my condition, before setting out immediately to rectify the matter.

Even today, writing these words after three decades of marriage to Luceiia Britannicus, I have not yet learned to be unsurprised by the ease with which she can abandon all semblance of the civilized matron, being normally the sunniest and most placid of souls, and revert to the implacable savagery of the threatened matriarch. From soldier and smith, I have evolved over those years into scribe and thinker, and for all that time I would have said, "Beware my wrath!" to anyone who thought to menace me or mine in any way. Nowadays, however, I see the folly in that. The strongest and most minatory words I could have uttered would have been, "Beware my wife!"

On this occasion, seeing me borne supine into the villa grounds, she came sweeping from the house like a late autumn wind, the strength of her arrival whipping the air from mouths that might have uttered words, and leaving the would-be speakers gulping for breath as she belabored them and buffeted about their ears. Within moments, I had been lifted from the cart and was being carried deep into the house, to where a makeshift couch was already being prepared for me amid the bustle of scurrying bodies building high fires in imported braziers and spreading rolls of cloth along walls and doorways to block out draughts. In vain I sought to protest that I was already on the mend. I was ignored and then deposited where my wife wished me placed, close to the fires. While people stripped me of the filthy clothes I wore, others brought steaming water to a metal tub that had appeared close by my couch, and as they lowered me into the makeshift bath, I was aware of my wife's disapproving eyes and downturned mouth as she surveyed the condition I was in. But having learned, even in those "early" days, the uselessness of protest in such cases, I gave up and surrendered myself to the almost orgasmic pleasure of the hot, artificially perfumed waters that engulfed me.

Later still, when I was once again in bed, warm, clean and pleasantly aware of the sleep that must overwhelm me presently, my filthy bandages all soaked and peeled away to be replaced with new, crisp, tightly bound white promises of health, I found myself so glad to be safely home that I took no offence when Luceiia, looking down at me once more, her eyes now filled with reassured confidence and love, shook her head and murmured something about my being too old for such adventures. The time had come, she said, for other, younger men to adopt the risks I had always assumed to life and limb. My place henceforth should be at home, here in the Colony, where my skills and abilities, and their value to the community, would not be hazarded. Youth, and its impulsive tendencies towards risk and danger, now lay behind me. In my haze-filled mind, I recalled that I had said much the same thing to myself, mere days before, in contemplating battle, and yet I felt I should protest her utterance of them. I knew I should, but I had not the strength and, at that precise time, I lacked the will. We were alone, finally, I knew, the others, servitors and friends and well-wishers, all gone. Luceiia lowered herself gently to the edge of my cot and kissed me, tenderly, her lips imprinting themselves on cheeks and nose, eyes and forehead, and her fingertips tracing the outlines of my face. Her gentleness transported me into oblivion.

II

WHEN I AWOKE the next day, I had begun to feel more like my normal self. I drank some hot, spicy broth for breakfast, and by noon I was beginning to feel hungry. By supper time, I was ravenous and had a large piece of bread and a small piece of meat with my broth, although Luceiia felt that I might be premature in tackling solid food after having not eaten for so long during my illness. I managed to keep it down, however, and from that moment on my recovery was rapid. The pneumonia that afflicted me had no doubt run its natural course, but I felt, and told my wife so, that it was put to flight by the pleasure of being back in my own home with my loved ones.

By the third day after my return home I was up, out of bed and walking for short distances. I had lost a shocking amount of weight, considering the short duration of my illness, and most of it was muscle. I was astonished to find myself as weak as a baby, and disgruntled when my physician pointed out that this was an inevitable demonstration of middle age. Luceiia fussed around me like a broody hen, of course, although I never saw a hen so beautiful, and kept close watch on me at all times, insisting that I spend most of my out-of-bed time sitting in a comfortable chair, well wrapped in blankets and close to a portable brazier containing a glowing fire made from my own charcoal, which threw out a highly gratifying amount of heat.

I was sitting thus across from Caius several days later, reading something of which I have absolutely no recollection. I know it was a book, but that is all I know because I do not think I ever read another word of it after Caius looked up and said, "Oh, I know what I forgot to tell you before you left on your last trip."

I shifted position, seeking a shred more comfort and tugging at the edge of my blanket in a futile attempt to pull some more of it loose from beneath me. It was effort wasted and I gave up in ill-tempered disgust, some of which may have crept into my tone as I said, in response to Caius's overture, "What?"

He caught the ungracious inflection and looked at me in surprise, obviously wondering what he had said to cause such a snappish reaction, while his patrician eyebrow arched so high that the skin of his forehead wrinkled above his right eye. I felt rather foolish.

"Pardon me, Cay," I said. "I did not intend to sound so ungracious. The tone of voice was not for you; it was merely frustration."

"Frustration?" The eyebrow did not descend. "Over what?"

I had to laugh, at my own childish anger and at his expression. "At this damned blanket. I'm sitting on it and I want to release some more of it from beneath me to wrap around my shoulders, but I can't pull it free and I can't stand up, because of the way Luceiia has it wrapped around me."

He was on his feet instantly, leaning towards me, hands outstretched to help me to my feet. Once I was standing, it became a relatively simple matter to shake the folds of the blanket loose and rearrange them the way I wanted them. When everything was absolutely proper and correct, we sat down again.

"So," I said, "what was it?"

"What was what?"

"What was it you forgot to tell me before I left to get the iron?"

He had lost interest in what he had been going to say and was looking at his text again, clearly desirous of resuming his study. "Oh, that." His voice reflected his waning interest. "It was nothing important, merely of passing interest. I received a letter from Marcellus Prello, a friend of mine in Gaul. Thank God there are still a few imperial mail ships getting through. Anyway, he wrote that he had been in Rome a few months earlier and had seen your old nemesis Claudius Seneca in the street. You don't know him, but Marcellus was one of the friends I asked for information on Seneca shortly after you first arrived here . . . How long ago would that have been?" The question was rhetorical, because he was already computing his own answer. "Great heavens, Publius, do you know you have been living here for more than ten years?"

I nodded. "Yes, I know. I've been married to your sister for almost eleven. But your friend was mistaken."

Caius's brow creased slightly. "What do you mean?"

I shrugged. "Simply what I said. Your friend must have been mistaken. He could not have seen Claudius Seneca."

He laughed. "Don't be silly, of course he could. He was in *Rome*, Publius."

I shook my head again. "No. It wasn't him. It might have been *a* Seneca— you've told me they're a prolific crowd. But it certainly was not Claudius."

Even as I said the words I regretted them. Caius was astonished by my reaction to a very casual statement, and I realized that I had committed a tactical error. I should simply have accepted his remark and said nothing. I held only one secret from him in the world, about this very thing. Now he came after me, his curiosity fully alerted.

"You sound absolutely convinced of that, Publius. How can you be so certain?" He paused, but not for long enough to permit me to frame a response before he continued, an edge of suspicion in his voice. "Since when do you keep yourself so minutely informed of the whereabouts and activities of Claudius Seneca?"

"I don't," I said, stubbornly. "I simply happen to know your friend was wrong. He made an error in identification. That's all."

A small frown ticked between the Britannican brows. "But how *can* you know that, Publius? Do you know for certain that Claudius Seneca was *not* in Rome at the time in question?"

A loud voice in my head was screaming at me to be careful in what I said. I decided to brazen it out. "Yes," I said, regretting more than ever having responded to Caius's initial comment at all.

He almost leaped on my answer, practically hectoring me. "I see. Then where *was* he, Publius? And when *was* the time in question? When was Marcellus Prello in Rome?"

Flustered, and beginning to feel a stirring of panic at being caught in a lie, I looked away, into the depths of the brazier beside me, unwilling to let him see my thoughts reflected in my eyes. He kept after me.

"Publius? Did you hear me?"

"I heard you. You are determined to have an answer from me, aren't you? Why? Why is this so important, Cay?"

My question took him by surprise; his face registered astonishment and disbelief that I would have to ask such a question. When he answered, the tone of his voice was that of a teacher explaining something self-evident to a struggling student.

"It is important precisely because of what you said, and the fact that you said it. I know you, Publius Varrus. You are not a devious man. I also know how you used to feel about Claudius Seneca, and you have not mentioned his name in years. Now, I bring his name up casually, mentioning that someone has seen the fellow somewhere, and your denial of the mere possibility of such a thing happening is immediate and absolute. Something strikes me as being wrong here, and, as an old campaigner, I have learned to trust my instincts in such matters."

I sighed and capitulated. "Very well, Cay, I'll tell you my secret. Your friend could not have seen Claudius Seneca because Claudius Seneca is dead."

Now it was Caius's turn to stare wordlessly at me and then into the fire. He cupped his chin in one hand, kneading the flesh of his cheek reflectively with the tip of his forefinger. When he did speak his voice was almost without inflection.

"Dead, you say? I can only assume you are convinced of the truth of that. You are sure of it, are you not?"

I nodded. "Yes, sure as I can be."

"And how sure is that?"

"Completely, beyond the shadow of a doubt."

"How? Who told you? And how can you be so certain it is true?"

"No one told me, Cay. I know because I killed him."

Caius sucked in his breath, stood up, turned on his heel and walked away from me, so that his voice drifted back to me over his shoulder.

"When?"

"Five years ago, just at the time we made the alliance with Ullic and his Celts and the word arrived that Theodosius had defeated and executed Magnus Maximus."

He turned back towards me and stood looking at me from the other side of the room. "Five years ago? And you said nothing? Why? How did you kill him? And when? You have never been away from the Colony for any great length of time, and Seneca has never been close to the Colony. Such a killing would require either careful advance planning and an absence that would require some kind of explanation, or the exact opposite, a sudden and explosive confrontation. I will not even entertain the idea that you could murder him from concealment. I am sure you allowed him an honourable death, in spite of the fact that in your eyes he had forfeited all claim to honour . . . But I have to ask myself how you could have managed his death without either Luceiia or myself noticing anything, and why you would have said nothing to either of us in all that time?"

I nodded, admitting the truth of what he said and acknowledging all of the commentary that he intended with his words. "After I had done it, I decided to tell no one," I said, clearing my throat in mid-sentence. "I decided the less said, the better, and I did not want to endanger you or Luceiia with knowledge of what I had done, even though—" I held up my hand, palm outward, to silence him before he could interrupt me, "—even though I was convinced that what I had done was correct and honourable and I had no thought of having done anything shameful. I had served as an instrument of justice, I believed, but I had no wish to boast of it."

"I see." Caius came back and sat down again in the chair opposite me. "You had better tell me everything that happened that day, Publius. Think carefully and leave nothing out. Assume that I know absolutely nothing of what you are going to tell me. Pretend I have never even heard of Seneca. This could be extremely important."

Impressed by his obvious sincerity and concern, I sat silent for a while, collecting my thoughts before beginning a none-too-brief narrative, telling him everything I could remember of the events leading up to and surrounding the death of Claudius Seneca. I had engineered Seneca's death myself, confronting him and killing him with savage satisfaction for his past deeds and the deaths of two of my closest friends.

I started with the original meeting—and the first fight—between myself and Seneca, almost fifteen years earlier, when I had been in the company of my good friend Plautus, then senior centurion of the garrison at Colchester, and ended with the final confrontation, in which I had forced Seneca to sign a parchment scroll admitting to his crimes and then given him a sword with which to kill me if he could. He failed. I stabbed him a mortal blow, left his confession where it could not fail to be found and departed the scene prior to the arrival of the military search party already summoned by one of my men.

As I told my long and unpleasant tale, Caius sat silently, staring into the coals. Not once did he raise his eyes to look at me. When I finished talking, the silence between us grew and stretched. The charcoal cracked and settled with a soft crunching sound and a puff of smoke and light ash. Finally he stirred and looked at me, heaving a great sigh and expelling it through pursed lips.

"And you never said a word, in all this time."

I shrugged my shoulders. "As I told you, I saw no advantage to you in knowing anything about it. I wasn't proud of it."

"I believe you, but were you satisfied with your vengeance?"

Again I gave a slight shrug. "I really don't know. I drew no pleasure from it, that much I can say with certainty."

"But you are sure you killed him."

"Of course I am! What kind of question is that? I don't kill many people. When I do, I'm usually aware of what I'm doing!"

He shook his head, a tightly controlled flick of annoyance. "I didn't mean that. What I meant was, are you sure he was dead when you left him?"

"As sure as I am that you're alive. I held the whoreson upright at arm's length, skewered on the end of my sword, and felt the life go out of him. I wanted to cut off his head—to execute him formally, I suppose—but I was too disgusted, so I just left him lying there. But he was dead, Caius."

"Mmm . . . And you left the signed confession right there?"

"Right there. Tucked beneath his arm."

"And you never heard about anything coming of what you had done?"

"No. Nothing."

"Did you not find that curious, or strange?"

"No, why should I? I knew what I knew. I knew what I had done, and I knew what must have happened once he was found. His family would have been informed of his disgrace and taken measures to ensure that the truth did not become widely known. They would have bought silence at whatever cost to protect themselves and their family name."

"You expected that? So you had no interest in establishing public disgrace?"

"No, none at all. What purpose would that have served? I merely wished him dead and his perfidy established and acknowledged among those who knew what was involved."

"Hmmm!" Caius rose to his feet and shook out the folds of the robe he was wearing, a draped garment cut and tailored to resemble the classical toga, but much lighter and more practical, opening down the front from neck to ankle, fastened with a series of small hooks and girdled with a belt of supple leather. He remained standing, bent forward and looking down towards his feet as he carefully readjusted the cloth and refastened the leather belt about his waist. I knew he was thinking deeply, using the activity as a mask for his deliberations. He was satisfied with his efforts, eventually, and turned towards the brazier, holding his hands out, absent-mindedly, towards the dwindling heat from the coals. I waited for him to speak, and at length he asked me a surprising question.

"Publius, do you remember our conversation on the first occasion that we met, that night in the desert in Africa?"

"Yes, I do. We spoke of many things that night."

"We did, and among them one thing that I had no wish to know of, at first. Do you recall?"

I smiled at him. "Clearly. The matter of the favour I had done for my commanding legate, the favour that earned me—how did you put it?—intercontinental and inter-legion transfer. You thought at first I had been involved in some kind of extra-legal chicanery."

"But I was wrong. You had been rewarded merely for 'straightening out' your commander's errant son. Young Seneca. What was his name?"

"The boy? Jacobus. I called him Jacob."

"Jacobus. That was my brother's name. What happened to him after you left, do you know?"

I shook my head. "I have no idea. I have not given him a thought since that night we talked of him. He was only the least of the Senecas. I presume he grew up and became a tribune; he had the makings of a fine officer, in spite of his family name. You will bear in mind that, in those days, I had no thought of Senecas as being different from anybody else."

"I remember." He heaved a deep, weary sigh. "We all learn through living."

The pause that followed was so long that I thought he had finished speaking, but just as I opened my lips to speak again, he resumed. "What would you say if I were to tell you he came to Britain?"

It was my turn to frown now, wondering what my friend was leading up to. "Jacob? I'd be surprised."

"How so? Surprised that I would be aware of such a thing?"

I hesitated, considering my answer carefully before I put it into words, for I was surprised to feel myself growing angry. The truth was that I knew Britannicus was as alert to the doings of the Senecas—all of them—as a barefoot man in desert scrub is wary of snakes and scorpions. His vigilance in that regard was all-encompassing, born of long years of personal enmity and generations of hatred and bloodshed between his House and theirs.

"No," I responded finally, "surprised that you would be aware of such a thing and not have told me."

He answered me with a smile. "Even if I thought the knowledge might be both unwelcome to you and unnecessary?"

"How could you *assume* it might be unwelcome, Caius? He and I were friends, once. But did he, in fact, come back?"

"Yes, Publius, he did. He arrived with the army Theodosius sent to restore order after the rebellion of Magnus Maximus." There was no trace of a smile on Cay's face now. "He is now deputy commander of the garrison at Venta Belgarum—I have been keeping an eye on him, as you can see. He is a Seneca, after all. Jacobus started out here in Britain as a squadron commander at Aquae Sulis, and among his first duties was the task of responding to a mysterious summons concerning the missing Procurator of South Britain."

"What?" I felt the blood draining from my cheeks, and a roaring noise began building up in my ears. "Jacob? A *Seneca* found Seneca? How do you know this? And why wouldn't you tell me before now?"

He held up his hand to silence me. "I would have told you immediately, had there been any substance to the story I heard, but there was none. The details came to me in a letter from a friend in Glevum, Decius Lepido. Did you ever meet him?" I shook my head and he continued. "Well, anyway, he is now chairbound, like most ageing soldiers, near retirement and confined to administrative duties. According to Lepido, the event was a false alarm. A mysterious message came to the garrison commander at Aquae, informing him that the body of the missing Procurator, Claudius Seneca, could be found in a specific place, indicated on a hand-drawn map. A search party was sent out immediately, but all they found was the place and three bodies, one of them still alive, none of them the missing Procurator. The official report of the matter crossed Lepido's desk the following month. He told me about it in his next letter, several months after that, and the only reason he mentioned it at all was that the leader of the search party was Jacobus Seneca, the Procurator's nephew. He said it reminded him of the old saying about setting a thief to catch a thief." He paused again.

"I remember thinking at the time that you might be interested in the reappearance of your young charge from Africa, quite apart from the news of Seneca himself, but you were away on one of your journeys when the letter arrived and it was hardly a major piece of important news. By the time you came back I had forgotten about it. When I did think about it again, much later, it no longer seemed worth mentioning. You had apparently forgotten all about the Seneca clan, and I thought it better to let sleeping dogs lie. So I said nothing. I can see now I was wrong."

I had listened to the last part of his explanation without really absorbing it. My mind was filled with the import of what he had said before that: *"Three bodies, one of them still alive, none of them the missing Procurator."*

"But that's impossible!" My voice was choked with phlegm. Caius raised an eyebrow at me, saying nothing. I cleared my throat and began again. "You said . . . your friend said, in his version of the story, that none of the three men was Seneca." Caius waited for me to continue. "But that's not true. He must have been mistaken."

Caius shook his head briefly. "No. He was quoting from the official report, Publius. Lepido would make no mistake about that. An official report is, *ipso facto*, the formal truth."

"There were three dead men in that clearing, Cay. None was alive." Another thought occurred to me. "What about the confession? Did he have anything to say about that?"

"What confession? The offical report made no mention of any confession."

"I left it under the swine's arm!"

"I believe you. But, officially, no confession exists, or ever did."

Unable to sit still any longer, seething with baffled anger, I sprang to my feet and began pacing the room, kneading my right fist in my left. Caius turned to follow me with his eyes, saying nothing, allowing me to follow the chaotic surging of my thoughts. Finally I stopped pacing and faced him again.

"Jacob grew to be a Seneca, after all." Cay's only response was to raise his eyebrow in that old, sardonic mannerism of his, and I continued. "I thought he was different ... thought he had the makings of a decent man ... but he's just as warped and evil as the rest of his brood. He found the body, suppressed the confession and covered the whole thing up. But how? How could he have concealed Seneca's identity? That doesn't make sense."

Caius ran his hand over his short, iron-grey hair from crown to forehead, pressing it down onto his brow with spread fingers as he sighed again. "But it does. It does, Publius. Think about it, and remember the people with whom we are dealing. Magnus's rebellion was over. New troops everywhere, all of undoubted loyalty to Theodosius, and all from overseas. Probably not one soul in the new garrison at Aquae Sulis had ever set eyes on Claudius Seneca, so when the man's own nephew denied that this was his uncle, who would contradict him? Officially, Jacobus Seneca brought back a nameless survivor who—"

"Impossible! I've told you, Cay, there were no survivors, other than me."

He stared at me. "Then why go to all the trouble of denying the identity of the corpse?"

"What d'you mean? To protect the swine's reputation, of course."

"Against what, Publius? All Jacob had to do was destroy the written confession, and Seneca was blameless. It would then have been a tragic end to a heroic figure: the noble Procurator, murdered by his abductors after a titanic struggle in an attempt to escape. That would have ended the mystery surrounding his disappearance very neatly, from everyone's viewpoint except yours."

"Damnation, that's not good enough, Cay." I was digging my heels in, mentally, knowing I was right. "There has to be another explanation. That whoreson was dead when I walked away from him, I swear it."

Caius shook his head slowly, unwilling to accede the point. "Then what other possible explanation could there be, Publius?"

I slammed my clenched fist into my palm. "I don't know, I don't know. But there has to be something, something devious and serpentine and reptilian. Something that would occur only to a damned Seneca, and we're missing it!"

Caius arrived at a decision. I saw it happen in his eyes, and then he snapped his head downward in a short, decisive nod.

"Very well, I'll grant that you may be correct, on the reptilian grounds alone. And we are not exactly devoid of resources in this. The truth is verifiable, although not immediately. I shall write to my friend Marcellus Prello again tonight and ask him to be more specific regarding this alleged sighting of Claudius Seneca in Rome. It may take a month or more to hear whether or not he has anything to add to his original report, but at least we'll know then, with some degree of certainty, if Prello spoke with conviction in his last letter, or if he was merely gossiping."

I felt better already. "Fine. So be it! But he's dead, Cay, and your friend Prello made an error of identification. I would wager on that. I don't know what motivated Jacob Seneca to do what he did in concealing the death of his unspeakable uncle, but I do know he did it. Claudius Seneca, may he be cursed anew by the ancient God of the Hebrews, is dead and burning in a firepit in Hades."

There was nothing more to be said at that time, I felt, but in spite of my surge of confidence, my peace of mind had been shattered for that day, and I ended up sleeping most of the afternoon away, lulled by a draught concocted for me by Caius's physician.

Within a matter of a few more days, however, a series of events was to occur that would drive all memory and all consciousness of Claudius Seneca from my mind.

III

THERE IS A beast in every man who breathes, a beast that is born in him and lives within him all his life, in a constant struggle for dominance over what he would prefer to think of as his "better self." I say that with complete conviction because I have had to come to terms with my own personal beast, and it now lies dormant inside me; dormant, but far from dead. It stirs, occasionally, reminding me of its presence, of its poison.

My beast's chains are strong—as strong as I, a maker of iron chains, could make them. I know to my own cost, nevertheless, that they are frighteningly fragile.

I have not always known such things, for it is not in my nature to dwell for any length of time on matters I cannot pick up and either bend or straighten with a hammer. I learned of the reality of man's inner beast only when I was a man full-grown myself, and I learned of it from my friend Bishop Alaric, after he and I had seen at first hand the depredations of one sad man's beast, which had caused him to run amok among his friends and neighbours, crippling and maiming before he could be overpowered. Alaric said at the time that the man, whom we both knew, had been "possessed by the beast." Hearing these words from Alaric, a man of God, I assumed he meant *the* beast, the Devil, and I said so. Alaric, however, quickly brought me to order on my misunderstanding.

It is too easy, he told me, with that simplicity of speech I so admired in him, to blame all our human griefs and ills on Lucifer. In doing so, he said, we can evade responsibility for our own actions, whereas the fault, in truth, is attributable to a lesser, more human beast that alternates constantly between lying dormant or raging savagely within each of us, male and female. The degree to which each of us subjugates our personal beast dictates the goodness, or the greatness, we achieve in this life.

This was a new notion for me, a disturbing, discomforting idea with which, I must confess, I did not rush to wrestle. But at that time I had not yet truly encountered my own beast and, try as I would, the closest I could come to seeing it then, or even sensing its presence within me, was in my own cold enjoyment of the kill, in war, I knew what that did to me—the feral enjoyment of battle and the sick revulsion that followed. But that was no beast, I reasoned; it was mere guilt.

Many years later, under the threat of rain, late on a cloudy summer afternoon that was dark with flies and heavy with omens, I was to recall that occasion, and that discussion, very clearly, as I gazed, horror-stricken, at the

47

signs of the victory of one more man's beast and recognized fully the hideous visage of my own.

Approaching this episode again has placed demands on me that are new and worrisome, because I must now write about the beast in man, and of the beast in me. I fear and loathe the task, but my course is clear: I may not deal in other people's faults unless I first lay bare, in full confession and acknowledgement, my own gross flaws. And so I must deal here with my friend Domitius Titens, and with the treachery I dealt him for his friendship.

Domitius Titens was our neighbour, the great-great-grandson, like Caius Britannicus, of one of the original villa builders in the region that we developed as our Colony. He was also my friend and an avid student of ironcraft. He would never have made a weapons-smith, but he learned quickly the artistic sleight of hand required to twist wrought iron into lovely, strong and decorative shapes.

He had been in the legions at the same time as Cay and me, and most of his soldiering had been done in the eastern marches of the Empire. He had served for years in Asia Minor and had ended up in Constantinople, at the Imperial Court, where he met and wed his red-haired consort, Cylla, bringing her back to his huge estates in Britain when his tour of duty ended.

Cylla Titens was, for a very long time, a part of my life that I could never bring myself to come to grips with. In the beginning, I thought of her as "Scylla," and imagined her to possess all the attributes of that mythological monster. She made my life a misery over a period of years, but I could never hold her wholly to blame for it. The fault was mine; Cylla was merely herself. Whatever power, for good or evil, she ever held over me she possessed only because I gave it to her, and it was that gift that rendered me incapable of dealing with her satisfactorily. She exercised a dark power with the dedication of a despot, and I was never able to break her hold.

Cylla and I never lay with each other. Never. Had I lain even once with Cylla Titens, I would have forfeited my wife and my honour, in my own mind, forever. I can state with certainty that Luceiia would have forgiven me had I strayed, because she told me so and I know she spoke the truth. But I could never have forgiven myself for such an atrocity.

Cylla Titens was everything I mistrusted and disliked in a woman, all smoothly disguised in the shape of what every normal man admires.

Cylla fascinated me. She was beautiful, with that headlong, dedicated devotion to her own beauty that left no room in her life for anyone or anything else of importance. Her body was her temple, and she worked long and hard to keep it long and hard. Beauty was life's blood to Cylla, and she was entirely taken up with protecting it. She never sat or walked in the sun, because she believed it dried and wrinkled her skin. And there was never any mention of Cylla and children in the same breath. Her self was the only thing she was true to, and she was determinedly dedicated to that.

I knew how faithless Cylla was; I had reason to. And she knew I thought her a shameless wanton. She never made any attempt to qualify the accuracy or the validity of my opinion. She did not feel she needed to. I lusted after her and she encouraged my lust, deliberately baiting the beast in me, drawing it ever closer to the surface with my own tacit consent.

There is a perversity in me that enjoyed the experience thoroughly, tormenting though it was, and the memory of some occasions that we shared can still choke me with desire from time to time, even though almost twenty years have gone by since I last saw her. The woman was temptation personified, and every blandishment she offered contained a challenge, I thought, to my ultimate moral strength. That, at least, is what I used to tell myself. In my arrogance, I deluded myself that I was ultimately invulnerable to her attractions, but there was always the chance that I would succumb.

Our perverse relationship was a secret between the two of us—guilty on my part, blatant and sexually self-stimulating on Cylla's. Between the two of us there were no pretences. Cylla's motivations were hers alone, as was the undeniable satisfaction she derived from the entire situation. My own were equally private. We never discussed them, save in the broadest, coarsest terms, in whatever space of time each particular set of circumstances permitted. We would talk then, mostly in whispers, and Cylla would act—perform, I suppose, would be the most appropriate word. I did nothing on these occasions but look and react in tense self-containment that was sometimes agonizing. We conducted our association with these constraints because they were within my control, and they were within my control because I dictated the opening rules of what was to become an elaborate and long-extended game.

It began when we first met, my first night in the Villa Britannicus, when I had just met and fallen in love with Luceiia. Cylla climbed into my bed that night and woke me from an erotic dream. Had Luceiia not come to my immediate rescue, knowing Cylla and what she was likely to do, I would have had Cylla Titens there and then, uncaring who she was. But nothing happened. Luceiia nipped that blossom before it could even bud, and I did not see Cylla again for almost a year.

When we did meet again, it was at a gathering of friends, a thanksgiving celebration for a full harvest. Again Cylla let me know, without words, that she considered me a potential and soon-to-be-possessed bedmate. I avoided her designs on that occasion, and for a long time afterwards, by the simple expedient of never permitting myself to be alone with her. And so we continued for another year and more, with the four of us, Luceiia and myself and Cylla and her husband Domitius, whom she called Dom, reunited at least five times at similar gatherings.

Let it be understood here that Cylla Titens was, as I have already said, more than simply attractive. She was wondrous to behold from a distance and she radiated an aura of sexual availability that every man in every gathering was aware of and responded to, with the singular exception of Domitius, her husband.

It was only on closer association with her that her unattractive elements became apparent, and it may be that many of those affected me alone; there were many men who seemed oblivious to her faults, focusing only on the sweet honey distilled between her thighs. She had, for one thing, a discordant voice. As long as she spoke quietly, it was not too difficult to listen to, but when she became animated, Cylla's voice developed a shrillness, a shrewish quality, that was most unpleasant. Unpleasant, too, was her attitude in dealing with or discussing people, events and topics that were not directly concerned with benefit to her. She could be, and was, more often than not, waspish, disparaging, disagreeable and condemnatory on everything she turned her tongue to, whether or not she knew what she was talking about. Cylla invariably declaimed her viewpoints, assuming an authority that was seldom justifiable. In short, her personality was markedly obnoxious, and I preferred to keep my distance from her.

Domitius, on the other hand, was literally besotted with his wife. He worshipped the ground she trod, and his worship could never allow him to consider that she might be less than perfect. He was a devout Christian, absolutely devoid of malice or mistrust, and his charity was endless. He was fully aware of his wife's vanity, her exclusive preoccupation with herself and her appearance and her outrageous expenditures to maintain all of these. None of this perturbed him. He laughed at all of it and considered himself blessed in being able to provide for all of her needs. Fortunately for Cylla, he also accepted as a part of life and happiness that his wife had to spend at least one week out of three taking the waters of the baths at Aquae Sulis. From time to time, to Cylla's great but unspoken annoyance, he would accompany her. Most of the time, however, Domitius was content to remain at home, running his estates, pursuing his own particular pastimes and leaving his beloved wife to her own reasonably discreet pleasures.

It was in the springtime of my third year at the Villa Britannicus, when we were taking the first cautious, exploratory steps towards establishing our Colony, that Domitius Titens visited my forge one day and became enthusiastically caught up in what I was doing.

He came by, originally, to discuss some family matter with Caius, and visited me in my smithy purely out of courtesy, to pass the time of day. He asked me what I was working on and I showed him, and then he asked more and more questions, showing genuine interest. I responded with enthusiasm, as any craftsman will, and the unforeseen result was that I acquired, in the space of one brief afternoon, a wealthy, dedicated apprentice who laughed at the soot on his snowy robes.

I have often wondered since how things would have differed in our Colony had I merely responded pleasantly that day and pleaded pressure of work to avoid his questions and be rid of him. But of course, recrimination is fruitless.

In any event; Dom had his own smithy set up and operating on his villa in a matter of months. It is not important that he never did become a good smith—it was strictly a pastime for him; what is important is that he gained years of great pleasure from the craft, he and I became close friends, and I started to spend time at his home, thereby falling into the bizarre, grotesque pattern of activities that was Cylla's game.

I think of it always as Cylla's game, even though I was as active a player as she in many respects. I can recollect with accuracy how the overt moves of the game developed, but the preliminary manoeuvres, and the evaluations that accompanied them, were Cylla's alone; I was totally unaware of them. From the outset, long before I knew there was a game, I was adamant that Cylla would never isolate me; there would always be someone nearby, someone within hearing distance. Cylla accepted this basic rule very quickly, and accepted also the corollary that I had not yet recognized: that no matter who might be around us, there would always be intervals, no matter how brief, when she and I would be together unobserved. It was on that acceptance that she built her strategy, and on that premise she moved her pieces with mounting authority, learning quickly what I would tolerate from her and what I would not. As things transpired, there was nothing, under the strict rules of the game, that I would not tolerate.

Cylla set out to make herself attractive to me—personably, intimately, hospitably attractive. And, in spite of my obvious disapproval of her, she was successful. There is no need to describe most of the things she did; they are contained in the armoury of every woman who takes aim at a man, and every adult is familiar with them. But Cylla handled these weapons with extra subtlety, sharpening them into instruments of incredible potency, and eventually stabbing deeply and accurately with them at the most outlandish times and with outrageous effrontery. Anyone watching would have said that she ignored me completely most of the time, yet when she did address me she was invariably pleasant, courteous and hospitable. Never a glimpse of the shrew for Publius Varrus! No one could ever have suspected that any bond, or any attraction, existed between the two of us.

Without contradicting what I have just said, I should mention that Luceiia had some short-lived suspicions in the beginning, right at the outset, before the charade had developed and before I had identified what Cylla was doing. It seemed to her, as a woman and my wife, that Cylla's conversion, in regard to me, from sexual predator to charming friend was *too* complete, and she remarked upon it to me one night when she and I were dining alone. She spoke merely out of perplexity and was not being in any way accusatory, and my response was terse, dismissive and absolutely truthful: "She knows I don't like her." Luceiia accepted that and never mentioned the matter again, for which I came to be extremely grateful.

And so Cylla disarmed me, almost to the point where I considered relaxing my vigilance. I started to feel more comfortable around her. I began to relax, to accept that she would not be offensive or put me out of countenance— she was one of the few people at that time in whose company I was still aware of my crippled leg. That awareness faded eventually, however, in the light of her consistent, considerate treatment of me and her ongoing deference. I began to feel at ease in her presence. She soon sensed that, and put her next move into effect. Slowly, and only very gradually, over a number of months, she brought *touch* into play. Not between us, except on one fleeting occasion. Cylla never touched me, nor I her, except for that one time. But she touched herself, and for my eyes alone, knowing that I was watching.

The first time she surprised me with an overt gesture, my reaction was to tell myself it was unintentional, that I had merely seen something not meant to be seen. Dom had brought me to the villa to show me a piece of work he had in progress, and he went straight to a curtained closet built beneath the sweep of the main staircase to rummage for the thing. Cylla had been crossing the vestibule towards the stairs as we came in. She smiled pleasantly, spoke a word or two without stopping and began to go upstairs. I stood in the hallway, waiting for Dom.

Cylla always dressed magnificently, and was celebrated for it. Her clothing was designed to drape in such a way as to conceal, yet sharply emphasize, the shape of her: her breasts, her flat belly, her thighs, hips and buttocks and the long, clean length of her legs. The stairway was brightly lit by a glazed, translucent skylight and Cylla paused about eight stairs up to call to Dom, reminding him that they were having guests that afternoon. She had paused with her right foot on the stair two steps above her left one, leaning forward and to her left to call down to Dom, who was almost directly beneath her feet. I noticed how the soft folds of her robe draped over her raised thigh, outlining it clearly and clinging to the limb. She continued to lean forward slightly, her head cocked to hear Dom's response, paying no attention to me at all, but as she stood, poised there for the space of several heartbeats, her right hand dropped to her thigh and stroked the smooth material of her amber-coloured robe, almost, it seemed to me, unconsciously, except that the stroking movement lasted one heart-stopping instant too long. The abstracted touch became an unmistakable caress; an invitation to look and admire; a lascivious little secret for me to carry away, having seen the incredible intimacy of the way her fingers curled to press the material against the soft, full undercurve of her thigh from just above her knee to the junction of her legs. Then Dom answered her and she was moving again, heading upstairs without a glance in my direction. I felt my crotch harden and heard my heart thump in my ears and I had to move quickly to meet Dom, hoping that he would not notice my obvious arousal.

That was the first clear move in Cylla's game, and it progressed rapidly from there. The second move came soon after. Standing beside Dom, her arms folded as they both looked down at the table on which I had spread the parchment I had brought to show him, she scratched idly with one thumbnail at her breast, bringing an amazingly large nipple into turgid prominence as I stood within arm's length of her. I saw the soft, yielding fullness of the breast and the urgency of that nipple's arousal and yet saw no sign that she was aware of my eyes. Dom, of course, saw nothing.

On another occasion, we were at a gathering of two dozen people, including Luceiia, in the main reception room of the house. By this time I had come to anticipate that Cylla would find a way, somehow, to do something, and I had even dressed in a long, light over-robe that would effectively conceal, I hoped, any excitement she might bring about. We were waiting for the servants to call us all in to dinner. The celebration was informal and everyone was having an enjoyable time.

Luceiia was deep in conversation with a group of Dom's elderly relatives who had come up from Sorviodunum and whose presence was the reason for the gathering. I had moved away from them to take a second cup of Dom's excellent Germanic wine from one of the servants when I became aware that Cylla was looking at me. She was sitting on a deep, high-backed couch and had just been in conversation with a couple of young girls who were now making their way across the room towards Dom. As soon as she saw me look her way, she averted her eyes and glanced around the room, and I knew she was looking to see if anyone was watching. As she did so, one of the servants banged loudly on a copper gong and announced that dinner was about to be served. Every head in the room except mine turned towards the source of the voice, and Cylla stood up.

I wish I could adequately describe how she did it. Her timing was perfect and her movements so deliberate, yet so quick, that I felt as if I had been kicked in the crotch. In less time than it takes to tell, she gripped the front edge of her couch, spread her legs wide so that the folds of her robe fell immediately and graphically between them and thrust her body forward in a long slide before pushing herself erect to stand spread-legged for a moment, her skirts swirling around her ankles. It was the movement of an athlete, but the spreading of her legs and that deliberate slide forward undid me, catching me by surprise as her manoeuvres always did. For an instant there was nothing in my world but the wanton urgency of those parted thighs and that thrusting, female belly, and then awareness crashed back and I looked around guiltily to see if anyone had seen me *see* it. No one was paying any attention and the entire crowd moved as one body towards the entrance to the *triclinium*, the main dining room.

I joined the exodus, my blood on fire, willing the pounding in my head to die down, but before it could I became aware of Cylla, at whom I had not dared look again, standing directly in front of me, too close, among the crowd. I stopped short, preparing to back away from her, but before I could do so, I felt her hand brush against me, locating me, and then the back of her hand pressing firmly against the jut of my phallus. I almost leaped away from her, but Cylla never touched me again, and she ignored me completely for the remainder of that evening. I calmed myself eventually, but lustful images swarmed in my mind for hours afterwards.

Now Cylla knew beyond doubt that her designs were working. She also knew, with equal certainty, that she could rely on my silence; and she knew, too, that she could count on my complicity in the game that had now begun in earnest.

I had absolutely no regard for Cylla as a person, and that saddens me

now. I considered her to be a thorough slut—everyone did, except Dom—
and I really believed, in my arrogance, that she was uncaring of my opinion.
She seemed, in fact, to revel in the knowledge of my real dislike of her,
perhaps because she knew that I would keep coming back in spite of it. Liking
and dislike, it seemed to me, had nothing to do with the game.

I never did doubt her enjoyment of the game, however; nor, for that
matter, did she doubt mine. But Cylla had an advantage over me: she knew
that I felt guilt because, for all my arrogant, self-deluding high-mindedness,
I was attracted to her wanton behaviour and could not master my lust. She
knew that she held my eyes, if no other part of me, clasped tight between
her lascivious thighs; she knew and enjoyed the agonizing depth of my guilt;
and she revelled in the knowledge that her depravity drove me to purge myself
of my frustrated seed by my own hand, since my then perverted sense of
honour would not let me willingly take my lust for Cylla home to Luceiia.

What cowards we men are! Here I am, writing of Cylla's depravity, when
it was mine. Eventually, before matters came to a head in a way I could never
have visualized, I was existing in a condition that must have approached
insanity, and I have often thought, in later years, that the dementia of my
lust reduced me, in effect, to the behaviour I might have expected of Claudius
Seneca, the man I detested most in all the world.

For several years, at the outset, we barely exchanged words at all. The
entire game was in the playing, with Cylla initiating and me reacting, both
wordlessly.

The end of that stage occurred early one autumn morning, when I had
dropped in at their house with some tools for Dom and had been invited to
break bread with them. The three of us were seated at a table in their private
quarters. We had eaten sparingly and were talking casually of nothing in
particular when I saw one of the signs I had come to recognize in Cylla as
she prepared to do something reckless and dangerous. When she became
excited her eyes glittered. There is no other word I can think of to describe
her look on such occasions; her gaze took on an almost luminous intensity,
and her eyes teared over, almost as though she were going to weep, except
that there was no hint of anything doleful about her. Her eyes filled with
dancing highlights, and she exuded an aura of barely hidden gaiety.

On this occasion, Dom noticed it too. He leaned forward and stroked
her cheek in a loving, uxorious caress, and Cylla turned and smiled at him,
a smile of utter sweetness, which she then bestowed on me.

"Publius," said Dom, "is she not radiant? I thank God daily for this
treasure He has given me. But she seldom looks this happy, and it must be
your presence that pleases her so. I must bring you here more often. Don't
you agree, my dear?"

Cylla did not speak. She merely smiled at me with that radiant, glittering
smile and I writhed in discomfort because both her hands were out of sight
beneath the table and I *knew* she was caressing herself.

I grew red in the face from guilt and fear that Dom might reach out to take her hand, and I moved quickly to stand up and take my leave.

"No," she said, both hands appearing above the tabletop, "you must not leave yet, Publius. Dom has something to show you." Dom's face went blank. "Don't you, my dear?" He blinked, and she continued as though speaking to a small boy. "Your plans for the new tessellated floor?"

"Ah! Of course, stupid of me." His face went blank again. "Where are they, my dear? Do you know?"

"Oh, Dom! They are either in your *cubiculum* or in one of the chests in your bedchamber. Bring them back here and we can spread them on the other table there."

"Yes, of course. Pardon me, Publius. I won't be long."

Cylla's hands were back beneath the table and, as Dom left the room, she made a motion which told me she had parted her skirts to free her legs. "Look!"

"No, damnation!" I stood up and walked angrily away from the table, angry at her and at myself. "Cylla, how can you do this to Dom?"

"To Dom? I am doing nothing to Dom. I'm doing it for you, look!"

I looked. Her naked legs were spread wide beneath the table.

"For the love of the sweet Christ! One of these days he's going to catch you!"

"Perhaps. But not today. I hid those plans too well. We have some time."

I turned my back on her, fighting to keep down the swelling in my treacherous crotch. I heard her stand up and move towards me until she stood in front of me, the perfect depiction of a decorous, dutiful Roman wife. She moved to the door of the room, looked out into the hallway and then came back to stand between me and the open doorway to the garden, so that her body was clearly outlined through her thin robe against the bright, early-morning sunlight. She stood spread-legged.

"Look, Publius." In my mind, I always hear her speaking in a sibilant whisper. "That's all you want to do, so look, and lust. Feel yourself grow hard and imagine what you could do inside me, how you would surge with spilling seed if only your iron will would let you." She pulled apart the skirts of her robe, revealing the beauty of her warm, soft, firm flesh, and showing me openly for the first time the breath-taking thick bush of red-gold hair at her centre. I gazed and grew hard, my ears straining for the first sounds of Dom's return. The glittering smile never left her eyes.

"Much as you might like to, you will never slide your hard smith's phallus into me, will you, Publius? That would be a sin against your wife. But your wife has been your wife for years now. She is beautiful, but she is familiar territory, no?"

I wanted to tell her not to soil my wife's name with her mouth but, God help me, I could only stare as she dug with one finger deep into her centre, churned it around and withdrew it, extending it to show me how it glistened with her juices.

"This is the unfamiliar, Publius. The illicit. This moisture that you yearn for is the forbidden fruit that keeps men young." She put the finger deep into her mouth, slowly sucked it clean and then held it out to me again. "This is why you look to me, to Cylla—because I can show you all the earthly delights, all the sinful excesses that wives do not deal in."

"Show them to your husband," I croaked, my throat swollen tight.

Her eyebrow went high, but neither in scorn, nor in derision. "He has no interest." I said nothing, and she smiled. "You do not believe me, do you? But why should I lie? What would I gain by it? Would it make you think me less wanton? Nothing could do that, could it? But that wantonness is what brings you here, so I accept your disapproval. Do you like this?" She ran her fingers through the bush of red-gold hair.

"Do that again," I whispered, almost choking.

"What? This?" She did it again, lingering long with that probing finger buried deep inside her before withdrawing it and offering it to me to taste. As I shook my head in refusal, I heard Dom returning. I watched her suck her finger clean again, knowing exactly how that hot mouth would feel around me, and then Dom walked back into the room, his head already bowed over the document he held unrolled between his hands. Cylla casually moved away from the revealing light of the doorway and I bent over the plans Dom laid out on the table, seeing nothing but the image of Cylla's mouth sucking on her finger.

That image, and the memory of her red-gold pubis stayed with me for days.

The ultimate move in the game, its final stage of depravity, happened in the late spring of the year of the raid in which I was wounded, mere weeks after Caius told me of the amazing and impossible report that Claudius Seneca had been seen in Rome. Cylla arrived at the entrance to my smithy one morning and asked if she might speak with me alone. This was unprecedented. She had never approached me so openly before. I quaked with apprehension as I stepped outside into the bright sunlight to speak with her, but she put my mind at ease immediately by handing me a package of drawings, the design for a smelting oven I had lent to Dom some time earlier and which he had promised to return that day.

"Dom asked me to return these to you. He has gone into Aquae Sulis."

I blinked at her, my eyes still smarting from the bright sunlight. "Aquae Sulis? Why didn't you go with him? You usually do, don't you?"

"Yes, but not this time. I have no need." I looked closely at her, but there was no glitter in her eyes. I relaxed, but she went on.

"Publius, I have a suggestion to make. I know you have no wish to go beyond looking. You enjoy looking. We both know that. Now I would like you to look in a different way. Would you like that? I think you would."

I felt myself frowning and stepped further from the doorway of the smithy, leading her by the elbow around the corner into a narrow, brick-paved passageway between some storehouses. When I felt sure we were far enough removed from the door to avoid being overheard, I asked, keeping my voice low, "Cylla, what are you talking about? What could be different? What more is there to look at? I know you as well as any man could know you, using only his eyes. How can you improve on that?"

"Cylla."

"What?"

"Cylla. My name. You said it. You never use it."

"No, I never do, do I?"

"Use it again, now."

She smiled, but it was a strange smile. Had I not known her so well, I might have thought it was an uncertain smile, almost tremulous. I said nothing, and she went on.

"We are here in your domain, Publius, and not playing the game."

"So?" I was confused, unable to understand what she was saying.

"So, after—what?—seven years of not saying my name, would you please me on this summer day by calling me by my name again? Just once more?"

I was surprised and, in consequence, more cruel than I care to remember. "Humph!" I grunted, feeling uncomfortable at this departure from the norm. "We were speaking of looking, Cylla ... Well, Cylla, I have watched you make love to yourself in every way, with everything from vegetables to the finest beeswax candles. What more is there to see?"

She gazed at me in silence for long moments and I tried to divine what she was thinking from the strange expression on her face, but then she laughed her old laugh and her eyes began to shine.

"Do I hear censure, Publius? Disgust? Come now, you love all of it. Cylla, your wanton Cylla, thrills you and excites you more than she disgusts you, does she not? No," she answered her own question, her voice becoming lighter with mockery. "No, perhaps not more than she disgusts you, but much more violently, far more pleasurably. I've seen you grow hard in spite of your disgust and your dislike of what you think of as your weakness, Publius, and I've watched you spill by hand the seed you would never give to me in any other way. But there *is* more."

"How? How can there be? What more?"

"Come to my house today and see."

"No. Not while Dom is away."

She gazed at me again. "I wonder if you will ever see what a fool you are in this, Publius. You will not betray your friend in his absence. You prefer to wait until he is nearby."

"That's enough, Cylla! Enough!"

She paused, then nodded. "Very well, then we shall choose another venue. Out of doors. In the woods."

"No! Against the rules. Not alone." I was growling through my temptation.

"I will not be alone. You will."

"What? What d'you mean?"

"What I said. I will be accompanied."

"My God, you're mad! Accompanied by whom? And what makes you think I would ever consider such a thing?"

"By a man. A lovely, stripling boy who cannot hear or speak, but lacks in nothing else."

"You *are* mad!"

She laughed again. "Mad? How? Because I invite you to watch? But I love having you watch me at my games, Publius! No one watches me better or more intently, more ravenously than you do. I truly thought you might enjoy watching someone else take for himself the pleasures you deny yourself. There would be no danger of discovery. You could watch and remain unseen! Think of it, Publius. The boy is deaf. He will not hear you approach to stand among the bushes, and he will make no sound, and I will bind his eyes so he is blind to all but the pleasures I will shower upon him for your pleasure." She paused, watching me closely, and when I said nothing she continued. "He is but a boy, Publius, though he performs like a stallion. He will be an instrument of pleasure, no more than that—a silent, unseeing, unhearing instrument, manipulable as any of the others I have used in the past. Except that he will use me as a mare, and I will use him to exhaustion. Think, Publius. He will not see you there. But I will. And you will finally see me used as the slut I am in your eyes—ravaged and ridden, stretched and clutched, sweating and writhing, kneeling over a living, piercing phallus, impaling myself as I look over his head, watching you watching me, both of us wishing it were you in me." Her voice softened. "No broken rules, Publius, no departures from the game. It will still be only you and I. But I shall cover his eyes tightly when it is done, because I want you, Publius Varrus, to watch a man's seed seeping from the body of your playmate at least once. Think of it, Publius. For your eyes and for your lusts alone, and none to know of it save I."

"Sweet Christ!"

She cut me short. "No preaching, Publius! I will be there, with the boy, by the third hour after noon. You know the standing stone at the south-east corner of our land. A pathway leads into the woods from there. Count your steps and keep them short as mine. A hundred and twenty paces from the edge of the forest there, you will see a holly tree on the left of the path. Directly behind that tree, some forty paces further off the path, there is a clearing with a mossy bank fit for the bedding of a god. Don't be afraid of making noise. Remember, the boy is deaf and mute. I will be listening for your approach, but I will not wait for long. With a naked youth and a long, strong phallus nearby, I find I grow wet very quickly and must scratch my itch." She paused and leaned closer to me, sniffing deeply. "You are grimy and sooty and sweaty and smelly. I like that. The juice is trickling from me, down my thigh, right now. I want to lean, or sit somewhere and do things for us. Is there a place nearby?"

"No, for the love of God!"

"No. For the love of lust. What about your smithy? It looks dark."

"Are you mad? Equus is in there, and a dozen other people."

"What's that place?" She nodded towards a door.

"Nothing. A storeroom."

"Show me."

"No! Cylla, for the—"

"Then I shall look myself."

She walked forward and pulled the door open. The room was tiny, with barely enough space for a man to enter and reach the shelves that lined the interior. She stepped inside and turned to face me, pulling the bottom of her beautiful, light-blue gown up over her long, clean-muscled legs. I groaned in despair and excitement. This time she was really going to go too far, but I had already seen the glistening evidence of her arousal on the inner surface of her thighs; she had not been exaggerating. Her fingers were already busy and her knees began to give way as her back slid down the shelf-lined wall. In the dimness of the hut's interior her eyes looked glazed, so intense was her excitement. She reached out one hand to me, wet with her body's fluid. I had never known any woman who could get so wet so quickly. I glanced from side to side in fear, but there was no one to be seen. And then Cylla began to moan, deep in her throat, something I had never known her do before.

"Stop that!" I hissed.

"I can't," she moaned. "It's being here, so close to your place. Step closer. Let me smell the smoke on you."

Terrified of being discovered, but completely incapable of resisting, I stepped closer and she closed her eyes, inhaling deeply and then whimpering in her throat as she gained release. I knelt down on one knee, no longer caring who might happen by. "Show me! Show me how wet you are."

"How wet do you want me?"

"As wet as you can be."

She stuck her tongue between her lips and smiled, and then squatted lower and squirted a strong jet of urine to splatter on the floor of the hut. As I gazed in utter fascination, she straightened up slowly, clutching her skirts high around her waist and simply allowing the stream of urine to run down her legs and soak her sandals.

"Is that wet enough for you? You see? There are still new things to look at. Give me your hand." I shook my head. "Then give me something, a cloth."

I straightened up and handed her the kerchief I wore around my neck, and she dried her thighs, rubbing the cloth thoroughly in the wetness of her crotch before handing it back to me. I raised it to my face and sniffed it. She stepped from the hut.

"Your turn. You need to do it. I'll watch. If anyone comes, I'll warn you and you can take something from a shelf for me." Her eyes were fixed on my crotch. "Do it, Publius. Now!"

I did, and it took only moments with her hungry eyes on me and the vision of what I had just watched her do. When it was over she nodded.

"The third hour. But no sooner. It would not please you to meet us on the path by accident. I will be listening for you. Remember: forty paces behind the holly tree."

Then she turned and was gone, leaving me to attempt to reconstruct my day and to struggle against the temptation she had dangled in front of me for that afternoon.

IV

I RODE HARD all the way to Cylla's tryst that afternoon, cursing myself and debating my own sanity with every beat of my horse's hoofs, and at the end of my journey I tethered the animal to a sapling just inside the forest's edge, about fifty paces from the entry to the path that would take me to the clearing. The sun had passed into the fourth hour of its afternoon journey and it threw my shadow directly ahead of me as I walked. By that stage I was numb; I knew only that I was lost in a wilderness beyond my understanding and completely beyond my control, but it was that last, pusillanimous thought that finally stiffened my spine and gave me the strength to stop in my tracks and turn around. I knew that if I went into the woods to that clearing, if I took even one step along that pathway, I would have forsaken the last remnants of my pride and honour; if I stooped so low as to watch Cylla with another man, I would be betraying not only my family and all I held dear, but my own manhood, giving up total possession of my immortal soul to Cylla's beast as well as to my own.

My horse stood cropping the sparse grass beneath the trees where I had tethered him, and I leaned my full weight against his side for a spell, smelling the clean, equine odour of him. He smelt exactly like a horse, exactly as he should, sweaty and wholesome, and there was nothing false or specious about him. He was a horse, full of a horse's strength. He had no truck with anything that was not fit for horses. When he rutted, he rutted straightforwardly, without subterfuge, and only with a mare who was in season; otherwise, he did as horses do.

I had a ludicrous vision of him gazing in fascination at another stallion rutting with a mare, and I began to laugh, quietly at first, and then with more and more abandon and less and less sanity as I was struck by the ridiculous folly of what I was imagining and I saw myself clearly for what I had become.

I ended up sitting on the ground between his legs, laughing uproariously and then suddenly weeping; like the sensible animal he was, my horse moved away, eyeing me uneasily, which made me laugh and weep the more.

I regained my senses eventually and felt better than I had in a long, long time. And I knew, with the clarity of absolute certainty, that Cylla's game had ended. I had found my direction again, after years of wandering lost, and it had been pointed out to me by a horse! How many times had Equus called me a horse's arse? Now I knew Equus was wrong, but it had taken a horse to show me what I was, or should be: I was a man, and a maker of weapons;

a smith and a soldier. I had no business with unmanly, lesser things, and from this day I would avoid them and regain the strength of my manhood.

I saw the fallen, rotting tree that I had noticed earlier, the reason for tethering my horse where I had. When you have a leg like mine, you watch always for easy means of mounting. I led him to it, climbed upon his back and pointed him away from the forest, down towards the stream among the bushes in the bottom of the valley. The trees here were sparse and small, no more than saplings; you could almost gallop among them.

On the bank of the stream, this time by an ancient, mossy stump, I dismounted again, took off my sandals and light leggings and then sat down, dangling my bare feet in the gurgling water. I watched tiny fish darting in the stillness of a lazy eddy by my side and let the soothing sound and touch of the cool waters wash me clean. And when I dressed again and left for home, it was without regret for Cylla or the game she was playing in the forest glade.

On the way home I was acutely conscious of the beauty of the day and of the scenery around me. The sprouting, unformed leaves had not yet lost their fragile newness and the moss of winter and spring was still bright green and moist; flowers bloomed among the grasses everywhere I looked and the air seemed full of butterflies and bees. At one point, I heard a crashing in the bushes and my horse shied nervously, scenting the bear that had already scented us and gone. I gentled him and then kicked him to a trot to get out of the area and leave the poor bear in peace; I had no quarrel with any animal that day. In this way, it took me far longer to get home than it had to arrive.

As I prepared to dismount outside the forge, I heard my name being called and turned to see one of the household servants running towards me, waving his arms. I stayed on my horse and waited until he ran right up to me, gasping for breath, with the news that Luceiia had been looking for me "for hours" and had sent him to the forge to wait for me and make sure that I went straight to her on my return.

As I strode into the villa, wondering what could be amiss, Luceiia came hurrying to meet me, her face pale, and I braced myself to hear bad news of the children or of Caius.

"Thank God you're here! Have you seen Domitius?"

I was taken off guard. "Domitius? Dom? No, he's in Aquae Sulis. He left this morning. Why?"

It was Luceiia's turn to frown and look nonplussed. "What do you mean, in Aquae Sulis? He was here less than an hour ago, looking for you."

My heart thudded and seemed to miss a beat. "Dom? No, he couldn't have been. He's away."

Luceiia was close to anger, impatient with my thick-skulled slowness. "Publius, listen to me! You have to find him. He is distraught. Something terrible has happened. I don't know what, but I'm afraid for Dom. He was wild, Publius, and there was blood on his clothes."

"Blood?" I was having difficulty taking in her words. "What do you mean, blood? How much blood? Whose? Tell me, Luceiia, in the name of God!"

She threw her hands apart in a gesture of helplessness. "I don't know, Publius! I don't know anything, except that something was very, very wrong and there was nothing I could do for him. He would not talk to me. He wanted only you and no one else. He was out of his senses, Publius—completely, totally undone. He burst into the house and I heard him shouting your name. When I came out to see what all the commotion was about, he was upstairs, rushing from room to room, all the while shouting for you.

"I went to him and told him you were out, but I don't think he even heard me. He looked awful, Publius. His hair was standing on end and his eyes were . . ." She broke off and raised a hand to her mouth as though to stop the words she knew would come out next. "Oh, Publius, I have never seen such eyes—filled with so much pain and rage and grief."

My mouth had gone dry and I could hear my heart beating in time to the dread wings fluttering in my gut.

"Then what? What did he say?"

"Nothing. Or almost nothing. He stopped shouting and looked around, blinking his eyes as though he didn't know where he was. Then he looked at me, and his face—I don't know how to describe it, Publius—it *darkened*, and he asked me, 'Did you know?' Then he looked around him again, and up at the skylight, and then he ran down the stairs and away, shouting your name."

"And no one followed him? You simply let him go?"

"At first, yes. We were all amazed, and he had a horse outside. I regained my wits as soon as he had gone and sent Paul the groom to follow him, but by then it was too late; Paul could not find him."

"Blood, Luceiia. You said there was blood. How much and where? Was it his own?"

She shook her head in an abrupt negative, as though dismissing my question. "I couldn't tell. He wore a cloak, fastened to the neck, covering him completely. I only saw a glimpse of his tunic, and it looked black. It was not until I saw his legs and feet, as he went out the door into the sunlight, that I saw it for what it was. Publius, his legs were *covered* in blood."

"Where was Cay during all this? And where is he now?"

Again the headshake. "He's not here. He went out earlier with a man, an old friend of his, who came here about noon. I don't know who he was. I was busy with the children and did not see him. Anyway, the servants said he was a stranger, but Cay knew him well from long ago. The two of them went off somewhere and have not come back."

"Sweet Christ!" I was already limping to the door as quickly as I could move, shouting back over my shoulder, "Call Equus and assemble a mounted party and make sure there's wagons and a medic with them. Tell them to meet me at the Villa Titens as quickly as they can, *and you stay here!*"

My horse still stood in the yard where I had left him. I flung myself across his back and had him running before I was properly seated. He was a strong animal and ready for another run. Now I whipped him to a gallop and put him to the shortest route towards the home of Dom and his faithless wife.

It took me half an hour, at full speed, to get there, and I was careless now of the poor brute beneath me, abusing him cruelly in my fear. As I went, I fought with my own imagination, telling myself it could not be as bad as I was fearing.

The first sign of tragedy was waiting for me at the villa gate: Carlos, Dom's manservant of many years, lay sprawled and disembowelled across my path. Behind him, some paces distant, lay another corpse, unknown to me. I looked further and saw more, four in all, in the entrance court. It looked like the aftermath of a raid, and I told myself Dom had been unmanned by discovering the scene unexpectedly, but even as my mind formed the thought I knew I was only deluding myself again. Dom, my gentle friend, had done this in the grip of madness.

The last of the corpses, this one a young woman, sprawled stiffly in her dried blood on the steps leading to the portico of the house itself, and I paused there, outside the door, dreading to enter, fearing what I would find. Rather than look too closely at the dead woman by my feet, I looked up at the sky. Night was approaching and heavy clouds had rolled in from the west, gravid with rain. *Perfect*, I thought. *You will need all your rain to wash away the blood here on this ground.* I drew my sword, for what reason I knew not, pushed open the doorway and stepped through into Hades itself.

A soldier grows inured to the sight of blood. It is part of his life; the spilling of it part of his occupation; and as he accepts blood and the spilling of it, he accepts as well the effluvia and the ordure that go hand in hand with the abrupt and violent, brutal severance of life. He learns to accept and ignore the stench of voided bowels and bladders; he sees without seeing the liverish, blue-white-purple glisten of entrails, and the sharp, pungent stink of visceral fluids assaults his nostrils only in passing. The soldier is endowed with this detachment in the same way that iron is tempered: by being immersed in fire and then beaten with heavy hammer blows. His tempering is in the fury and the terrors of battle, where nothing may exist in his mind that might distract him from his most sacred, dedicated need: to survive.

Remove the stimulus of dire, frenzied struggle, however, and transport the man, along with all the chaotic slaughter of the battlefield, into the confines of a quiet, spacious, well-lit family home, and you amplify ten-thousandfold all the cumulative horrors he has been able to ignore throughout his life. The result is waking nightmare: horror and loathing beyond description.

I had never really known, in spite of all my experience, just how much blood can spill from human bodies. Every wall in the interior of that house, it seemed to me, was polluted with blood: it was everywhere, smeared and splashed in thick, dark gouts from which grim trickles ran towards the floor, which was completely awash in thick, black, coagulated sheets and puddles of gore. It was a scene from Tartarus, lacking only leering, gibbering demons.

I would not have been surprised to see demons. I looked for them, but only their minions were present, the flies. Beelzebub himself, the Lord of the Flies, had been here recently but was now gone, and only his servants remained, their buzzing drone filling the air like the moans of tormented souls.

I stood just inside the open portal, my feet in blood, as though I had frozen to the floor, and my scalp crawled and I found myself fighting to draw breath as the scene seemed to revolve slowly around me. I counted seven bodies, all household servants, all butchered horribly. The broad stairway to the second floor, the stairway where I had first seen Cylla touch herself, was a dried river of blood. I made a mighty effort and succeeded in flexing my fingers, which gripped my sword hilt so tightly that they were in pain, and then I moved towards the stairs, looking down to place my feet carefully, trying to ignore the charnel-house around me.

There was another young woman lying at the top of the stairs. She had been almost completely decapitated and it was her blood that drenched the steps. Cylla's bedchamber lay along the passage to my right, Dom's to my left. I went to Dom's room first, turning the handle cautiously and pushing the door open with my foot. It swung back slowly, revealing an empty chamber, clean and miraculously free of blood.

It seemed to take me an age to retrace my steps, past the dead girl at the stair head and along to Cylla's room, where I found the door wide open. An open window faced the door directly and I saw the curtains stirring sluggishly, too heavy with dried blood to flap in the strengthening breeze from outside. I stepped inside and vomited immediately, my whole being revolted at the sight that greeted me.

Cylla and *someone*—I presumed her young deaf-mute—had been destroyed on the bed, hacked and slashed almost beyond recognition, and their dismembered bodies piled together in a heap. In my first glance I saw severed arms and legs, a gutted male torso, and Cylla's head, wide-eyed and screaming, her lustrous hair glued to her skull with blood and her lips drawn back from her bloodied teeth in a rictus of terrified realization of what was happening to her. All of that I saw, and then I threw up, bending over with my hands upon my knees, my sword still gripped bone-tight. Reeling with nausea, and fearing I might fall into the blood, I staggered backwards, groping behind me for something to support my weight, and I found Dom. My hand touched his face, warm and alive, and I recoiled with a scream of fright, my sword arm swinging high to strike my assailant down.

But I did not strike. For I saw his eyes immediately, then his face, and then his condition. He was wedged almost upright, hunched over, his knees almost giving way, in a corner behind the door, and he was dying. His left hand hung by a flap of skin from its wrist, where he had chopped it off, and most of his life's blood was already gone. His eyes were ghastly in the whiteness of his face, but they seemed clear and lucid. He knew me. We remained there, immobile as statuary, for what seemed like a very long time before I lowered my sword. Dom's own sword, a fine, sharp one that I had made for him, lay by his feet. When I moved, so, too, did he, gesturing with that grotesquely flopping hand towards the bed and its horrid burden. The movement brought a feeble jet of blood spurting in my direction and I remembered another handless arm that had saved my life in battle long ago, allowing me to be crippled rather than killed.

"Cylla . . ." His voice was little more than a wheeze of sound. "She mocked me, Publius . . ." I remained motionless and he went on. "Railed at me . . . Laughter . . . Struck me . . . Tried to kill me." His eyes looked towards the bed and back to me. "Said everybody knew, Publius . . . everybody knew . . . servants . . . friends . . . all knew. Did . . ." He sagged, then drew his head back with a great effort, fixing me with rapidly glazing eyes. "Did you . . . ?" His strength gave out and he fell to his knees before me like a supplicant. Then his eyes rolled back into his head and he pitched forward on his face. I did not bend to feel for a pulse. Dom was dead and the better for it.

I can remember walking from that house in a state of absolute calm, picking my way with care to avoid the blood as much as possible. I crossed the courtyard to the gate where my horse stood waiting for me, far enough removed from the smell of blood to be unaware of it but sidling nervously, nevertheless. The first, heavy raindrops fell and turned into a downpour as I squatted on my heels against the wall outside that dreadful place. And in my mind I saw nothing of the slaughterhouse, only my good friend Dom looking at me with his incomplete question: "Did you . . . ?"

We found a gibbering, hysterical survivor in the cellars, a woman who had managed to escape with only a minor slash wound. She told us of Dom's rampage, of how he cried only *"Did you know?"* before he cut down each living soul he met, and, when he could find no more to kill, ran screaming from the villa.

We burned the Villa Titens and all that it contained, removed its stones and ploughed the ashes under, leaving no sign of its existence in our lands.

It did not occur to me until long afterwards that Cylla could not have been in the forest glade that afternoon.

V

THE TITENS AFFAIR affected everyone in the Colony, drawing a cloud over our little society, a pall that coloured every aspect of our lives for a long time. It seems strange to me now, however, that Caius and I barely discussed the matter after the first shock had worn off. We spoke of it in detail in the days that followed that dreadful afternoon, but then, by mutual consent, we consigned it to the past along with its principals. We had too many other things claiming our attention, all of them concerned with the ongoing life around us, for which we were responsible.

Luceiia, however, continued to think about the Titens household and the situation that had prevailed there, and, as in all things she turned her mind to, she considered it logically, analytically and exhaustively, arriving in due course at a conclusion she wished to share with me. That sharing became a night-long discussion that lasted well into the dark hours before dawn, with the two of us seated on either side of a glowing brazier in our chamber while the rest of the household slept. Luceiia did most of the talking. I listened, for the most part, and attempted to disagree with her on several points, but she demolished my few objections with ruthless, implacable arguments founded on solid logic and I finally had the good sense to stay quiet, listen and absorb what she had to say.

I remember it began almost innocuously. I had been aware for several days that something was bothering my wife deeply—she had been withdrawn and unusually taciturn; not ill-tempered or waspish in any way, but definitely unlike her normal, sunny-natured self—but my awareness had been mitigated to some extent by the knowledge that everyone in the Colony was concurrently undergoing the unsettling aftereffects of the Titens catastrophe. On that particular evening, we had retired slightly later than was normal. There had been a chill in the air all day, and Luceiia had ordered a brazier set up in our sleeping chamber, on the stone slabbed fireplace in one corner of the room. We stood side by side for a few moments in the firelight, not touching but merely warming ourselves by the glowing brazier, and then, as we were beginning to prepare for bed, our peace was rudely shattered by a chorus of drunken, bawling voices from the night outside. The suddenness and abnormality of the disturbance took me outside immediately in search of the perpetrators, cursing to myself as I struggled into my cloak and emerged into the cold night air. I found them without difficulty and gave them the rough edge of my displeasure, dispatching them homeward amid besotted apologies and a few sullen mutterings.

When I returned eventually to go to bed, I was very surprised to find Luceiia still awake and fully dressed, sitting by the brazier.

"They're gone. Why aren't you abed, love?"

"I couldn't sleep."

I misunderstood her. "Why not? They were drunk, and loud, but I told you, I sent them on their way. They won't bother us again. Come, let's to bed."

"I told you, Publius, I would not be able to sleep. I have too much on my mind."

I stopped in the act of moving towards her and hesitated there for a moment before seating myself on the bed, my cloak still folded over my right arm. "What's wrong, Luceiia?"

She shook her head, a tiny, exasperated gesture. "Nothing, everything. I've been thinking about Cylla Titens and that whole sorry mess."

That was not what I wanted to hear, then or at any time. My conscience would never be at ease over the entire matter of myself and Cylla Titens, and my apprehension flared in recognition of the fact that Luceiia appeared to have identified Cylla, the wife, and not Dom, the killer, as the progenitor of the disaster. She was correct, of course, but I had heard no other woman state the case so openly, although it had become common talk and knowledge among the men. Before I could begin to recover my wits, however, or even start to grapple for a response to what Luceiia had said, she continued speaking.

"This was simply more of the same. It's growing worse."

Now I was confused. I had no idea what she was talking about.

"What d' you mean? More of the same *what*?"

Luceiia withered me with a glance that seemed to me composed of equal parts of pity and scorn. "*Degeneration*, Publius! Surely you can see what's going on here, all around us? You can, can't you?"

I could only shrug and shake my head, wide-eyed at her evident concern and anger.

"*Ooh!*" Now evidently completely exasperated, she spun her head away from me and gazed into the coals, leaving me to try to decipher her meaning. After a space of long moments, during which I sat in bemused silence, she straightened her back and sucked in a deep breath before turning to face me again.

"Very well, let's play questions and answers. Two days ago, the day before yesterday, you came home angry and upset. Do you remember?"

"Of course I do. What of it?"

"What had angered you?"

"Someone had stolen several tools from the smithy."

"Why did you assume they had been stolen? One of the others might simply have mislaid them."

"No, that never crossed my mind. The lock had been forced on the shed where they were kept, and the same thing had happened in the wine storage room. Wine had been stolen, too, and it looked to me as though the tools stolen from me had been used to break the lock on the wine room."

"Ah, I see. Tell me, when was the last time we were disturbed here in our own home at night by noisy, drunken louts?"

"Never. This is the first time it has happened . . ." Perception began to dawn, although I was amazed by what I thought I perceived. "Luceiia, are you suggesting that those men tonight—"

"Were the men who stole your tools and then the wine? No, of course not. That would be absurd."

"Then what in the name of—"

"Publius, I am saying that there are things happening around here, in our own Colony, that should not be going on; things that have never happened before; things that anger and frighten me. Theft has always been *unknown* here! I've lived here all my life and have never known anyone to steal anything, unless it was theft committed by strangers, outsiders stealing merely because an opportunity presented itself. But no one on this villa has ever stolen anything from any other. There is no *need* to steal, Publius! But stealing is becoming common. So is brawling; men fighting over petty, stupid differences that shouldn't merit violence of any kind. You may think I am being foolish, and until tonight I would not have made this comment, but it seems to me—and to many of the other women around here—that men are drinking more."

"That *is* silly, Luceiia. Men have always drunk and always will."

She flared up. "I know that, Publius Varrus, and don't you call me silly! Don't belittle me, and never take me for a fool, for that's the last thing anyone could call me. I am Luceiia Varrus in marriage, but I have always been and will always be a Britannicus in my mind and in my nature, and we were *never* fools!" I sat blinking at her, mildly astounded by this newly revealed facet of my wife, as she continued, in a softer voice, "I was referring to *public drunkenness*, not to mere drinking. We are seeing—and you would, too, were you to look—an upsurge in public wantonness unprecedented in these parts." She saw the protest forming in my eyes and cut it short before it reached my lips. "Yes, *wantonness*, that's what I said. Domitius Titens would never have slaughtered anyone had his wife not been a wanton bitch, constantly in heat. God knows it took him long enough to see it, but when he did, he reacted in the only way his nature would allow him to. His life, his manly notions of honor, dignity and self-worth had all been destroyed, and yet he might have learned to live with that, to bear it with some kind of stoicism, had he been stronger. But he was suborned and completely undone by his realization of the *public* manner of his shame. Had he killed his wife, and even her adulterer, none would have thought the worse of him. But once he had seen her flagrant attitude, he must also have perceived his own shortsightedness in all that had gone before. He was driven insane, Publius, by the *public* wantonness she flaunted, and by his knowledge of the *public* depth of his humiliation." Luceiia paused, drawing a long, shuddering breath.

"But Cylla's wantonness is no more than a symptom of what we are facing. It is mirrored and reflected by the other, lesser, but no less invidious things that are occurring: the fighting, the stealing, the drunkenness, the evils that are sneaking into our lives . . . There is a man here in our Colony who is a living, ravening beast, incestuously cohabiting with his own daughters."

"Luceiia!" I could not keep the disapproval from my voice. "You can't *say* things like that without corroboration! Do you know it to be true? Can you prove it?"

"I have no need to prove it! I *know*! The women who have told me are all my friends and none of them would lie in such a thing, but they know that *men* will do nothing about it."

I shifted in discomfort, unwilling, suddenly, to pursue the difference in viewpoint she had specified, and to cover my concern I rose and hung my cloak on a peg. She watched me as I did, and then she spoke again, this time in a much more gentle tone. "Bring that other chair over here and sit beside me." When I had done so, she smiled and leaned towards me, touching my hand, cupping it in her own.

"Publius Varrus, you are my husband and a good man. But that very *goodness* inhibits you from seeing other men as being less well intentioned than you. You judge all men as being good, in essence, but that simply is not true. I have been thinking now for weeks, ever since the Titens massacre, of how I could bring these matters that concern me—that terrify me—to your attention. Now I have begun." She smiled and sat up straighter. "When I have finished, you may go to sleep and think upon what I have said."

I shook my head in perplexed acceptance, and settled down to listen to what turned out to be one of the most astonishing and logically flawless situation analyses I had ever heard. My amazing wife confounded me with an oral dissertation on public morality, social structure and civic, as well as personal, responsibility that left me deeply disturbed and quite unable to sleep. By the time we did eventually go to bed that night, shortly before dawn, I was convinced that what she had been telling me was accurate and correct in every respect, little as I might like it. My unreserved acceptance of her views, unfortunately, led directly to one of the few altercations I ever had with her noble brother.

It began abruptly, two days later, after two long days of thought and a good night's sleep, while I was telling him about the long talk his sister and I had had. I was gravely concerned by some of the things she had said and some of the issues she had raised, and I suppose the depth of my distress and anxiety came through clearly to Caius. He listened to what I had to say, courteously as always, at least in the early stages of my talking. As I went on, however, I could see that he was becoming more and more upset by what he was hearing until finally, unable to listen any longer, he held up a hand to restrain me. I stopped in mid-sentence, surprised by his reaction.

"You want to say something?"

He glared at me. "No, nothing. Not now. Not until I have had time to settle my thoughts and consider your words."

I was mystified. "Then what's wrong with you? You look as though you would like to flay me alive."

He exploded into anger, slapping the table violently and leaping up so suddenly that the stool he had been perched on fell over backwards.

"Damnation, Publius, I can't believe what I'm hearing! Do you know what you are telling me? Can you hear yourself? Have you listened to your own words?" He spun on his heel and walked across the room, his hands clenching and unclenching in agitation, while I stared after him in amazement.

My own concerns were deep, but I had thought about them long and hard before deciding to talk to Caius and I had tried to present them as dispassionately as I could. Now I was seeing a reaction I thought totally out of proportion to the tenor of what I had been saying, particularly since he had not allowed me to finish what I had begun to say. He swung back to face me, his face contorted by an anger I had not seen in him for years, and I felt myself frowning as I wondered what had caused it. He did not leave me wondering long, and his next words broke over me like cold water.

"Where in Hades has your training gone? Have you lost your manhood? You were a soldier once, Varrus! An officer! A supposedly intelligent commander of men! Don't make me doubt you now. Women's words and women's sentiments and women's pleadings suit you ill. You need to spend more time among your fellows and less among your womenfolk listening to old wives' tales and fears. You're growing soft and feminine!"

The injustice of these words infuriated me; my own anger swept up around me in a red haze and I found myself straining towards him, fighting an urge to beat him to the floor. I took no more than one half step, however, before the discipline of years stopped me. Forcing myself to contain this thundering surge of rage, I bent down slowly and righted the stool he had upset, holding it very tightly in both hands and setting it securely in place before allowing myself to look at him again. His face was still suffused with anger, as, I knew, was my own. His lips moved to form new words, but now it was I who cut him off with a chop of my hand, and whatever he had been about to say remained unsaid. I could hear my heart beating in my head and I waited until the pounding died down before I spoke. It took a long time, and neither of us moved in the interval. Finally, when I felt that I could speak without shouting, or without my voice shaking, I swallowed hard and willed myself to whisper, "Those are not words I expected from you, my friend." And having said that I turned and walked slowly from the room, leaving him alone with his inexplicable anger.

During the following hour I walked alone in the woods, going over what I had said to him and trying to identify the reasons for the astonishing effect of my words. What had I said? Certainly nothing that could be considered incendiary or demeaning; nothing that I could even classify as being unmanly or feminine, even though the arguments I was presenting had originated with my wife. So what, I asked myself over and again, could possibly have upset Caius so much?

I had told him that Luceiia was concerned that our colonists were losing touch with the morality necessary to communal living. The words sounded pompous to my own ears, now that I thought about them, but even so, could that have been the cause of his fury? Pomposity? Or was it the moral stance? Had he taken offence at that, misconstruing my words as a personal attack on his own morality? Surely not, I decided.

I had been describing Luceiia's concerns. She had been talking in generalities most of the time, but she had pointed out a number of specific instances in support of her claims, some of which I had been aware of, but many of which I had known nothing about. All of them had worried me, but several had been really frightening. The Titens family's situation was, strangely enough, the easiest for me to accept, in spite of my own role in it, for it embodied the entire situation in miniature. And Luceiia had assured me that the particular instances she cited were only random examples of a widespread and growing disease in our Colony.

I had told Caius some of this, and I had said that, in Luceiia's opinion, and now in my own, we, as the leaders of the Colony, were faced with a moral responsibility to ensure not only the physical welfare and well-being of our people, but also their moral, if not their spiritual welfare—an uncomfortable responsibility, certainly, if adopted, but an incontrovertible one.

I had then told him Luceiia had convinced me that the ancient laws and morality of Rome were no longer flexible or versatile enough for our times. The context of the times had changed, I said, and was still changing, and it seemed to Luceiia, and to me now, that the rules of the society we were building called for a more simplistic, more personal and more intimate set of laws and regulations.

It was at this point that Caius had interrupted me angrily, but examine it as I might, I could not find any reason for the ferocity of his rejection.

Eventually, after an hour or so, I had cooled down enough to return to the villa. I saw no sign of Caius and made no attempt to find him. I excused myself to Luceiia, claiming to have work to do, and took myself off to my forge with a cold roast fowl, a loaf of bread and a skin of wine. I ate alone and worked until nightfall, when I made my way back to the house to find Caius waiting for me in the family room. He stood up as I entered and I stopped on the threshold, looking at him and trying to gauge his mood. He shrugged and turned up his palms, with a curiously shamefaced look in his eyes.

"We need to talk, Publius. As friends."

I put down the bag I was holding and crossed towards the couch by the fire, and he turned to watch me as I passed him. My anger had long since disappeared and the room was warm and cosy with flickering light and dancing shadows.

"Where's Luceiia?" I asked.

He moved to sit across from me. "With the children. She will leave us alone for a time. I told her how ungracious and offensive I was to you this afternoon and she will not come in until I have stewed long in my own juices and made my apologies to you for my—"

"Forget about that, Caius." I cut him off, standing up and moving towards the table where I had seen a leather bucket filled with ice and salt and a stone jug of my favourite Germanic wine. Ullic's people brought us cartloads of ice from the mountains every spring, cut into large blocks and insulated with straw and, stored with care in the whitewashed cool room of the villa, it kept our stored meat and poultry fresh through the heat of the summer. It also served to cool our best wines on festive occasions.

"No apologies are necessary between us, Cay. We have been friends too long. I angered you, you angered me. Things like that happen, sometimes." I picked up the wine jar, feeling its icy coldness and reaching for two cups. "Why the best wine? This is celebration stuff. What are we celebrating?"

He smiled, wryly. "My apology? My dear sister thinks that I should admit to failings more often. She seems to think it makes me more human."

"You told her what we argued about?"

"Yes. I was surprised you hadn't already done so."

"I wasn't ready." I poured for both of us and handed him a cup. "I would have told her eventually, but it was too soon and I hadn't had time to think things through." I tasted my wine. It was perfect. Chilled and delicious. "What did she have to say?"

"Not much, at first." He raised his cup to me and sipped his own wine. "God, this is nectar! No, she had little to say at first. I knew she was ashamed of me and angry at me for turning my tongue on you, but she was remarkably patient and showed her usual forbearance."

"Yes," I murmured, "but your sister is a remarkable woman. I've told you that before now, more than once. So, you discussed her . . . conclusions? Civilly?"

"Civilly, and thoroughly."

"And . . .?"

"And she is absolutely correct, of course. We have a problem of some magnitude, one that will have to be addressed."

"Hmmm . . ." I sat down again in my favourite chair. "Addressed by whom?"

"By all of us, Publius. Initially by you and me, I suppose, working together with Luceiia. Eventually, however, this is going to demand the involvement of everyone in our little society."

I moved to a more comfortable slouch, holding my cup carefully so as not to spill a drop of wine. "Why did you get so angry with me?"

"I don't know." He grimaced, tacitly admitting to the lie. "Yes, I do. I suppose it was fear."

"Fear?" I could not keep the surprise out of my voice.

"Yes, Publius, fear!" He sat down across from me and was silent for a few moments, staring into the fire, then he continued. "I've been aware for some time now that there are changes happening here, Publius, changes we can't control; changes I don't like; changes in the way people are thinking and behaving." He paused again and sipped at his drink. "On the surface, many of them don't seem very profound or serious. But they are. And the remedies are dangerous in and of themselves."

"I don't follow you."

He smiled, a small, enigmatic smile. "Oh, you will when you start to think about it."

"About what? What danger? There's no danger involved anywhere that I can see."

"Isn't there, Publius?" Caius sat up straighter and leaned forward, looking me directly in the eye and balancing his right elbow on his knee. "Then look at your own reservations from this perspective: the matters you brought to my attention this afternoon are all concerned with the common everyday things people do. Luceiia has noticed a . . . what was her word? Laxity? That was it. A laxity in the structure of life around here. And now you agree with her, since she brought it to your attention. I agree with her too. She's absolutely right. But it's not just here, Publius. It's not just on our villa. It's everywhere. It's in the towns we visit, in the cities and in the villages, and it's growing all the time. Have you put a name to it yet?"

I shook my head. I was fascinated because he had already taken me far beyond the boundaries of my own thinking. He carried on without waiting for an answer.

"It's called anarchy, Publius."

Now I responded, laughing in disbelief. "Anarchy? Cay, you can't be serious!"

But Caius was not laughing. "Yes I can, Publius, and I am. Oh, it's a very small degree of anarchy at this point, but it will spread like a pestilence."

I laughed again, trying to ease him out of this train of thought, but he was not to be put off and he silenced me with an upraised hand.

"Please, Publius, let me finish. I find no humour in this, now that you and my sister have forced me to confront it."

"Really, Caius!" I was still trying to laugh this off, to put it aside as trivial. "We said nothing of anarchy. Luceiia was upset about one of the carpenters, a drunkard who terrorizes his wife and children. You know how she is about things like that."

He nodded, his face troubled. "Yes, I do," he muttered, his mood changing instantly. He shook his head regretfully. "She still hasn't recovered from the deaths of the children, has she? And it's been, what? Four years?"

I thought for a while before answering his question. "Yes, it's been four years, and no, she hasn't really recovered, Cay, not deep down inside. I don't think she ever will . . . She blames herself—still thinks she was the cause. And she can't forgive herself for not having seen things developing sooner. She really believes she should have been able to prevent it."

"But that's nonsense!"

"Of course it is, I know that ... we all do, even Luceiia, most of the time. Thank God for that, at least. But once in a while, she changes back to the way she was just after the children died ... something sets her back, reminding her ... and it usually happens when she hears about some child being mistreated or falling sick."

We sat in silence for long moments, each of us remembering.

During the long winter of the year in which I had killed Claudius Seneca, a withering sickness had swept through our lands. Its onset had been like the normal winter sniffles, but this illness was a killer, developing into high fevers, congested lungs, muscular spasms and paralysis. Very young children and old people seemed to lack the strength to resist it, and in our region alone scores of them died. Our household had been among the first hit, and Luceiia had convinced herself that she was responsible for bringing the contagion back from a journey she had made into Aquae Sulis shortly before the outbreak.

Three of our four daughters caught the sickness, and the two eldest, Victoria and Rebecca, born a mere eleven months apart, had died of it, Victoria mere days before her ninth birthday. Veronica, our third child, had just turned six at the time, and we thought for a while that we were going to lose her, too. But she survived, and the following year, she and her younger sister, Lucilla, were joined by another, Dorathea, our "gift from God" when one was most needed. Veronica, now our eldest, had been named after her aunt, Veronica Varo—wife to Quintus Varo, Cay's brother-in-law—who had been the first woman to welcome me on my arrival in the west, the year I fled from the wrath of the Senecas.

"Apparently," I resumed, picking up the thread of the conversation, "Lignus mistreats his children. That's what set her off in this instance. She suspects him of incest with his daughters. And of course, apart from that, she is worried about the rash of thefts that has broken out lately. Theft was unheard of around here until just very recently, and I understand her concern. Now all those things are worrisome, Cay, but I would hardly say they represent *anarchy*."

"Wrong, Publius. They all do. Each of them and all of them are symptoms of what I am talking about." He heaved a short, gusty sigh of frustration. "Don't you see? It's all part of what we're supposed to be preparing for, Publius—the breakup. The armies have deserted this part of Britain, for all intents and purposes. The garrisons are gone, to Londinium and Venta and Lindum, because that's where they're needed to hold off the enemy. The enemy is increasing in numbers and in ferocity from all directions, and the supply of reinforcements to us from overseas is nil! Every able-bodied soldier is on full alert—non-stop active duty. The military administration can't afford to leave domestic forces in non-priority locations, so they've pulled out the smaller, local and provincial garrisons and sent them where they'll be put to best use. That's fine, and it's sensible, and it's inevitable, but ... but, Publius, there is one additional, unprecedented fact involved here: when the garrisons

leave the provincial centres, for whatever reason, the machinery for enforcement of the law leaves with them."

I blinked and gazed at him, saying nothing, and he continued.

"The magistrates still rule, in name, but without the military they have
no means of enforcement. Can't you see that?"

I considered it for a few moments and then shrugged. It seemed to me
he was making too much out of a temporary inconvenience, so my response
was dismissive.

"No, not really. Criminals are still being transported to where they can
be punished, just as they've always been, aren't they?"

His response to that was scornful. "Criminals! We're not talking about
criminals, here, Publius, we're talking about ordinary people who commit
minor transgressions. Tax evasions, civil contempt, common assault, unruly
gatherings, public drunkenness—that's where the rot sets in. Murderers and
arsonists will still go under escort for punishment to the nearest military base,
but the smaller, petty offenders are going unpunished and unchallenged,
because it's simply too much trouble to check them.

"In direct consequence, the boundaries between right and wrong are
being blurred. The emphasis—even among the ordinary, common people—
is changing from 'Don't do that, or you'll be punished,' to 'Don't get caught
doing that . . .' That represents a major change in people's attitudes, Publius,
and hand in hand with it walks corruption. Judges and magistrates begin to
take bribes. Some always have, but they were held in some kind of restraint
in the past by the presence of the army. I had a letter on the subject from
an old friend in Aquae Sulis. The situation there is disastrous. There are
armed factions springing up in several places around the town, ostensibly
organized to augment the military forces there in an ongoing war against a
highly organized band of brigands. These brigands have become so bold, and
the military forces in Aquae are so powerless against them, that people are
in fear of their lives from day to day. They have no certainty of justice. They
no longer have redress for any wrongdoing they suffer."

"Wait, Caius, wait." He subsided, and I bit my lip, choosing my words
carefully. "I don't doubt what your friend tells you is true, but that's in Aquae
Sulis."

"It's happening elsewhere, too."

"I'm sure it is, but what bearing does that have on us here, in the Colony?
I don't see the connection. Isn't that why we are here? To isolate ourselves
from the rest of the country and the dissolution that's bound to come when
everything breaks down?"

"Of course it is, but no isolation can ever be complete, Publius. Our
people still have contact with the outside world. And what we are discussing
is an attitude. It's an abstraction, but it is all-pervasive, and it is beginning
to affect us here in our sanctuary. We are sinking into lawlessness."

I still thought he was over-reacting, but I had no doubt of his sincerity.
"Lawlessness," I responded, "that's a big word, Cay, and I don't think things

are that serious. You said yourself it's only now beginning to concern you here."

"That's true, I did. So?"

"So what?"

"So what are you suggesting?"

He had taken me by surprise again. "Me? I'm not suggesting anything. Or if I am, I suppose it's that we should do something about it, find some way of stopping it."

"I see." His enigmatic smile was back in place. "And how does one stop lawlessness?"

I blinked at him, suddenly beginning to sense where this was leading, and becoming aware of an urgent need to consider seriously what I was saying. "By making new laws, I suppose . . . to replace the old ones."

"Exactly. And you don't think that's dangerous?" His smile was wider now but there was no humour in it.

I was nonplussed, unsure of my footing, conscious of deep waters ahead of me. "Dangerous? Not particularly. What's so dangerous about it?"

"Tell me, Publius, what's the difference between a rule, a regulation and a law?"

He had me floundering now, and I could not answer him because I did know the difference. I shrugged and he took pity on me, his mirthless smile intact as he continued.

"Would you agree that a rule is a relatively mild, informal guideline prepared by, say, a society or a guild for the governance of its members? Nothing too formal or demanding, except that refusal to abide by it might result in the member's being mildly disciplined or even, in the last resort, being asked by his peers to withdraw from the society?"

I nodded in agreement.

"And then, as a soldier, you know that a regulation is a much more stringent form of rule, laid down by the army, and disobedience to the regulation involves physical disciplining of the culprit under martial law. And the guarantee of punishment is supplied by the authority of the imperial legions? Agreed?"

Again I nodded.

He continued. "A law, on the other hand, is an absolute rule, drawn up by the State, and failure to abide by it draws down absolute punishment, administered resolutely and with the full power and majesty of the State behind it?"

"Agreed. That sums it up." My voice was very quiet.

"Very well, then, Publius. You were talking of making new laws for our Colony. Let's stay with the definitions we agreed upon. Now, did you mean rules? Regulations? Or were you really talking about laws? And whichever of them you meant, had you given any thought to how they might be drawn up? Or implemented? Or enforced?"

"Good God, Cay," I whispered, "I see what you mean."

"Do you, brother?" He took a deep swallow from his cup. "I wish I did."

I drank from my own cup, and suddenly the wine seemed flat and tasteless. "We don't have that kind of authority, do we?"

"No, Publius, we do not. Nor, I think, would we want it. We have power, in that we own this land, in common with the other villa-owners. As such, we control the Colony and are accepted as its leaders by the people who live here, but would we want those powers extended to embrace the power of life and death? I submit that neither you nor I, nor any of the others, would, or could, be comfortable with that kind of power."

"How so?" I was surprised again. "We've all held that power before, in the legions."

"Yes, but only as deputies."

"That's true, you're right. But we have to do something, if what you suspect is the truth. So what can we do? Where do we start?"

Caius got up and moved to the brazier to feed the fire. "We have begun. All we can do is talk about it and try to see some way to draw up a set of rules that all of us can live by. We have to assume the responsibility for being the catalytic force behind the movement, for while I have reason to fear what we are contemplating, there is no doubt in my mind that we are correct. And we will not be able to do this alone. The enormity of such arrogance would be self-destructive." He turned back to face me. "The laws exist already, that goes without saying. No need to invent new ones. But we lack the means of prosecution. We must have some means of *enforcing* the laws, Publius . . . and that is going to be a fearsome responsibility and a dreadful and daunting task."

"We'll have to set up some new kind of governing body."

"Absolutely. But it will also have to be a representative body. It can't be just you and me. The colonists would never accept that, nor would I wish them to. We could, however, extend the powers of the existing Council to cover legislation."

"You mean found a real Senate, along Roman lines?"

He grimaced. "Possibly. Something like that. That was our original intent, when we first talked of establishing a Council to govern the Colony."

I stood up now and moved closer to the brazier, extending my hands towards the heat. "I remember, but we decided against that degree of sophistication. Do you really believe we could go back to that now? It would be a major departure from all we've done since those days, Cay. A really big change. You think it could be done?"

"Of course it could, but it would have to be done in the right way, with the proper preparation and spirit."

"But what about enforcement? We'd still have to set up some form of disciplinary force. Our own soldiers?"

"Hardly, Publius. A military dictatorship?"

"What, then?"

"No idea. As I said, it's going to take a lot of talking and a lot of sober thought . . . But a strengthened Council, endowed with the bona fide senatorial authority to apprehend transgressors might be the answer . . . particularly if it were backed up by some form of tribunal . . ."

I could practically hear his mind clicking as he pursued the pros and cons of what he was saying.

"Yes, that might be it, Publius . . . a tribunal . . . a systematic method of exercising the voice and judgment of the colonists, in conjunction with the Council. Public trials, and accountability for persons accused of public—even private—mischief. But no powers of life and death, none of that nonsense. Banishment only. The ultimate punishment would be banishment."

I was dubious. "You really think that would be enough of a deterrent to criminal behaviour?"

He grinned at me. "Today? Probably not. But in five or ten years from now, when the world has gone to Hades, who knows? Let's bring Luceiia in on this now. We could use her common sense."

I think none of us could really have suspected that the discussions begun that evening among the three of us would become the basis for the entire system of law throughout our growing domain in the years that stretched ahead, although that is exactly what happened.

Luceiia, when she joined us, dismissed most of our concerns about lawmaking as being premature. Cay, she pointed out, was the owner of the villa and its lands and *ipso facto* had an absolute right to determine the code of conduct for everyone living on those lands, as did the other villa-owners on theirs. The Council was a relatively new body and was functioning reasonably well in its current form. Best to let it continue as it was and to let its authority and its functions determine themselves with the passing of time. As the population of the Colony grew, the scope of the Council would expand naturally to reflect that growth. Cay and I exchanged glances and agreed with her; she was right again.

At one point she stopped talking quite abruptly and sat deep in thought for some time before glancing shrewdly at her brother and then at me.

"Both of you are concerned about interfering with the rights of other people, aren't you? You can't see clearly where moral supervision, for the want of a better expression, stops, and plain interference and meddling begin. Am I correct?"

She was, as far as I was concerned, but as I cleared my throat to answer her, Caius began to speak.

"Yes, Luceiia, you are, as usual. I am particularly concerned about the carpenter Publius mentioned. It is an appropriate case, in this context. You say he is a drunkard. He would probably respond that he is a hard worker who enjoys a jug of ale or wine, or both, after he has finished his day's work. I do, too. So does your husband. We may simply be able to hold our drink better than this carpenter. Should we condemn him for that? Can we? You suggest he bullies and terrorizes his family, and that he is incestuous with his daughters. That latter is only hearsay, is it not? Is there any proof that he does?"

Luceiia shook her head.

"I thought so. So there is nothing to be done about that, at the present time. We can do nothing until someone complains. Nothing at all. On the matter of beating and terrorizing his family, however, he could respond that he disciplines them. How am I to react to that?" Cay was frowning, a deep line of thought creasing the space between his eyebrows. "I believe in discipline, and I believe that discipline has to be harsh if it is to have any effect. How am I, what right have I, to tell any man how to govern his own household? Could I have told Domitius Titens to discipline his wife? Or to look to her chastity? By what right, other than that of an officious and interfering neighbour? He would have drawn his blade on me, and who would have blamed him? His domestic life was none of my concern; it could never have been any of my business, simply because it was his and his alone. You know the laws governing adultery. He could have whipped the flesh from her bones with complete impunity and no man would have thought the worse of him . . . As it was, he went berserk and slaughtered his entire household."

"Someone should have stopped him, Cay."

"Luceiia, that is absurd. Someone would have stopped him, had anyone known what he was going to do. As it is, no one could possibly have known, not even the man himself, until the deed had begun, by which time he had lost his reason."

Luceiia nodded her head decisively. "That is exactly the point I wished to make. There will always be the unknown, which will transcend all the laws and all the rules. But there will also be signs and indicators pointing towards the unknown, Caius. Warnings, if only we can identify them. We must be attuned to them, somehow. We must—we have to be on guard against that which is not normal, and know what to do to stop it before things go too far. There must be rules, Caius, and there must be people, people like you and Publius, whose duty it is to enforce those rules and to make informed decisions as to when and how and by whom those rules are being broken."

"That is . . ." Cay's voice tailed away for a beat, and then resumed, "That is not fit work for men, Luceiia."

"Nonsense! Of course it is!" Luceiia's voice was scornful. "Not only that, it is work for extraordinary men, men who are above being influenced by pettiness. And it is necessary work, brother. But why shouldn't it be women's work, too? Extraordinary women?"

Both of us stared at her, but it was I who asked her, "What do you mean?"

She stared at me, wide-eyed. "What do you think I mean? Admit women to your Council and let them share the duties of the guardians of the law. You will find, I think, that they will be more conscientious and more judicious about reporting the kinds of things that concern all of us, and they will not be swayed by many of the concerns that influence men."

"And what are those?" I was smiling, amused by the novelty of the idea she had suggested. The look she threw back at me was scornful.

"Come, husband, you and I have talked about this often. The things that matter—really matter—to women are a world apart from those that matter. to men. Our two systems of values are totally different. Men are concerned with conquest and commerce. Women are concerned with other things: family harmony, thrift, domestic strength and the raising of children to be whole, strong, healthy adults. If you agree these things have value, then you must see that the input of women to the governing of this Colony must have a purely beneficial effect."

"Sister," Cay's voice was respectful, "I think we would have difficulty selling that concept to our colonists, but you have ended this discussion on a wondrous note. Let's talk of other things, for now, and think long and hard on what you have just said. I believe you may have taken us far along the road to a solution to our problem. I don't know many better judges of character than you, and I would back your judgment against any man's. If we had three or four women like you, we would be in very capable hands."

"Brother," said my wife, "I can introduce you to ten tomorrow, and will be happy to do it . . ." The inflection of her voice as she stopped clearly indicated that there was a "but" attached and still unspoken.

"Good. I want you to do so. I look forward to it, in fact." Cay's frown broke into a great grin. "But while you are gathering your delegates, could you perhaps give some thought to how we might convince the councillors of the worthiness of your idea?"

"Of course I will." She smiled her own, determined little smile. "Leave that to me. I'll find a way, perhaps not by tomorrow, but I will find one." Luceiia drained her cup and turned it upside-down as a signal to me. I got up and poured more wine for all of us from the jar, which was now sadly depleted. As I did so she continued.

"But I had not finished what I was saying earlier. I want you to listen to what I have to say about the carpenter." Cay's brow quirked into a scowl but she ignored it and continued speaking, her voice implacable. "This is an evil man, and I know both of you would prefer not to think about him, but I believe you have to consider him as a special case." She held up a hand to forestall any interruption. "Please, let me finish. He has a small son who sometimes plays with Veronica and the other children." She looked intently from one to the other of us, fastening her gaze finally on her brother, knowing that he was the one she had to convince. "Caius, children will play together, no matter what we tell them to do to the contrary. And because they play together, they learn together. That is the way of childhood and of nature. And they learn the bad as well as the good." She stopped again and her face was pale with restrained emotion. "I love my children, Caius, and I love *children.*" Her emphasis was clear and unequivocal. "Childhood, God knows, is short. I want my children to enjoy it as much as they can; they will have all of the rest of their lives to see the squalor and injustice of the world they have to live in. But it infuriates me when I see my daughter Veronica weeping and distressed and terrified by what has happened to her little friend, who has had his limbs bruised and broken by the drunken brute who fathered him. My daughter has no need to see such things, and neither do any of the other children. Nor do they need to see the mother and sisters of one of their friends brutalized and beaten by a ravening beast." Luceiia paused again and looked from Caius to me and then back to her brother. "I am not telling you what to do, but surely you can see that some kind of example has to be made of this man. There must be some way of forcing him to behave differently."

"What?" Cay's voice was low and sombre. "What would you suggest? How can we do anything about it? What right do we have?"

"What *right*?" Luceiia's voice was withering in its wintriness. "Whose rights are we talking about here, Cay? Who is right in this case? Don't his children have any rights? Doesn't his wife?"

"That's beside the point, Luceiia," her brother interrupted her. "I am saying that Publius and I cannot take it upon ourselves to discipline another man for the way he treats his family. We have no right to do that."

"Then what right do you have? Is he not one of your tenants?"

"No, he is not. He is a colonist and he contributes his work to the Colony. He's also a free man."

"Then tell me, what would you recourse have been if he were one of your legionaries and behaved this way?"

Cay's response was instantaneous. "I would have had him flogged."

"Then flog him now, Caius, or you risk seeing others following his example."

"Nonsense! You are making too much of this, Luceiia."

At that point I intervened, seeing the wrath that was building in both of them. I suggested that we think upon what Luceiia had said and consider our options in the light of the seriousness of her charges. I also suggested that I would make a point of visiting the carpenter in question and having a talk with him. Both of them seemed satisfied with this, and we went on to talk of other things until the fire finally burned down without anyone making a move to replenish it and we all went to bed. The last thing Luceiia said to me before we slept was that she was glad I was going to speak to the fellow.

VI

ALTHOUGH I HAD fully intended to talk to Lignus the carpenter the next day, as I had promised Luceiia, I had forgotten in the enthusiasm of our discussion that I had also promised to ride into Aquae Sulis with Victorex, one of the colonists from Terra's villa. He was bound for the market there, hoping to buy a stud horse he had heard would be for sale, and I had volunteered to accompany him. It was a long and tedious journey to make alone, and I had business there that I had been putting off for some time.

We travelled in a fast, light cart, pulled by two horses, and had a pleasant journey together, talking of horses all the way, since Victorex seemed to have no other interests. When we arrived, however, Victorex discovered to his great disappointment that his hoped-for stallion was nowhere to be found. Unwilling to waste his journey completely, he went to make more inquiries and discovered that its sale had been postponed simply because its owner could not make the journey into town for that market day. Freshly determined to succeed, Victorex set out to find the owner's villa and make a private purchase, leaving me to make my own way back to the Colony in the cart. He would ride back on his new stallion, he said. I spent the night with him in Aquae and set out for home the following morning as soon as the sun rose above the horizon.

The journey back took the whole of the day. The weather was beautiful and I made excellent time on the road, but I was still almost seven miles from the Colony as darkness fell, forcing me to reduce my speed. I usually prefer to camp out rather than attempt to travel at night, but this night was mild and the sky was cloudless and moonlit and I was on my home ground, so I decided to keep going. I stayed on the main road south for another three miles and kept up a good pace to the point where the road came closest to the Colony. There I struck out overland, much more slowly, but travelling as the crow flies rather than taking the longer, more circuitous route offered by the track from the highway to the villa.

The only sounds I heard for the next hour were the squeaking of the cart's springs and axle and the muffled thud of my horses' hooves as I threaded my way between clumps and thickets, managing to find solid, grassy passage. When I saw the moon's reflection shining from the waters of the Dragon's Pool, I knew I was home, and my head was full of pleasant thoughts of hot bath water and hotter food when I heard an unearthly, wailing cry from the bulrushes that fringed the water. My blood froze like a child's who has heard

too many stories of ghosts and monstrous apparitions, and the fine hairs on
the back of my neck stirred with horror. I have never been a superstitious
man, but there have been occasions in my life when I might have been
converted, and this was one of them. The night that had been so clear and
brightly lit by the moon a moment since was suddenly dark and filled with
menace.

Even tonight, as I write these words long miles and years from the sight
of it, I know the Dragon's Pool is still deep and dark, bordered by sedge and
reeds and scrubby willows, its surface probably concealed by a curtain of
mist. Tales told around the fires on dark, wintry nights still speak of ancient
slaughters and chaos and the souls of drowned and murdered people dragging
themselves from the deep waters in the darkness there to bewail their lost
lives on earth.

My heart told my doubting mind that I had indeed heard such a sound.
My horses had heard it, too, and that appalled me; they stopped in their
tracks and one of them whickered softly, and their ears twitched around as
they sought to locate the source of the strange noise. I sat motionless, willing
my heart to slow down and behave normally, telling myself I was far too old
to be frightened by noises in the night, however strange they might be. But
it came again, and this time, even as my heart leaped in fear, I recognized
the sound as being natural and human: a woman's voice, or a child's. My
fear died, and yet I hesitated to call out, unwilling to break the silence, waiting
for the sound to be repeated again.

It came again, and broke the tension that held me. I saw only the mist
upon the water and the sedge, but I had heard clearly enough to know that
the voice had come from close to the water's edge. I stood up and looked,
but I could see only that the fog hung thickly enough over the lake and its
shoreline to obscure my vision, so before going anywhere I moved to the back
of my wagon and took out my tinder-box and the deep clay pot of oil-soaked
rags bound tightly around dry sticks I carried for making torches or fires.
Within moments I had ignited some dried moss and blown it into flame,
into which I dipped the edge of the oily cloth wrapped around one of the
torches. Only then did I move away from the cart, holding the flaring light
above my head as I approached the waterside. The full moon at my back
threw my shadow grotesquely ahead of me as I walked. There was no noise
now, except for the flaring of the burning torch. I called out, "Who's there?
Where are you?" and heard nothing. No sound at all. I moved closer to the
water, cautiously, beginning to think again that I might have given in to folly,
since any human in distress would have responded to the approach of help.
But there was nothing. With mounting uneasiness, I transferred the torch
to my left hand and drew my sword, taking some satisfaction in the slithering
sound it made scraping from its sheath.

I called out several more times, standing still each time and listening for
a response that did not come, and at length my feet sank into the mud by
the water's edge and I could go no further. The reeds surrounded me in a

tall, dense sea reaching higher than my waist. If there was any living soul ahead of me, he or she must be afloat and so beyond my help. I turned around and saw my horses and cart where I had left them, and I began to make my way back. My shadow lay behind me now, and I had not walked six paces when I saw something I had missed on my way in. There was a trail through the reeds where someone, or something, had dragged itself along, moving from my left to my right. In the clear moonlight I could see quite clearly now where the path of my own entry crossed over the broken and flattened reeds. I swallowed a mouthful of gummy saliva, flexed my fingers around the hilt of my sword and followed the path to my right for a few paces. Then, appalled, I saw the light of my torch reflected in a gleaming eye and I dropped into a fighting crouch, sweeping my sword up in a hissing arc and bringing my torch in a flickering, roaring swing down and around in front of me at the same time. What I saw in that instant stunned me and I hung there, suspended, gaping at the spectacle of a small, naked and incredibly dirty and blood-stained child, a boy, whose single, staring eye was filled with terror and the certainty of death.

In a moment I was on my knees beside him, trying to sheathe my sword and jam the base of my torch firmly into the mud at the same time. The boy shrank from me, a terrified moaning emerging from his mangled mouth as he tried to escape, digging his right heel uselessly into the slick mud, pushing himself frantically backwards to hide again in the rushes. I grasped at his leg to hold him and instantly identified the splintered, bloody end of a broken thigh-bone against my fingers. His entire body jerked in agony, his breath exploding in a solid grunt of pain, and he fell back, unconscious.

I snatched up my torch again and held it by him, looking intently at what the light now disclosed. The boy could have been no more than seven or eight years old and had been brutalized, savagely beaten to the point where he should have been dead. Shaken by that realization, I bent to his tiny body and listened for a heartbeat, but all I could hear was the flickering of the flames of my torch. I felt for a pulse and found one, faint but steady, beneath the point of his jaw. But the child was cold, chilled and naked. Cursing aloud, I got up and made my way as quickly as I could to the cart, where I unpacked my new cloak and then led the horses back down to the edge of the reeds. I wrapped the still-unconscious child in the cloak, doubling the length of it up from his feet, and then I threw my torch out into the waters of the lake and carried him to the cart, where I emptied the long tool box, dumping its contents on the ground, and then lined the bottom of it thickly with all the clothes I had. He was a very small bundle and fitted perfectly into the box. I climbed up onto the driver's seat and headed for home again, moving as quickly as I could without jarring the box or its occupant any more than I had to.

It took me an hour to complete the journey. I ran into the house, carrying the boy and shouting at the top of my voice for assistance. The family had just finished dining and the servants had entered to clear away the debris from the dining room, which was still brightly lit by a roaring log fire and dozens of lamps and candles. I placed my pathetic burden directly on the table, sweeping whatever was there into a shambles on the floor and unwrapping the folds of the cloak in which I had swathed him. Only then, in the brightly lit *triclinium*, did I really see how badly used the child had been. He was coated from head to foot in thick, slimy mud mixed with his own blood. His left leg had been broken in two places that I could see, and his right arm was twisted out of alignment. A large flap of skin and flesh had been ripped on his left breast and his little ribs were plainly visible in the wound. His mouth had been smashed; his teeth had punctured his lips and his lower lip had been torn almost in half. His scalp was deeply lacerated and dried blood had scabbed in his hair.

Luceiia took one brief look at me on my arrival, waited only to see that what I was carrying was human, small and injured, and immediately disappeared in the direction of our living quarters, calling out orders as she went to summon our medical staff and to fetch hot water and clean cloths and towels. The servants bustled to carry out her commands as Caius approached the table and looked and was speechless, as shocked as I have ever seen him. His face went pale and he clutched at the table for support as he gazed down at the boy, and then he turned and walked from the room, and I knew that he was going to vomit up his outrage. I had no time myself for outrage or for anger then; there was too much to do if we were to save the life of the child, who was now in a deep comatose state. Only later, when there was nothing more to do but wait, did I begin to seethe with fury.

Our physician, Cletus, had ministered to battle-damaged men for years. He bathed the boy carefully and thoroughly with mild soap and hot water before dusting the wounds and fractured limbs with healing herbs and setting and splinting the shattered bones. The child, deeply unconscious, showed no signs of pain throughout this procedure. Cletus then shaved the child's head, using my skystone knife, the sharpest blade in the Colony, to reveal the lacerations on the small scalp and to allow him to wash and clean the head wounds thoroughly. After that, he gently cleaned the broken mouth and fastened the torn, flapping lower lip with two tiny knots of twine, sewing the pieces together as delicately as a woman. Only then did he turn his attention to the wound in the boy's side, stretching the ragged flap of skin back into place and stitching it, too, firmly, with pieces of thick thread. All of that done, Cletus then swathed the patient in clean bandages and placed him in a cot in his own quarters, where he could maintain vigil over him for the remainder of the night.

Throughout the entire proceedings, Luceiia had been silent, responding only to Cletus's demands for this or that article of his healing craft. I had had nothing to say either; all my attention was focused on the boy and the physician. Finally, when the child was in bed, with cloth-wrapped bottles of hot water packed around him, Luceiia and I retired together to our family room. Someone, knowing we were still afoot, had kept the fire burning and the lamps and tapers lit. Caius had gone to bed. I went to the stone chiller and poured us each a mug of Equus's cold ale, taking it to the couch, where Luceiia sat staring into the fire. She took the mug from me but made no effort to drink. I sat down beside her and drank deeply, barely tasting the brew but grateful for its coldness.

My mind still could not accept the enormity of what I had seen this night. I had no illusions about childhood; few children were as well beloved and happy as ours were. Childhood, for the mass of men, was not supposed to be a happy time. It was a time to be passed quickly by; a time of harsh discipline in earnest of a harsher life ahead; a training time for manhood, or for womanhood. It was a time of learning the difficult lessons and essential skills that had to be learned well and quickly if the child was to survive to see full growth, to father and rear children of his own while he was yet still young enough to pass to them the lessons he had learned. The disciplines and punishments of childhood were severe, as they had to be; none but the very wealthy could afford to nurture and protect their progeny from life itself. Children who did not learn to cope were spoiled, in the worst sense of the word; they seldom survived.

But what had been done to this child was infamous. Had I known any full-grown man to treat another man in such a way and leave him in such condition, without direst provocation, I would have had him flogged. To treat a child like this, no matter what the provocation, was inexcusable. I felt that I would give much to find the nomad ruffian who had done it. I drank again and stared into the flames, seeing the boy's poor, broken face before me.

"I wonder who he is," I asked aloud, and instantly I felt Luceiia stiffen beside me.

"Are you saying you don't know, Publius? You don't know who this child is?"

There was wonder and disbelief in her tone. I turned to look at her.

"No, of course I don't. How would I know? I found him beside the lake. He had been abandoned there by someone. I would dearly like to know by whom."

Luceiia stared at me wide-eyed and her face went hard as stone. I felt an absurd swelling of guilt and some formless shame.

"Luceiia? What is it, in God's name? I told you, I don't know the child. Don't you believe me?"

She continued to stare at me, her eyes almost unseeing, her face frozen in that strange expression, and I thought she truly believed I was lying to her.

"Luceiia? What's wrong with you? I tell you I don't know the boy. Why would I lie to you?"

She finally looked away from me, down at the mug in her hand, and raised it to her lips, but she had barely begun to sip it when she jerked it away from her mouth with a grimace of distaste and held it out to me with a small shake of her head. Mystified, I took the mug from her, watching as she stood up and crossed distractedly from the couch to the small table where the brightest lamps burned. She leaned over and picked up a lamp and then turned back to me.

"It's Simeon," she said. "I warned you this would happen."

"What?" I was dumfounded, and confused. I had no idea what she was talking about.

"Who's Simeon? What are you talking about, Luceiia? We . . . I know no one called Simeon. Simeon who? And what warning? You warned me? About what?"

"The carpenter." Her voice was a whisper, drained of emotion. "Lignus. The mad one. The drunkard. I told you of my fears about him. You and Cay. You promised to visit him and talk to him. I told you I feared for his family, what he might do to them some day. The boy is his son, Simeon. He sometimes comes to play with your own children, Publius, and yet you say you do not know him?"

"By the sweet Christ!" I rose to my feet, my entire body chilled. "You thought I knew this? And did nothing?" I gazed around the room, unsure of what I would do next, seeing the familiar ornaments and objects of my home as though they were strange to me, and then my reason reasserted itself and my fury found focus on new, grim fears. I remembered that I had removed my sword-belt on entering the sick bay and I strode to fetch it. When I returned, buckling it on, Luceiia was still standing where I had left her, holding the lamp. She looked at me in puzzlement.

"What are you doing? Are you going out?"

"I am. Where does this fellow live, exactly, this carpenter?"

She shook her head as though clearing it. "Behind the last of the stone houses, to the south, in a wood hut in a clearing in the forest."

"Do we need horses, or can we walk there? How close is it?"

She blinked at me, shaking her head again. "Not far. It's only a short walk through the village, to the far end, towards the hill fort. But it's dark, are you going there now?"

"Of course I am going there now, and so are you. Christ alone knows what scene from Hades we'll find awaiting us when we get there, but I'll need you there in case there's work for women. He has a wife and daughters, does he not?"

She nodded, her expression more alert now.

"Good," I went on. "Now, tell me exactly how to get there, and then rouse up some help and follow me by road. I have no time to wait. You have some time to make your arrangements, but there is none to waste." I paused as a thought struck me, and then continued as I saw the rightness of it. "I'm going first to the barracks to find some soldiers to go with me. I want this to be official, rather than personal. Our man may still be there and he might choose to fight. I hope he does. Get Caius up again. He will want to oversee this. Ask him to summon some of the senior members of the Council and wait here for me to come back. In the meantime, when you come, bring

Gallo and two other servants, the strongest, and one of the wagons, a big one. We may have to use it to carry bodies. But hurry, love, we've wasted enough time already and we may be far too late with far too little help."

A very short time later, I stopped about fifteen paces in front of the carpenter's hut, just at the edge of a screen of bushes and saplings that surrounded the clearing in which the dwelling stood. Holding my torch high with my right hand, I signalled with my left to arrest the six young soldiers I had commandeered and brought with me. They had been playing dice in the barracks by the villa. I had already told them what was involved here as we walked, and that I was unsure of what we might find awaiting us. At first glance, however, we could see nothing sinister. The hut was a sturdy one, as one might expect the home of a carpenter to be. It was dark and peaceful, and smoke from a damped-down fire wisped gently through the hole left for it at the peak of the roof. The building had two crude windows, both covered with thick wooden shutters, and a heavy, latched door that looked as though it would be barred on the inside. I wondered what lay behind it as I stood there looking at it for long moments. Finally one of the soldiers cleared his throat tentatively and I interpreted it correctly as a signal either to do something or let them get back to their interrupted game. I spoke to the decurion in charge.

"You stay here with your men and wait. Keep them here for the time being, among the bushes and out of sight from the hut. I'm going to go in alone. It doesn't seem like there's any danger, but you can never really be sure of these things. There can be few situations more lethal than a bad domestic disturbance. Wait until I call you in, and when I do, if I do, come fast and be prepared to subdue this man and take him prisoner. You understand me? Take him prisoner. No matter what happens, or how violent he gets, I want him alive. Is that clear?"

He nodded, and I stepped from concealment and walked towards the hut, stopping again only when I was directly in front of the door. This time I listened for noises from inside, but I heard nothing. I drew a deep breath, shifted my torch to my left hand and pounded on the door. I heard an immediate babble of voices inside, all female, and then a rough, explosive male voice telling them all to be quiet, whereupon there was immediate silence. I knocked again, feeling a surprising and profound relief at knowing the women were alive, at least, and realizing only then that I had been dreading to find a charnel-house resembling the Villa Titens on the day of Dom's final madness. Then I heard movement inside and a clatter and cursing as someone knocked over something heavy. A few moments later light flared, gleaming through the space behind the shutters on the windows, and the same rough male voice came to me in a shout, asking who I was and what in Hades I wanted at this time of night.

I kept my voice level but raised it sufficiently to be heard behind the door.

"This is Publius Varrus, from the villa. I wish to speak to Lignus the carpenter."

Another hiss of muffled conversation and another oath from the man silencing it. I waited. Finally the voice came back at me.

"What do you want with him?"

"Words. And I don't want to shout through a door. Open up."

There was a pause, then, "Step back, away from the door. How do I know you're who you say you are? Step back and let me see you from the window."

I took two steps backwards and stood in the open, my gut tensed against the arrow or the knife that could easily come seeking me. One of the shutters on the window to the right of the door opened slightly, I saw a shape peering out at me and heard him grunt as he recognized me. The shutter opened further and he leaned out, his head sweeping from side to side as he looked around the entire clearing as far as he could see.

"Are you alone?"

"Do you see anyone else here?"

"Humph. What do you want? You should be abed like every other honest man."

"I will be, soon, but I want to talk to you, and the matter is important."

"Well then, talk, I'm listening."

I knew I had to tread carefully here. It was imperative that he leave the window and open the heavy door, otherwise any attempt to take him into custody might be bloody and wasteful. I drew myself erect and voiced my disgust in the tone of my next words.

"I have urgent need of a carpenter. An immediate need for which I am willing to pay well. They told me you were the best. But I will be damned if I am going to stand here shouting to you like a huckster in the middle of the street, broadcasting my affairs to all ears while you huddle in the warmth of your hut like a lazy boar. Go back to bed, Lignus, I'll find another carpenter."

I turned on my heel and began to walk away, and his voice stopped me before I had taken two paces.

"Wait! Wait, damnation! I'll open the door."

He pulled the shutter back into place and a moment later I heard the heavy bar on the door being removed. I stepped forward again as the door began to open, but he held it only partly ajar with the weight of his body and stuck his head through the opening. When he spoke this time, his voice was quieter, less surly.

"What is it then? What's this urgent need you have? You've never called on me before."

Even from the little of him that was visible, I could see he was an enormous bear of a man, half a head taller than me, with a heavy, rank beard and a great, swollen belly. He did not seem to be drunk, but I was close enough to notice that he stank of sour, dirty sweat and his breath reeked of something like fish oil; I felt my stomach heave, partly through revulsion, but mainly because of the anger I bore towards him. I moved closer.

"Can I come in?"

"Eh?" Plainly I had caught him unprepared. He had not expected me to enter, or even to wish to enter. He glanced around the clearing again before clearing his throat and denying me. "No! No, I'll come out. Give me a moment."

He closed the door in my face and I heard him muttering to someone inside, another voice arose, and then came the sound of a blow and a muffled, female cry of pain. My rage flared up again. I dropped my hand to the hilt of my sword and swung my torch around my head, making the flames flare up. When he opened the door to come outside, I thrust the flaming end of my torch towards his face, making him gasp in surprise and leap back, throwing up his hands to shield his eyes. I pushed the door wide with my shoulder and followed him inside, drawing my sword as I went.

The heat inside the hut was stifling. I was aware of two guttering lamps, a large, glowing fire and several moving bodies drawing back in fear from my intrusion, but I kept my eyes firmly fastened on the carpenter. His surprise was short-lived and his face clouded with anger as he tensed himself to leap at me. I threw the point of my sword up towards his throat.

"Don't," I warned him, and the venom in my voice held him back. "Don't even begin to think about tackling me, or I'll spill your guts on your feet." I moved closer to him, backing him up against the wall, and saw fear in his eyes. "You think I'm deranged?" I prodded my point towards him. "You think the man you're facing has lost his mind? Well, perhaps I have. I found your son tonight, you drunken whoreson, out by the lake."

He blinked at me, confusion mixing now with the fear on his face. "Who? Simeon?"

"Aye, Simeon. They tell me that's his name."

Truculence emerged in his eyes now and grew into a scowl. "Simeon? That's what brings you here?"

"No, the beating you gave him brought me here."

"Then be damned to you! He's my son and I'll treat him any way I want to, when he needs a lesson in manners—" He would have said more, but I cut off his words by pressing the point of my blade against his throat.

"Manners? He needs manners so badly, at his age? How old is he? Eight? Seven? You stinking piece of offal! The boy is at the villa, and he may be dead by now.

"No one believes he can survive the beating you gave him. He has a shattered leg, so even if he lives, he'll never walk properly again. And his arm is broken, and his ribs, and perhaps his skull. His teeth are broken, and he may have lost an eye, and his lower lip was torn off, and he's what? Seven? Eight years old? Did he put up a good fight, pig? Did he tax your strength? Or did he scream for mercy? Look in my eyes, you gutter-dropped son of a whore, and ask yourself if you can see much promise of mercy there, and then ask yourself again what I might do if you give me half a reason to restrain you."

I stopped, my eyes on his, and saw fear again and the beginnings of panic in them. Not breaking my gaze, I spoke over my shoulder to the women in the room, one of whom was sobbing wildly. "You women, get outside, and shout to the guard to come in. Move! Quickly!"

There was no response to this, and so I jerked a glance towards them. There were three of them, all huddled on a huge wooden bed in a litter of smelly bedding.

"Did you hear me? Go outside, now!"

"We can't!" The one who had spoken kicked her leg and I heard the clink of chains. Startled by the sound, I made the error of looking towards it, and that was all Lignus needed. He was big as a bear, but now I discovered he was also quick as a cat. I saw him spring sideways away from me, along the wall to the corner of the hut, and I barely had time to turn my sword awkwardly, thrusting for my life against the thick iron bar that had suddenly appeared in his huge hand and would have broken me in two had it hit me. As it was, it smashed the sword from my hand, numbing my whole arm and sending me reeling across the room to trip over a wooden stool and sprawl full-length on the straw-covered floor. I rolled as I landed, but I had no momentum working for me and the giant was on me immediately, bringing his weapon down in a fearsome swing at my head. He missed, and the impact of the blow against the floor jerked the bar from his grasp. I managed to clout him across the side of the head, back-handed, with the torch that was, somehow, still in my left hand. I lost my grip on the torch, but my blow had been lucky enough to stun him, knocking him down as his beard and hair ignited from the oil-soaked rags, wreathing his whole head in flames. He began to scream and beat at the flames, and I added my own shouts to his screams, summoning my soldiers.

All three women now began screaming, too, and as I struggled to my feet I saw why. My lost torch had landed in a pile of straw and wood shavings in another corner of the room and long flames were already shooting up the wooden walls. Lignus's head was a cocoon of rolling flames, and I snatched up a pot of water sitting by the hearth and dumped it over his head as the first soldiers came crashing through the doorway. I grasped the first two men and pushed them towards the sprawling giant on the floor.

"You two! Get him out of here and keep him safe. Tie him up. The rest of you, get these women to safety." I saw the decurion in charge removing his cloak, preparing to try to smother the raging flames in the corner, but I knew it was already too late for that. I seized him and spun him around, away from the fire. "Forget about that, it's too late now. Those women are chained to the bed. Get them out of here or they'll all burn. Break the bed apart if you have to."

I moved to help them, and we did have to break the bed apart, although only two of the women were chained to it. The third woman, whom I presumed to be the mother, was unbound, but she hampered all of us, clinging to her naked daughters as though to protect them. The bed was massive, solid and impossibly heavy, strongly built by a carpenter who, whatever his faults might be, knew his craft and took good care of his creature-comforts. Someone found a heavy maul and an axe on the floor beneath one of the windows, but by the time we succeeded in bursting the frame of the bed, shattering the corner joints with the heavy hammer, the small room was filled with flame and blinding, choking smoke and we were all in danger of being overcome. Finally, the women were being removed and we all withdrew, but as I turned to make sure everyone was out ahead of me, something flashed and burst, belching smoke and sparks into my face. I was snatching a breath at the time and inhaled what seemed like pure fire before I was overtaken by an uncontrollable spasm of coughing that racked me with tearing pain and deprived me of any sense of direction. Panicked, I turned completely around, twice, looking for the doorway but completely unable to pierce the swirling smoke, and then my knee gave way and I fell forward, and my head hit the floor within half a pace of the doorway through which smoke and long tongues of angry flame were now roaring. Hands grasped at me and hauled me through, out into the cool night air, where I coughed and retched and clutched myself in agony for what seemed like an eternity.

When I recovered a semblance of self-possession and opened my eyes, I found that my head and shoulders were supported in the lap of my wife, who was bathing my face with a wet cloth. I blinked at her and shook my head, surprised that I had not been conscious of being cradled, or of being bathed.

She frowned and leaned close to me. "Publius? You passed out. Are you in pain?"

I shook my head again and tried to reassure her, but my voice would not work. I pushed myself up from her lap, supporting myself on one elbow, and looked around me. There were dozens of people in the clearing—soldiers, and ordinary colonists of all ages. Behind me, the carpenter's cottage was an inferno, but no one was making any attempt to fight the fire. I felt dozens of eyes on me and pushed myself up until I was sitting. I coughed again, trying to clear my throat, and Luceiia offered me a cup of water. It hurt to swallow, but the result made the pain worthwhile. I gulped the entire contents of the cup, feeling the cooling, healing water spread inside me.

"Thank you," I rasped. Then I stood up and looked around more carefully. Luceiia had stood, too, and now held my elbow, supporting me against the slight sway in my stance.

"Lignus, where is he?"

"The soldiers have him in custody. He is badly burned, and in great pain."

"So is his son. Where are the women?"

"In the wagon. I brought some clothing and blankets."

"Were any of them burned? The women?"

"No, and they are warm and cared for, although they are terrified out of their wits."

I frowned at her. "Terrified? Why? Have they been harmed?"

"Of course not, Publius. But they are frightened by all that has happened. These are women who are not used to being seen, and now they are the centre of public attention. They are distraught. And they are still afraid that they will have to live with him tomorrow, after all this has died down."

"Tell them they need have no fear of that, wife. None at all."

"I have told them. They do not believe me. All this has been too sudden and they have lived in fear of him too long. One of the daughters is heavy with child."

I looked at her, seeing the stillness of her face. "His child?"

"You can't be surprised, Publius? I told you about it long ago. This only confirms my suspicions."

I was quite inexplicably at a loss for words, and I found myself making excuses for the man, suggesting that it might be someone else's child, and that we were condemning him unjustly, but Luceiia had no patience for that.

"In God's name, Publius, whose else could it be? He kept them chained to his bed, did he not?"

I sighed and conceded that she had the right of it. "He did, aye. Incest is common enough, God knows, for all that it's condemned. But this chaining of his daughters to their stall, like cattle . . . I think I'll flog him personally in public."

"No, husband, you will do no such thing. You will commit him to trial by the tribunal of the Colony. The tribunal we have talked so much of setting up. He will be tried by his fellow citizens and banished from this Colony, to return only upon pain of death. His trial will mark the birth of our new system and provide sufficient unity of outrage to cement its laws. We may have reason to be grateful to Lignus the drunkard."

"Lignus the murderer, if his son does not recover. How is the boy?"

Luceiia shrugged and a frown darkened her face. "I do not know. He was still unchanged when we left home."

"Well," I said, looking around me again, "let's go and see how he is now. We'll leave some soldiers here to make sure the fire doesn't spread, but I think there's little danger. Thank God there is no wind tonight, the woods are wet after the rain of the past few days, and there are no other houses nearby. It should be safe enough. Let me go and organize things here and send these people home."

Lignus would have been a piteous spectacle, had there been an ounce of pity in my soul. Luceiia had not exaggerated, he had been badly burned about the face and head. I lodged him in a stone hut, under heavy guard, when we returned to the villa where, with an ill grace born of my resentment, I went looking once again for Cletus and directed him towards yet another patient in dire need of his healing arts. Then, and only then, did I go looking for Caius.

I found him waiting for me in the *triclinium*, seated in front of a blazing fire with ten of the twenty-two councillors, far more than I had expected him to rouse, grouped around him. They were talking animatedly, but fell silent when I strode limping into the room.

"Ah, there you are, Publius!" Cay rose to his feet immediately and waved me towards an empty seat placed beside his own. I could tell by the tone of his greeting that he had been discoursing already while waiting for me. His voice rang with the orotund, slightly exaggerated resonance that he used to sublime effect when dealing with gatherings he wished to dominate.

"You must have smelled the concoction Gallo is serving us. Your timing is excellent and you probably need a hot drink, for the warmth of it, if not the stimulus."

As I moved to be seated, two of the household servants stepped forward bearing trays of steaming mugs filled with Gallo's personal specialty for long, dark nights: hot milk flavoured liberally with strong honey mead. I gulped one down completely and helped myself to another as Caius resumed his seat and continued speaking in his formal, gubernatorial tone.

"I've been telling our friends here about the discussions you and I have been having recently, concerning the increase in lawlessness that seems to be surrounding us." I noticed that he specifically ignored Luceiia's role in these discussions. "And I have apologized for rousing them from their beds at such an ungodly hour, except that the seriousness of tonight's events does indeed warrant such extreme actions."

I cut short whatever it was that he had been leading up to. "It warrants more than that." I looked around the faces in the room, but spoke directly to Cay. "How is the boy?"

He cleared his throat. "I believe his condition is stable."

"No improvement? He's still comatose?"

"Yes, I am afraid he is. There has been no improvement that I am aware of."

"Have you told these people what happened to him?"

"I have."

"Have they seen him?"

"No, I did not think that was necessary. There was nothing to gain by it; nothing to see except a small boy swathed in bandages."

"Hmmm!" I made a show of counting heads, though I knew from the first exactly how many were present. "We have twelve councillors here, out of twenty-two. That gives us a quorum. I think we should convene an extraordinary meeting of the Council here and now. Were all the others invited?"

"Yes, but for one reason or another they could not come." Caius cleared his throat, with some embarrassment, I thought. "I must confess, though, my summons was not worded with sufficient strength to indicate a Council summons."

"How could it have been? No one had thought of having one then. The idea only occurred to me now. But I believe it necessary that we meet here, formally, right now. We have ample and sufficient reason and there are some imperatives that have thrust themselves upon us in the past hour. If we tackle them resolutely, now, while the situation is still unfolding, we may solve all of them and save ourselves a long and weary task in time to come. Does anyone object?"

The councillors merely shrugged and muttered, but they were amenable enough. They had to be, and I knew that, because they did not really know what the agenda of the meeting would be. The only objection came from Caius himself. "It is very late, Publius. We could be here all night."

I recognized this as a mere formality. I could not, however, define the origins of the small, half-amused smile that had twitched at the corner of his mouth before he began to speak, and I made a mental note to ask him later what had prompted it.

"I doubt it. I would like to outline the situation now in force, as I see it, and make a few specific recommendations for action. If the councillors present approve those recommendations, we should all be in bed within the hour. If there are any serious misgivings voiced, I shall vote to adjourn until the full Council can meet tomorrow, in which case we can still be abed within the hour."

Caius shrugged his shoulders. "That is agreeable to me. Is anyone opposed?"

No one was, and we went directly into formal session with Caius chairing. He gave me the floor and I went straight into the tale of my discovery of Simeon by the lake. I described the child's injuries in graphic terms, attempting deliberately to enlist their horror and outrage. Then, while they were still wide-eyed with disgust, I went on to describe the events that had followed: the scene in the cottage, the women chained to the bed, Lignus's struggle to avoid arrest and the fire which, had Lignus's hut been closer to other buildings, could have been disastrous to the Colony.

Having fixed that image of the possible outcome of these events firmly in the minds of my listeners, I outlined once again the minute but steadily noticeable decline towards anarchy that was becoming apparent in the towns of the region, and even in our own small Colony. I related the story of the dilemma that would face us as lawmakers and law-enforcers as Caius had first described it to me, repeating his device of distinguishing between rules, regulations and laws, and I emphasized the need for an authoritative and supportive stance from the Council in bringing these matters before the colonists and obtaining their moral support in what we were attempting to do.

I told them that if, as I suspected, they were in agreement with the concerns and sentiments I had expressed, and if they could accept Caius's and my own analysis of what was wrong, and if they could in fact identify potential difficulties ahead for our Colony as this atmosphere of moral lassitude continued and expanded, then they must clearly see where those concerns would lead all of us as councillors. I exhorted them to take a firm stance on this issue and to do so immediately, tonight. Lignus the carpenter, I argued, had presented us with a perfect opportunity to move decisively towards ensuring the safety of everyone in the Colony. Ours was ostensibly a Christian community. Christian law was simple, I pointed out; it has only ten real rules, the Commandments, and Lignus had broken almost all of them. If his son were to die, he would be guilty of the murder of his own child. His cruelty was so appalling and his disregard for any of the basic laws of society was so profound that his conduct endangered everyone around him, even though he had as yet caused no damage to anyone other than his own family. But, and I hammered this point home with my fist on the back of a chair, if a man will brutalize his own family, could anyone be foolish enough to hope that mere compunction would prevent him eventually from harming someone else's family? Lignus had not merely transgressed, I told them, he had gone far beyond the bounds of common, human decency. The entire populace would rise up in outrage against his crimes. We, the Council, could use that outrage as an opportunity—one that we hoped would never be repeated— to further our own designs for the protection of our colonists and citizens.

I spoke for almost half an hour and no one interrupted me, and when I had finished there was silence for a spell. I had stood up, under the spell of my own eloquence, my tongue loosened and made fluent by the potency of the meaded milk and my thoughts sharpened by my unquenched anger at what had transpired. Now I remained standing, waiting for a reaction to my diatribe.

It was Vegetius Sulla who broke the silence. He was the eldest son of old Tarpo Sulla, a vigorous and outspoken member of our original Council who had died several years earlier. Unlike his fiery father, however, Vegetius spoke seldom and never without forethought, so men invariably listened carefully to what he had to say.

"Your argument is strong, Varrus. I agree with you, but what exactly are you suggesting we say and do? Be specific. Let us vote on it. I doubt, however, that we'll be abed this night. If we back your suggestions, then we'll have to prepare to present them tomorrow for some kind of ratification by the Plenary Council, at least, if not the full Colony in general assembly. I think tomorrow is going to be too important to this Colony to be embarked upon without detailed plans and strategies."

Sulla's words brought a murmur of assent from the others and I looked at Caius, silently offering him the floor. He moved his shoulders in a slight shrug and indicated with a wave of his hands that I should continue. Continuing, however, was the last thing on my mind. I had prepared the way for him, and I knew he could outline our discussions and our intentions more precisely, more concisely and with far more authority than I could.

"Good, then I will yield the floor to Caius Britannicus. In the meantime, I request your permission to leave for a short time. I should go and check on our prisoner and on the comfort of his womenfolk. He was badly burned, but not too badly injured, I hope, to enable him to avoid standing trial at a public tribunal. I will come back and report to you as soon as I know what is happening. Caius?"

I left the room as he stood up to speak and made my way directly to the stone hut where Lignus was being held. It was well guarded and well lit. Cletus was emerging as I arrived and I drew him aside, out of earshot of the guards.

"Well? How is he? Will he live?"

"Yes, he will." Cletus looked at me strangely. "Do you care, Publius?"

"Yes, Cletus, I do, but only insofar as I have need of him to help us in the governance of this Colony. I want him well enough to stand up on his feet, erect and visible, to be condemned by a public tribunal."

"Ah! I see . . ." Cletus's voice trailed off, and then resumed. "When?"

"Tomorrow? Is that possible?"

"My dear Publius, anything is possible, according to the good Bishop Alaric. Probability, however, is something different. Nevertheless, I think he will be well enough to stand alone for a short time tomorrow. What will happen to him after that?"

"He'll probably be banished. Exiled from the Colony and forbidden to return upon pain of death."

"No execution?"

I tried to read the expression on the physician's face, but it was too dark where we were standing, and so I merely shook my head. "No execution. Unless the boy dies. Then the father dies, too. Will the boy die?"

"He might. I do not know. Only time will tell us that. But if Lignus is not to die tomorrow, he will be able to stand trial. He will not, however, be strong enough to leave the Colony right away, nor for at least a week, more probably two. Unless, of course, you carry him to the edge of the lands and leave him there, in which case he will die tomorrow, or the day after that."

I spat, vainly trying to clear my mouth of the metallic taste of anger. "He's the barbarian, Cletus, not I. How badly is he burned?"

Cletus yawned and rubbed his eyes with the heels of his hands. "Not as badly as he appeared to be when first I saw him. His hair and beard are gone, but the flames were doused before the burns could penetrate too far. One side of his face, though, will be scarred. Was he splashed with oil?"

I grunted. "No, but I hit him with a torch. It had been soaked in oil."

"Of course. That's what would have caused it. His left ear is badly burned and may be completely lost."

"If that is all he loses, one small ear, he can think himself blessed. Where are his wife and daughters, do you know?"

Cletus shook his head. "No, I saw them with Luceiia, but that was before I came here. They must be up at the villa." He yawned again, hugely, and mumbled something about checking on the boy and then getting some sleep before dawn came.

I thanked him and went to find Luceiia, finding as I walked that my own eyes were feeling gritty and heavy-lidded. I drew several deep breaths of clean night air to clear my head, thankful that the slight breeze that had sprung up was blowing from the villa towards the smouldering ruin of Lignus's hut.

Luceiia was with the boy, whose condition was unchanged. She told me that she had had the carpenter's women washed and lodged in the servants' quarters, where they were now in a drugged sleep, thanks to one of Cletus's own sleeping potions. There were others around them and they would be well cared for. I told her, in turn, of what was happening at the impromptu Council meeting in the *triclinium*, and then I kissed her, sent her to bed and returned to the meeting, where I discovered that the proceedings were over. Caius had made his recommendations and they had been unanimously endorsed. There were some four or five hours of darkness left, and everyone had agreed to reassemble at the tenth hour in the Council room.

Word had already been issued that the following day was to be a holiday; no work parties would go out that day and a general assembly of the colonists would be held in the middle of the afternoon. New laws would be proposed by the Council for the well-being of the Colony, and after the need for them and for their preparation had been agreed upon and they had been adopted, a public tribunal would be convened to judge the case of Lignus the carpenter.

By the time the last of our visitors had said good night, I was reeling with fatigue, overwhelmed by a sense of anticlimax. Caius came to me and put his arm around my shoulder.

"Well, brother," he said, "this was a good night's work. We made great headway here, in one short session. Perhaps we should be grateful to our drunken carpenter."

"Huh! I'll show my gratitude tomorrow when I vote to commute his sentence of execution to one of banishment." I broke off, remembering. "You were laughing at me tonight. Or you were smiling. Earlier, just after I arrived, before I started talking. Why? Was I amusing in some way?"

He laughed aloud. "Ah, so you noticed! No, you were not amusing. I was merely surprised, and very pleasantly so, by the change I suddenly noticed in you, Publius, that is all."

"Change? What change? What kind of change?"

"Improvement. When you strode into that Council meeting and took it over from me, with total correctness and confidence, I suddenly realized how far you have come since you first arrived here. The Publius Varrus who came here originally would never have thought to take the floor from Proconsul Caius Britannicus. He could have done so, at any time, but he was not ready; he was not yet sufficiently at peace with himself. Nor would that same Publius Varrus have dreamed of facing, or haranguing, or influencing, or even bullying the august members of the colonial Council." He was laughing again. "Tonight, I saw you accept yourself and your role here for the first time, Publius. I saw you exercise your power in this Colony, and I grew even prouder of you than I was before. And that made me smile, but with pleasure, and the rightness of it."

I was staring at him, but as I heard his words I knew he was right. I had taken charge, completely, not as Varrus the centurion-turned-tribune, but as

Publius Varrus, Councillor, Citizen and leader. "Yes," I said, "but I was outraged. I have to get to bed, Caius."

"And so do I, my friend. But I hope your outrage lasts. If it does not, I may have to find ways to renew it regularly. I like what it does to you."

I thought Luceiia was asleep when I fell into bed, but she was awake, waiting for me, although she made no sound as I slipped out of my clothing and climbed beneath the covers to mold my shivering body against the contours of her back, snuggling against the warm, comforting smoothness of her and passing my arm gently over her waist to nestle between the warm mounds of her breasts. Only a contented married man can appreciate the privilege of such moments. His less fortunate unwed brethren cannot be privy to such bliss, because their singular estate simply precludes the ease-filled, familiar and familial intimacy necessary to such sensations. Lesser men, single and unmarried, too frequently must sleep alone, and when they do have partners to share their couch, their own lusts and the need to demonstrate their prowess combine to rob them of the sheer pleasure of simply sharing bed and bodily warmth at any length. Their time abed with those women they may have from time to time is too demanding, too athletic, too filled with novelty and imperative demands and requirements. Only the well-wed man can know the simple, priceless luxury of sliding into bed, exhausted from his labors, on a chill, cold night, to find it filled with the welcome, wondrous, undemanding warmth of a sleepy, scented, softly yielding spouse who squirms and nestles close against him, offering her presence as both solace and reward for his endeavors.

That thought was in my mind before I realized Luceiia was awake. My tiredness was such that my bliss was overwhelming, but then I felt her hand close over my own, which lay inert upon her breast, and squeeze my fingers closed.

"Has everyone gone home?"

I pulled her close against me and spoke with my nose between her shoulder blades, kissing her skin and smelling the sweet perfume of her hair. "Aye. Caius had finished everything when I returned. We meet again in the morning, with the others of the Council, in full session. Everything's arranged. Tomorrow is a holiday. No work parties. General convocation in the afternoon, and we'll try the carpenter thereafter . . ."

Her voice woke me again. "Are you asleep?"

"Hmm? Think so, love . . . Very tired . . ."

She moved against me, thrusting her bottom deeper towards me and drawing up her right knee so my thigh filled the junction of hers. "Too sleepy for this?" she murmured, moving against me.

"Mmm," I mumbled, aware of the heat of her against the skin of my thigh, her hand leading my own downward from her breast and lodging it in the fold of her belly and upraised leg before moving back towards me to slide down into the tiny space between us, spread fingers flexing against my skin.

And as awareness grew, my sleepiness abated rapidly, although languidly, luxuriously and without unseemly urgency.

Later, in that tiny space of time between my being vibrantly, ecstatically awake and crashing backwards into sleep, she bent and kissed my nose, easing herself voluptuously in the saddle of my loins and brushing my chest with the tips of her breasts.

"Now I suppose you'll go to sleep? Well, before you do, Master Varrus, I want you to know how proud of you I have been tonight, and how glad I am to be your wife . . . Had you noticed that, that it pleases me to pleasure you?" I merely smiled at her in the moonlight, lacking the energy to answer in words. She kissed me again, pouting her lips to pillows of moist softness, blessing my face: lips, nose, eyes and forehead. "Sleep now," she whispered, raising herself so that I felt the cool night air against the warm moistness of me, and then resuming the position she had occupied when I arrived. I remember her sitting up again, too, tugging at the bedclothes to bring them higher on the bed.

At least, I think I do.

VII

LIGNUS THE CARPENTER had his moment of public infamy at the third hour of the following afternoon, when he was arraigned and brought before the full tribunal of the Colony Britannicus, held erect between two soldiers who were as big as he was. His head was almost entirely swathed in bandages and it was obvious to everyone assembled in the main courtyard of the villa—and the crowd included every man, woman and child in the Colony—that he was in great pain. His suffering brought him little pity, however, for his only son still lay comatose in the villa's sick bay, and the spectacle of his bruised and abused wife and pregnant and beaten daughters had scandalized the entire community.

The justice dispensed to him was swift and quickly summarized: In that he was responsible for brutalizing and savagely beating his own son, crippling him and leaving him in a condition closer to death than life, and in continuing danger of suffering death from the abuses he had undergone; and in that he physically chained, constrained and incestuously impregnated one of his own daughters and cohabited incestuously with the other against the laws of God and man; and in that his actions and the consequences of those actions occasioned a conflagration that endangered and might have affected the entire Colony, he, Lignus the carpenter, was proscribed and banished from the lands entailed by the Colony under penalty of instant death, to be executed immediately upon his being discovered in future within the bourn of the Colony or any of the lands owned by or attached to it. His wife and daughters were absolved of any guilt or willing complicity in his atrocious conduct and were offered the option of remaining in the Colony and living by what work would be provided for them after his departure. They accepted the offer without hesitation.

There was a corollary to this verdict, however, made in recognition of the fact that the man was physically unable to travel at the time of sentence. He was to be lodged, under guard, within the Colony for a maximum of twenty-one days, or until Cletus the physician pronounced him fit to travel, whichever should be shorter. After that he would be escorted to the boundary of the Colony by the high road to Aquae Sulis and there cast out.

The entire tribunal lasted less than half an hour, and it was a fitting end to a day that had seen some miraculous advances in the method of government of our Colony.

The Plenary Council had convened at the tenth hour, as scheduled. By then, the word had gone out among the members who had not been present the night before, and the new ideas had fallen on fertile ground. It seemed there were very few councillors who had not been reflecting, with varying degrees of worry, on the worsening situation in the town and cities of south-west Britain. In a fiery two-hour session, the councillors unanimously and immediately endorsed the initial decisions reached the previous night at the impromptu session. It took longer, however, for them to agree in principle to an analysis and examination of Caius's suggestion that the Council be expanded and altered to include the guidance and counsel of women in specific areas, mainly affecting the morale, governance and well-being of the colonists and their domestic conditions. This was a chewy mouthful for the councillors to swallow, but the majority ended up admitting that, if the guiding principles of such involvement were well thought out and disciplined, and properly administered, the idea could have much merit. Luceiia and three other women were elected by the councillors to consult with the Plenary Council on how these matters might be conceived and achieved.

The assembled colonists, for their part, roared their approval of every suggestion put forward by the Council that day, and when Cletus delivered a report on the status of the boy Simeon, who was still unconscious, a silence filled with sympathy fell on the crowd and lasted for a long moment. When the public meeting was finally adjourned after the tribunal, very few people left the gathering place. Everyone wanted to talk about what had happened and what had been resolved during the day, and soon fires were being lit and food prepared, and the activities of the day took on a holiday atmosphere that lasted well into the evening.

Young Simeon regained consciousness just before sunset, to everyone's relief and great pleasure, most particularly his mother's, and Cletus ventured a qualified prognosis of eventual recovery, although the lad's broken leg was so badly smashed that he would probably hobble worse than I did for the rest of his life. That night, after a late supper, while Luceiia was supervising the bedtime of the eldest of our brood, Caius and I sat in companionable silence on either side of a blazing fire in his study. He was reading a letter that had arrived the day before from our friend Bishop Alaric, who was in Verulamium. I was mulling over the thoughts that had occurred to me after reading the same missive. Alaric had written about the latest escalation of enemy raids on all sides of the country. In what appeared to be a general response to an abrupt curtailment of the flow of funds from the Imperial Exchequer, he informed us, the Colonial High Command in South Britain had been recently forced, yet again, to cut back drastically on its policing duties. The news, while not surprising, had angered me. This nonsense of troop withdrawals and reallocations had been going on for several years now, and we were well aware of it. It was no secret that the garrisons had been pulled out of many of the minor forts, and we knew that, in spite of bureaucratic protestations of "interim measures only, pending the return of victorious forces from the continent," these moves were permanent.

From my own, personal perspective, the worst thing about all of that—

apart from the legal ramifications of the loss of the punitive arm of the law, which had been causing us so much concern—was that many of these supposedly minor forts were strategically located and essential to the defence of outlying areas of the country. When the soldiers were withdrawn from these, there was nothing to prevent incursions by pirates and marauders.

The most glaring example of this we had seen was the closure of the main fort at Cicutio, in south-central Cambria, and the withdrawal of troops from Dolocauthi, to the north-west. Dolocauthi was the biggest gold mine in the Western Empire, and when the troops were withdrawn from there, the word spread quickly. A line of forts, joined by a high-quality road along the south side of the Cambrian peninsula, was still being maintained, to keep the seaborne Scots from Dolocauthi, but it was a poor second-best to a strong, garrisoned fort on the spot.

Dolocauthi itself did not interest me personally and would not had it been a thousand times bigger, but it had come to symbolize two things: the stupidity of the High Command, who decided in the first place to withdraw the garrison without shutting down the mines—no doubt seeking to placate carping, middle-level government officials—and the colossal stupidity of the Hibernian Scots, who knew no difference between a gold mine and an iron-ore pit.

Caius put down Alaric's letter and sighed, moving the taper back to the centre of his table. I watched him for a few moments before breaking in on his thoughts.

"What are you thinking about?"

"Oh, I don't know. Alaric's letter depresses me. I was thinking of garrisons, and the lack of them. For all the good it seems to do nowadays, my friend, the Garrison of Britain might as well not be here. Never enough men in any one place, and never enough time to arrive at where they ought to be before it's too late." He paused. "You know, Publius, there is something I've been meaning to ask you about for some time. Do you remember the horse you brought back from Glevum?"

"Of course." His question surprised me. I was amazed that he should remember.

Five years earlier, we had taken to sending our wagons north towards Glevum twice a year, to buy up ingots of iron and lead. From Glevum, we would travel back to the Colony through Corinium and south through Aquae Sulis, gathering extra luxury items that were otherwise notably absent from our Colony. The return of the wagon train from Glevum had quickly become a semi-annual event looked forward to with eagerness by everyone, until the word spread, within three years of our first such journey, that the garrisons had been withdrawn completely from the inland forts, and reduced in the coastal forts. Within the following year, Hibernians by the boatload were spilling into Cambria, searching for the fabulous gold mines of Dolocauthi. To the best of my knowledge, they never did find Dolocauthi, but they terrorized every miner in the country to the extent that the flow of iron into the Glevum markets had dried up completely.

That was a blow to us; to me personally. It meant I had to start looking elsewhere for my iron. It had been on the last of those Glevum journeys, about a year earlier, that I had found the horse Caius referred to.

We had been searching to the north of Glevum itself for pockets of iron production, and on a spring afternoon we crested a hill and saw a raid in progress on a farm in the valley below us. The fighting was over, if there had been any at all. There were raiders everywhere, and the flames were just starting to spread in the buildings. I sounded a call on my horn and led my men down the hill in a charge. The raiders saw and heard us coming, and they ran. There were three of us on horseback that day, and we pursued them, easily outdistancing our soldiers, who had no hope of catching them. Within a short space of time we were in bowshot range of the fleeing raiders, and we managed to drop half a dozen of them at no risk to ourselves before we ran out of arrows and had to turn back.

The only living being left on that farm had been a stallion, a heavy black with wild eyes. And he was alive only because of his wildness. Two other horses lay slaughtered. He alone had kept his distance. We chased him, those of us who were mounted, and finally managed to loop a rope around his neck and bring him back with us.

"What happened to it? It was a stallion, wasn't it?"

"Aye. And a fine one. I still have him, but he's too wild to ride."

"You mean he's in the stables? Here?"

"Well of course. Where else would he be?"

"Hmmm." His face assumed one of those strange Britannican expressions I had come to know so well and which, I knew from experience, normally resulted in an increased work-load for someone, usually me. His next words hinted eloquently of fermenting thoughts and yeasty processes occurring within his brain. "A stallion. Publius, what do you know of breeding horses?"

I looked at him, recognizing the tone and wondering what was coming next.

"Nothing, apart from the obvious. You need a stallion and a mare, and they handle the rest themselves."

"Nothing more?"

"What more could there be, Caius? It's natural."

"Publius, when I want a clown, I'll hire one," he snapped.

I shrugged, grinning at his short temper. "Pardon me. What's on your mind?"

"Adrianople," he said, mollified slightly by my ready apology. "Adrianople and Alexander of Macedon."

I waited for more, and when nothing was forthcoming I prompted him. "Forgive me, but I don't follow you. What connection is there between Adrianople and Alexander?"

"None, Publius, there is none. Not yet. Apart from the obvious, as you said to me. But my mind tells me there should be. Are you hungry? I could eat something."

"There are some pears there, on the table. Permit me." I rose and took the bowl to him, then watched as he selected one, took out a small clasp knife and began to pare the skin from it. He was obviously deep in thought, as was I, wondering about the "obvious" connection between Adrianople and Alexander that I had evidently missed.

"Varrus," he asked me after a few moments of silence, using his old, army tone, "what is the major difference between our cavalry and our foot-soldiers?"

I barely had to think about that. "Speed," I answered. "Speed and ease of manoeuvring."

"And which would you say are the better troops?"

"The infantry, naturally."

He looked up and smiled at me strangely. "Why? And why 'naturally'?"

I thought he was twitting me. "Are you serious, Cay? They are more dependable, more adaptable, more solid in every way."

"Why?"

I blinked at him, wondering where this discussion might be taking us. "For many reasons. What are you driving at, General?"

"Just answer the question, Varrus. Why more solid?"

I thought about it for several moments. "Well, for one thing, infantry are more . . . permanent. They stay in the field longer and have the ability to prepare their own defences. Fortifications. They're more stable. They have fewer needs. A foot-soldier need only look after himself. A horseman has to look after his animal, too. And in the final analysis, infantry are a solid, unified force. Horsemen are individuals."

He barely gave me time to finish. "But you have just finished telling me that mounted troops have the advantage of speed and the ability to manoeuvre more quickly."

"Well . . . they do, under certain conditions. In hill country, a man on foot is far more dependable."

"*If* he holds the high ground."

"Aye." I nodded.

"Then what about Adrianople? Heavy concentrations of horse in that engagement wiped out an *entire* Roman army."

I shook my head. "No, that was a fluke, a trick. The army's commander must have been negligent in the first place."

Caius was frowning, shaking his head. "Do we know that, Publius? Really? I doubt it. There are no flukes in war. Trickery is a legitimate principle of warfare."

I shrugged, beginning to feel very mildly exasperated. "I don't see where this is leading us."

"You will. Tell me, what would you say was the difference between Alexander's cavalry and ours?"

Again I paused to think before answering. "Discipline, I suppose, if any-thing. And tactical deployment. Alexander refined his father Philip's tactics, which were already superb. But apart from that, the major difference was that the Macedonian cavalry was heavy cavalry of a kind that we don't use today. Big horses, carrying heavily armed men. All trained to operate in concert."

"Like hammers, Varrus?"

He had surprised me again. My mind jumped backwards, twenty-odd years, to the special unit, "the Hammers," that Caius and I had assembled to smash back the Caledonians after the Invasion of 367. I nodded, slowly. "Yes, I suppose you could say that. Like hammers. Or like one big hammer."

There was the vestige of a smile on his lips. "Now do you see what I'm thinking, Varrus?"

"I think I'm beginning to."

"Imagine the effect, Publius." His voice was excited. "Imagine the effect of a squadron, or even more, a cohort, of heavily armoured soldiers, mounted on big horses and trained to ride as a unit. Not skirmishers, Publius, no, nor mounted archers, but front-line troops—shock troops! Imagine a solid line of mounted spearmen riding at the gallop against a boatload of Saxons caught on land. Can you see it?"

I could. I could see it clearly and something stirred in my gut, but I had to be sure that I was seeing what he was seeing. "Spearmen? You mean with *sarissas*? The long, sixteen-foot spears Alexander's Companions used?"

"Why not? Or even axemen. But trained to fight together, as one force, like an infantry maniple. Could it be done?"

I was seeing a solid wall of charging men on enormous horses. "Why not? They would require a lot of training, but it could be done, if you had the horses." I stopped short, disappointment sharp in my breast over the death of my own sudden enthusiasm. "Unfortunately, we don't. Not the kind of horses we would need—big, heavy brutes. They would have to be massive to carry heavily armed men. Ours just aren't big enough. And we would need so many of them! Hundreds."

He laughed aloud and rose to his feet. "We shall have them, Publius! We'll breed them! Big horses! By the hundred!"

"No, Caius, hold up!" I felt it my duty to interrupt, to bring him back to earth. "That would take years!"

"Of course it will. No doubt of it, none at all!" His voice was fierce and jubilant. "But we have years, Publius! We'll start tomorrow. And the first thing we have to find is someone who has knowledge about horses, and I know just the man. You remember the bailiff who was tending Terra's villa when he bought it? Fellow called Victorex, or Victrix, or something? Terra told me his father used to run a hippodrome in Gaul. The son learned about horses as a child and was a horse physician of some kind. I'll have Terra send him over tomorrow, and we'll ask him what he knows of breeding. He knows horseflesh, from all accounts. He may just be our man. You, in the meantime, can concern yourself with finding out all you can about Alexander's methods."

I grimaced. "How will I do that? I know of his campaigns and his battles, and a little about his strategy. But there's little or nothing in our books about his actual tactics—how he deployed or trained his men. We Romans have never concerned ourselves with cavalry tactics of that kind."

"Not until now, my friend. Not until us."

"Anyway," I went on, "I don't like the *sarissa* idea. Those things were too cumbersome—six paces long and useless after the first charge. They had to drop them then, and use swords. I don't like that at all."

He nodded. "Nor do I. Find me some way of keeping hold of a spear so that it can be used after the first attack. Our men should be able to kill with it again and again, as often as is needed to win a battle."

"Hmmm," I said. "Sounds like you want a short spear."

"I don't know what I want. But you may be right. A short spear with a two-edged blade. Something that will cut as well as thrust. Something that will let our horsemen fight from horseback without having to dismount. That's what we need, and that's your department. See to it, please, and let me know as soon as you have solved the problem." The bridge from infantry to cavalry had already been built in the mind of Caius Britannicus.

"Let me think about it," I told him. "I'll talk to Equus, too. Perhaps between us we can come up with something."

"Good." He was standing close, leaning over me, his hands clasped in front of his chest, making little explosive noises as he brought the hollows of his palms together unconsciously again and again. "Excellent, excellent. Now let's go and find some more food. That pear was excellent, but I want meat. Thinking makes me hungry. In the meantime, I want you to think about that spear."

I laughed and stood up, stretching. "I will. I don't know what I might be able to come up with, but I'll think about it. You just reminded me of something else, though."

"What's that?"

"I'm due to meet that merchant again, Statius, the one who's collecting iron for me in the north-east. I arranged to meet him again in Noviomagus next month. I'd forgotten. You reminded me of it when you made me think of the Glevum trips we used to make."

"Is that important?"

"Very important." I grinned at the memory of the merchant's expression when he had seen my bag of gold *auri*. "You should have seen his face when I pulled out the money to pay him! Now that he knows how mad I am to exchange gold for iron, he'll probably have ten wagons loaded to overflowing. I hope he has, I'll gladly take them off his hands."

Cay frowned. "That much? Do we need that much?" His tone made me smile again, but I wiped the smile off my face as I answered him.

"As much as I can get, Cay, and then ten times as much again. You were the one who made me worry in the first place about what's going to happen in the future. Now I am convinced that your prophecies were short of the mark. If things keep deteriorating the way they have been, iron is going to be worth a hundred times its real weight in gold, and there's going to be little time or opportunity to mine it, smelt it and carry it here from wherever we might find it. A storeroom full of gold ingots will give you no more than indigestion when you have to grow and make your own food because there's no one left to buy from, Cay. But with a storeroom full of iron ingots, I can make all the tools we'll need to grow and harvest our own food and fight off anyone who tries to steal it from us."

He was nodding in agreement as I spoke. "You are correct, as usual, Publius. I can be very dense at times."

"No, not dense, brother. You were simply not brought up to see that iron might someday be worth more than gold, that's all."

"God! Was anyone?"

"Of course, I was."

"Oh. Silly of me, I should have known. So when will you leave?"

"In about three weeks."

"Just in time to take Lignus with you."

I shook my head in disgust. "By the Christus, I hope not! But you are probably right, and if I have to, then I will. But he had better behave himself until he gets out of my sight."

"He will, my friend, he will." Caius yawned and stretched. "Aye! I think I shall forgo that food after all. I am ready to sleep. I had no more than three hours last night and I'm too old for that. Good night to you, and don't forget to think about my two-edged spear."

VIII

WELL, I THOUGHT about that spear. I thought of little else for a long time. I worked on it and worried over it day and night for months after that evening, not knowing it was to be another ten years before the discovery was made that would revolutionize our way of waging war, and even longer before we would recognize what we really had.

Victorex, the bailiff from Terra's estate, took to Caius's ideas before he had even finished outlining them, for horses were this man's life. He even looked like one. He was tall and bald except for a thick corona of stiff, straight, dun-coloured hair that encircled his head above his ears like a cropped mane. He had long, pointed ears, large, pale eyes that were slightly too close together and a face that seemed to fill up his whole head. His nose was long and flat and his big, oblong teeth seemed squeezed together at the front of his mouth. And he had no chin. A strange-looking character, altogether. The first time Equus saw him he said, "My God! And they call *me* Equus!"

Victorex was the perfect man to put in charge of Caius's new project, and he could not wait to get started. The first thing he did, after he had moved his belongings from Terra's villa to ours, was to examine every head of stock we had. Within a week he had divided them all up by sex, weight and colour and begun to devise complicated plans and charts for his "bloodlines," as he called them, and for his breeding stables. All told, including the horses from the other villas in the Colony, we had twenty-seven stallions, about fifty mares and a number of geldings, mules and horses too old to be useful. Victorex selected the three finest stallions and the ten biggest, strongest mares as breeding stock, to be kept at the villa. The rest he allocated to the various farms that made up the Colony. Caius had informed all of our people of his plans, and if there were any ill feelings over this relocation of stock, they went unvoiced. The word went out, too, that every expedition that left the Colony had to keep constant look-out for new stock. No plugs or swaybacks were wanted, but all horses judged to be suitable for breeding purposes were to be bought at a fair price and brought back to the Colony.

The first opportunity came on my next excursion to Noviomagus to meet with Statius, but we found no horses on that journey other than the nine pairs we bought from him, complete with wagons loaded with iron ingots. Caius had been correct, in his usual manner, about our timing on that trip. The twenty-one days of grace accorded to Lignus the carpenter expired as we were preparing to leave the Colony, and he was granted another two days in custody so that we could escort him safely off the Colony's lands. His son

Simeon was recovering slowly, and there was now every reason to expect that the boy would grow healthy again, although his leg was broken and twisted beyond even Cletus's ability to repair. Lignus's burns, on the other hand, had been largely superficial and were healing quickly, except for the oil burn on his left ear, and hair had already begun to grow on the rest of his head, leaving him with a mangy, scabby look that I thought well suited to him. He still stank like a goat, too, and I ordered him forcibly washed before I would allow him to approach my train.

We were taking only two wagons with us on the outward journey, to carry the salt and provisions we intended to pick up along our route, and Lignus sat chained in the bottom of one of them as we marched away. No one came to see him off or to wish him well. We took him far beyond the boundaries of the Colony and left him, free of his chains at last, just outside the small town of Sorviodunum, where four main roads intersect.

From there onward, relieved of his company, our journey to and from Noviomagus was direct and uncomplicated, and we avoided being seen from any of the towns we passed by. We concluded our business with Statius quickly and to his immense satisfaction, and contracted to meet with him again just prior to the start of the new year. With the proof of our madness and riches, this second exorbitant payment of gold safe in his hands, Statius would have been happy to bring his next shipment of iron all the way to our Colony, but I balked at the thought of him knowing where to find us and our gold. I told him that I had to come back to Noviomagus then anyway on other business.

Five days after leaving Statius in Noviomagus, we were back on our own lands, and I was pleasantly surprised to find that my old friend Bishop Alaric had been installed as a house guest during my absence. He was the first person I saw among the small group waiting to welcome me home, standing straight, tall and white-haired beside Caius. He had brought joyous tidings with him on this visit, but no mention was made of them to me at that time. Luceiia had missed my arrival, being away from the villa on some business connected with her emerging Council of Women, but Caius assured me that she would be home presently, and I went about the business of overseeing the unloading of my wagons and the disposal of the goods they held before making my way to the bath house to wash the stains of the road from my pores.

When I entered the house again, I found Caius seated by the window in his study, poring over one of a pile of tightly rolled parchments, all sealed with wax, that lay on the table in front of him. Curious, I asked him what he was reading and he reacted with the euphoria of a man who has just found buried treasure. The parchments were all letters from his son Picus, written over a period of years and dispatched by a variety of military couriers from all parts of the Empire, in care of Plautus at the garrison in Colchester. Plautus had been transferred to Londinium since Picus left Britain, and the postmasters at Colchester had taken very little interest in forwarding letters to him. Eventually, however, a large number of letters had been delivered to Plautus in bulk, and he had duly forwarded them to Alaric, knowing they would come, in time, to Cay. Having waited years to receive them without even knowing of their existence, Cay had now determined, he told me, to wait a little longer before permitting himself the pleasure of reading them, teasing himself with the self-discipline of not yielding to his impulse to rip them open and wallow in them. Now, however, he yielded slightly, permitting himself to read one of them. I grinned and left him to his pleasure, knowing he would give them to me to read later, and deriving great pleasure myself from the knowledge of how much this sudden wealth of correspondence meant to him.

Picus was Caius's only surviving son, his first-born, and Caius doted on him, although he had seldom mentioned his name in the past few years. He had had other sons, Marcus and Paulus, twin boys, but had lost them, along with his beloved wife, Heraclita, and his only daughter, Meleiia, to a nameless plague that had almost killed him, too, and had decimated his entire command at the outset of his last posting, his Proconsulship as Commander-in-Chief of the imperial garrisons in Numidia. Only Picus had survived the holocaust untouched, uncontaminated by the pestilence. Upon their return to Britain at the end of those five dreadful years, Picus had joined the legions as an ordinary soldier at the age of sixteen, maintaining the unbroken, centuries-old tradition of his family. His father's rank and his family name meant nothing at that stage. Any advancement Picus might achieve thereafter in his military career would be won on his own merits. Shortly after that, however, to his father's undying grief, the boy had fallen under the spell of the upstart Emperor from Britain, Magnus Maximus, and had gone sailing off to Gaul, still but a simple legionary, to help that ambitious warrior secure his imperial crown. Since then, no word had come from Picus and Magnus was long dead, his armies shattered and his followers proscribed. Now the reason for the years of silence was explained, and Caius Britannicus was rejuvenated by the tidings from his son.

After dinner that evening, when Luceiia and the two women who would be staying at the villa that night had retired to Luceiia's new *cubiculum* to discuss their Council business, Caius, Alaric and I sat alone in Cay's study, and I caught up on all the happenings that had occurred while I was away. Cay was not ready yet to discuss Picus's letters. The pleasure of them was still too new, too solitary, too precious to share, and Alaric and I understood how he felt. Neither of us pressed him, and our talk was desultory as a result.

"Philip Ascanus was here, right in the Colony," Caius said, suddenly, during a lull in the conversation. "Arrived the day after you left."

"Who?" I had heard him perfectly well, but the impact of his words was so outlandish that I had to ask him to repeat the name.

"Philip Ascanus. You remember him?"

"Remember him? Of course I remember him. How could I forget? What was he doing here?"

"He came to claim his patrimony." Caius's voice was dry as a desert wind and I was floundering for a foothold among my swirling thoughts.

"Patrimony? What patrimony? Have you spoken with him? I am amazed that he would even dare come near you, after the way you dealt with him when you last saw him. How long ago was that? My God, Cay, that's twenty years ago—more, closer to thirty."

Caius grunted. "You are growing old, my friend, and like an old man, you are starting to exaggerate. Unfortunately, what you say is not far off the mark, but it's not quite twenty years." He paused and cleared his throat, managing to inject disgust and distaste into the sound. "The man has improved none in the interim, however—nor would he, I fear, given another ten years. He is still a charlatan and a blusterer, though more daring and more insolent than he would have presumed to be with me twenty years ago. But then, I never found him guilty of a lack of daring."

Alaric was looking from one to the other of us, curiosity stamped on his face, and I explained to him, "Philip Ascanus served with us for a short time before the Invasion, back in '67. He was a bad officer, the worst kind. A brutal bully and a homosexual torturer. Starved his men and spent the money for their rations. Caius straightened him out the only way possible—had him court-martialled, stripped of his rank and expelled from the Legion."

"I should have had him hanged," Caius drawled, his voice bitter.

"I don't understand," I said, turning back to face him. "What in the name of all the ancient gods was he doing here? What's his business?"

His eyebrow went up in surprise that I should ask the question. "What does he want? Why, his own good, of course. Apparently, he thought to be our neighbour."

I was astounded. "Are you serious? How?"

This brought a wordless grunt from Caius, who sniffed and replied, "Apparently, one of the villas to the north of here was acquired by an uncle of his, who promptly died, leaving the place to his favourite nephew."

"Good God! And now Philip Ascanus is here?"

"Was here. He didn't stay."

"Which villa? Is it one of the ones close to us?"

"Close enough," Cay said. "I thought of disputing his claim in the courts, when he told me why he was here. But then I reasoned that I was merely being petty. The uncle never took possession, formally, but he paid the purchase, nonetheless, so the villa and its lands go to his only heir."

"Philip Ascanus!"

"Philip Ascanus. Apparently he lives close to Glevum. Received the news of his uncle's death from your friend the tribune there."

"Scala?" I had met Tribune Marius Scala during one of my trips to Glevum some years earlier. He was a pleasant fellow and our friendship, though brief, had been a delightful one.

"That's the one."

"Good God." Another thought occurred to me. "How did you find out all this? Are you telling me he actually came here, knowing this was your house?"

A chilly little smile flickered across Cay's mouth and his aristocratic drawl became more pronounced. "No, not quite. He seemed quite genuinely surprised to see me here. Quite severely disconcerted, as a matter of fact. Bereft of words. Looked as though I had caught him in the act of buggery again. It would have been quite laughable except for the fact that nothing the fellow did could ever amuse me. I was the last person on earth he could ever have dreamed of seeing here, and he was most upset to find himself a supplicant on my doorstep. He thought he had come to deal with you, you see. Your friend Scala left him with the impression that this was your estate."

"With me? My estate? Why would Scala do that?" I stopped and thought about it. Scala could easily have taken the wrong impression from me; after all, I had spent less than a week in his company and there had been a lot of things going on, including some sustained drinking. I shrugged the thought off and continued. "Even so, I'm surprised Ascanus would have the gall to face me, knowing that I know what I know about him. What did he want to see me about?"

Caius shook his head, his little smile spreading wider. "I've no idea. He was probably looking for information about the area and the district. Yours was the only name he knew, and he had that from your friend Scala. But there's no question of him having the gall to face you. It would never have occurred to him that he might know you, and he would probably not have recognized you had he met you face to face. Bear in mind what you just now said, Ascanus was a bad officer, the worst kind. Such men do not recognize, or even think of, the soldiers under them as living, human beings of import. He was told to look for the villa-owner Publius Varrus. If he remembered anyone of that name at all from his past and long-forgotten army days, it would only be a lowly centurion. Centurions do not own villa estates, Publius. You forget that his time with our unit was before you won promotion in the field and before you came into your own wealth from your grandfather. Philip Ascanus would never have made the association between a common soldier of twenty years ago—a mere subaltern risen from the ranks—and a man of wealth and power today.

"Anyway," he continued, grinning, "he knows who you are now. I told him all about you and warned him that you would not be pleased to see his face again. He knows that he is not welcome on these lands and he will not return uninvited. Believe me."

I attempted to erase the frown from my forehead. "You don't mean you're prepared to accept him as a colonist, do you?"

Caius smiled again. "No, not at all. I think the possibility of that is very slight. In fact, I no longer think it is a possibility. I believe his vision of a life in the country began to dwindle the moment he found himself face to face with me, and died altogether when he learned you were here with me. The thought of propinquity to two people who know the truth about him—and who would have no compunction in condemning him—would be unbearable to the man."

"So you don't think he'll be moving to the Colony?" I was grinning now, too.

"I do not. But I do think my agents should be able to buy his villa for a reasonable price, now that he no longer has dreams for it."

I shook my head. "He'll never sell to you, Cay."

"He'll never know I'm involved. He will take the cash and forget about the place."

"Hmmm!" I mulled that one over, trying unsuccessfully to focus my mind on my twenty-year-old memories of Philip Ascanus, but I could only recall a faintly paunchy, dissolute body and a weak, pasty face with an incipient double chin and a pouty mouth. No eyes and nothing definite to fasten on, not even hair colour. I realized that Cay was correct. Ascanus would sell, and we would acquire more land.

"What's the place like, his villa?"

"Excellent. Not as large as some, but very well staffed and well run. I went and looked as soon as I found out Philip had returned to Glevum." Caius stood up. "No, stay where you are, I'm only stretching my legs," he said to Alaric, who had moved to stand up with him. Alaric subsided and Caius crossed to the big hearth, where he threw a new log on the fire before turning to look back at me.

I was frowning again. "And that was all? He gave no reason for coming here to our villa?"

"Only that he came looking for Publius Varrus, and that Scala had given him your name."

Caius left the fire and came back to sit again at the table, resting his hand on Alaric's shoulder as he passed. He moistened the tip of one finger and dipped it gently into the small pot of salt that still sat in the centre of the table, then transferred the finger to his mouth, licking the salt off absent-mindedly. He glanced over to where Alaric sat watching and listening.

"Alaric? What do you think of this conversation?" The bishop blinked his eyes slowly and thought for a few moments before he began to speak.

"Well, my friends," he said at last in his moderate, deliberate tones, "I hear strange and unexpected sounds and great bitterness coming from two people whom I love and respect. I hear you ascribing a sinfulness worthy of eternal damnation to a man whom neither of you has seen or heard of for twenty years, while both of you admit to each other, and to me as witness, that neither of you has any reason to do so, other than an old dislike. I hear no charity in you, my friends, and I hear none of the forgiveness that the Blessed Christus begged us to apply to our enemies."

Caius and I regarded each other with wry looks.

"Alaric's right, Cay," I said.

Caius heaved an enormous sigh. "I know," he replied, "I know he is." He shook his head, sighed again and rose to his feet. "And we will take his unspoken advice, and talk of other things. Another cup of wine, either of you?" As he poured he said, almost to himself, "But tomorrow, I will send word to my agents in Londinium and Glevum that I wish to buy his villa anonymously, for a fair price." He put the wine jug down firmly. "I will send one of our fastest couriers, first thing in the morning."

And so it was arranged that our Colony would increase by the size of the Ascanus estate, and the three of us spent the remainder of the evening talking pleasantly of other things.

The following morning, I set out on my monthly rounds of the Colony estates. The day passed slowly and uneventfully, one of those plodding, rural days unmarked by anything but drudgery, hard work and meticulous, painstaking efforts to maintain an inventory of crops in progress, grain supplies in hand and the multitudinous details of keeping a growing community alive and well-fed. I was homeward bound by late afternoon, and it started to rain, spattering heavy drops, as I entered the boundaries of the land belonging to the Villa Britannicus proper. Looking up at the suddenly leaden skies, I blessed Luceiia's foresight in convincing me to take along my cloak. The day had started well, but early in the forenoon dark, scattered clouds had started blowing in from the west, and I had begun to realize she had been correct the night before when she had predicted heavy rain by afternoon. Now all the rifts between the clouds had been sealed up and it looked as though this was not a shower that would blow over quickly. I was riding in a cart, since I had decided to drop off a load of new tools to several of our outlying farms, but Equus had taken the leather covering off the day before, to mend a rent in it, and it had not yet been replaced. It took me only a moment to retrieve my heavy cloak from the box on the back and I swaddled myself in it completely, pulling the cowled headpiece well over my head and slipping my hands through the vents provided for them before taking up the reins again. A cold, gusty wind began to blow the rain in sheets, but I remained sheltered beneath my cloak as both wind and rain picked up in strength, throwing themselves uselessly against the thick, tight, wind-and waterproof weave of the warm garment. For all that, the rain was icy and my bare hands were chilled and stiff from holding the reins by the time I eventually reached the gates of the villa and turned thankfully into the courtyard.

I had been driving fast, driven by the weather, and when we arrived my poor horse was coated with mud and steaming like a *sudarium*. The rain had stopped somewhere along the way and the clouds overhead were broken again, showing widening reaches of blue sky. I threw my reins to a groom and my wet cloak to Gallo, Caius's major-domo, and ran into the house, calling aloud for Caius. He was not there. Nor were Alaric and Luceiia. The house was empty, except for servants. Frustrated, I then made my way directly to the smithy, but Equus was gone too, on a visit to one of the other villa forges. Thoroughly deflated, I went back to the villa, where Gallo informed me, politely, now that I had time to listen, that Caius and Alaric had been collected by a wagon sent for them from the villa of our friends, the twins Terrix and Fermax, widely known as Terra and Firma. They were to be guests of the twins for dinner and an entertainment that night and would return to the villa in the morning. My wife had gone, he also informed me, with several of her women on a mission of mercy to the home of yet another neighbour whose wife was having great difficulty in birthing a child—her fourth. Even my three daughters were gone for the day, out on a visit to some friends at another villa, accompanied by their nursemaid, Annika. I asked after the boy, Simeon; had he been left alone? No, I was told, he had been moved out to the home of his mother, now that she and her daughters were comfortably settled in a new home and the boy was out of danger. Defeated, I decided to bathe and asked Gallo to organize some food for me and replenish the brazier in Cay's study.

An hour later, bathed, fed and warmly dressed again in loose, comfortable, indoor clothes, I sat down at Cay's desk by the window and gathered my patience to wait for someone to come home.

It was growing dark by the time I heard the noises that told me my children had finally arrived home from their excursion with their nurse, and I went looking for them, unusually excited by the prospect of being able to spend some time with them, without other pressures demanding my attention. Luceiia and I were regarded as peculiar by some of our friends, in that we tended to spend a great deal of time with our children, enjoying them as much as we could. But other priorities seemed to intrude more and more all the time, and time spent with the children was something that happened all too seldom nowadays. I felt my usual surge of pleasure in seeing that they were all happy to see me: Veronica, the eldest at ten, Lucilla who was bewitching at seven, and Dorathea, breathtakingly beautiful and four years old, but feverish this evening and sniffly with a cold.

We were still together when Luceiia arrived home from the birthing with the news that Margaret Lupidus, one of our newest colonists, had safely given birth to twin daughters who seemed to be identical. This was not good news. Twin sons had been revered in Rome since the birth of Romulus and Remus, but twin daughters were a burden to any family and were not looked upon with favour. Luceiia and I shared a cup of wine after the children had gone to bed and drank in commiseration for the Lupidus family, which now consisted of five living daughters from seven birthings, none of which had yielded a son. We loved our daughters dearly, but few families could afford a brood of girls as well as we could. There were times when I longed for a son, but I made it a point of honour never to mention that to Luceiia.

When our single cup was empty I rose to replenish it and told Luceiia the story of my day on the land, amusing her with the comments and observations of the farmers, who, like all farmers everywhere, tended to see life from a different viewpoint than other men, and frequently to hilarious effect. Finally I leaned over and kissed her.

"It's early enough to be sinful. Come to bed with me."

"Why? Are you tired?"

I laughed aloud at the tone of her voice. "No, but it's a cold, wet night and I want your heat."

She sniffed disdainfully. "Heat I have, and to spare, but it's a beautiful night and not cold at all."

"It's pouring!"

"Nonsense, the rain stopped hours ago. The weather is beautiful and the sky is clear. There will be a moon tonight."

I blinked at her. "It must be wet somewhere," I said.

"It will be. Come."

We stood up together and my throat was choked with lust, but propriety still made demands of me.

"What about dinner?" I asked, rasping the words.

"What about it? There's only us. Everyone else is gone. I told Gallo I would cook for us in our own chambers. What would you like for dinner?" Her voice was low and throaty, intimate.

"You."

"Well, Master," she replied, smiling, "dinner is almost ready, awaiting only a few, last-minute touches."

Soon, we lay panting on our bed like a pair of newlyweds, too impatient for each other to bother with removing our clothes. I was more than ready, and as I entered the loving warmth of my wife's body my mind was filled with the need to control my surging seed. Luceiia took me smoothly, and I lay securely lodged, fighting to empty my mind of where I was and straining to relax and make no movement. But I knew it would be to no avail; my mind and my body were united to defeat me, and I felt the pressure mounting, spurred by the sheer sensations of such hot and moist containment. And then I was saved and yet frustrated by the sound of a howling, childish wail from somewhere deep in the house. Luceiia froze immediately, her head cocked to one side, the transition from lover to mother instantaneous.

"It's Dora."

"I know," I said, willing her to ignore it. "Annika will see to her."

"No, the child's sick. She has a fever."

"She has a cold, that's all. My problem is more urgent."

She ignored me for a moment, head cocked, straining to hear, but the cry was not repeated, and at length she relaxed and returned her attention to me.

"Problem? You have a problem? What problem?" She moved her body delightfully, then. "Oh, that problem?"

I sensed her smile as she moved in the darkness beneath me.

"Well, my love, that one is easily dealt with." She reached down towards her waist and pulled her skirts higher, then seemed to flex her entire body and wrap it around me, gripping me with her thighs and grasping me by the ears as she pulled my face down and filled my mouth with her hot, thrusting tongue. I felt her belly writhe and rise to meet me, her body opening and engulfing me like the hot waters of a bath, and I exploded, losing all awareness of everything except the crashing roars of ecstasy in my head. Then, while I was still spent and gasping, I felt Luceiia move beneath me and away from me, slipping her body free from mine.

"Don't go to sleep, I want more," she whispered.

I rolled onto my side. "Where are you going?" But I knew, and she was already gone. The lover had merely abetted, not replaced, the mother.

I lay there for a long time, recapturing my senses, and then I rolled off the bed and adjusted my clothing so that I could stand comfortably before crossing to the window and opening the shutters. It was a warm, mellow, late-June night and it bore no signs of the torrential rain that had poured down for so long earlier. I hitched up my robe and threw one leg across the sill and perched there, feeling the coldness of the stone against my naked skin and listening to the sounds of the early night as I thought of the pleasures I had found in the woman I had married. My loins were empty, almost achingly drained, and I luxuriated in the joy of satisfaction, idly attempting to recall the furious sensations so recently stirred up in me by my lust. But that was fruitless, of course, since our minds and bodies are no more capable of remembering fleeting pleasure than sudden pain, and I soon became distracted by the sounds out in the night. I could hear voices, nearby, man and woman, though I could discern no words, strain as I might, before they moved off and died away and a cacophony of barking dogs sprang up to fill the night with chaos and comfort. And then, somewhere far off, a nightingale began to sing, and I sat for a long time, entranced by the beauty of the sound, lost in a land of fantasy that knew no rhyme or reason until a drunken voice broke out beneath me, startling me with its suddenness, bellowing a tuneless song that spluttered into silence and was followed by the sound of a body falling heavily, and then more silence. The nightingale began to sing again and I shifted restlessly, moving my now-cold buttocks in complaint against the harshness of the stone window-sill.

I had not heard Luceiia return, but suddenly she was behind me, running her fingers through my hair and breathing gently on the soft skin at my neck. And, all at once, the passions that I had sought in vain to recall came back to me, overwhelming in their urgency. I withdrew my leg from the cool night air and returned to our bedside, my hands, my lips, my awareness filled with the reality of Luceiia, and this time, we took the time to remove our clothes before offering our nakedness to one another. Our coupling now was wondrous and filled with love and leisure, the joining of two lovers who enjoyed perfect familiarity each with the other's body. We melted together, moving in loving fidelity and reaching that peak together that leaves both partners hanging between life and death, knowing that happiness is achievable on either side of the divide.

And suddenly it was I who was raised, tensed on one elbow, my head cocked to hear again the alien sound that had jerked me back from the edge of sleep.

"Publius? What is it? What's wrong?"

"Shh! Listen! What's that noise?"

"What noise?"

I sat up, my face pointed towards the open window-shutters. "That noise! Listen!"

It came again, a man's voice, raised in a shout of panic, faint and far off, smothered by distance, but now taken up and repeated by another, nearer, and then another and several more. I leaped from the bed and ran to the window, leaning out, straining my ears, and heard the dreaded word, "Fire!"

"Fire," I said, over my shoulder to Luceiia. "They're raising the alarm. There's a fire." I could see nothing, could smell no smoke, but my guts churned in apprehension. "Quick! Light a lamp." I began scurrying to find my clothes in the darkness, dragging them on somehow and running from the room before Luceiia was able to find the tinder-box.

I emerged from the main door to find the courtyard already filled with running bodies and saw a horseman thunder into the yard and head straight for me. He saw me and leaped down from his horse's back, almost falling at my feet. I grabbed him and held him erect.

"What, man? What is it? Where's the fire?"

"The granaries," he gulped, drawing a deep breath. "The granaries, Commander, up on the hill! Four of them are in flames."

"Four of them? Damnation! Where were the guards? Are they all blind up there?"

One granary alight was a tragedy; four meant catastrophe. We would be hard-pressed to save enough food for the coming winter. I gripped him firmly by the shoulder and seized his horse's bridle in my other hand.

"I'm taking your horse. Give me a leg up, quickly."

He hoisted me up cleanly, and I fought for a moment to control the animal, which resented having someone new leap onto its back so soon after shedding one rider. Finally I brought it under restraint and swung it around in the direction I wanted to go.

"Summon every man in the Colony," I yelled at the rider. "Every soldier, every colonist. Get them up to the hilltop as quickly as they can run. Who's fighting the fire?"

"Only the soldiers who were on duty up there. There's no one else nearby."

"Damn and blast! I'm going up there now. Get the others on the road as quickly as you can. Tell them it's going to be a hungry winter if they're slow." I put my heels to the horse, and as soon as we were on the pathway that rounded the south-west end of the villa I saw the baleful, smoky glare of the fire on the hilltop ahead of me.

The hours that followed are hazy in my memory, so intense was the frenzy with which we fought the blaze. It burned with an ugly, sullen fury, refusing to be mastered, its roots smouldering deep within the piled banks of dried grain. I remember clearly, however, that I found signs, early on in the struggle, that the burning piles had been soaked with oil before being set alight; around the edges of the conflagrations, there were scatterings of grain, kicked away from the flames by the first discoverers of the catastrophe, and they were glued into clumps, held together by the viscous, flammable stuff poured over them by the incendiary madman who had done this.

That knowledge, that there was a madman among us, startled me into realizing that there might well be no men at all left down at the villa, and that this madman, whoever he was, would almost certainly not be up here at the fire.

The man working beside me was Erasmus Sita, a young giant and a decurion in our colonial forces. Sita was huge and strong, a full head taller than me with a mighty breadth of shoulders. I tugged him by the arm and motioned him to step away with me, back from the noise of the fire and the smoke. He leaned close to hear what I had to say. I ordered him to select ten of the youngest, strongest soldiers he could find and take them at the double, forced-march pace, back down to the villa as quickly as he could. He was to find Luceiia and make sure that she was in no danger, and then he and his people were to remain at the villa, standing guard and at the ready for anything that might develop. I saw the puzzlement and curiosity in his eyes and I waved towards the fire.

"This was deliberate, Sita. There were four separate fires here, now threatening to grow into one big one. Somebody set this place alight on purpose. I don't know who and I don't know why, but I don't want to be caught unawares if the whoreson has other plans for tonight. So get down to the villa quickly, but take the longer route down, not the main path; that way you'll avoid the people coming up. If they see you going back, it could cause confusion. But get there quickly. You understand?" He left at a loping run and I saw him begin to pick out his men.

I remember then that I left him to it and turned my attention to organizing a bucket-chain from the unfinished cisterns in the fort, and that there were not enough men available to make it work. And I remember the arrival of the first newcomers, a trickle that grew to a flood as the flames rose higher and the wind sprang up again to whirl blazing sparks towards the four minor granaries that were still untouched by the fire.

The granaries themselves were no more than stout wooden boxes, bins pitched at the seams and raised on stilts to protect their contents from the damp earth, and covered with heavy, sloping roofs. They burned disgustingly well. I don't know when I realized we could not win, but I think the awareness came only slowly to me. Dense, awful smoke swirled everywhere, roiling obscenely upwards. It filtered everywhere through the piles of grain, ruining the food forever, even before the wooden side panels burned through, allowing the grain to gush out onto the ground. In a short time, all our vigilance was dedicated to protecting the four silos that remained.

I staggered off at one time, away from the searing heat, in search of some clear air, my insides raw and burned from inhaling the smoke-laden air close to the fire. I found a wooden saw-horse to lean against, and someone handed me a jar of water. God! I remember still how good it tasted. I drank deeply and then sat there for a while, looking at the activity going on around me. I was exhausted, but then, everyone else was, too, by that time.

Too tired to move, I stared at the men around me and wondered if it was one of them who had set the fire in the first place. I knew them all, and I had to accept the possibility, but I found it hard to believe that any of them could deliberately wreak such malicious damage. And yet someone most definitely had. Then came a crashing roar mixed with screams of agony as one of the bins collapsed in flaming ruin, sending burning bursts of sparks in every direction and catching at least one fire-fighter unaware. I plunged back into the smoke and lost track of time again.

There came a time, at last, when there was no more to be done. The fire was as close to being under control as it would ever be. There was no hope of extinguishing it completely; the scattered piles of grain would smoulder for days, unless it rained again. I delegated a crew of soldiers to police the area and guard against new outbreaks, promising them they would be relieved in four hours. In the meantime, dawn was breaking and everybody else began to go home in search of sleep. I climbed up into a wagon that was crowded with weary men, all of them crusted in soot and grime, the whiteness of their eyes and teeth startling against the blackness of their faces. My nostrils were clogged with soot and the stink of burning. I do not know who was with me in the wagon, or whose back it was I leaned against. Before the cart reached the bottom of the hill I was asleep. I think everyone else was, too.

The man I was leaning my back against woke me by leaving the cart, but I shifted my position and dozed off again immediately, and then somebody was shaking my shoulder and calling my name. I opened my eyes and looked at my tormentor. His face was black and strange-looking, and as soon as he caught my eye he gestured sideways with his head, saying nothing. Groaning, I pulled myself erect, saw that I was home and began to climb stiffly down from the cart. I reached the ground, looked up to thank the carter, and only then realized that everyone was staring over my head at something behind me. I turned, and my guts churned as I saw a body spread-eagled face down in the dim half light of dawn, at the bottom of the steps to the main doorway of the house. The door lay open, and there was no sound to be heard. My tiredness vanished instantly, but my legs were unwilling to move from where I stood staring, and I felt fear and panic washing over me.

Somehow, I took the first step, and my paralysis was gone. I began to move quickly towards the sprawled shape and, before I was halfway towards him, I knew who had set the fire. I recognized him, left him where he was and veered away, heading directly into the house. As I set my foot on the bottom step, young Sita emerged from the doorway and paused in surprise at finding me so close.

"Commander," he said, "I didn't hear you coming."

"My wife, where is she?"

His eyebrows rose. "In her chambers, Commander."

I swallowed my relief. "And my children?"

"Asleep." He nodded towards the corpse. "You saw that?"

"Aye." I walked back to the body and turned it over on its back. Lignus the carpenter would set no more fires. He had been warned he would die if he ever came back, and he had. The tragic part was that he had cheated death for long enough to be able to do what he did. Outrage, anger and deep hatred for this man and all that he had stood for swept over me, so that I had to close my eyes and take a deep breath to control myself against the urge to kick his corpse. And then I noticed that all of his blood seemed to be on his back. There were no wounds on his front. I looked up at Sita.

"Did you do this?"

He shook his head. "No, Commander, but I had the body brought here."

"Brought here from where?"

"From where he died. The cottage where his wife and daughters are lodged. He tried to get them." He grinned, a small, nervous grin. "Unsuccessfully."

My thoughts were racing. "How did you know to search there?"

"We didn't. We heard the noise as we came through the village. Women screaming and crying. I decided we had better take a look at what was happening, and there he was, dead."

"He was alone? No accomplices?"

"He was alone there, sir, no accomplices that we could find, and we've searched the entire area."

"Who killed him?"

He cleared his throat. "Your wife, Commander. The Lady Luceiia. It was all over when we arrived."

"What?" I looked down at the body again, unable to believe what I had just heard. "Luceiia did this?"

The young decurion nodded, wordless in the face of my shocked surprise. I shook my head to clear it and then remembered the men on the wagon, watching this. I turned back to them.

"Thank you, my friends," I called out. "You can go home now. It's all over." I pointed to the body on the ground. "This is Lignus, the carpenter. He set the fire and he died for it." I turned back to young Sita, looking again at Lignus's body and wondering how my gentle wife had been able to do this thing. "I must go to my wife. Is she well?"

He nodded. "Perfectly well, Commander. Completely in control. She showed no signs of falling apart, and no compunction over what she had to do."

"Hmmm." There was nothing more I could say. I moved to walk away and then remembered. "One more thing." I touched Lignus's remains with my toe. "You'd better detail someone to bury this refuse somewhere out in the fields or in the woods; can't leave it lying around here to stink. And now good night. We will talk further tomorrow—later today, I mean. Good night, Sita."

"Good night, Commander." He snapped me a perfect, punctilious salute and marched away about his business.

As soon as I had watched young Sita out of sight, I made my way indoors and went directly to our sleeping chamber, aware of the noises of women somewhere at the back of the house. Luceiia was not in our chambers. In the middle of an emergency situation, she would have fires of her own to tend to. I had to restrain myself from searching her out immediately, to find out from her what had happened and how she had come to kill, and to be able to kill, Lignus, but I knew I would be interrupting whatever important chore she was attending to at such an ungodly hour. I would find out everything I needed to know in the morning. I realized all at once that it was now light enough for me to see myself, though dimly, in Luceiia's big, polished-bronze mirror against the wall; I leaned close to the mirror's surface and peered at my reflection. I was filthy, my clothing, my skin and my hair all black, thick with soot and ashes, and my nostrils told me I stank of sour smoke. I was in no condition to get into my wife's bed, yet neither was I in any condition to go looking for hot water. I dragged a woollen blanket from a pile in the chest at the foot of our bed and set out to look for a comfortable couch to lie on.

Luceiia opened our bedchamber door as I reached it and was surprised to find me there. She came to me directly and threw her arms around me, ignoring my filthy condition and my weak attempts to save her from contamination. She spoke through her kiss. "Where were you going?"

"To find a place to collapse." I held up my blanket for her to see. "I'm in no condition to lie on anything clean. Where have you been?"

She told me that she had organized as many of the women as she could find, turning them towards the preparation of food and drink for the men returning from fighting the fire. I had to ask about Lignus, then, and what had happened down here at the villa.

Her first instinct, she said, had been to join the group heading for the hilltop, but then she had realized that if this was a major fire, there would be a need for food, bandages and medical assistance. She began assembling her own women and delegating tasks, the first of which was to split up and find all the women colonists remaining in the cottages around the villa. She had gone herself on that errand, and one of her calls was to the cottage that now housed Lignus's wife and daughters. Luceiia had been accompanied by two of her own women, and they had heard screams and sounds of struggle from a long way off. Not knowing what was wrong, they had emerged into the clearing in front of the cottage to find one of Lignus's daughters, the pregnant one, lying bleeding on the threshold of the hut, with the noise of strife coming from inside. Luceiia had pushed her way into the hut and seen Lignus in a corner with his back to her. He was struggling furiously with the other sister while the mother lay bleeding and moaning on the floor. He had thrown his sword on the floor to free his hands and was now punching brutally at the body struggling against him. Luceiia realized that he must have started the fire on the hill to give himself time and opportunity to avenge himself

on the women. Without even thinking what she was doing, so great was her
anger, she swept up his sword from where it lay on the floor and; holding it
two-handed in front of her with the hilt against her breast, ran at him and
thrust it into his back with all her weight behind it. The point had slid cleanly
between his ribs and into his heart, and he had fallen dead at her feet before
he had time to turn around fully to see who had killed him. Moments later,
Sita and his soldiers had arrived on the run.

When she had finished talking, I stared at her for a few moments in
silence, thinking that we little knew the people we loved. What she had done
was completely in character and should not have surprised me at all; she was
the sister of Caius Britannicus and an imperious aristocrat of the old order,
accustomed to taking charge, to making decisions and to being obeyed. But
she was also my wife and I loved her deeply as a woman, so I seldom considered
the steel that underlay her womanish exterior.

She was gazing at me, waiting for me to speak. I kissed the end of her
nose. "Good for you," I whispered. "How do you feel?"

She touched the spot I had kissed with the tip of one finger. "How should
I? I am tired and hungry, but I feel as if I could carry on forever, or for as
long as it takes to clean up this mess Lignus has caused." She paused and
squinted at me. "If you really mean how do I feel about having killed Lignus,
then the answer is that I don't. I would do it again without thinking, as I
would destroy any animal threatening my family or this Colony. Lignus was
not a man. He was a wild beast, mad and dangerous. What about you? How
do you feel?"

"About Lignus, nothing. About the fire, anger and concern but no great
urgency yet, although if we don't get a good harvest this year it's going to
be a long winter. About you, I feel proud and wonderful. About sleep, I'm
not capable of feeling anything. I'm on my way to find a quiet corner where
the soot and grime that crusts me can do little damage, then I'm going to
collapse and slip into a coma."

She thrust her face into the hollow of my neck and sniffed deeply. "You
do smell rather smoky." She pushed me away and smiled up into my eyes.
"I know you don't want to hear this, but you might sleep far better after
being bathed and massaged. I know it seems like too much trouble at this
moment, but life will be much the better for steam and perfumed oils and
a brisk pummelling. Hmmm?"

I nodded my head, scrubbing at my eyes with the heels of my hands.
"Very well, my love," I muttered, "you are correct, as usual. I'm going, I'm
going."

I have no recollection of entering the bath house or of removing my
clothes, but I do remember walking through the *tepidarium*, where I splashed
cool water all over myself, dislodging some of the soot that covered me, and
into the steam room where, for the next quarter hour or so, I luxuriated in
the intense heat, feeling the dirt and the grit being washed away by the
natural rivers of my own sweat. I ended up with a series of plunges into the

hot and cold pools before subsiding and lying face down on the masseur's plinth, regretting his absence as I imagined how he would go to work mercilessly on my ill-used body. But he had been up at the fire too, working as hard as everyone else, and would be sound asleep somewhere. I could have sent for him—I even considered it, half-heartedly—but in the end I did not have the heart to disturb his rest, wherever he was.

I dozed off, eventually, then awoke again, plagued by the discomfort of the plinth I lay on. I felt cleaner and more presentable, but I was dead tired as I made my way towards my own chambers. Luceiia was still not abed, but our little invalid Dora, our four-year-old daughter, lay in our bed peacefully asleep, her thumb stuck deep in her tiny mouth. I bent over and touched her cheek, marvelling, as I always did, at the miraculous softness of her skin and the utterly helpless innocence of her trust. I dropped my clothing where I stood and crawled into the bed beside her, cradling her tininess in my arm before I fell asleep.

BOOK TWO

THE
REGENT

IX

Father,
Greetings from an errant son, whom you have probably consigned long since to perdition for a lack of filial attention, if you do not believe me already dead.

I am alive, healthy and well, and hope, with guilty optimism, that you are, too. How foolishly we treat the rushing passage of time! I deeply regret having permitted so many years to pass without making any serious attempt to write to you. I remember you telling me, on many occasions, how difficult it is to write down one's thoughts so that they reflect, accurately, one's feelings on any particular subject at any one time. Words, you told me, are but ungainly tools, ill suited to the use of serious, intelligent men. I have often recalled, with bitter irony, the scepticism with which I dismissed, in my youthful omniscience, the import of those words. I now know, as the result of many long hours of effort, how accurate your observations were.

This missive, which I must believe you will someday read, will no doubt impress you with its clarity and the apparent ease with which it has been written. Disabuse yourself of any misconception, Father; I am as awkward in my efforts to write today as ever I was. The letter you read now is no more than a painstaking copy of the last of many scribbled, much-altered, often-perspired-upon scraps of parchment and paper, laboured over on many a night by the agued fluttering of an almost lightless lamp.

I know you will have little need to be reminded of the discomforts involved in writing a letter on campaign. I have been on campaign endlessly now for years, ever since leaving Britain with Magnus Maximus, and throughout that time it has ever been too easy to find reasons for never having enough time to write. It has been several months since I decided to end that condition, and it has taken me until now to produce something I consider fit enough and substantial enough to send to you after so long a silence.

I am in Constantinople, serving on the personal staff of Flavius Stilicho, Count of the Domestics, Commander of the Emperor's Household Troops. You might be amused to know that I have met Theodosius now on several occasions and have endorsed, in my own mind, the verdict of Publius Varrus, who declared that Theodosius was, "for all his faults and personal shortcomings," an able administrator and a fine

129

soldier. In those days, Theodosius was Count of Britain. Now he is Emperor and still, again in Varrus's words, "a grandiloquent and pompous pain in the arse!" But he is, above all, an able Emperor and a notable judge of men . . .

That I can write such words in a letter will give you some idea of the import of my posting and the security we enjoy in our communications. All of that is due to the personality and influence of my commander, Flavius Stilicho. It is he whose privilege and personal seal attached hereto enable me to write my mind thus openly, and it is he who has finally made me wish to write to you, for many reasons, although mainly to tell you about Flavius Stilicho himself, and the privilege and honour I enjoy in being close to him.

Father, you would take Stilicho to your bosom! He is all that you hold honourable in the Roman tradition. He is half Vandal, his father a low-born captain of mercenaries. And yet, for all that, by the strength of his own intellect and the astounding abilities he has demonstrated in his short career—he is but twenty years of age, seven years younger than I!—he has completely won the affection and esteem of Theodosius and is married to the Emperor's favourite niece, Serena. She, too, fell victim to the charm of Stilicho.

If, as I suspect, you and Publius Varrus have just exchanged mutual snorts of "Nepotism and privilege!" you must withdraw them. I swear this is a man among men, for all his youth—a military genius on the level of Alexander.

I met him just over a year ago, in the late summer of the second year of Magnus's campaign in southern Gaul. Things had been going well for Magnus (as they still are, I hear) and we had won many victories against all sent against us. My own mind was not at peace, however, with the way the affairs of our army were developing; the Magnus I had known and admired in North Britain was neither the man nor the Emperor I followed now in Gaul. Greatness had worked great changes in him, and as far as I could see, none were improvements.

One afternoon, on a routine patrol ahead of the army, my party unexpectedly encountered a fair-sized group of the enemy, men and officers. We discovered them first, fortuitously, and I was able to entrap them. In the course of the fighting I found myself matched against a young tribune, barely out of boyhood, richly appointed and uniformed, who fought like a madman—a very skilled madman, be it said. Luck was with me. He slipped in the grass, and I had his life in my grasp and my sword at the ready. Thank God I could not bring myself to kill him at that moment! Telling him to live for another day, I clubbed him with the hilt of my sword and left him lying there. Moments later, we were surrounded and outnumbered by an army of newcomers sent, as I discovered later, to meet and escort the party we had attacked. I was taken prisoner with my entire force and brought to the camp of Proconsul Glaucius Mamilias. As you will have deduced, the boy I spared was Flavius Stilicho.

He sent for me later and questioned me closely. I felt, although I know not how to describe it, an affinity for the man, youth though he was. He told me he was just returned from Persia, from the Court of King Shapur III, where he had been the personal ambassador of Theodosius himself. On his return to Constantinople he had been dispatched immediately to form some intelligent appraisal of the rebel Magnus and his modus operandi, and to divine a method of defeating him.

You may imagine my astonishment as I listened to him speak, although I must tell you it never crossed my mind to doubt him. The reverence in which he was held was all too apparent. The Proconsul himself deferred to this young man!

In short, Flavius Stilicho thanked me for his life and offered me manumission—for all my men—if I would serve with him and give him my allegiance. He assured me I could do so with honour, for he would require me neither to divulge information concerning Magnus's plans nor to bear arms against the soldiers among whom I had fought my way across Gaul. Father, I did not even hesitate before accepting his offer. I knew, somewhere in my soul, that I was born to fight beside this Flavius Stilicho. And I had decided long before then that I was unhappy in the ranks of Magnus Maximus. I chose to be Stilicho's man, and my soldiers all chose to follow me.

Since that day, I have not looked backward. Offered the chance to leave and wait for Stilicho elsewhere, far from Magnus, I chose to remain with him. Three months later we were in Asia Minor, and for the next nine months we went soldiering wherever Stilicho was needed. Then, three months ago, Theodosius promoted him to Commander of the Imperial Household Troops, and we have been in Constantinople ever since. I suspect we will not stay much longer. Stilicho lives on horseback and detests the confinement of a city, and besides, there are too many battles to be fought throughout the Empire .

My rank is now that of prefect. I am a cavalryman, and a cavalry man by conviction. But that is another story, and I am presently composing another letter—this one is already too long—in which I will tell you of the developments in Stilicho's mind, and in my own.

Farewell, Father.

My love to Aunt Luceiia, and to the tribe of small Varri who, I am sure, run all of your lives. I shall send this in care of Pontius Aulus Plautus, Publius Varrus's friend in Colchester, by military courier. He will see that it reaches you from there.

Your dutiful son,

Picus

I read that first letter from Picus four times without pause, from start to finish, when Cay eventually passed it on to me. I had been awaiting it impatiently for a long time, schooling myself to be calm. Cay had received no fewer than fourteen letters in all, none of them short and none of them showing, externally, any sign of order, process or continuity. Picus stood revealed, by the end of all of them, as a highly conscientious and able correspondent, but an unthinking one in that he seldom gave any indication of the dates on which he was writing. In consequence, his father had to read all of his letters in random order as they came to hand, and only after that could he begin to place them in some kind of temporal progression.

He then extended to me the privilege of reading them as a series of consecutive observations. And they were fascinating. The first of them, of course, was probably the most moving of them all, emotionally. But the second amazed me, recalling to my mind instantly a comment, by our friend Alaric, to the effect that God has willed it that no great idea should ever occur to one man alone. When the truly great developments in mankind's progress appear, they always seem to appear simultaneously in many lands, promulgated by many intelligent and visionary people.

> Greetings, Father,
> Already, having completed the first step, it seems this writing task grows easier. I suppose that is due to the difficulties I had with my first attempt, when the array of subjects to refer to and deal with seemed endless. This letter, by comparison, is much simpler; it has but one major component.
> Father, I wish to write to you of horses—horses, cavalry and the way in which a single man's perception of the importance of both may alter history. The man in question is, of course, Flavius Stilicho— nothing I write to you in future will be untouched by his influence, even should he die tomorrow, which the gods forbid!
> I know you are aware of the debacle at Adrianople some years ago, in 376. That was the year I first joined the Eagles. Irrespective, however, of your own personal judgment on that affair, I have to regurgitate in here, since it has a direct bearing upon the entire tenor of this letter.
> The officially sanctioned story of that fiasco, as I am sure you will recall, is that the Imperator Valens, co-Emperor at the time with Valentinian, was careless and silly enough to march a consular army of eight legions—40,000 men!—through hostile territory without taking even the most elementary precautions. His army then, in extended line of march along a lakeside, was surprised by a migrating tribe of Ostrogoths who, being mounted on horseback for their journeying, seized the moment and the day by charging at Valens's host in an undisciplined but deadly, densely packed mob. Their concerted attack, completely unexpected, rolled Valens's extended legions up like a parchment scroll before they had time even to think of deploying into line of battle.

It was a fluke, we are told, one of those unforeseen and unforeseeable developments that, in war, must simply be accepted and accommodated.

Flavius Stilicho will have none of that. He asserts—and none who listen can argue against his thesis or his logic—that it is inconceivable that any haphazard attack by an undisciplined rabble, no matter how huge their numbers or how densely packed their mass, could totally demoralize and destroy an entire Roman consular army of 40,000 men, killing all of them, including an Emperor and his entire staff.

That such a thing happened is incontrovertible. How it happened, how it could happen, is a matter open to the wildest conjecture. How it is likely to have happened, however, is a conjecture that one might analyse quite pragmatically, and Stilicho has succinct ideas and opinions on that topic. From those ideas and his deliberations concerning them, he has drawn a number of conclusions, and upon those conclusions he has constructed an amazing calendar of future events. Being privy to his thinking, and without any disloyalty or fear of being censured, I have decided to apprise you of Stilicho's thoughts, knowing that they will interest you both generally and specifically, and knowing also that the effort of detailing them for you will assist me personally in assimilating them.

His deliberations and his findings, stated categorically, follow, and I must inform you, regretfully, that the language and the clarity of thought are Stilicho's alone:

i. Valens and his army, although culpable of dereliction by default, could not collectively have shown the degree of mindless, suicidal ineptitude so clearly alleged in the official version of the incident. Valens had superb generals, legates and distinguished senior officers attached to his staff. Even had Valens been patently insane on the level of a Nero or a Caligula, his commanders would still have retained their military competence and responsibility for the army.

ii. Rome has conquered the world by the excellence of her legions, the greatest military force history has ever seen. Roman armies—Rome's foot-soldiers—have been invincible since the days of Gaius Marius and Julius Caesar; the only defeats sustained since then by Roman armies have been at the hands of other Roman armies.

iii. The catastrophe at Adrianople, therefore, was epoch-making: the greatest defeat of a Roman army by a non-Roman force in more than half a millennium. To categorize it as anything other than an unfortunate and regrettable mischance would be an admission that the barbarian forces threatening the Empire are capable of repeating their performance at Adrianople whenever and wherever they please. Obviously, such an admission is officially beyond consideration. The capacity, therefore, to inflict such damage has been attributed to hazard and ill fortune—the fact that the barbarians simply happen to have been on horseback at the time of the incident, an eventuality unprecedented in the annals of Roman warfare.

iv. Rome has never relied upon cavalry, other than for the provision of mobile screens of skirmishers and mounted archers to protect the legions while they deploy in line of battle. The cavalry function has always remained, more or less, in the hands of Rome's allies in Germany and Africa. To the Roman military mind, in fact, cavalry has always been deemed an inferior military presence, operating without the rigid discipline and training required by massed infantry formations. To this day, since the beginnings of Rome, there has always been something less than Roman about cavalry and cavalry troops.

Such are the findings of Flavius Stilicho; from them he has developed the following propositions:

v. That any Roman worthy of the name will discern the four foregoing points for himself, after even the shortest period of analytical thought on the matter, and will accept the verity of the situation and the dominant peril it implies, namely:

vi. That no Roman worthy of the name who has even the slightest knowledge of military matters can seriously doubt the existence of brilliant, clear-thinking generals, equally capable of analysis and action, in the territories of the barbarians. It follows logically and inevitably, therefore, that the action against Valens's army at Adrianople will be recognized by such men for what it was: an overwhelming victory against a supposedly invulnerable force, won by the simple expedient of falling upon the Roman cohorts with sufficient speed to ensnare them before they could deploy on their own ground and in their own battle lines, and then overwhelming them with a sheer mass of men and horseflesh. Granted that realization, at some time in the future, if not now, Adrianople will be emulated and repeated, and the day of the Roman legion as it now exists will be over.

That phrase, Father, "as it now exists," contains a seminal thought. Flavius Stilicho has the kind of mind that confronts potential disaster and circumvents it. His propositions continue:

vii. That, accepting the inevitability of such a development, it is incumbent upon the senior legates of the imperial staff to begin immediately searching for effective means of precluding such a possibility, and to do so not by staring gape-mouthed into the future but by searching diligently in the past for an answer.

viii. That the greatest military genius of ancient times was Alexander of Macedon, called The Great, who refined the heavy cavalry techniques of his father, Philip of Macedon, and used that heavy cavalry to conquer the world.

ix. That since the cavalry in general use today consists of light skirmishers mounted on light horses, and the large, heavy horses used by Alexander and his troops are unknown in Roman military life, every *effort should and must be made—immediately and without delay—to collect such horses, from wherever they may be found throughout the Empire, and to begin a program of breeding them selectively while training and equipping new, large bodies of troops to be the nucleus of a new form of warfare in the Roman world. And—*

x. That within one decade, or two at the very most, fully 25 percent of the fighting strength of every imperial legion in the field should consist of such heavy, tightly disciplined, highly manoeuvrable cavalry.

Father, I had the privilege of being present when Stilicho outlined his findings, his conclusions, and his recommendations to the Emperor. Theodosius looked at him, frowning, and asked, "Do you really believe this?" Stilicho merely inclined his head. "So be it," said the Emperor. "Let it be done." And the world as we know it—a thousand years of military history and tradition—changed.

This has been a long letter, Father, but I have enjoyed the writing of it, and I think I have but little now to add. I know you will give it serious thought, and I know you will see the portent of it. We began the task of conversion to cavalry that same night, although it has been largely a paper task to this point. I am embroiled in it, and already we make great progress. Our major difficulty has been finding men— officers senior enough and flexible enough in their thinking (strange how those two seldom go together) to envision what we are about to do.

I shall write again, as soon as I have substance to report. Take care of yourself, Father, and convey my respect and good wishes to all whom I hold dear.

Picus

"Strange how those two seldom go together . . ." It pleased me considerably that Picus should be so evidently the son of his father. That one little observation, whimsical and acerbic at the same time, demonstrated to me, more clearly than anything else I had read, that our boy had a pragmatic and slightly cynical head on his shoulders. Pragmatism is all very well on its own, I find, but it is too often humourless. When it is salted with a healthy and subtle hint of cynicism, however, the result is often humour, wit and irony. Those who possess such a blend of spices in their character are seldom boring.

I was rereading this second letter from Picus as I walked to a meeting with Victorex, our Master of Horse, and I was smiling at my thoughts as I turned into the huge yard that fronted the main stables. There I found a spectacle that made my smile even wider and my pleasure greater, and I stopped and leaned against a gatepost to watch what was happening.

Victorex, due mainly to his strange appearance and his almost complete disregard for the concerns of normal men and women (he was obsessed with things equine to the exclusion of all else), had made few real friends in our Colony, and he seemed more than content with that. He had, however, within a very short time of his arrival here made two staunch friends in the Villa Britannicus, both of whom shared his fierce love of horses and neither of whom seemed even slightly aware of the strangeness of his appearance.

The first of these was my daughter Veronica, and the other was my wife. Veronica, now a beautiful, vivacious ten-year-old, had been besotted with a love of horses ever since she was old enough to tell a horse from a puppy. Her mother, I later discovered, had had the same passion as a girl but had forgotten it, by and large, on entering womanhood. In the past few years, however, her childhood love had been rekindled in the heat of her daughter's enthusiasm, and since Victorex had arrived to take over our horse-breeding program, both of them had spent all of their free time with him and his horses.

Victorex blossomed under their concern and attentions. He was still as surly and ungracious as ever with ordinary mortals, utterly impatient with their trivial concerns, but he clearly considered my wife and daughter as possessing that extraordinary status enjoyed only by himself and his beloved charges. And thus, according them that recognition, he deferred to them in wondrous ways. His whole demeanour—his entire behaviour—had altered dramatically in the short months since his transfer to the villa. He now took trouble with his clothes and with his personal hygiene . . . matters that had seemed quite beneath him before the visits of Veronica and Luceiia became daily occurrences. It was true that he still slept in the stables, but he no longer smelled so pungently, so succinctly, *of* the stables.

Now I found him at the centre of his training circuit, pivoting slowly, holding the end of a long lead-rein attached to the bridle of a beautiful black pony that circled him at a pretty canter, bearing my daughter on its back. The child's face was glowing with pleasure, and the great slabs of Victorex's teeth were exposed in a huge grin as he shouted instructions to her. As I watched, she drew her legs up beneath her and pushed herself erect until she stood, perfectly balanced, on the pony's back, the reins held loosely in her left hand, her right held slightly out and away from her body. It was lovely to behold. Her movements, her control and her poise were so perfectly correct, so natural, that what I had seen, and the danger involved in it, became apparent to me only long afterwards, by which time I knew that, had any real danger existed, Victorex would never have permitted the attempt. Knowing I was watching her, she made two complete circuits of the yard; then dropped back astride her mount and kneed him out of the circuit, directing him effortlessly to where I stood. She brought him to a halt and slipped lithely to the ground, where she hugged him briefly around the neck and then rushed to me, her eyes dancing with excitement. As I swept her up in a hug, she spoke into my ear.

"Daddy, isn't he beautiful? His name is Bucephalus, the same as Alexander the Great's horse, and Victorex says he's giving him to me for my very own. Isn't that wonderful?"

It was indeed, and surprising. Much as he loved his horses, Victorex owned none of them. They were communal property and therefore not his to dispose of. As I sniffed lovingly at the warm, clean scent of my daughter's hair before setting her down again, I was aware of Victorex approaching, his head cocked to the side as though listening. As he came, he gathered up the long lead-rein in loops, arranging them in his right hand. He read the expression on my face accurately and spoke to forestall me.

"Master Varrus." He nodded his greeting. "Beautiful day."

I returned his nod. "Victorex. That's what I was thinking, too, until I discovered that you had presented my daughter with a communal gift."

He frowned and shook his head, trying to stop me. Veronica took a step backwards and looked from me to Victorex, her face troubled.

"What's wrong, Daddy? What is a communal gift?"

Victorex answered her. "It's a gift from many people, Magpie."

Magpie? That was new to me, but I looked at my raven-haired, white-skinned child and saw the rightness of it immediately. She was frowning, speaking directly to Victorex.

"But you said the gift was from you, to me."

"And so it is. Now take Bucephalus inside and rub him down. I have to speak with your father. And be sure you don't miss any part of him. He deserves the best you can give him."

"I know, and he shall have it, and he knows that, too. Don't you, boy?"

The pony whickered and nudged her with his muzzle and she laughed, although her expression was still slightly uncertain. "He knows I have some honey for him, but he doesn't know where it is. Will you still be here when I've finished, Daddy?"

I nodded to her. "Take your time. I have things to talk about with Victorex, but if we finish before you do, I'll wait for you and we'll walk home together."

Victorex and I watched her lead the pony away, and I found myself admiring the lithe grace of her and marvelling at how quickly she was growing.

"Bucephalus . . . beautiful pony," I said, finally, when she had disappeared inside the stables.

Victorex sniffed. I was not included among his elite, obviously. "You remember the stallion I went off to buy for Terra, the time we rode into Aquae together?" he said.

I turned to face him. "Yes."

"Well, I found it and bought it, but I found another horse, too—same place, same time. A brood mare, beautiful. She was for sale, so I bought her. With my own money. First horse I ever bought. But I fell in love with her."

It did not seem at all strange to me that he would phrase things that way.

"Where is she now?"

He nodded towards the stables. "In there, with the others." He cleared his throat. "Now, you take that li'l Bucephalus. That horse is perfect. Perfect shape, perfect colouring, perfect proportions, perfect temperament. That's a beautiful li'l horse. In fact, that li'l horse is perfect for anything you want it to do, 'cept work, or breeding. It's too damn small. An' yet it's perfect. An' it's perfectly useless, too, unless you happen to know a ten-year-old li'l girl who's perfectly suited to it." He sniffed again and I felt myself squirm inside. I knew what was coming now, and I felt small and mean-spirited as he continued.

"Now, thing is, I've been given a job to do, and I've been told to be ruthless. No room in this operation for extra passengers. If a horse can't work, an' can't be bred, I have to get rid of it, you follow me? That means kill it." He hawked and spat.

"I don't like killing horses. People I generally don't care about, but horses matter to me. Most of 'em are worth more'n most people. And I object most particularly to killing beautiful horses. The li'l horse wasn't mine, but Magpie had already fallen in love with it. How was I going to kill it now? So I traded my mare for the li'l fellow, and now he is mine, and nobody can tell me what to do with him, and I'm giving him to Magpie."

It was my turn now to clear my throat. I felt foolish and ungracious. "Forgive me, Victorex," I said. "I wronged you. I should have known better."

He laughed. "How? You don't know me at all, Master Varrus. In your place, I'd have thought the same thing. I just didn't want you upsetting Magpie."

"Magpie." I savoured the name; it was perfect, like the "li'l" horse—perfectly suited to my lovely daughter. "Where did that name come from?"

"Not me. That's what her friends call her, didn't you know? It's just about—"

"Perfect."

We both laughed. "Look," I said then, "at least let me reimburse you for your mare. It's not fair that you should lose your purchase price."

He looked at me with an expression of pure pleasure and his next words made him a third friend in the Villa Britannicus.

"Lose my price? Are you blind, Master Varrus? The happiness in that li'l girl's face has paid me ten times over already, an' I haven't even given her the horse yet! I don't want money, and what need do I have of a horse? I've got a hundred of them and I'm breeding more." He shook his head. "No, Master Varrus. You keep your money and just let me do what I want to do, the way I do it best. You love that li'l girl, I know you do, but I'm inclined to think of her as something very special too. And she's not afraid of me. That's worth a lot. You'd be amazed how many people think I'm mad, or dangerous."

I held out my hand. "Well, here's one who doesn't. Thank you. From now on, you run your stables as you see fit, and I'll be content if you simply keep me informed. My job is to train the men to ride your horses so together we can build something new in this country—the best men, mounted on the best horses anyone has ever seen. I know you won't tell me how to do my part, so I promise not to interfere with the way you do yours. Do we have a bargain?"

We had a bargain.

Some time later, walking back to the villa with Veronica, I asked her about her new name. It shamed me slightly that I had not been aware until now that she possessed one. I had been thinking of her all these years as my daughter, too blinded by my fatherly love to see that she was also a wholly formed little person with her own identity.

"So, young lady," I asked her, "how long have you been Magpie?"

"Oh, forever, Daddy. It used to be *The* Magpie, but it was shortened to simply Magpie a long time ago."

"And why The Magpie?"

"Because I'm all black and white and I like to wear green and my eyes are green and shiny, of course! And I was a terrible thief when I was little."

"A thief? What did you steal?"

"Oh, everything . . . at least, everything that was bright, or shiny and pretty, just like a real magpie. But I always gave the things back . . . most of the time because I had to."

"I see. I had no idea we had a thief in the family."

She smiled up at me and my heart swelled. "Well, not a real thief. I mean, not a robber or a brigand. I wouldn't steal money, and the things I stole were only mostly borrowed. You see, everybody knew when something pretty went missing just where it had gone. I could never really get away with anything."

"Did you try?"

"Try what? To get away with anything?" She paused, her brows wrinkled. "You mean did I ever really, really try to steal something?" She shook her head, dismissing the thought. "I don't think so, not really. I might have, when I was really tiny, I can't remember. But one day Mama came and took away one of my very favourite treasures—my most beautiful comb, with coloured glass in the handle. She just took it. She said she wanted it and she was keeping it. I was very angry, and later I was very sad. I really missed it . . ." Her voice died away, and she took my hand and pulled me to a stop, then made me squat down so that she could talk directly into my face. "And then, the next day, Mama gave me back my comb and told me that whenever I took something that belonged to someone else, I made them feel just as hurt and just as sad as she had made me." Her expression was very solemn and serious. "I never stole anything again, after that, and for the longest time I wouldn't even borrow anything from any of my friends, even with their permission."

She tugged my hand then, indicating that we should continue walking, and as we went she concluded, "They stopped calling me *The* Magpie, after that. But Magpie never went away, and I'm glad, because I like it. Of course, only my special friends call me that. Other people still call me Veronica."

I felt almost jealous—excluded. "I've never heard it before today," I said. "I suppose that means I'm not really a special friend . . ."

"Oh, Daddy!" She stopped again and looked at me with what I defined instantly as loving exasperation. "You're my *father*, for goodness' sake! You're my *specialest* friend, more than even Victorex. You can call me Magpie any time you like."

"Thank you, Magpie," I answered. "I will." I felt absolutely euphoric.

By the time Victorex had spent two years in his new position, he was heading up a self-sufficient operation with the sole purpose of breeding horses. He had five very happy stallions and upwards of seventy mares in various stages of pregnancy, plus a fair number of foals. He had already started weeding out his future breeding stock. Only two of the foals from that first crop, one of each sex, were judged by him to be worth keeping. The others were all marked as workhorses as soon as they were able to walk. Victorex estimated that by the end of ten years he would be starting to produce big, strong horses. In twenty years, he would be producing large numbers of them.

He knew what he was doing. We did not, so we left him to do it.

In the meantime, with those animals Victorex would allow me to use, I began working on new techniques of training and deploying mounted men. It sounded easy when we were talking about it, but making it work was another matter altogether.

I already had a central body of men trained to operate on horseback, the nucleus of my new force. Every trainee was an expert at vaulting onto a horse's back, fully equipped. This should have been an advantage, and it was, but only to a clearly delineated degree. Now all I had to do was to untrain these men, completely and absolutely. I had to make them forget everything they had been taught, except how to stay on a horse once they were mounted—and even that, I found, was easier to think about than to achieve.

The men I had to start retraining were bowmen, archers, light skirmishing troops. I was trying to change them into heavy cavalry. That meant that the light, leather armour they wore was no longer strong enough to do the job they would have to do. So, remove the light, leather armour and replace it with regulation iron or bronze helmet, breastplate and a heavy kilt of iron-studded leather. They were going to be in close combat with an enemy on foot; their most vulnerable parts, therefore, were their legs. So, replace bare legs and light sandals with metal greaves and armoured boots strong enough to withstand a sword thrust or the swing of an axe. I had now increased the weight of each man by about thirty pounds, overall.

In addition to all that extra weight, I also had to consider that the shields all horsemen then carried were small, flimsy affairs of toughened leather, suitable for deflecting a spent arrow or a thrown stone but of no value in stopping a heartily swung axe or a close-hurled arrow or spear. So, change the light shield for a heavy-duty, utilitarian shield suited specifically to a mounted man rather than a standing legionary.

Added to all of this, I had also to bear in mind the fact that we were breeding bigger horses. Not simply taller horses, but *bigger* horses.

In its simplest terms, the problem I was faced with came to this: I had to take ordinary men, used to performing the ordinary task of mounting a horse in a vaulting spring, load them down with an additional forty to fifty pounds of dead weight and ask them to hoist that up on to horses that were bigger, and wider, than any they had ever ridden before.

And that was just the start of it. I was also asking them to forget about all the advantages they had learned were associated with being mounted on a fast, high-strung animal who could respond to the sway of a body or the pressure of a knee and swing its rider out of danger immediately. Instead, I was asking each of them to make himself consciously, individually, an immobile brick, an unmanoeuvrable unit in a solid wall of living horseflesh. I was asking each of them to advance, revolve, change direction and generally perform as one inanimate part of a single, solid mechanism. A living unit. Not men, but a wall of horsemen. That meant that, in the last analysis, if Caius Britannicus or Publius Varrus were killed by a well-aimed or lucky arrow, he would be dead and gone, but his horse would continue to function as part of the striking force, held in position by its neighbours on both sides. Many of my men found that a chilling and unnatural thought. All of a sudden, in their eyes, riders had become expendable. The horse had become all-important.

That, of course, was nonsense. But in the beginning, at least, that is how they saw it, and that is the perception I found myself having to contend with.

I persevered with it, however, and soon found that there were some of my men who began to show clear leadership capabilities in the new techniques early in the process. Whenever I found one of these, I promoted him on the spot, thereby instituting, although I did not realize it at first, a whole new hierarchy of leaders—cavalry officers.

Nothing that changes the order of things as radically as we did happens overnight. The process I am describing here in a few words took years to achieve. Life in our little Colony meandered very quietly during those years, for the most part, with only an occasional reminder of the strife in the outside world penetrating to shadow our peace, in the form of reports by Alaric or one of his visiting priests on what was happening abroad. In this way we learned of the death of Valentinian, and of the rebellion of Eugenius, another would-be emperor thrown up from the ranks of the armies to challenge Theodosius. Theodosius, however, had Stilicho—ably assisted by our own Picus Britannicus—to take his part, and Eugenius was crushed by a mighty army assembled in the west.

Then, two years later, came the news that stunned us all, and, fittingly, we heard of it from Picus, whose letters were now arriving regularly.

Father, greetings,

This letter will reach you, I hope, ahead of the news it contains. I have been involved in what has been described by some people as a civil war between two of the strongest, most able men in the Empire, and the information I have to impart to you in this letter will, I have no doubt, amaze and trouble you. Theodosius is dead. He died tonight, less than an hour ago, and his death has plunged the Empire into a schism that will rock the world.

I have not mentioned this previously in any of my letters, but the meteoric career of Flavius Stilicho has been influenced, constrained and strangely paralleled, although to a far lesser extent in my judgment, by another Flavius—one Flavius Rufinus, of whom I doubt you have ever heard. Flavius Stilicho and Flavius Rufinus have been rivals since the day young Stilicho made his first step towards prominence. Until then, Flavius Rufinus had enjoyed the full warmth of the Emperor's favour, unchallenged by anyone. Rufinus defined Stilicho as a rival immediately, and has since done everything in his power, short of declaring overt hostility, to thwart his progress. Recently, however, mere months ago, all of that changed. The rivalry between the two flared into open animosity and outright enmity, and Theodosius, astute and deft manipulator that he is, has been using this situation to his own unique advantage. This culminated in an imperial proclamation—six days ago, as I write this—that has exploded in the courtly Roman world like a thunderbolt.

As I am your son, I know you will forgive me, despite your interest and impatience, for playing the orator and deferring my announcement of the content of this proclamation until later. It is more important, I believe, that you first understand the background to the antipathy between the two Flavians.

The two are diametrically opposed in almost every aspect of their personalities, and there are some who argue that Flavius Rufinus is the better man. I am not an adherent to that belief, nor could I be, even were I to know Stilicho only by repute. Where Stilicho will grasp a new or alien concept almost before it is uttered, and be prepared to act upon it, Rufinus will labour hard and long to define and assimilate it. That exercise completed, however, Rufinus will act every bit as firmly and decisively as Stilicho ... he will merely have allowed more time to elapse. Both men are natural leaders of immense ability, and each is idolized by the troops he commands; but where Stilicho is shrewd, deliberate, logical and painstaking in his dealings with everyone, regardless of rank, Rufinus is emotional, precipitate, illogical and impulsive. All other differences fall into insignificance, however, beside the fact that Flavius Stilicho possesses a deep and abiding sense of justice, and an innate humaneness—attributes that simply do not exist in Flavius Rufinus.

It was this last, major difference that caused the open rift between

the two, and although the details of the spark that caused the conflagration vary widely according to the source, there is enough of commonality
among the stories to make eminent and acceptable sense.

Flavius Stilicho, as you know, is a Vandal by birth, his father a
captain of Vandal mercenaries and his mother a Roman lady of impecca-
ble ancestry. Flavius Rufinus is a Gaul, from the ancient territory known
as Cisalpine Gaul. Stilicho absorbed his military knowledge from his
father, originally, and began his career, for a very brief time, as a
military tribune. Rufinus joined the Praetorians as a boy, while Stilicho
was still a baby, and worked his way inexorably upwards until he
became the Praetorian prefect of Illyricum, on the northern Adriatic. The
outstanding abilities of both men brought them early to the attention of
Theodosius . . . in the case of Rufinus, long before Theodosius became
Emperor.

The story goes that word reached Rufinus, about a year ago, that
one garrison of mercenaries, ostensibly within his territorial jurisdiction,
had mutinied and was holding the town it garrisoned, in open revolt
against the Empire. The same story came to the attention of Flavius
Stilicho more than a month later, but Stilicho's version—which I read—
contained significant differences to the version reported by Rufinus. In
the dispatch sent to Stilicho, by the personal hand of the district
paymaster (this happened, by the way, on the Illyrican borderlands, an
area plagued by infestations of bandits) he was informed that a local
garrison, seconded from one of Stilicho's own legions, had been on
duty without pay for almost two years. On three separate occasions,
paymaster's trains, each one more heavily guarded than the one before,
had been waylaid and destroyed before they could reach the garrison.
The mercenaries had finally announced to the local authorities that,
until they were paid in full, they would do no more soldiering, perform
no military duties and permit no trade goods to leave the region. Stilicho
reacted quickly, ordering the paymaster, no matter what the cost, to set
this situation to rights and pay the garrison. Alas, he was too late.

The garrison, mercenaries as I have said, were Vandals, and the
significance was not lost on Flavius Rufinus. He besieged the town,
took possession of it and promptly slaughtered the entire garrison and
populace, after which he razed the town, as an example, he said, to all
potential mutineers and those who would abet them. Apparently unable
to let pass the opportunity to humiliate his rival, he himself brought
the word to Constantinople several months ago.

I was present in the audience chamber with Stilicho when Rufinus
reported his actions to the Emperor, and it was the first word any of
us had heard on the subject. Father, you could not imagine Stilicho's
fury. I would never have believed him capable of such headlong, damn-
the-consequences intensity of feeling, and I thought I knew him well.
He had to be physically restrained from attacking Rufinus, in the

presence of the Emperor himself! And even thus restrained, facing Theodosius's temper and his long-standing championship of Flavius Rufinus, and knowing his life to be hanging in the balance, Stilicho told Rufinus he was unfit to live and call himself a soldier, warning him moreover that when Rufinus died, it would be at Flavius Stilicho's hands, no matter who or what the instrument might be.

Of course, as you may imagine, the Emperor excoriated Stilicho, but a blind man could have seen that Theodosius enjoyed the confrontation! He sternly warned them both to keep themselves apart, under pain of his displeasure, and terminated the audience with no more than a mild censure of Rufinus for the atrocities that had enraged Stilicho.

Then, six days ago, His Imperial Astuteness made his proclamation. Theodosius had been unwell for months, though this was concealed from all but a few, and he was no longer a young man. But he was able, and he was cunning. He announced his partial abdication in favour of his twin sons, Honorius and Arcadius. The boys are mere infants, of course, far too young to rule. However, for the ultimate good of the Empire, Theodosius decreed that each twin would, upon his death, rule one half of the Empire, Honorius the western half, from Rome, and Arcadius the eastern half, from Constantinople. In their minority, the boys would be served, and the halves of Empire governed, by two Regents: Flavius Stilicho with Honorius in Rome, and Flavius Rufinus with Arcadius in Constantinople! In the meantime, until Stilicho and Rufinus could settle into the business of governing, Theodosius would continue to supervise the Empire at large.

What a mind, Father! At one step, Theodosius had preserved his sons' succession and doubled the Empire's chances of survival in the face of aggression, even though the doom-sayers immediately began bewailing the destruction of the Empire as men have known it. Neither Stilicho nor Rufinus will flag in their protection of their charges, and each will watch the other very closely. The Empire is in strong, but mutually inimical hands. Of course, Theodosius had no intention of dying so quickly. But die he has, and we must live now with the aftermath of his plotting.

I wish I could receive letters from you in return, but I must either ask you not to write or charge you to say nothing in your letters that might be construed by anyone as being treasonous or contumacious. The security I enjoy in my writings is now outgoing only. Anything coming to me must undergo close scrutiny by the enemies of Stilicho and his Western Empire.

Farewell. I will write again soon.

Picus

X

ASTOUNDED BY THIS latest news from Picus, we girded ourselves and prepared for mighty things to happen. But nothing did. Life in our isolated Colony went on with its own placid rhythm, and I continued to work patiently and painstakingly with my own fledgling army. Then, in the following summer of 394, Picus's words came home to us with a new urgency.

Word came from Ullic's kingdom that pirates were landing in force along the south side of the estuary to the north of us, and we received three separate delegations from towns and villages to the south and west, beseeching our help in defending their lands from the Saxon and Frankish raiders who were descending on the coasts like swarms of flies. We also had it on good authority, from Bishop Alaric and his priests, that Saxon raiding parties had been wintering for the past two years on coastal lands to the south-east, not even bothering to sail home, and thereby catching advantage of the spring months to raid and plunder, thanks to the scarcity of military garrisons in that region. Things were going rapidly to Hades, and we were emerging as the only pocket of organized resistance in the whole south-west of Britain.

Ironically, our biggest difficulty now was maintaining our defensive role. The temptation to go marching off to war was very strong. I know; my own hot head was attuned to it. Only the level thinking of Caius Britannicus kept us in check. His was the voice that kept reminding us of the prime purposes of the Colony: self-sufficiency and survival.

Even so, we sent forces out to help our neighbours when we could, and it was this neighbourly attitude that finally brought us to the official notice of the military authorities.

We had known right from the outset that by maintaining a private military force—even if we did call it quasi-military—we were placing ourselves outside the law. In legal terms, all men within the Empire fit to bear arms were automatically soldiers and owed their loyalty to the Emperor himself. The fact that there might be three or even four Emperors at any one time was academic; it had no bearing on the law. It followed, therefore, that any private citizen equipping or maintaining an armed band of soldiers—even if they were private retainers—was, *ipso facto*, usurping the loyalty these men owed to the Emperor. He was depriving the Empire of troops.

The rich had, of course, been maintaining private "security forces" of their own for centuries. This was a known and accepted fact. In the space of a few years, however, in our quiet little Colony we had accumulated and trained, outfitted and equipped a genuine army of close to a thousand men. Three things had enabled us to do this in safety. The first, of course, was that our original plans had been devised with the full cognizance and support of several of the most senior officers in the armies of Britain. The second was tied directly to the first and was well understood by all concerned: our "army" was being prepared in accordance with a plan; it would not be mobilized, or become effective, until after the regular legions had been withdrawn from Britain, if such a catastrophe ever occurred. The third thing that had protected us was our isolation. We were far off the beaten track, and in the early years, at least, we had taken great pains to maintain secrecy and security.

As the years passed, however, circumstances changed. We worked our trainees hard, and their training demanded that they be uniformed, to give them that sense of belonging so necessary to military units. Then, as a diplomatic gesture to please our valuable ally in the north-west, King Ullic Pendragon, Britannicus changed the uniforms from plain homespun to a military red, giving our men a visibility beyond anything they had had before. That visibility became even more pronounced after the regular military authorities started pulling garrisons out of the forts in the west to concentrate them in the south-east on the Saxon Shore, in the area south of the Wall in the north, and around Londinium, which had for a long time been the administrative centre of the region called South Britain. The removal of these garrisons led to increases in raiding, and that led us more and more into open defensiveness, increasing the risk of our being "noticed" officially. It had to happen sooner or later. It happened in 396.

One bright-eyed young staff officer in Londinium had heard about our exploits and saw in them an opportunity to impress his superiors with his efficiency. He prepared a report on "a rebellious group of bandits and deserters in the west, operating to the south of Glevum." We had his report almost before his superiors did, thanks to Plautus, who had been on duty at the time and saw the document. A small expedition was detached from one of the Cambrian garrisons to investigate the report, and it found no trace of any organized bandits south of Glevum.

It was sheer bad luck that the young officer in command of that expedition happened to dine with a magistrate in Glevum. In the course of that dinner he picked up some genuine information about us and our activities and he included that information in his report to his superiors in Londinium. This time we had the information before he even sent off his missive. One of Alaric's priests sent the word to us, directly from the clerk who wrote out the officer's report. In it, the young tribune stated that he had "every reason to believe that the rumours of organized bandits operating south of Glevum are, in fact, references to a commune of civilians living to the south of Aquae Sulis, who have organized themselves along quasi-military lines in order to defend themselves and their farms against Hibernian raiders." He went on to say that he had been given no indication that these people were involved in any lawless activities, other than the intrinsically lawless taking up of arms in a semi-organized fashion. He said that he had been able to obtain no clear indication of the numerical strength of these people, having heard estimates ranging from a hundred men to several thousand. His personal opinion was that the figure of as many as a hundred might be grossly exaggerated. He did recommend, however, that in the interests of the Senate and the People of Rome an investigation should be conducted into the condition of the citizenry in that part of the country, which was outside of his own immediate jurisdiction.

On the whole, it was an excellent report, submitted by a man who was unusual in that time in that he was both an officer of the army and, at the same time, thorough, fair-minded and conscientious in the performance of his duty. The news of his report hit the Colony the way my skystone must have hit the ground. Britannicus summoned an immediate emergency meeting of the Council, and it was a stormy session.

Caius had a very strong and surprisingly uncharacteristic belief that he always adhered to in the Council's sessions, and it amazed me that it never failed. He believed absolutely in letting the Council solve its problems in its own way. He would sit back and remain generally apart from the debate, interfering only when it was necessary for the sake of order. He maintained that, no matter what the problem under discussion might be, the Council had the ability to solve it among its members. The final decision on Council matters never originated with him, but it was he who chose the Council members, and he took an almost indecent pleasure in co-ordinating their separate abilities to work together for the good of the Colony. The only rule that governed these sessions was one stating that no one could leave the meeting until the problem facing the Council had been solved to the satisfaction of two-thirds plus one of the members present.

The session dealing with the tribune's report was the longest I ever sat in: it lasted ten hours.

On this occasion, the words of sense and settlement came from Vegetius Sulla, the eldest son of Tarpo Sulla, who had died several years earlier. Vegetius, himself a man of forty-eight, had served a full twenty-five years with the legions in Gaul, in Africa and on the German frontier. He was a man of few words and wide experience who seldom spoke up in Council, but was always listened to when he did. The arguments had been going on for hours and some there had almost come to blows. Feelings were running very high, and there was total confusion in the Council room. No progress had been made in more than six hours.

I noticed Vegetius stand up from his seat and move away to a clear space in one corner of the room, fumbling in the leather pouch that hung by his side, and I watched, intrigued, as he drew out a stone of some kind, attached to a length of cord. He shook the kinks out of the cord and then, holding the end of the cord in his right hand, he began to swing the stone in circles around his head. As the stone picked up momentum, it suddenly began to emit a warbling, whistling noise that grew and grew to become a shrill, ear-bursting, wailing shriek.

All other noises in the room died away as people turned in open-mouthed stupefaction to stare at him. He moved his right arm out from the vertical and caught the whirling stone with a loud smack in the palm of his left hand. I could feel myself grinning from ear to ear, though I had no idea what he was up to. The silence in the room was astounding.

Vegetius looked around him at the staring faces and opened his left hand, letting the stone fall to dangle at the end of its cord.

"I got this when I was serving in Germany," he said. "The barbarians beyond the borders there make them. Their children use them as toys. You hear six or seven of them going at night out there, it can scare you. But it's harmless." He began to swing it again, harder and harder, until some clapped their hands over their ears. Then he let it go. It flew across the room and blasted to shards a vase on a table against the wall. In the stunned silence, tiny pieces of the vase pattered like raindrops. He spoke into the stillness.

"At least, it looks harmless. Fact is, it kills. When did any of you last see one of our warships?" No one answered him, and he continued. "They're blue, you know. So are the crews' uniforms. In some kinds of light, you can't even see them. But they are there, believe me, in full view and extremely dangerous."

"Vegetius," said Britannicus, gently, "I think you have a point you wish to make. If we all sit down, will you explain it to us?"

Vegetius smiled. "Happily," he said. Everyone sat down. Still smiling, Vegetius walked to the front of the room, retrieving his missile on the way. He paused and looked all around the room before he spoke.

"We have a problem. Several of them, in fact. We have an army that we should not have raised or trained; uniforms that we are not supposed to be wearing; fortifications that are not supposed to exist; cavalry that we're not supposed to possess; and a military expedition on its way here from the east to find out who we are and what we have." There was utter stillness now.

"My suggestion is this. Things are not always what they appear to be. We should take advantage of the time we have left to us before our visitors arrive, then show them what we have and let them see for themselves that we have nothing."

That speech created quite a stir. Some people thought he had lost his senses, for there seemed to be no logic in his statement. Then someone asked him how he proposed doing what he suggested.

"Simple," responded Vegetius. "We start with the most obvious. Disband our army. Send them away."

"A thousand men?" The question from the floor made the idea sound ridiculous, but Vegetius leaped on it.

"Why not? If we send them away now, the signs of their having been here will be gone by the time our visitors arrive."

"But where could we send a thousand men?" someone else wanted to know.

"Anywhere, man! But not in one great block. We split them up, send them out on exercises. Ullic could use some of them in his hills against the Hibernians for a month. Two or three hundred, I imagine. Another two hundred could lose themselves in the moors down to the south-west. Another hundred on the plains around Stonehenge."

"That's only five, six hundred. What about the others?" Everyone was throwing questions now.

Vegetius shook his head in disgust. "How many of them really live here? On the farms and in the cottages? A hundred? Two hundred? That's less than two men to a square mile of the Colony. So we'll be well staffed! As long as we're careful to conceal ourselves, to be as close to invisible as we can possibly be, we can lose another four hundred in plain sight."

Caius spoke up. "That still leaves a hundred men and a very visible fortification on the hill behind us."

Vegetius grinned. "Yes, Caius, it does—for now. But don't lose sight of the war galley."

"Forgive me, Vegetius, but I don't know what you mean."

"I mean that if we do it properly, we can hide it."

"Hide it?" Britannicus sounded astonished. "Hide the fort?"

"Why not? If the navy can hide a fleet of galleys in plain sight, why can't the army hide a fort?"

"God in Heaven!" said Britannicus. "How would we do it?"

Vegetius looked at Britannicus, almost seeming not to see him, his brows puckered in thought, his eyes far away from this room. "I have an idea, Caius, that will work—I know it will, if I can only find the proper key. It's not difficult. All it will take is imagination, conviction and luck." His voice dwindled almost to nothing and he scratched the point of his chin with the tip of one finger. Every man in the room watched the gesture, waiting for him to continue. "We once hid an entire legion in Gaul, in broad daylight, and an army marched past within a quarter mile of us and didn't see us." His voice trailed off again for a few moments before he shook his head abruptly.

"No. That won't do it. We used nets with twigs and branches woven into the mesh. These walls are too high, and they're on top of a hill . . . Caius, can you see the walls and the fortifications from the rear of the hill?"

Caius shook his head. "I've no idea. I don't think I've ever been behind that particular hill. Why? Is it important?"

"It could be. Does anyone know?"

"Aye, I do!" This was Terra. "Firma and I were hunting out that way about a month ago and he remarked that, from the valley floor there, you can't see any indication at all that there's anything built up on the hill. We talked about how difficult it would be to get up or down the hillside from that direction. Didn't we, Firma?" His brother nodded.

"Good." Vegetius was pleased. He opened his pouch and dropped his whistling stone inside, and then he crossed the room again to the table that had held the shattered vase. There was an open codex there, its pages covered by pottery shards. He wiped them off with his hand and stood there, looking down at the book, his back to the room. Everything about his posture made it clear that he was deep in thought. Finally he turned to face the assembled Council and leaned back, resting his buttocks on the edge of the table.

"Is Father Andros in the villa today?"

"He was, earlier," I answered. "I spoke with him just before I came in here. But that was several hours ago." I wondered what he had in mind. Andros could do things with parchment and a stick of charcoal that verged on the magical.

"Well, at least he's not far away. Caius Britannicus, I have a suggestion to make to you and the Council. If you accept it, you will break precedent. I do not suggest it lightly. We are faced here with a major crisis. The fact that this Council has been in session for—how long? seven hours?—without resolving anything, only serves to emphasize the gravity of the situation.

"I have an idea that I believe will work. But I'm going to need some time to myself and the help of Father Andros to straighten out some of the lines of it. So I suggest that we adjourn this Council for, say, two hours. I promise you that at the end of that time we may reconvene with a reasonable chance of ratifying my plans."

There was an uncomfortable shifting as the other twenty men in the room took stock of this proposal, and eventually all eyes turned to Britannicus. I had never heard the Council chamber so quiet.

Caius cleared his throat and spoke to everyone. "What Vegetius says is true. To accept his suggestion would be to create a precedent that might become dangerous. We have to ask ourselves if we dare to violate our own rule, the only rule that governs our participation in this Council. Since our beginnings we have ordained that none may leave a Council meeting before all business facing the Council has been dealt with and resolved. This has allowed us to deal successfully with the dangers of procrastination. Successfully and, to this point, effectively. Do we dare to do otherwise now?

"On the other hand . . ." He paused, marshalling his thoughts. "On the other hand, what Vegetius is proposing is not a complete negation of the principle governing that rule. He is asking for time and the privacy to nurture and develop an idea that, whatever its substance, is absolutely germane to the problem facing us today.

"He is not asking for an overnight adjournment, merely for thinking space. All of us here have been unable, in the space of seven hours, to come up with any ideas at all. We are not simply lacking a solution; until Vegetius phrased it so succinctly, we had not even arrived at a definition of our problem. Vegetius Sulla has been ahead of all of us in defining, appreciating and, I hope, dealing with the problem. What he is saying to us is that all of our arguing is interfering with his capacity to think constructively. He is telling us that in the space of two hours we may eat, renew ourselves and return to this Council meeting refreshed and able to evaluate the worth of the plan he will then propose to us. So. How do you vote?"

The meeting was adjourned for two hours by unanimous consent.

XI

VEGETIUS WAS LATE in re-entering the Council room, and it was a measure of the high regard he had won for himself among our colonists that his twenty-one peers remained calm, talking quietly among themselves as they awaited his arrival. Eventually, some quarter of an hour late, he came bursting into the room and strode to the front, followed closely by Father Andros, our resident artist whose skill in drawing had amazed all of us for years. Andros clutched an armful of rolled parchments, and Vegetius began to speak even before he had reached the front of the room.

"My apologies for my tardiness, my friends, but you will see that we have not been idle since leaving you. Father Andros and I are going to show you some pictures. But first I want to remind you of the things I talked about earlier: the whistling stone—a children's toy and a deadly weapon for those skilled in its use; the naval galley that, painted blue, can disappear from sight in the full light of day; the Roman legion in full battle array that rested completely undetected by an enemy less than a quarter of a mile away, again in broad daylight."

He paused, and everyone in the assembly hung on his words, waiting for him to continue.

"None of these phenomena appears to be what it really is, given the proper—and by that I mean the carefully contrived and arranged—conditions. Their deadliness becomes invisible. Not just because they are made to look less deadly, *but because they have been rearranged . . . disguised in such a way that men can look right at them and simply not see them.*" He stopped, waiting for a reaction, and got none.

"Do you understand what I am saying?"

Torquilius Linus, formerly a very successful lawyer, and one of the most distinguished-looking men in the room, coughed uncomfortably and spoke softly in his rich, baritone voice.

"I believe I do, Vegetius. I think you are telling us that you can conceal an entire hill—a mountain, almost—from human view. I must also say I do not believe that to be possible."

Vegetius clapped his hands together loudly. "You are absolutely correct, Torquilius. It is not possible. But that is not what I'm saying at all! I am saying that with effort, determination and careful planning, we will be able to *alter the appearance* of the hill to deceive men's eyes, by breaking up and concealing from view the outlines of the fortress—at least from here, a mile

152

away." He turned to Father Andros. "May I have the first drawing? The view
today."

Andros handed him a fat scroll, and Vegetius unrolled it and held it up
where we could all see it. There was an audible, concerted intake of breath
at the reality of the landscape depicted on the parchment. We were looking
at a perfect rendering of the view of the fort hill from the courtyard of the
villa. Andros had a gift that verged on the magical; with a few slashes of
charcoal, he had captured the scene perfectly, so that the walls of the new
fortifications stood out, clearly defined against the contours of the hill. He
allowed us to admire it for no more than a few moments before he released
the bottom of the parchment, permitting it to roll itself up into a tube again.

Wordlessly, Andros handed him a second scroll, which Vegetius displayed
in the same way. It was almost an exact replica of the first drawing, except
that it was scored with hundreds of vertical stripes, and I realized what had
been wrong with the first one.

"Can anyone identify the difference?" Vegetius's voice was hard-edged.

"Yes," I said. "The scaffolding was missing from the first drawing." A
recent development, the newly erected scaffolding around our rapidly growing
walls had altered the appearance of the fort quite radically over the previous
months. I hesitated, unsure of myself. "It's not quite right in this one, either.
There's something missing. I think."

"You're right, Varrus. But what is it?"

"The horizontals!" Firma's voice came from right behind my head. "The
platforms of the scaffolding are missing."

"Good man, Fermax!" Vegetius released the bottom and let the scroll
roll up on itself, already reaching behind him for a third, which Andros had
ready for him. "Now, what about this one?"

The parchment he held now had vertical slashes scattered down the
hillside in random fashion, far below where they had appeared before. Nobody
said a word. The puzzlement in the room was almost palpable.

Wordlessly, Vegetius released this scroll and took a fourth from Andros's
hand. This time, as he unrolled it, holding it high, there was a shocked mutter
of reaction. The entire scene had changed. The hill was still there, but from
a point about two-thirds up its flanks it was cloaked in a curtain of greenery.
Bushes and trees completely hid the walls from view.

"You see, my friends? Magic! But all good Romans know there's no such
thing as magic." He rolled up the scroll and reached for another. "Now," he
said, deepening his voice dramatically. "Look carefully!"

There were six—what? cylinders?—arranged randomly on the parchment.
That was all. Six vertical cylinders. He closed the parchment. The next scroll
showed one cylinder, close up, with branches of trees and bushes, their cut
ends showing, tied around it like the staves of a fasces tied around the axe
handle.

"There's your magic, my friends." There was no doubting the conviction
and the satisfaction in Vegetius's tone. His voice rang clearly throughout the

room, convincing its hearers by its very resonance. "Take enough men and enough rope, cut enough branches, tie them around enough uprights, stand far enough away, and you will see a forest created where there was none before. As the uprights descend the slope, the branches tied around them mask the bareness of the ones above. Pile bushes at the bottom, back off for a mile or so and, until the branches all die, you have what appears to be a living forest."

He fell silent, letting what he had said sink in. Britannicus finally broke the long silence that ensued.

"Vegetius, that would *work*! How long would the branches stay green?"

Vegetius shrugged and shook his head. "I don't know, Caius Britannicus. Two days? Three at the most, I would think. After that they will probably start to look very dry. But even then, it might not be noticeable from a distance. They'll be dead, but they might still appear green from down here. I wouldn't care to leave them for more than a week, though."

Caius was tugging at his chin, his brows furrowed in thought. "What about the top of the wall? What if you can't get your 'trees' as high as you'd like?"

"I would alter the shape of the top of the wall itself with dirt." He looked around him for information. "How wide is it on top? Six feet?"

"Closer to nine," said Tullus, one of the stonemasons.

Vegetius nodded approvingly. "There you are, then, three good paces. Ample room to build hillocks to break up the straight line. Given time, we could cut sod and cover the raw dirt, too."

Everyone in the room sat in astonished silence. Then, hesitantly, one of the newer Council members raised his hand for permission to speak.

Britannicus nodded to him. "Speak out, Horatio."

Horatio cleared his throat, and when he addressed Vegetius his voice was strong. "I believe that this idea might work. But it seems to me that it will take a lot of organizing, and much depends on the timing of the thing. Do you agree?"

"Aye, I agree completely," Vegetius said. "The whole thing depends on timing, as I see it. What's your point, Horatio?"

"The greenery, and the time needed to gather it. It takes a lot of trees to make a forest. Even a false forest. And you said that, once cut, you would not want to have to trust the greenness for more than a week." He looked around at the faces of the Council members. "We talk of sending our men away. But we will need them to gather the greenery in enough quantity to mask the top of the hill. Especially if it all has to be collected and put together in a matter of days."

A buzz of agreement and speculation broke out among his listeners, and he raised his voice above the noise, silencing everyone. "I am not trying to find fault! I do believe this can succeed. All I'm saying is that we will have to plan carefully. It can be done! But we must make sure that it is *we* who control the timing of the whole thing."

"Horatio, think of what you're saying! That's impossible!" This was a shout from Varo. "We have no control over the timing. Are you suggesting we ask the people in Londinium to tell us when they'll be sending their investigators?"

Horatio's answer was immediate. "No, not at all! I'm not! But I am suggesting that not one person here, Vegetius included, has thought to mention that we have almost a hundred heavy horses to hide, as well as a thousand men. I say let's hide the soldiers in the fort itself and use the horses in our planning. We can hide them, *and* use them!" Horatio turned to me. "Varrus! Would it make sense to send our cavalry along the roads leading to the Colony, to build fires and watch for the approach of whoever it is that is coming?"

I nodded, non-committally. "Sounds interesting. Go on."

"Well," he was growing enthusiastic now, "there are only three ways we can be approached by road, am I correct? From the north, by way of Glevum and Aquae Sulis, from the east through Sorviodunum and from the south by the coast road? If we were to send out our cavalry, with orders to split up along the various routes and build signal-fires close enough to be visible to the next man along the line, then we could go to meet these 'investigators.' The news of their approach would reach us then as quickly as it takes a man to see a distant fire and light his own."

"Aye," I nodded, "that makes sense. But why send horsemen?"

"Because they can stay here longer, working, and then get to where they are going more quickly. They can get away more quickly, too—fade into the countryside and make their way back here slowly and safely after our visitors have left. That way, we do not have to hide the horses."

"By Hephaestus, Horatio, you're right!" I was up on my feet, limping to the front of the room. "Signal-fires should give us three, maybe four clear days' notice of their approach, if we can pick them up far enough in advance. And while we are waiting for the signal, we could have every man in the Colony working on the job! We might as well keep the soldiers here, for if we can't hide the fort, we can't hide them, either. We should be able to finish the whole thing in two days' hard work, let our men scatter and then look as innocent as babies under our tree-topped hill when our company arrives! Vegetius, Horatio, I commend you!"

My own excitement transmitted itself to everyone there, and a chorus of cheering ensued. Vegetius was the one who restored order by pulling out his whistling stone again, forcing everyone to be quiet to make him stop the fiendish noise.

"All right," he finally said, when all was quiet again. "It occurs to me that we have more work ahead of us in the next few weeks—if we have that long—than ever before in the history of this Colony. We have a lot of preparations to make. So let's get to it. Britannicus, the floor is yours."

Britannicus stood up, a smile on his face. "I thank you again, Vegetius

Sulla, on behalf of all of us." He looked around the room. "Are we all agreed that the plan Vegetius proposes is the one we should adopt?"

"Aye!" It was unanimous.

"And are we all equally in agreement that Quintus Horatio's amendment to it is sensible?"

"Aye!" Again unanimous.

"So be it. Now we must plan the details."

Towards midnight, the plan was finished. Caius assembled a general meeting of the entire Colony at the main villa the next day to explain exactly what was happening. Directly after the assembly, work began on several fronts. Men were set to work building ramps to give access to the top of the walls, and others were set to digging dirt and piling it on top of the walls of the fort to break up their regularity. Others were cutting sod to mask the newly piled dirt, and still others were planting uprights, tree-trunk tall, on the side of the hill. All others not involved in this back-breaking work—women and children and old men—scoured the countryside finding copses and suitable woods that could be plundered, when the time came, in such a way that the depredations would not be noticeable to a stranger.

Britannicus reckoned that we had at least ten days available to us for preparation before the authorities in Londinium had time to receive the report, digest it, consult on it, arrive at a decision and finally dispatch an investigative force of some kind. Which meant that the cavalry could be put to work for a week, too, before being sent out to stand guard.

As it turned out, it took the authorities three weeks to make up their minds and act. We filled in the extra two weeks by adding more and more uprights to the hillside. Some of the work parties were put to work digging up real saplings and transplanting them, so that the hillside really did begin to look like a forest coming back to life years after a great forest fire. Bushes, ripped from the earth and dragged to the hillside by horses, began to transform the place. At even less than a mile, it became very difficult to make out the lines of the tops of the walls.

In those three weeks, our colonists performed a feat that was almost magical, and they were helped by the Celts, who came in hundreds, once the word of this insanity had spread, to see for themselves what was going on. Underneath it all was an almost hysterical anticipation that it might all be for nothing. If the authorities decided not to investigate the young officer's report, we would all have broken our backs ruining a perfectly good hill!

I was at dinner with the family one night, at the beginning of the fourth week of our preparations, when Britannicus's steward interrupted us with the news that our closest signal-fire was ablaze, and that messengers had already been sent to alert the other villas of the Colony. Our people assembled at the main villa throughout that night, and by dawn the last stage of the operation was launched as everyone who was able set about the final task of cutting green branches and lashing them to our makeshift tree trunks.

Britannicus was finally up on his feet again, after having been confined to his bed for over a week with a badly sprained back, from trying to lift a tree trunk that was too heavy for him. As soon as I had seen everyone off in an orderly fashion I headed back to report to him, but as I was entering the main gates of the courtyard I heard the sound of a galloping horse, and I turned to see one of my own men, on a badly blown mount, thundering up behind me. He reined in when he saw me and jumped from the back of his almost lifeless horse. His knees gave way as he landed, so that he stumbled and I had to catch him. He was breathing almost as hard as his horse, and I had to steady him until he regained his breath.

"What is it, man? What's wrong?"

"Cavalry, Commander! Heavy cavalry." He shuddered. "Coming from Londinium. Overland. They're not on the road, and they're coming fast!"

"How fast, man? How long do we have?"

"A day, Commander. Maybe two. No more. They will be here by the morning of the day after tomorrow. We lit the fires as soon as we saw them, but then we had to pass the word from man to man by mouth. Almost killed the horses."

"How far apart were you spaced?"

"Three, four miles. Depended on the terrain. We had to be able to see the next man's fire."

My mind was racing. "How many men in your chain?"

"Thirty-nine. I'm the last of them."

"How long did it take to get the word to you?"

He shook his head. "Don't know, Commander. Some of the lads took off as soon as they had lit their fires, as they were supposed to. One fellow had to ride three posts before he found a man with a fresh horse. All of us rode flat out!"

"Damn! You did well. What's your name?"

"Septimius Severus, Commander."

"We all owe you a debt, Septimius Severus. Now get some rest. You've earned it. Where are the others?"

"All split up, Commander, as ordered."

"What about the men on the other routes? Do you know anything of them?"

"No, Commander. But the word was that as soon as the signal-fires were seen coming back towards the Colony, the other men were to send their fires out to the ends of their routes. So everyone must know by now that the game is on."

I nodded. "Good. Go and find a bed, and get some sleep. I have to get word to our workers that they only have today to finish the job. Thank God we had two extra weeks."

I hurried inside to tell Britannicus what was happening, and to get word out to our people in the fields that our visitors were fast approaching. I spent a long, wearying day worrying about the speed they were coming at, and wondering if we had enough manpower to finish the job in time. I need not have worried. Our people outdid themselves, and long before dusk they were adding the finishing touches to an amazing piece of human wizardry. The hill was forested. The fort was gone. There was no sign of any human influence on the hill behind the villa.

None of us had any sleep that night. The commissary operated at peak capacity from dusk until dawn, and as our soldiers were provisioned they dispersed into the night to conceal themselves in the newly hidden fort. By dawn, everything that could be done had been done. Our army was dispersed or hidden and the signs of our frenzied preparations were covered and cleaned up. There was nothing to do but wait and try to behave normally.

The morning passed, and the midday changed into afternoon. Britannicus and I sat on a bench in the courtyard, sharing the warmth of the afternoon sun and doing our best to be casual, pretending that we were both at ease and contented.

We had no idea where our "guests" were, or when they would arrive. We had decided not to spy on their advance after the first sighting, reasoning that it was enough to know that they were coming. Victorex had come by late in the morning to ask us when we wanted to start moving the horses out of his breeding farm—we had quartered a large number of our workhorses there, rather than take the chance of the empty paddocks attracting attention. He had assumed that the cavalry would want to quarter their mounts there, forgetting that we were not supposed to know they were coming. He was most abashed when I pointed that out to him, but his understandable error made all of us realize how easy it would be to betray ourselves and our readiness for this visit. So, on that long afternoon we filled our waiting time with a review of everything that might, or could, go wrong.

We were aware that everything—the success or failure of our entire scheme—depended on the calibre of the man in charge of this investigation. We could anticipate that whoever he might be, he would be thorough in his inquiries, but we felt confident that, given an ounce of luck and a particle of good breeding on his part, we had a fair chance of disarming his suspicions. We were confident, too, that he would come directly to us. There was no other place on the road that he could stop. He would not be interested in towns—and there were none closer to us than Aquae Sulis, anyway. The few villages in the area were full of our own people, who would direct any strangers to us, and all of the other villas close to our own were controlled by us. Our visitor would have to come to us and deal with Caius Britannicus, Proconsul and Senator of Rome.

No one in the region would betray us, we knew, because everyone for miles around depended upon our good will and our support. If loyalty to the Empire dictated to any man jealous of our strength that he denounce us, the fear of losing our military presence and assistance would keep his agonizing within his breast. At least, that is what we hoped.

In the middle of the afternoon, unable to sit still any longer, I made my way to Victorex's stables to see for myself that all was as it should be, and almost an hour had passed before by the time I returned. By then, however, our guests had been announced. Shortly before I returned, Caius heard the blast of a trumpet in the distance and the sounds of a party of mounted men coming along the road leading to the main gates of the villa. He told me later that he sucked in a great, deep breath and went to meet them.

There were five in the advance party: a grey-bearded centurion, a trumpeter, a standard-bearer and two outriders. They came at a gallop right up to the gates, where Caius awaited them, and drew to a halt. The centurion did not dismount; he looked down on Cay from a horse several hands higher than any we had bred.

"Proconsul Caius Britannicus?" He looked unsure of himself.

Caius spoke. "I am he. Has it become customary nowadays for a centurion to talk down to a Roman senator?"

"Your pardon, Proconsul." The man had meant no disrespect. He flushed, and his eyes switched from Caius to his troopers, than back to Caius again. "Escort will dismount!" All five of them slipped heavily to the ground from the backs of their horses, the standard-bearer achieving this feat with some difficulty, to Cay's eyes, because of the size and length of the great scarlet standard he carried. As the man stiffened to attention again, Caius eyed the standard.

"What emblem is this?" he asked. "It is new to me."

The centurion saluted. "New to the whole world, Proconsul. Ours is a new unit. Heavy cavalry. Fresh arrived from Armorica by way of Gaul."

"What are you called? Your unit, I mean."

"Lead Equine Cohort, seconded from Thirty-fourth Legion on special duty, Proconsul."

"Lead Equine Cohort! I see. The Thirty-fourth Legion, you say? Welcome, and what may we do for you, Centurion?"

The man cleared his throat. "We have been sent ahead to request your hospitality, Proconsul. We have been on the road from Londinium these five days past, and our commander would like to rest here for a while with you, if you can accommodate us."

"Five days from Londinium?" Caius sounded surprised. "You have made good time. Where are you headed?"

The centurion cleared his throat again. "I regret I am not at liberty to say, Proconsul."

"No, I suppose not. A heavy cavalry unit, you say? Since when has Rome had heavy cavalry?"

"Since only very recently, Proconsul. A few years."

"Hmmm." Britannicus's grunt no doubt sounded unimpressed. "Who is your commander, and how many of you are there? Not a whole cohort, I trust? How long will you be staying?"

"No, Proconsul, three squadrons only. Marcellus Vicere is our tribune, and we have one hundred and thirty-eight men and horses, Proconsul."

"One hun—?" Britannicus told me later he felt like an actor in a play. He widened his eyes and made his voice reflect what he called singular astonishment. "Do you have grain for your horses?"

"Aye, Proconsul, in the commissary wagons. And food for our men."

"Oh! I see." Cay now allowed himself to appear mollified. "Well, that's not so bad, I suppose. I think we can look after you. For one night, at least." He turned to one of the gawking servants. "Nestor, find Gallo and tell him to prepare enough meat to feed a hundred and fifty extra men tonight. Tell him I don't care where he finds it, even if we have to borrow it from our neighbours. We can repay it later. Tell him we have company from Londinium, and bid him have his people set up tables in the fields behind the villa of Terrix and Fermax." He held up his hand to detain the man and turned back to the centurion. "You said one hundred and thirty-eight horses?"

The man shrugged and nodded at the same time. "One hundred and forty-four, Proconsul, with the wagon horses."

Britannicus turned back to Nestor. "Send word to Victorex, as well, that we will need his walled pastures. If he has workhorses there, send them to the farms and leave them there tonight."

Nestor bowed and left at the run.

Caius turned back to the centurion. "How many officers are with you altogether?"

"Five, Proconsul. Four regular and one . . . guest."

"A guest? On a patrol? Who is this gentleman?"

The centurion flushed and looked away into the distance. "I . . . I do not know his name, Proconsul."

It was an obvious lie, according to Cay, and he ignored it. "And you? What is your mark among these mounted troops?"

The man smiled, pleased to have the subject changed. "The same as it has always been, my lord. Senior Warrant Officer. Lead Cohortal Spear. *Pilus prior.*"

"Good. My greetings to your commander. He and his officers are welcome to share our roof tonight, and to dine with us. When your people arrive, my man here, Rollo, will show them where they are to be quartered." He nodded his dismissal and turned as if to leave before swinging back again to the centurion. "How long before your people arrive?"

The man shrugged. "Perhaps two hours, Proconsul, perhaps more; we came to warn you at top speed, to allow you time to prepare. In truth, I've no idea how far they are behind us now, but they will be here before nightfall."

Caius nodded again and left them standing in the road, surrounded by gawkers. He had not taken three steps, however, before the *pilus prior* called out to him.

"Proconsul, your pardon, sir, but I am sore set. Could I use your latrines?"

Caius's eyebrow went up at this astonishing request, but he was too polite to rebuke the man. "Of course you may. Rollo, show the centurion where to go."

As Caius passed through the gates of the villa, he was congratulating himself on having handled the meeting without raising suspicion. He felt, he told me, that he had achieved just the correct mixture of surprise and indignation, tempered with a touch of well-bred impatience, and he believed that if all of us could maintain the tone he had established, we should be able to emerge from this entire exercise in control of the situation. He knew the *pilus* had lied when asked about their "guest" on the patrol, but he also knew the reason for the lie, because the "guest" was the Imperial Inspector. He was not surprised that the man had clearly been placed under orders to say nothing about the true purpose of this visit.

I returned about then to the villa, emerging from the woods to the east just in time to see Caius's shape disappearing through the villa gates. I took note of the standard party, but made no effort to hurry, and when I was no more than a hundred paces from them I saw their commander stride out through the gates, spring nimbly up onto his big horse, then wheel his men and ride off at their head. They did not even notice me.

I found Cay still standing on the front steps of the villa, staring in perplexity at something he held in his hand. He was turning to enter the house when he noticed me, and he stood where he was until I joined him, leaving my horse ground-tethered. The object in his hand was a thickly folded square of papyrus, and he was tapping it fretfully against the back of his left wrist, still frowning bemusedly, when I reached him. I indicated it with a nod of my head.

"What have you there? Did they deliver it?"

"Yes," he said. "But strangely, and it makes no sense."

I laughed. "Neither does what you just said. How did it go?"

"Hmmm?" He looked at me as if I were speaking Greek.

"Your meeting with them. How did it go?"

"Oh. Very well, I think. They had no idea we expected them. But this . . ." He waved the folded papyrus at me. "I know not what to make of this. Most extraordinary."

I put my hand on his shoulder and turned him towards the door. "Come, I'm parched. Let's have a cup of wine while we discuss it."

A few moments later, the first edge of my thirst dealt with, I refilled my cup and slid down into a couch.

"So. Tell me what happened."

He did, relating the entire conversation with the *pilus prior*. When he told me of the man's request to use the latrine, I laughed aloud, but Caius cut my laugh short.

"No, Publius. It was a ruse, for some obscure purpose. Look at this." He held up the papyrus again. "Rollo took him to the latrine and then came back bringing me this. The man wanted me to have it without anyone else's knowledge. The message it contains is nonsense. The word from the *pilus prior*, delivered to me by Rollo, was that he had brought this secretly, for my eyes only, as a favour to a friend. But who that friend might be, or what his purpose is, is beyond me."

"What?" I stood up and held out my hand and he passed the message to me. I flipped it open and read the words aloud. "*When the primus pilus speaks of God, remember God and take heed. He rides with the* pilus prior." It was signed "PPPP"—a signature well known to my eyes—and I read it in full: "Pontius Plautus, *primus pilus*."

Caius was mystified. "Plautus? But what does he mean? Your friend makes riddles, Publius."

Then suddenly his eyes went wide with alarm and he grasped me firmly as I swayed and almost fell. I felt the blood drain from my face and heard a great roaring in my ears.

"Publius! In God's name, what's wrong?"

His voice seemed to reach me from far away, and I felt him lowering me back to my seat on the couch again.

Eventually, after what seemed an age, the whirling, roaring sensation behind my eyes died down and I shook my head to clear it, but when I spoke my voice was almost a croak. "In God's name, you say . . . you're right, but you don't know it. That's what Plautus is telling us. God rides with this *pilus prior*. The devil-spawned whoreson's alive! Your friend in Rome was right! It's Seneca! It's Claudius Seneca! Deus is what his friends called him that day, the first day we crossed blades. Plautus was there! Deus! God! It was their blasphemy for Claudius. Plautus was with me and heard it. Caesarius Claudius Seneca rides with the *pilus prior*! He is the Imperial Inspector."

Caius was thunderstruck. "No, it can't be! He's dead. You killed him, you convinced me! It's impossible that this could be him. Seneca? Here? That animal? No, you are mistaken. He couldn't be."

I shuddered, getting hold of myself. "No. It's him. It has to be, Cay. Plautus is not a subtle man, yet this is a cryptic message. The whoreson is alive! I refused to accept the evidence that he was still alive because I didn't want to. But he *must* have survived—how, I'll never know—and now he's coming here. There's no other possible explanation of this message, Cay. Plautus obviously sent it with this *pilus prior* as the only means he had of warning us. No one else would understand it, but to me it's unmistakable, and Plautus knew it would be."

He was frowning, biting his lip, thinking furiously as he moved to close the door to his study against interruption. "Very well," he said eventually, accepting my view and signalling to me to be quiet and let him think. "It is pointless to argue with you, especially on this. I was supposed to follow up on the matter with further inquiries, but I never did. Damnation! Now we have to think this through, and we have only an hour."

I followed him with my eyes as he began to pace the floor. I slumped in my couch, my mind racing like a cataract but achieving nothing in the face of my outraged disbelief. Finally he stopped pacing.

"Well, there is no other alternative. You will simply have to go into hiding until these people leave. It is unfortunate, this development, but it does not alter the situation materially. Nothing need change, other than your absence. I shall handle everything else alone."

I shook my head. "Everything has changed already, Caius. You do not know this man."

"Nonsense! The man is a Seneca and I know the breed far better than you do. He may be slightly more dangerous, less predictable, than his fellow spawn, but he is far from invulnerable to the presence of a Britannicus. I shall wrap him in coils of silken hospitality that will befuddle him because he will not expect fair treatment from me."

"No, Caius! Our entire plan was based on the assumption we would be dealing with a normal soldier—an officer and a man of breeding, a professional. None of it holds together any more, because now you are dealing with a madman. Seneca is insane. He's capable of anything. He could have you executed just to satisfy his own mad lusts. You'll see—no rules will apply in this except his, and he'll invent those as he goes along. I've learned a lot about this man over the years. He is demented. Inhuman."

He cut off my babbling with a viciously upswept hand. "No matter! I am a Proconsul of Rome and a senior senator to this filth, in age at least. Do you expect me to be cowed by him? A Seneca? Now be quiet, please, and let me think."

He started to pace again and I forced myself to sit quietly and stifle my inordinate fear. I am no stranger to fear of many kinds, but this fear turned my bowels to water. I fixed my eyes on Caius, trying to empty my mind, and as I watched him he seemed to shed years visibly, transforming himself into the Britannicus I had first known.

"Varrus," he said at length, the use of my old name confirming his transformation, "I have a plan, and I think it's a good one. Bear with me just a little longer." His eyes were glowing yellow and I waited, reflecting that his plan had better be a good one. He stopped pacing and turned to me, his eyes seeming to bore into my soul. "Will he remember you, do you think?"

"Remember me? He'll have me crucified as soon as he sets eyes on me!"

"Nonsense!" His immediate frown and humourless expression left no doubt that Caius Britannicus was not disposed to take this matter lightly. "Be serious, Publius! From what you told me about your last confrontation with him, he was confused and almost blind, after having spent a week wearing a blindfold. Is that not so?"

I had to think about that for a moment or two. I knew that what Caius was saying was correct, but I also had a nasty feeling that he was about to recommend that we put some arcane theory to the test, with my life hanging in the balance. I conceded, but let my hesitation reflect my lack of confidence.

"More or less," I said, unwilling to be too enthusiastic. "But he saw me clearly enough when we fought. Don't forget he was trying to kill me."

Caius nodded, his face preoccupied with what were obviously portentous thoughts. My misgivings increased. I was seeing portents of my own.

"You told me also that he never knew your name. Do you still hold that to be true?"

"Yes."

"You are convinced of that?"

I nodded. "Yes, Cay, I'm convinced, but I was also convinced I'd killed him."

"Hmmm! Water under bridges, Varrus." He pursed his lips, evidently considering and rejecting several things he might say to me in extenuation of his point. Finally he nodded abruptly. "Excellent. So be it. I have a plan that will work, providing your name means nothing to him."

"What is it?"

"It is the essence of simplicity. We will hand you over to him."

I blinked, feeling that I was missing something here, some essential element of logic. "I beg your pardon, Caius," I said, my voice as casual as I could make it, "but has it occurred to you that he might choose to have me executed out of hand as soon as he lays eyes on me?"

"No, it has not occurred to me, simply because the idea is ludicrous," he snapped. "You will be my prisoner, and thus safely beyond his jurisdiction."

"*Your* prisoner? What does that mean?"

He was smiling now. "Think about it, Publius. He has come here to search for bandits, outlaws, rebels under arms. We, supposedly, know nothing of his mission. What if . . ." He paused and then continued, warming visibly to his idea as its possibilities became clearer in his mind. "What if he should arrive here to find the troubles over? To find me preparing to leave for Londinium, to see to my affairs there and to transport a prisoner, a very important prisoner, a bandit leader whose depredations have been terrorizing the entire countryside hereabout. You will be that prisoner."

I was unimpressed. "Cay," I said, "I can't share your enthusiasm for this scheme. To my eyes, Seneca's first move is so obvious it hurts my neck even to think about it. He will promptly relieve you of your prisoner, on his own authority, and execute me then and there for the crimes you have just described. That's what I would do in his position, even without the personal hatred between us."

"Absolute nonsense, Varrus! This authority of his you talk of, what is it? Whence does it come? He *was* Imperial Procurator, once, and we both know how he handled that assignment. Now he is little more than a glorified messenger, sent on an errand to do someone else's bidding. I shall not permit him to usurp my rights. I outrank him in every way."

I shook my head, sceptically. "Not in his eyes, you won't."

"Damn his eyes! I would remind you of one thing, Publius." Caius's voice crackled like ice. "His eyes are the eyes of a Seneca, which makes them less than infallible. I am senior to him in the eyes of everyone who is sane, and that *pilus prior* of his is no madman. I promise you, Seneca will have no choice. If I have to exert my influence over the troop commander, this Marcellus Vicere, to go around him, I will not hesitate. Seneca will have no choice but to offer to escort me back to Londinium, or to permit me to make my own way there, with my prisoner. And I will take along a band of my own retainers—our best men—to escort me safely there and back. Naturally, their sole function will be to look after your welfare. You will come to no harm, my friend, I promise you."

I was far from reassured. "What happens, then, when we arrive in Londinium? Bear in mind, if you will, that I'm still proscribed for the alleged murder of Quinctilius Nesca in Aquae Sulis, and for the slaughter of his bullies. They'll hang me for that, if nothing else."

He waved that aside. "Nonsense! That's the point of the whole exercise. We will take our witnesses to prove you were nowhere near Nesca that night, and I will use every office of my rank in your defence, including my personal oath and guarantee as a senator and Proconsul. All charges will be quashed, I promise you. It will be my word and my reputation against Seneca's. Do you doubt the outcome?"

I made a wry face. "Cay," I said, "I've known you for a long time now, and I've never known you to be really wrong about anything of import. Not yet."

"Then this is no time to start doubting me, Publius. This opportunity could be a godsend. It could solve all our problems. Wait and see. Seneca will be so happy to have you under guard, he will accept my story completely. He will have absolutely no idea of my real intent, and we will have him out of here and on his way home without suspecting a thing about our walls. Later, once we are safe in Londinium, I'll do an about-face on him that will leave him stunned. What do you think?"

I could not say what I thought. I expelled my breath noisily through puffed cheeks and shook my head.

"Well?" He was insistent. "Will you do it? It will mean rough treatment for the next few weeks, but it will save the Colony, and it will clear your name."

I got up and poured myself a cup of wine from the jug on the table, staring pensively into the drink as I reviewed everything he had said. "My name has never been clouded, Cay. It has never been known to my enemies. All they've had is my description. Truthfully, I'm not transported with joy by your idea. I wish I had your confidence in my welfare." I emptied the cup in one gulp. "At the same time, from every other viewpoint but my own, I can see that it will work. It's brilliant. I only wish somebody else could perform my role in it. But you're right, it has to be me. Nobody else would do for Seneca's well-being what I will . . . I only hope you're equally correct about the rest of it."

He threw his arms around me. "I am. Trust me."

"I'll trust you." I found a smile for him from somewhere. "But your sister's going to have your balls for this."

He smiled briefly, a wintry little grin. "Leave Luceiia to me. She is my
sister and she knows what duty means, and what it sometimes entails. In the
meantime, you are going to have to change into other clothes. Old clothes,
and dirty. You have to look as unsavoury as your calling would make you."

I looked him straight in the eye, smiling. "No great difficulty in that, for
a smith. Charcoal, soot, smoke and ashes and old, sweaty, smelly clothes. I'll
look disreputable enough, even for you." Suddenly my smile dried up and
my stomach churned and my voice lost all its levity. "This is really going to
be rough, isn't it?"

He clasped my hand. "Aye, my friend, rough, but temporary."

I grimaced, then tried to change it to a smile, but ended up by wincing
as I grudgingly acknowledged the unwelcome certainty that had been niggling
at my consciousness for some time now. "Brother," I said, "I'll tell you
something now—something you don't know. The prospect you outline, grim
as it is, does not frighten me nearly as much as my next task, for you are
wrong in what you've said, in one respect. I must be the one to tell Luceiia,
not you. And when she learns what is afoot here, her reaction is going to be
something I would rather not behold. For once, I promise you, duty and its
obligations will have less than no effect on her."

Caius was frowning by the time I had done. "What d' you mean?"

"I mean that my wife, who is only incidentally your sister in this matter,
is about to be infuriated beyond telling, and she has every right to be. She
will be outraged, scandalized and vengeful, bitter and very deeply hurt over
what she will see as a betrayal."

"Betrayal? I don't follow you. Betrayal by whom?"

"By me, Caius, by me! She places great import upon honesty and openness
between her and me—always has, since the beginning of our time together.
And now I have betrayed that trust, with silence and needless secrecy. Luceiia
has no knowledge of my last attempt to kill Seneca, Cay—none at all. We
talked about it, you and I, but we both believed him dead, as you said
moments ago. I never did tell the story to Luceiia because the Titens massacre
and the Lignus beating of the boy burst upon us one after the other. I forgot
all about it . . . willfully, I admit, but completely. But we were wrong. The
whoreson is alive and now he is here, and our only plan to deal with him is
to hand me over to him as a prisoner. Your sister is not going to accede to
that with any speed or ease."

Caius had blanched as the import of my words sank home, and now he
placed his cupped hands over his eyes, speaking between his wrists. "I had
not thought of that, Publius. God help me, it had not occurred to me, and
you are right. She will never forgive us."

"Oh, she'll forgive you, Cay, providing your plan succeeds, but she might
not me, no matter what the outcome."

He lowered his hands from his face. "What will you say to her?"

I shrugged. "Whatever I must. Pray God on my behalf to send me the right words, although I doubt that even He could find those. I'd better go and do it now. I'm growing more apprehensive and cowardly by the moment."

I found Luceiia in her family room, arranging dried flowers in a basket. She glanced up at me in surprise, frowned, then quickly lowered her hands from what she was doing, squinting slightly as she gazed keenly at me against the afternoon sunlight.

"What's wrong, Publius? Why are you here? Have they arrived?"

I shook my head. "No, not yet, but they are on their way." I moved towards one of the couches with all the resolution I could muster. "But I have something to tell you, and must tell you now. Come and sit with me."

She moved to join me, saying nothing, merely scanning my face with narrowed eyes. I found myself dithering over my first words, flapping my hand ineffectually, but then I drew a deep breath and plunged ahead, determined to shoulder my way through what I had to say. I succeeded merely in being prolix, indeterminate and pompous.

"Luceiia, something has . . . happened . . . something you will not like . . . an unforeseen development of great moment. Something both ominous and frightening, and it is made worse because of something else I have not told you."

Her expression had become much more intense, eagle-eyed. "Say what you mean, Publius. Has someone been hurt? Is it Caius?"

"No, no, nothing like that. It has to do with this inspection; something we could never have suspected . . . and with me, and you—"

"In God's name, husband, tell me what it is! Your tongue-tied floundering is frightening me. What is this something you have not told me about? It has to do with the inspection, you said. Tell me!"

I caught my breath, then spoke in a rush. "The inspector is Claudius Seneca, whom I had believed dead. Plautus sent us a warning of his coming— a written message delivered to Caius in secret by the *pilus prior* who rode with the advance party."

She pressed the back of her hand to her mouth in dismay. "Are you sure of this?"

"Completely. Absolutely. There could be no mistaking the message, which was meant for my eyes alone. Plautus said, God rides with the *pilus prior*. Seneca's friends call him god—Deus—as a short, blasphemous form of Claudius. Plautus was with me the first time I encountered him and we heard them use the name. I could not be mistaken. Seneca is the inspector sent to find signs of treason in our Colony. Think you he will fail to find them, vicious and demented as he is, once he hears the name Britannicus?"

She sat gazing at me in silence for a space of heartbeats, then asked what we intended to do now. I shrugged and told her Caius had come up with a design to thwart him, but that before I could tell her about it, I must tell her of another matter. She pressed her lips into a kissing shape, but they betrayed no sign of softness.

"You have a secret, then, husband?"

I nodded, miserable.

"And you now wish to share it with me?" I could only nod again. "That is . . . unfortunate," Luceiia said, her voice now strangely gentle and her eyes filled with concern, "since I must assume it is this emergency that brings you to unburden it . . . And that must leave me wondering—you will agree, I'm sure, when you think of it—how many other secrets you conceal within your breast, awaiting similar emergencies. Mmm?"

I squirmed. "There are none now, no others"—liar that I was, the face of Cylla Titens laughed at me within my mind as I hurried on lest she pick up that treacherous *now*—"and I had never meant to mention this one aloud, since I believed it could cause only needless grief and quarreling . . ."

"You had better tell me."

I gulped. "Seneca. I tried to kill him and he saw my face."

"So? I knew that, Publius, but that was long since, before you came here."

I held up my hand to stop her. "No, I mean another time, a few years ago, here in the West, close by Aquae Sulis, just at the time we first met Ullic, when you wanted to accompany us, do you recall?"

She was frowning in puzzlement. "I recall that, clearly, but I don't know what you are talking about otherwise, although I noticed that you said you thought him dead."

Slowly at first, haltingly, then with increasing fluency as the tale progressed, I told her the whole story of what I had believed to be the death of Seneca and the establishment of his guilt: how I had sent men to abduct him from his hiding place in Aquae Sulis, then kept him captive in the forest glade, and finally how I had killed him, as I thought, and then been too disgusted to strike off his head. She listened in absolute silence, her face pale now, but betraying nothing of her thoughts even as I explained the reasons for my silence at the time and ever since. When I had done, she sat stone-faced, thinking deeply for what seemed to me an endless time.

"And Caius knew of this?"

I shrugged my shoulders, feeling worse by the moment. "Only recently, directly before the Titens affair drove all thought of everything else from our minds . . . I meant to tell *you* at that time, as well . . ." My voice shriveled, its futile, useless words making me hate myself.

"You should have struck off the head, husband," Luceiia said eventually, "and you should have told me at the time it happened. Failing that, you should have told me any time thereafter. Any time but now."

I nodded, filled with anguish and with shame, feeling juvenile and inadequate, but she was not yet done and the outlines of my ignominious fall had not begun to form, let alone harden.

"We have been greatly damaged here, you and I," she continued slowly, before I could find words. "And I know not how extensively the damage done might spread." She inhaled an enormous breath and squared her shoulders, thrusting her breasts into prominence before subsiding again as she exhaled, a deep, vertical crease appearing between her brows. She tapped a fingertip between her breasts, against the bone. "Something has broken, in here, I think . . . and needlessly, Publius . . . Something that was precious and fragile . . . I never thought to see you as less than the giant of a man I wed . . . Immaturity . . . and insecurity . . . were never words I would apply to you before today and this sad little secret with its myriad poisoned barbs . . . Do you understand that what you physically *did* to Seneca is unimportant, Publius? Do you see wherein the tragedy of that now lies? Claudius Seneca is barely human. His death would have been a blessing, in everyone's eyes. But that he, of all people, should be the cause of *this*, to *us*, through *silence*, defies credence . . ."

"Luceiia—"

"Shush!" She jerked up a peremptory hand, silencing me, after which I sat in chastened silence while she gazed at me with remote, but deeply troubled, eyes. "We will talk about this, later, Publius, just you and I," she whispered, eventually. "I think we must, if we are to have the slightest chance of continuing to live the life we thought to live . . ." There was a dull, strangely lifeless undertone in her voice that abruptly chilled and terrified me. Hearing it, I began to appreciate truly, and for the first time with some degree of objectivity and accuracy, how deeply I had erred in this; how gravely I had endangered the central truth of my life, its very keystone: the love I had shared with this woman. And everything I felt was amplified by the guilt that devoured me over Cylla Titens. What if *that* specter were to spill out into the light someday, I asked myself.

All thought of Seneca and his inspection had been driven from my mind by my appalled terror. My heart pounded frighteningly within its cage, and my tongue felt like a dry stick in my mouth. And in the midst of this, Luceiia stood up and spoke now like the Commander I was supposed to be.

"For the moment, however, there are other matters to concern us. You say Caius has devised a plan to deal with this human offal. Tell me about it."

I swallowed hard, sucked at my tongue in an effort to moisten and unstick my mouth, and attempted to speak, dreading what I must say next, but she interrupted me yet again, stopping me before I could begin.

"No, wait! I cannot listen yet." She drew herself even more erect, not looking at me. "I may seem very calm, but in my mind I want to scream and rage and fight with you. I need time . . . to be alone. You tell me this is Caius's plan. Well, I want to hear it from his lips. Go now and bring him here. While you are gone, I'll try to master myself. Go!"

In my guilt, incapable of doing otherwise, I bowed formally and left her standing by the couch, and my soul was filled with the cold, impersonal detachment of her dismissal.

I could not find Caius at first, and by the time I did, a quarter of an hour later, I had regained sufficient composure to conceal the despair-filled extent of my misery from him. In response to his questions about Luceiia's reception of my confession, I mumbled something about the volcano not yet having had time to gather sufficient forces to erupt, and he accepted that without demur or comment. When I informed him that Luceiia did not yet know what his plan was, however, and that she was waiting to hear it from him in person, his equanimity was visibly ruffled, and I took a certain malicious and selfish pleasure in observing that even the Proconsul was not immune to his sister's wrath.

We had barely entered the room when Luceiia accosted him. Her demeanour was still cold and aloof, so I could not tell how successful her attempt to "master herself" had been. Her initial comments, however, were not encouraging.

"Publius tells me Seneca is on his way, within hours of here, and you have devised a plan to thwart him. Will it endanger me and mine?"

Caius cleared his throat, evidently deciding upon the spur of the moment to proceed with circumspection. "That is a blunt greeting, my dear, but I see what concerns you. You and the children will be safe enough, although the presence of any Seneca entails a certain peril to all of us."

"Then have him killed the moment he appears."

"Have him—?" For the first time since I had known him, Caius Britannicus was at a loss for words. He turned to me, wide-eyed, seeking support that did not exist. "But, Luceiia, my dear sister, that is neither possible nor practical—"

Luceiia was on him like a lioness. "Balls, brother! It is both! And more than either, it is the sensible, sane thing to do. In terms of possibility, my husband, here, can bring him down from half a mile away, with one shaft from his bow. In practicality, it will solve all our problems, protect all our people and rid the world of a disease. This is a rabid animal we are discussing, not a man at all."

"Luceiia . . ."

"Don't appeal to me, Caius; just have it done. I doubt that anyone among his escort will blame you."

"In God's name, Luceiia, think what you are saying! He is an imperial envoy. To harm him would be treason, bringing death and outlawry."

"And what exists for us if he is left alive to look about him, you senseless man? A fortress! and a private army in pretty uniforms! Treason, bringing death and outlawry! Our entire way of life here is a treasonous offence against every law of Rome. For God's sake, brother, can you not see the need to strike the iron while it glows red hot? Kill him from afar, then blame outlaws and face it down! Your influence is every bit as great as his. Greater, in fact, for you have men's respect. Kill him, Caius, and brazen it out with your Proconsulship, before he can be the death of all of us."

"That is insane. I have never heard you sound like this before, Luceiia. I find it hard to credit."

"I have never been threatened this way before! And I find your stupidity in this equally hard to credit. This man may be your enemy and you may treat him with your male nobility, God help you, but when he brings his verminous existence into *my* lands, threatening me and my children with dispossession and ruin—" She cut short her tirade, making a visible and strenuous effort to calm herself, after which she resumed in a more normal voice. "This plan of yours, may I hear its outline?"

"Of course you may, if you will promise to hear me out and not interrupt me like a fishwife, in the telling of it."

Her nostrils pinched as she drew breath at that, but she nodded, and Caius proceeded to outline his idea, clearing his throat again before commencing, and clearly expecting to be savaged at any point as he went on. Luceiia sat and listened as silently as she had promised, however, her face growing more and more flinty with each detail she heard.

"So," she said eventually, when her brother had finished speaking, her voice soft and yet chilling. "You would save my life and my children's lives— everyone's life, in fact—by offering my husband to this monster—falsely, of course—as a helpless prisoner, relying on your probity and strength to counterbalance and defeat his insanity? Is that what you are telling me?"

Caius grimaced and nodded. "You put it harshly but, yes, that is what I am saying."

"And what about you, husband? Are you prepared to put your trust in this scheme—to be offered, helpless and in chains, to Claudius Seneca?"

I nodded, feeling more in control of myself now. "I think it will work."

"You do? Then you are a fool, my love, and more so than my noble brother, for it will be your life in the hazard, here." Her eyes flicked back to Caius. "There will be a point at which you should know whether or not this can succeed. When will that be?"

"Tonight, within moments of Publius's first appearance on the scene."

"What will happen then?"

"There will be a clash of wills, of personalities, between myself and Seneca, and an assignation of loyalties by the officers in the imperial party. They will side either with me or with him."

"Hmm. What if Seneca attacks Publius immediately upon seeing him? He's mad enough to try."

"He will die, before he can even approach him. That might be the best thing that could happen, for he would be in flagrant violation of all the laws of conduct and hospitality."

"And what will it take to convince you that your plan has any chance of success?"

"The disposition of the loyalties of Seneca's escort, and their acceptance of my rank and station."

"And if they cleave to Seneca?"

"Publius will escape during the night, and the imperial party will be killed the following day."

"How?"

"I shall recall our forces tonight and attack them. We outnumber them by five to one."

"And after that, when they fail to return to Londinium?"

"Then we must take our chances. Nothing will have changed from your scenario. We will face death and outlawry. But I don't think that will happen."

"Oh, you don't. I see." I found myself disbelieving how cold and distant my wife had sounded throughout all of this exchange. "One more question. What if Seneca accepts what you say here, for the sake of appearances, and then kills Publius out on the road?"

"Not possible—no, let me restate that. It is possible, I grant, but highly improbable in the extreme. My decision to proceed will be based upon my interpretation of the calibre and trustworthiness of the officers of the escort. If I am not satisfied, we will not go. If we do go, Publius will be guarded night and day by our own people . . . Our very best people."

His sister turned away from him and walked across the room to the fireplace, where she stood staring down into the empty brazier for a long time. Finally she turned and looked from one of us to the other.

"Did you know, Caius, that there was a time when I feared having you discover that I had become a wealthy woman by inheriting the fortune of our Aunt Liga? I knew you disapproved of her, a woman, a Roman woman who had never married, earning all that wealth through commerce." She shook her head. "I was afraid that you, as a man, would disapprove of me, a woman . . . I know now that the difference between us, between men and women, is not one of sex, but one of *species*. We are different *animals*. And you men, I now know, are weaklings beside us, in matters such as this. Disapprove of that, brother." She looked now at me. "Go, then, play your silly, pointless, honorable games and dance the dance of destiny by your own rules. How long will you be gone?"

I shook my head, glancing at Caius. He shrugged.

"Three weeks, perhaps four."

Luceiia nodded. "Very well, I require that time for my own purposes. I have much to think upon. But know this, both of you. I will take no part in any of this foolishness. I have no wish to be involved in any way other than those I have to suffer as things are. Do not look for me to participate in any aspect of this folly, from this time forth. Go with God, both of you, but without me or my blessing. And, Caius, if you fail, if you lose my husband, don't come back."

She stalked from the room and left us staring at each other, round-eyed.

XII

IT WAS ALMOST dark by the time Vegetius Sulla opened the door of the stone hut that had become my prison. I was lying on the straw-covered floor, my arms and legs aching from the chains I wore. My left eye was swollen completely shut and crusted with blood where Vegetius himself had hit me with his sword hilt earlier. He stepped inside and squatted beside me.

"They're ready for you, Publius. The audience is assembled and the circus is prepared. Caius has told them all about you and how we captured you, and of our plans for you. Now they're waiting to see you. How do you feel?"

I tried to lick my sore lips, split by a backhanded blow when they first brought me here, and croaked, "Give me a drink." It tasted like nectar. I swallowed and spat. "How do I feel? That's a damned stupid question. How do I look?"

Vegetius winced. "Awful, and you stink like a goat, too. Exactly like a filthy, evil bandit who has been properly beaten since being captured."

"Good, that's how I'm supposed to look."

"Can you stand up?"

I tried. "No. You're going to have to help me."

He snapped a command and one of our young soldiers stepped into the hut and stopped there, his eyes widening as he looked at me in horror.

"Help the prisoner to his feet."

The young man bent to obey, handling me as if I were fragile, sheer reverence in his eyes. When I stood upright, Vegetius shoved a spear shaft through the space between my bent elbows and my back, pinioning me and stretching the chain on my manacled wrists across my belly.

The young soldier's eyes worried me.

"Wait!" They stopped and looked at me and I spoke to the young man, mouthing my words carefully with my broken lips. "Look, lad, this is being done for a purpose. Was that explained to you?" He nodded. "Good. Then get that look off your face. If they see it in there, you'll betray all of us. This is only mummery, but it has to look genuine. Remember, I am not Publius Varrus. I'm a captured rebel—a murderer and a bandit. I am a prisoner, and if you feel anything towards me at all, it should be indifference mixed with malice. Understand?" He nodded again. "All right then, make your face a mask and knock me down, hard. Then haul me back up and drag my butt in to Caius Britannicus."

He looked to Vegetius for confirmation.

Vegetius nodded. "Do it, hard, and treat him like cattle from now on. If these people suspect our motives, he's a dead man."

The young man set his jaw and swung the flat of his sword, knocking me off my feet and out of action.

I regained my senses as they dragged me in front of Caius and his visitors. I had two guards, one on either side of me grasping each end of the spear shaft across my back, carrying it on their shoulders so that my feet swung clear of the ground and all my weight hung from my tortured shoulder joints. I did not have to worry about acting, for my predicament and the pain it caused were very real. I heard someone snap an order to halt and the two guards carrying me stopped short and lowered my feet to the floor. My knees folded and I would have fallen had they not taken up the tension again and held me erect. I bit down hard, trying to pull myself together, and I heard what sounded like someone moaning in the distance. "Luceiia," I thought, "be strong! Don't let them see your pain." But the moaning went on, and I realized that it was me. I stopped it and hung there, supported by my guards.

"This is a general?" The voice was loaded with disdain. It was deep, and quite pleasant in pitch. I could not place it as belonging to the Seneca I remembered.

"No," Caius answered, "not a general, Claudius Seneca, merely a leader of rebels, that is all."

"He doesn't look much like a leader to me."

Caius sounded as though he was pleasantly relaxed, sprawling backwards in his chair as he spoke. "I will admit he looks a little more worn and a lot less warlike than when we took him. Without his armour and his weapons, and without his rebels, he has shrunk to human proportions. A week ago, however, I can assure you his reputation was fearsome and his depredations formidable."

The deep voice sounded bored. "Formidable out here in this backwater, perhaps. Elsewhere, he would have been a gnat to be swatted casually. The fellow is obviously a deserter. Hang him, I say, and have done with him."

"No." Caius again. I was surprised by the ease with which I could hear them discussing me. I was very close to their table. "No, he should be taken in an open cage to Londinium, to serve as an example, as I have said. He is a rebel. His humiliation should be public, and spectacular—used to discourage others from emulating him. To hang him out of hand would serve no useful purpose."

"I disagree." There was a note of petulance in the heavy voice now. "He would be dead. Deserters are to be executed immediately upon apprehension."

"This is no deserter, Senator. At least, I do not think so. He is a veteran, certainly, but I doubt that he deserted. The fellow is crippled. It is an old wound and a grave one; it would have ended his service."

"Nonsense, Caius Britannicus! He could have taken a wound at any time."

"Not that one, Senator. Not if he were a deserter. It would have killed him. He could not have recovered from a wound like that outside of a military hospital."

There was a long silence after this when no one spoke at all, and I could feel the eyes of all of them on me. Then that voice spoke again, sullen, like that of a spoiled child speaking through an adult's mouth.

"By all the ancient gods, Caius Britannicus, you are a tedious man! My men have travelled with me all across this land to draw some blood and you have robbed them of their just satisfaction! How could you have done all you have said, fought the engagement that you have described, and taken but one prisoner?" He paused as though waiting for a reply, and when none came the strangely whining, petulant, bass-voiced complaint continued. "You have no answer? Then let me tell you what I think. I think you might be making more of this than was the case. I think you would like us to believe that you have won a major victory here, when all that happened was a minor squabble. I think that tomorrow we will ride with you to view the ruins of this rebel's camp and count the bodies of his slain companions, and I think that we had better—"

"Claudius Seneca!" Caius's voice cracked like a whip. "*I think* I will be happy to do as you suggest, but *I also think* that when I have done so, you should be prepared to render me a fair apology for any slur you might have thought to cast upon my honour! *I also think* you might be slightly overtired after your long and exhausting journey. I do *not* think, however, that you would wish me to think you are questioning my truthfulness."

There was no disguising the challenge carried in the emphasis of his words. Seneca remained silent, and Caius continued. "And while we are discussing thoughts so freely, think upon this. My men are not soldiers of Rome. They are farmers and artisans, solid and seldom impetuous. When they are threatened, however, they retaliate. When they are injured, they exact revenge. And when they have been angered thoroughly enough to seek revenge, they do not think of taking prisoners! We do not have jails, nor jailers here. I called for the rebel leader only. The man you see before you is the only prisoner here. Their general, as you called him. Their limping, crippled god—their savage, grey-haired Vulcan! He will hang soon enough, but in Londinium, and I will take him there myself. Take him away!" This last was to my guards, who began to swing me around.

"Wait!" The voice almost squeaked. The bait was taken. I drew a deep, painful breath. "What did you say, Britannicus? What did you call him?"

"Call him? Vulcan, I called him, after the crippled god."

"Is that his name? Vulcan?" The venomous, hissing voice now reminded me of a serpent. "Hold up his head! Let me see his face!"

I felt fingers take hold of my hair and jerk my head back painfully. Through the tears that instantly flooded my eyes, I saw the man approach me, gliding almost sideways as though prepared to leap away again to safety at any sign of threat. Closer he came, and closer, peering into my blood-and-dirt-encrusted face, seeking a memory.

"It could be," he whispered. "Stand away from him!" He was shrieking now at my guards. "Let him stand alone!" I felt the support go from me and took my weight fully on my own feet. Seneca stepped back from me, his arms stretched out towards me, fingers beckoning. I blinked my eyes clear. Caius stood crouched behind him, ready to spring. Everyone else at the table looked incredulous. I fastened my eyes on Seneca, whose own were blazing as he whispered, "You! It is you, isn't it? Come, walk to me, you whoreson!"

I swayed, but made no move towards him, recalling Plautus's words that first time we met him: the face of a god and the personality of a pit viper. Today's god had a badly broken nose. He began circling to my left, out of my view, and I ignored him, looking instead at the strangers in the group around the table. There were four of them, all young, all watching Seneca as children would watch a new-found, ugly lizard. Suddenly, he grasped the end of the spear shaft, wrenched me violently around and pushed me with the flat of his foot. "Walk, you whoreson!" I stumbled forward and fell face down. As I lay there he kicked me full in the side, and I heard Caius shout his name. A wave of nausea swept over me and I almost fainted. I could hear him ranting above me, and then the two guards were hauling me back to my feet again. Seneca had his back to me, gesticulating wildly, shouting at the group around the table. I swallowed thickly, trying to swallow all my pain.

"Seneca!" I did not have to say it loudly. He froze in mid-gesture and turned slowly towards me, an expression of almost comic recognition on his face at hearing my voice. I forced myself to smile. "You sorry pederast. I gave in to my disgust and left you to die last time we met, instead of killing you outright as I should have. Next time I have you on the blade of my sword, be certain I shall cut off your head the way I would any other serpent's."

His eyes flared and he screamed and a knife appeared in his hand as if by magic. He flung himself at me, but fast as he was, Vegetius Sulla was faster and had him in an arm-hold before he could close on me. The whole room erupted and I heard Caius roaring, "Get that man out of here! Back to his cell! Chain him to the floor!"

They dragged me away.

Hours later, in the dead of night before dawn, Caius came to me and sat beside me on the floor, stroking my hair and laying his hand on my neck.

"Well?" I croaked. "How did we do?"

He shook his head. "It could not have gone better for us, Publius. My only sorrow is that you have to suffer like this."

I grunted. "If it will confound that rabid son of a mangy bitch, I will take ten times as much. Didn't I tell you? Is he not wondrous to behold?"

"He is a mad dog. His soldiers are in terror of him." He shook his head. "Publius, he is far worse than you had described him, and you never lacked fervour in condemning him."

I straightened my legs slightly and groaned with the pain of it. "What happened after I left?"

Caius sighed. "We calmed him, finally, but he and I had harsh words. Fortunately, he had placed himself so firmly in the wrong that even his own officers had to side with me. I waved my Proconsul's baton and dictated the law to him. He hates me now, I think, far more than a mere Britannicus. He hates me almost as he does you."

"Aye, it does not take much to earn his hate, from all I've heard of him. Be careful, Cay. He is an ill man to cross."

"So am I, Publius, so am I. But I am not stupid, and so I will be careful, for both our sakes. He left the dining room in extreme anger, but he went to bed eventually, and will sleep well, aided by the last cup of wine he had."

"You drugged him?"

He nodded. "That way he can be trusted not to do anything impetuous." He stopped and squeezed my shoulder. "But you have not heard the good news! Seneca came to Britain to prepare the way for Stilicho's arrival! There has been a major invasion again, from the north, and the young officer told me that Stilicho came in person to put it down. He should be in Londinium by the time we arrive there. That means Picus will be there, too. As Regent, and as Commander-in-Chief, Stilicho will hear your case upon my insistence. We have won before we've set out, Publius!"

I made to move and winced again. "Don't say all your prayers of gratitude prematurely, Cay. You still have to get me there alive. Don't ever lose sight for one moment of the fact that this mad whoreson has a lot of vengeance to work out on me—for spoiling his pretty face, and then for abducting him, exposing his treason and forcing him to acknowledge it. All of those will be larger in his sick mind than the fact that I then tried to kill him."

"You'll be alive, my friend. Now try to sleep. Tomorrow morning I will have you brought before me formally for arraignment in the murders of Quinctilius Nesca and his men, for assault and mutilation upon Seneca as an ambassador of Valentinian and for rebellion and banditry. Any one of those charges is serious enough to guarantee you safe conduct to Londinium for trial and execution."

"Thank you, Caius," I said. "That makes me feel much better. I can sleep easy now."

It was a long, brutal journey to Londinium, and I saw it from the worst of all viewpoints.

Seneca flatly refused Caius's proposal that I be permitted to ride, strapped to a horse. He insisted that I should go on foot, or be dragged behind a horse.

Caius objected, arguing that this would slow the entire column down intolerably and that he had affairs to deal with in Londinium that would not permit delays of any kind. Besides, he contended, I was his prisoner and he wanted me fit to be tried and hanged at journey's end. He suggested that they build a cage on the bed of a cart and confine me there.

Seneca objected to what he termed the luxury of such a conveyance. I was a criminal taken under arms, and therefore under sentence of death

already. I must be made an example to everyone meeting us on the road—
Caius's own original contention—so there could be no hint of softness in
the treatment accorded me. On this point Caius could not reasonably disagree,
and so they compromised. I would travel on a cart, but in a manner of Seneca's
devising. Caius told me this in the dead of the night before we were to leave.
He felt terrible, I could see, about the way in which I would be forced to
spend the next week, but I shrugged my shoulders and told him to put it
out of his mind. I would be riding, even on a cart. That had to be better
than walking the entire distance to Londinium.

I must have been mad to think so, knowing that Seneca had the ordering
of my passage.

Nevertheless, I slept well that night, aware that the men who guarded
me would be my own. All of them knew what was happening, and I would
have trusted any of them with my life without a moment's thought. It occurred
to me just before I fell asleep that that was exactly what I was doing.

They took me out before dawn and allowed me to wash in cold water
before leading me to my cart. I blinked at it in the pre-dawn light, seeing
only the single pole that had been sunk into the floorboards and fastened
securely with braces. Only my own men were around as they helped me up
on the flat bed, and there we waited for a space. Finally Draco, the chief of
my guards, spoke in a low voice.

"I don't like this one little bit, Commander. Not one bit, and neither do
the others. You say the word and we'll have you out of here in no time."

I grinned at him in the greying light and stretched my arms straight
downward, not wanting to look too relaxed in case we were being watched.
"Don't worry about it, Draco. It's better than having to walk. I'll be all right."

"You think so?" His voice was an angry growl. "I doubt it. We're waiting for
chains. That whoreson wants to keep you standing all the way to Londinium."

"So? Then I'll stand. I've spent half my life standing, usually over a forge."

"Aye, but not chained to the damned thing. You are to be chained to
that post. You won't be able to fall down, even if you pass out."

"Then I won't pass out. We'll be in Londinium within the week. After
that, everything will be fine."

"Hum! I hope you're right. But a week's a long time to stay on your feet."

"I'll manage it."

I could see his face clearly now. There was an expression of doubt and
concern stamped on his features. "I hope so, Commander Varrus, I hope so.
But I'll tell you, the moment you pass out, or one of these fancy horse-topping
bastards starts to abuse you, that'll be the end of it. We'll spill blood."

I reached out and laid my hand on his arm, swiftly and cautiously. "No.
You will not. But I thank you for the concern, Draco. I think the only time
you will have to worry for my safety is at night, and even then, there should
be little danger."

"Aye. Here comes their armourer."

I heard the clank of chains and the sound of hobnailed sandals approaching, and one of Seneca's centurions came straight towards us and vaulted nimbly up to where I waited. I was looking curiously at the apparatus he held in his huge hand but could not make it out clearly, except for the coils of chains. He left me little time to wonder what it was, for he dropped the long length of chains on the wooden deck and hoisted the thing up to my gaze.

"Right. Let's see you get out of this, rebel," he snarled.

The apparatus was a pair of thick, wide leather belts, one much longer than the other, joined by two short lengths of chain. These chains were attached to each of the belts by strong rings through the leather. He buckled the larger of the belts around my waist, tight, and then attached the smaller one to the thick post behind me. I stood motionless until he was finished, and then tested the strength of my binding. It was solid. I could sway my body no more than two handspans to right or left, and had no hope of sitting down. The thought of just relaxing occurred to me, and I bent my knees, letting the whole of my body weight drop into the belt. It was thick and solid, catching painfully beneath my rib-cage. Little hope of comfort there.

"All right, take off those irons on his wrists."

I held out my hands and Draco unfastened the light manacles I wore.

The centurion chuckled and jumped down from the cart again. "You're going to love this, rebel."

I watched, uncomprehending, as he raised a thick, heavy iron ring that had been fastened to the side of the cart directly to my right and fed one end of the long chain through it. It was a big ring. Big enough for the manacle on the end of the chain to pass through it easily. And it was a thick, heavy manacle, too. Much bigger than the ones Draco had just taken off me.

"You're just going to love this," he said again, talking to himself more than to me, and he sprang back up onto the bed of the cart, breathing slightly more heavily now. I was looking at the chain. It was almost six paces in length and it was strong. I knew, because I had forged it myself, though someone else had added the manacles to it. He squatted at my feet and reached across to thread the manacle on the other end through a matching ring on the opposite side of the cart, pulling it firmly through and straightening up to face me.

"Now," he said, and he smiled so that I wanted to kick him in the balls. "Let's have your wrists. Hold them out."

I did. I had no choice. The manacles were tight, biting at my wrists, which had always been thick.

"Now, one wrong move and I'll smash your lights out," he grunted, fumbling at his belt with one hand while he held the hinged clasp about my right wrist with the other. He produced a length of iron wire, again my own, I suspected, and held it in his teeth while he drew out a pair of small tong-like pincers that had also been stuck in his belt. Then, his breath coming more and more rapidly as he concentrated, he threaded the iron wire through the bolt holes of the manacle and began to twist the ends with the pincers, drawing the halves of the bracelet together until I hissed with pain. When he was satisfied that it was tight enough, he repeated the procedure with my other wrist. I gritted my teeth in silence, but I knew then it was going to be a long journey.

"Good!" He stepped back and surveyed the job he had done. "Now!" He knelt at my feet and took twin grips on the chain, pulling it both ways through the ring bolts at the side of the cart until my arms were taut. He gauged the tension of my arms, and then released the pressure so that they sagged a little. "That's better! We don't want it too tight, do we?"

"Don't we?" I asked, trying to keep my voice unconcerned. "Why not?"

"Well, rebel, we have to leave you room to sway with the wagon."

He ignored me then and returned to his work and I watched in wonder as he drew carefully at the chain in each of his hands, gauging and adjusting until at last he had two links touching, one protruding from each of his fists, with the remainder of the chain, the middle part, piled beneath.

"Here. You. Give me a hand here!"

Draco had been standing by all this time, watching in silence, and I could see from his face that he was about to explode. I frowned at him, catching his eye, and shook my head warningly, indicating that he should do as the centurion demanded. He knelt beside him, his face a study of disgust.

"What?"

"Hold these links while I bind them together." He repeated his trick with the iron wire, binding the links together strongly, and I still could not see the purpose behind this. The chain was far too long. It would have been a simple matter to measure the length needed and shorten it. Draco thought the same thing. "Why not just shorten the chain?" he asked.

"Ah!" said the centurion. "That's what I thought, too, at first. But then the Lord Seneca pointed out to me what it was he wanted. Look closely at the join here. What's beneath it?"

"His feet."

"That's right! Well done, lad! His feet. But they're not going to stay there, are they? We're going to ask him to move them. Aren't we?" As he said this, he whipped a short, heavy hammer from the back of his belt and rapped me painfully on the instep. I whipped my feet away, awkwardly, for I could hardly move, and then watched in disbelief as he hammered two long nails into the floor of the cart and then bludgeoned them over until they held the chain firmly in place directly beneath the point where my feet had been. And then it became deadly clear what he had been doing as he shovelled the remaining pile of chain directly beneath me, knocking my feet aside again with his hammer so that I would have fallen but for the way I was bound.

"We want to give him something to stand on, don't we? So he won't get splinters in his feet from these rough boards. There you go, rebel. You're all set. Enjoy your journey."

Draco was staring open-mouthed, just beginning to grasp what had been done, but I was far ahead of him. I would have to stand on these chains all the way to Londinium. My feet were sore already, thinking of it.

The entire villa staff turned out to see us leave, and they all stared solemnly and silently at the spectacle of me chained erect and dirtier than any of them had ever seen me before. I kept my chin up and tried to look at nobody directly. Luceiia was nowhere to be seen, but I had not expected her to be. Nevertheless, I looked about in search of her, hoping against hope, my chest aching with the knowledge of what I had done to her with my accursed, self-willed secrecy, and the extent to which I had destroyed her trust in my truthfulness. Unable then to bear the thought of her hurt and anger, I forced myself to pay attention to other things, emptying my mind of self-pitying thoughts as well as I was able, and staring straight-faced at the orderly bustle of the assembly all about me.

Caius came and looked at me and how I was bound, and his mouth tightened to a lipless line. Afraid he might betray himself, I spat at him, playing my part and willing him to silence, and he shook his head in a tiny gesture of furious disgust before walking to his own wagon.

As the wagon-driver climbed into his seat and the cavalcade formed up, I looked around me for one last time, raising my eyes to the forested hill in the middle distance. Its top shrouded in heavy, low-lying cloud, it looked magnificent, and there was no sign that it held anything but forest. And because of the furore my "capture" had caused, there was now no danger of its being detected for what it was. As I gazed at it, a heavy drop of water landed on my face and it began to rain. Someone shouted a command from the head of the line, and the entire cavalcade began to move out. My driver cracked his whip and we took our place in the middle of the column, with Seneca's troops ahead of us and my own men falling in behind. We left in a clatter of hooves and creaking of cart wheels, but nobody uttered a word. Not even Seneca, whom I had expected to gloat.

We had no sooner started to move than I discovered the true extent of my plight. As long as the road was even, my position was bearable, at least in the beginning. On uneven surfaces, however, it was impossible for me to keep my balance. The unevenness and hardness of the chains directly beneath my feet was agony, and I had constant cause to regret that my legs were so dissimilar in length and strength. I tried kicking the chains from beneath my feet, but they were nailed in place, so that even with the pile of them pushed forward, the two straight lines from right and left cut cruelly into my soles. And after a time, the pain of being unable to hold my arms straight down became unbearable and my muscles screamed in agony. I began to fall, at least as far as my chains would permit me before pulling me up short. My wrists bled and scabbed over and bled again from the jerking of my irons each time the cart lurched enough to upset my balance.

It rained almost without let-up for the first two days and nights. I slept chained to my stake. I pissed where I stood, unable to direct the flow, but I managed to restrain my bowels for two days. Some time during the third day, dying in my own stink and pain, I lost consciousness.

The pain in my wrists brought me awake again and I opened my eyes to find myself lying by the side of the road, looking up at the damnable cart with its upright stake. It was not moving, and neither was I. I was aware of someone holding my head, and of angry voices shouting somewhere close by. My stomach spasmed and cramped and I vomited without the strength to turn my head. I felt myself being turned over, quickly, and the motion brought a sullen dizziness that sent me spinning into blackness again.

When I next opened my eyes, I was in a prison: a huge, stone, vaulted room with heavily barred doors and only a hint of light coming through a tiny, barred window high up on one wall. I lay there amazed and took my time looking around me, making no sudden moves. A cresset fluttered in an iron brazier above my head, its flames jumping wildly in a breeze that must have come from the high window. I was alone in the huge room. No other prisoners. I moved my arm stealthily, expecting to feel the tug of manacles, but there was none. I was unbound.

Slowly, for I was in no hurry to jump up, not knowing where I was or who my hosts might be, I explored the place with my eyes and my hands. I was lying on a thin mattress on a stone bench. Directly above my head, dangling towards me as though to mock, a set of manacles hung on rusted chains from a great ring set into the wall. On the far side of the room, close by the barred doorway, a pile of fresh-looking straw had been thrown on the floor. Beside it lay a metal bowl and a jug that looked as though it might hold water. I saw more manacles hanging on the walls all around the room. Six more cressets flickered and guttered, throwing fitful shadows on the walls. The rippling of their fluttering flames was the only sound in the place. I sniffed deeply, searching for smells, and smelled only a lingering unpleasantness that seemed ingrained in the walls—a mixture of unwashed bodies and the aromas they produced.

I raised myself cautiously onto one elbow and a wave of nausea swept me, making me shudder and grit my teeth to keep my stomach in place. I fought the urge to retch as my eyes teared over, making my vision swim. Grimly, I hung there and forced my rebellious body to submit to my will. I had been sick enough, obviously, to have come to this place with no recollection of anything beyond that last stark vision of the cart looming above me. I would be sick no more. At last, when the dizziness subsided, I was able to turn my head. The stone bench I lay on ran the entire circumference of the room, except for the wall the door was set into. It was a big room. I had no idea where I was, but I began to suspect that it must be Londinium. I swung myself up to a sitting position with great, grunting effort and earned another fit of weakness for my pains, this time accompanied by a pounding ache deep inside my skull. I attempted to ease my legs off the side of the bench so that I could rest my back against the wall and they *fell* off, almost overbalancing me with their sudden, uncontrollable weight. Fear flared in me like a new-kindled fire. I was as weak as a baby!

I sat there helplessly, drawing deep, ragged breaths, afraid to put myself to any further tests. I knew without a doubt that if I attempted to stand up I would fall to the floor. My mind was racing uselessly, trying to come to terms with this weakness, trying to close upon a reason for it, trying to reconstruct what must have happened to me. It was hopeless, and I succeeded only in frightening myself further. I knew only that if I was this weak, I must have been close to death. I forced myself to close my eyes and breathe deeply and regularly, battling my panic and trying to rally my strength. And then I began to cough. And once I started, I could not stop myself. The coughing racked me, harsh and painful, tearing at my lungs and stomach muscles. I almost fell from the bench, stopping myself only by bracing my arms against the edge of my seat. Great, gurgling globs of phlegm rattled in my chest and surged up in my throat and I barely had the strength to spit, so that saliva dribbled from my chin. Eventually the spasms weakened and died down and I sat there, uncaring, grateful only for the lessening of the torment.

"So, you're awake."

The voice came from the doorway. I raised my head and peered to see who spoke, blinking my eyes to clear my vision. It was a soldier, obviously one of the guards. A stranger. I tried to focus on his uniform, searching for some clue to his identity, but I saw none. He wore the simple, unadorned leather harness of the standard garrison trooper. I watched him as he crossed towards me, making no attempt to close the door behind him. He stopped about two paces in front of me, looking down at me from what seemed to be a great height. I licked my gummy lips and tried to speak, to ask him where I was. Nothing came out. He curled his lip and sucked noisily at a morsel of food caught between his teeth. I waited.

"You're a tough bird, for a rebel. We all thought you were dead, for sure. But you're too damn mean to die, aren't you?" He expected no answer and waited for none. "Here." He turned and recrossed the room to the door, picking up the jug and bringing it back to me. "Try drinking this."

I took the jug, and half full as it was, it was all I could do to raise it to my lips. It was wine and water mixed, and it tasted like nectar. I sluiced it around my mouth and felt it cleanse me.

"That's enough! Don't want you puking all over the floor." He took the jug away from me again but placed it on the floor where I could reach it. Now I could talk, I felt.

"Where am I?"

"Londinium. In the Imperial Prison, awaiting trial and hanging."

That was not cheering news. "Where are my friends?"

"What friends? You have none. Some of your guards have spent time down here with you, though. You're a very valuable prisoner, it seems. They don't want to lose you. Not to sickness, and not to Seneca's people."

"Is Seneca here? Why am I not chained?"

"Not chained? Damnation, we're not barbarians! We don't chain corpses any longer. And no, Seneca's not here. This is a prison, didn't you hear me? Seneca lives in a villa. Go to sleep while you can. Your own guards will be back soon. They told me to call them if there was any sign of life about you. Are you hungry?" I shook my head. "Well, there's food in the bowl over there if you are. I'll bring it over." He did so, leaving it beside the water jug. "Sleep, rebel." His voice was not unkind. "It'll help you regain your strength, now that you've come back to life. And don't even think about escaping. You couldn't walk across this room."

He turned to leave and I stopped him. "How long have I been here?"

He made a face, shaking his head. "Don't know. You were here when I took over this duty. That's a week ago. You'd been here for about a week before that."

Two weeks! Where was Caius? What was going on here? I lay back on my pallet and tried to take his advice, but I did not expect to sleep.

Next thing I knew, however, I was waking to find Draco looking down at me. Before I could open my mouth in greeting, though, he turned to the two men with him and growled, "You were right. The whoreson is alive. I didn't think he'd make it." To the man on his right he said, "Check him. Carefully. Caius Britannicus will not thank you if you promise him an execution after all and then let this swine die."

The man addressed, obviously a physician from his looks and dress, stepped forward and began to palpate me, turning me over gently to reach the back of my ribcage. His fingers on my skin were cold and prodding and none too gentle. He finished his examination by laying his hand on my forehead and then turning up my eyelids and peering into my eyes.

"Well?" Draco's voice was an ill-tempered growl. "What?"

The physician straightened up with a sigh. "He will live to die at your pleasure. But he is still extremely weak. You should not try to move him for at least two days, and he must be well fed from this time on. Hot broths and potions of strong herbs. I will bring the herbs."

"To Hades with your herbs. He won't need them."

"He needs them! If you wish to have your trial and your execution and your general amusement with the man, you will have to build his strength. Try to move him now, abuse him at all, and I will take no responsibility. He should be dead already. He will be if you do not do as I say. Hot meat broths and herbal potions. On your head be it, otherwise."

Draco threw me a venomous look filled with such hatred that even I believed it. The physician glanced at the other man who stood with them, a simple soldier, and then back to Draco. "Why do you hate this man so much?" he asked.

"Hate him? The whoreson killed my wife. Get out, both of you. Out!"

They left abruptly, and he stood above me, watching them until the gate of the cell closed heavily. I lay and watched him, attempting no move while his eyes remained fixed on their departing backs. When he was satisfied that they were gone, he stooped and picked up the drinking jug, bringing it to my lips and supporting my head with his forearm. The water and wine mixture tasted as good as it had the first time I tasted it. When I had drunk, he laid my head back gently on my paillasse.

"You hate hard, Draco," I said. "I didn't know you ever had a wife." My voice was behaving normally now.

He half grinned and shrugged his shoulders. "Blame Britannicus. He has turned all of us into mummers."

"Mummers? Why? What has happened?"

He moved and sat at my feet on the ledge that supported my mattress, leaning back against the wall and fixing his eyes watchfully on the door in the far wall.

"Lie still and keep your eyes closed, as though you were asleep again. But listen closely, I don't want to speak too loudly. How much do you remember of the journey?"

"Rain," I said. "I remember rain and pain. That is all."

"That's all? You remember nothing after we cut you loose from the chains?"

"Draco," I said, "I don't even remember that. The last thing I recall is lying on the roadside, looking up at the cart and being sick. After that there is nothing until I woke up here."

"Well, we thought we were going to lose you and we nearly had a war with Seneca's people. He almost threw a fit when we started to take you out of the chains. He was going to kill me. Then Britannicus came up and those two almost came to blows. Seneca tried to attack Britannicus, started to draw his sword."

"Against Britannicus? What happened? Was Caius hurt?"

"Nah!" He shook his head, his eyes still fixed on the doorway across from us. "I'll be back."

He stood up and moved quickly across the large cell. I turned my head to watch him as he reached the doorway and leaned close to the bars, checking that no one stood there listening. He came back and sat again.

"The officer. The regular commander. He stopped Seneca before he even got his sword out. Saved his life. Grabbed him and wrestled with him. Threatened to have him in chains in your place if he didn't start behaving like a Roman officer and a patrician. Marched him off under escort to his own place in the train and apologized to Britannicus."

"You say 'saved his life.' How? Would Caius have beaten him to the thrust?"

Draco shook his head. "No. But I would. I was angry enough to kill him. I told you he was going for me when Britannicus came along. I had my dagger out as soon as he turned on the old man. It would have been between his ribs inside a heartbeat if the other officer, Tribune Vicere, hadn't jumped on him."

"I see." I thought about that. I remembered the angry voices I had heard on regaining consciousness there by the roadside. "So then what happened?"

"That's when we started play-acting. More to drink?"

I shook my head and he helped himself to a mouthful of wine and water, and then I lay there and listened intently as he told me the whole story.

Draco had been true to his word, it seemed. He had watched me closely in my impossible situation, braced upright as I was and unable to relax or defend myself against the onslaught of the incessant, chilling rain for two days and a night. When I finally turned up my eyes into my head and collapsed against the restraints that bound me, he had been less than three paces from me and had estimated correctly that I was not going to recover this time. He had leaped up onto the bed of the cart immediately and set about sawing through the leather belts that held me imprisoned, paying no heed to whether he was being observed or not. As it turned out, his actions went unnoticed until the last leather strap gave way, allowing me to sprawl in an unconscious heap on the bed of the cart, tethered only by the iron shackles and chains around my wrists. It was the noise and the sight of my falling that finally attracted the attention of the regular soldiers and brought Seneca, fuming with anger, down around Draco's neck.

At first, he had ignored Seneca's ranting entirely. He had taken up a heavy maul from the bed of the cart and set about hammering at the iron ring set into the side of the cart, through which my chains were threaded. As soon as he had pounded it loose, he threw the maul across the cart to another of our men on the opposite side, who set about loosening the second ring. It was this flagrant refusal to recognize his presence and authority that snapped something inside of Seneca, and Draco might well have died then and there had Caius not turned up to intervene. Seneca, however, was not to be gainsaid. He saw his vengeance on me about to be thwarted and he was not prepared to let that happen. The second ring gave way, Draco dragged me from the cart and lowered me to the ground by the roadside, Seneca aimed a kick at him and Caius stepped between them. Seneca was deranged. He started to draw his sword from its scabbard, apparently with every intention of attacking Caius, and he was leaped on at that point by the officer in command, Vicere, who promptly placed him under restraint and had him removed from the scene by an armed escort. It was during this angry confrontation that I had briefly regained consciousness and been sick before passing out again.

Marcellus Vicere, it seemed, was an honourable man with no hint of vindictiveness about him. Having made the decision to place Seneca under arrest, at least temporarily, he was able to look objectively at my situation and consider it from the viewpoint of Caius, who was adamant that I must survive the journey in a condition to stand trial for my crimes before a military tribunal. He called a halt to the progress of the train and allowed his physician to examine me. But he was too late. The physician had been unable to recall me to consciousness and a high fever had set in. All that they could do was keep me warm and reasonably comfortable for the rest of the journey and hope that I would survive the passage.

Two nights later, while the party was encamped, another of our men, by the pure good fortune of being in the right place at the wrong time, was able to interrupt an attempt on my life. He had come off picket duty and passed by the tent where I was being held just in time to see a muffled figure slip furtively through the tent opening. He investigated and found the intruder in the act of trying to smother me. They struggled and the interloper managed to escape. The soldier who should have been guarding me was nowhere to be found, and was not seen again; a thorough search of the surrounding area next morning yielded no sign of him, so it was concluded that he had been the unsuccessful assassin.

Everybody knew who had suborned the man, but there was not a shred of evidence to support the knowledge, nor a hint of proof.

From that time onward, however, it was the retainers of Caius Britannicus who stood guard over me. Caius had told his men that they should appear, to all men and at all times, to hate me virulently, so that only their own loyalty to Caius kept them from killing me themselves.

I survived my fever and lung congestion, and they brought me here to this prison, where I had struggled against the sickness now for two weeks. Caius had been almost distraught with apprehension lest I should die, and had detailed his men so that at least one of them was always on duty, watching over me, even though the danger from Seneca seemed safely past now that we were in Londinium and I was an official prisoner of the Empire.

When Draco had finished his story there was silence between us for a few moments, and I found my eyelids drooping in spite of any effort I made to stop them. He told me to sleep, that he would still be there when I awoke, and I slept.

Some time later, I have no idea how long, I awoke to hear him arguing with someone, although I could not make out what was being said. Finally, I heard his footsteps returning and heard him muttering ill-naturedly about a waste of good food and drink on an unnatural whoreson. I lay with my eyes closed and waited patiently for him to "rouse" me. He did. We were alone again.

"Here, Commander, drink this. It'll set you up." He was holding a steaming bowl of beef broth with herbs and spices in it, and at the first sip of it, the saliva squirted from beneath my tongue. I was ravenous. When it was all gone, I felt much better, stronger already.

"I'll get you some more later. How do you feel?"

"Better," I said. "Have you sent word to General Britannicus that I am recovering?"

He nodded. "Aye, but he won't have received it yet. He rode out with the Regent, Stilicho, this morning, and has not returned."

"*Stilicho*? Stilicho is here?"

Draco grinned. "Aye, Commander, Stilicho is here. Here, there and everywhere. He has not spent two days in Londinium, they tell me, since he landed in Britain nigh on a month ago. General Britannicus waited for over a week for him to return. Stilicho came back four days ago, and the General was only able to gain audience with him this morning. He went to wait on the Regent shortly after daybreak, was cloistered with him for three full hours and then rode off with him to the south. I know not where they went, nor when they'll be back."

I thought about that for a time. "Good," I decided eventually. "The longer they remain absent, the stronger I shall grow." Another thought occurred to me, and I posed the question to him as soon as it formed in my mind. "What about my case? Do you hear anything of it?"

He grinned again and shook his head. "No, Commander. Nobody talks about you. You are not the most famed brigand of the ages. Few people know you are here, apart from ourselves and Seneca's people. And Stilicho, now, I suppose."

I looked around the huge cell. "Why am I alone here? Do you know?"

"Aye, I know. When Stilicho arrived this place was full. He emptied it. Tried everyone, hanged most of them and let the others go free. No one else seems disposed to try his hospitality."

A cold shadow seemed to pass across me, chilling me again momentarily. "What is he like, Draco, this Stilicho? Have you seen him?"

He shook his head. "Nah. He's the Emperor's Regent, Commander. Ordinary people like us never see the likes of him, even from a distance. But that's acceptable. I hope never to see him, or the Emperor. It would only remind me of how I resent the riches of others."

I found the strength to smile at his little joke. "Now," I asked him. "What happens now? Will Caius come here, do you think?"

"Be sure of it, Commander. His orders were clear. He was to be informed of your condition the moment you showed signs of regaining consciousness. From that time on, no less than two of us are to be on duty at all times for your protection."

"Two, plus the regulars outside?"

"Aye, for the time being."

I moved to sit up, but I still felt very weak. I knew that the best thing I could do for myself now was to rest until my next hot meal came, to conserve my energies and build up my strength. I thanked Draco for his kindness and begged him to allow me to rest.

XIII

DRACO WAS WRONG. Caius did not come to see me. Now that I had regained consciousness, however, my recovery was a quick one. I gained strength by the hour, helped by the nourishing broths and eventually by the solid, wholesome food that Draco and the others made such a show of begrudging me. I knew that Caius had returned to Londinium with Stilicho late on that first evening, because he sent word to me that he was back and happy to hear that I was better, but he did not come himself. The following day, Draco brought me a letter written in Caius's familiar hand. I read it immediately, sitting up on my bench now without effort. It was terse and unsigned.

I rejoice that you are better and improving rapidly. You frightened all of us for a while. I may not come to you; the dangers are too great. Be assured that I have not been idle on your behalf. Much has been done. More remains to be done. You will be brought to trial soon. Have no fears. This travesty will soon be dealt with and forgotten by all of us. Rufinus is dead. Your enemy has no friends in the Empire now. Do not be tempted to keep this. Give it back to the messenger to return to me.

I read the missive three times before re-rolling it and handing it back to Draco. "What dangers are too great?" I asked him.

He shrugged. "Seneca's the danger. He has men everywhere. If Caius Britannicus were to visit you, it would be reported, and that would do no one any good. Seneca's completely fooled, we think. He has no idea of how we really feel about you. He believes that you really are the rebel we said you are."

"So? I can understand that. But who is Rufinus? I know the name but cannot place it with a face or a position."

"Regent in the East as Stilicho is in the West."

As soon as he said the words, I remembered. Picus had told us in a letter how Theodosius had split the guarding of his twin sons between his two finest commanders, Flavius Stilicho and Flavius Rufinus. Divide and conquer. While each of them lived, there could be little danger of the other usurping the children's thrones.

I pondered that one. "What has that to do with Seneca?"

Draco grinned and shrugged his shoulders. "Nothing, and everything.

189

Seneca was a spy for Rufinus, it seems. Set to keep watch on Stilicho. Now Rufinus is dead."

I gaped at him. "How do you know that?"

He grinned. "The General told me. Stilicho told him." I was not the only one of Cay's veterans who still referred to him as "the General."

"Stilicho knew? And did nothing?"

"Couldn't. Devious reasons, I'm told. Too many people could be hurt if he did anything. So he put up with it. And with Seneca."

"Britannicus told you this? To tell me?"

"Why else? None of my affair."

"How did Rufinus die?"

Draco made a face and shook his head, indicating ignorance and indifference.

"And Seneca knows nothing of this?"

"Nothing. Only Stilicho knows. And Britannicus, and me, and now you."

I was mystified. "Why would he tell me this? I am to be tried soon. How soon? Do you know?" He shook his head. "Does Caius Britannicus know?" Again a head shake. I tutted in frustration and waved him away, and he left me alone to practise walking and struggle with my thoughts, which were far from tranquil.

Two days later I was awakened by my regular guards and told that I was to be indicted before a military tribunal that same morning. They hauled me upright, bound me with walking chains around my ankles and shackled my hands behind my back. I was almost sick with terror, and more than aware of the weakness in my legs, as they marched me out of my cell and up a long and winding stairway, where I teetered insecurely alongside the vertiginous depths of the stairwell. A long passageway at the top of the stairs led to an inner courtyard, and the brightness of the morning sun blinded me after the gloom and darkness I had become used to. But even as we walked, I felt myself grow stronger, and soon I was stepping almost normally for me, feeling the tug of the chains and hearing their metallic rattle at every step I took. The dazzle left my eyes and I began to see again, and the first thing I saw was my own filth-encrusted tunic; and then, out in the brightness and the clean air, I smelled my own stink and it was almost enough to make me retch. The tribunal, I thought bitterly, would really be impressed by my appearance.

I had a surprise in store, however, for my guards led me directly to a bath house where they undid my chains and stripped me and let me bathe in cold water. When I had finished, they threw me a bundle of clothes that were clean, compared to those I had discarded. None of the six men escorting me spoke or took his eyes from me for a moment. When I was dressed, they chained me again and we continued our journey towards the central complex of the military headquarters buildings. With the wash and the change of clothes, I felt better than I had in weeks, and I began to tell myself that I could feel confident in Caius's judgment. But I was difficult to convince.

There was no doubt that the Imperial Presence was here in Londinium.

Even in the alleys and rear passageways of the buildings there were Imperial Household Troops everywhere. Security was absolute. My escort passed me through a series of checkpoints, each progressively more thorough, until we entered one building and found ourselves in an anteroom of some kind, where my six guards handed me over formally to a centurion and two Household Troopers, all resplendent in the crimson and sky-blue uniforms of the Emperor's personal guard. The two troopers flanked me, and we proceeded along another dark passageway, which came to an abrupt end at a heavy door. My guards stepped closer to me here, each holding an arm as the centurion opened the door and led us through.

We were in the tribunal, a large room shaped like an amphitheatre and lined with stepped seats arranged in a horseshoe, all facing a dais at the end of which sat a long table and three high-backed chairs. Every head in the room turned to look at me as I stepped through the doorway. There must have been fifty officers present, all in full-dress uniform, each of them holding his helmet formally in the crook of his left arm. The assembled tribunes of the seat of power in the province of South Britain. At first, the faces were all the same, indistinguishable one from the other, but then a few of them, the older faces, started to become familiar. At the front, seated beside the open space reserved for me directly in front of the dais, sat Caius Britannicus and Caesarius Claudius Seneca. As my eyes focused on Seneca, a wave of hatred and loathing swept completely over me, making me lose all awareness of who and where I was. Strangely, the sight of Caius had no effect on me at all, not even one of relief.

My escort tugged me forward and I moved to the front of the room, my chains noisy in the utter silence. I ignored the faces around me—their arrogance, curiosity, hostility and disdain—and forced myself to look only straight ahead, fixing my eyes on a spot on the wall ahead of me. Aware of the figure I must have presented in my prison clothes, I braced my shoulders and stood as tall as I was able.

They must have been waiting and watching, for as soon as I had come to a standstill in front of the dais, a door opened in the wall behind it and a group of brilliantly dressed senior tribunes entered and made their way up onto the rostrum. I found myself face to face with Flavius Stilicho, Commander-in-Chief of the armies of Imperial Rome, and now Regent to the young Emperor Honorius.

There was no mistaking him, in spite of the fact that his dress was identical to that of his companions. I suddenly remembered Caius remarking, years before, that dress has a way of fading to insignificance under the aura of the truly great men of any age, and this man's entire demeanour stamped him as unique. We had been talking about greatness, and Caius had said that men of destiny carry about them the pristine qualities of the great predators they frequently resemble. Here was living proof of that. Theodosius had carried himself with the bearing of a great tiger-cat. Julius Caesar is always portrayed with the aspect of an eagle. Flavius Stilicho was a Vandal hawk. The image sprang immediately into my mind on seeing him. He was compactly built, giving an impression of great strength and agility, and his bare forearms were thick, roped with heavy, clearly defined muscles. His face was lean and saturnine, with huge, dark, almost black eyes. His mouth was small and clear-lined, the lips firm and full above a strong, dimpled chin. His face was dominated by a small, savagely hooked nose. That nose, in fact, dominated his whole appearance, with his eyes and his broad, high, unlined forehead. In spite of his youth, for he was only twenty-nine at this time, his hair had begun receding from his temples, leaving a pointed peak at the centre of his brow, and even from where I stood below him, looking upwards uncomfortably at his eminence, I could see the intellect that lay behind that brow and blazed through his dark eyes.

The group of seven arranged themselves so that four remained standing, arms folded on their breasts, behind the three chairs. Stilicho stepped forward and took the central chair, flanked by the remaining two tribunes. But he did not sit. His eyes swept downward to where I stood below him, and I saw something stir in their depths, although I could not have described what it was. He looked at me, deep and long, his eyes now expressionless, and then he moved his gaze around the tribunal, ending with Seneca and Caius. There was not a sound in the great room. When he finally sat, everyone else sat, too, except me, my guards and the four standing tribunes on the dais behind him. Stilicho pursed his lips and then spoke, addressing the room at large.

"This is a military tribunal; as Commander-in-Chief, I sit in judgment. This is also a civil tribunal; as Regent of his Imperial Majesty, Honorius, I sit in judgment. The matters before this body today are complex and involve both military and civil questions. The prisoner before us stands accused of serious crimes." He looked down at the parchment he had been holding and unrolled it. "I shall enumerate them.

"One: It is alleged by Caesarius Claudius Seneca that the prisoner, unknown to him by name, did fourteen years ago, in the company of another man, also unknown to the complainant, commit an unprovoked assault upon Claudius Seneca in a public *mansio*, while Claudius Seneca was engaged upon the private business of Valentinian, then Emperor. In the course of that assault it is alleged that the prisoner broke the complainant's nose and mutilated his body by carving a letter V upon his chest.

"Two: It is alleged by Caesarius Claudius Seneca that the prisoner, whose name was still unknown to the complainant, was recognized in the town of Aquae Sulis two years later and ordered to surrender himself to Quinctilius Nesca, uncle of the complainant and a magistrate of this province. The allegation states further that in trying to avoid capture on the pre-stated charge, the prisoner brought about the deaths of two of Quinctilius Nesca's retainers and murdered the magistrate himself, by strangulation, during the night that followed.

"Three: It is alleged by Caesarius Claudius Seneca that upon his arrival at the home of Caius Britannicus, former Proconsul of Numidia, and Senator of Rome, he found the prisoner, under the name of Vulcan, being held by the Proconsul prior to being brought here to Londinium to stand trial on charges of brigandage and armed rebellion." He stopped and looked up, nodding towards Caius. "Senator Caius Britannicus is present here. Those are the charges as delivered to this tribunal. Are there any comments?"

"Yes, my Lord Regent!" Seneca was on his feet, his face slightly flushed, an arrogant sneer on his lips. "It is a minor matter, but one that requires clarification. You neglected to state in your reading that Senator Britannicus sustains the charges."

Stilicho gazed at him in silence for long moments before replying, his face devoid of expression. "I neglected nothing, Senator Seneca." He looked down briefly, hesitated, and looked up again. "No, that is not quite true, although the neglect has no bearing on the matters before us. I neglected to mention before the start of these proceedings that I have been informed of the sudden death of the Regent of the Eastern Empire, Flavius Rufinus. He will be missed."

There was a concerted hiss of indrawn breath at this and I turned my head quickly to see the effect of the announcement on Seneca. I was delighted to see the blood drain visibly from his face, and I began to feel more sanguine about the outcome of all of this, although I was still mystified. Stilicho ignored the effect of his announcement on Seneca and continued speaking, his voice clear and crystalline, ringing throughout the tribunal.

"As the personal representative and Regent of the Emperor Honorius, I am entitled, should I so elect, to decide these matters at my sole discretion and announce my judgment. I have chosen not to do so for a number of reasons. I appointed the Legates Larrens and Titanius, here present, to assist me in compiling and assessing the evidence and testimony we could amass concerning these charges, some of which are very old. We have been engaged in that pursuit for the past forty-eight hours. Our joint findings are as follows."

He fell silent for a moment, staring intently at the document he still held open in front of him, and then he raised his head and spoke again into the silence. "In the matter of the assault, fourteen years ago, the Legate Larrens has led the investigation. Legate?"

Larrens rose to his feet and, to my utter amazement, proceeded to detail testimony offered and formally attested to by Plautus regarding the details of the assault and the provocation leading up to it. Seneca stood through all of it as though carved from stone. When Larrens had finished his recital, Stilicho stared stern-faced at Seneca.

"Now," he said, "there is one other piece of testimony that this tribunal does not have, but it is my understanding that it can be produced within days if Senator Seneca so desires."

I found myself holding my breath, wondering what this could be as I waited for him to continue. He did, his eyes unwavering on Seneca.

"The owner of the *mansio*, his wife and his two sons still live there. There is little doubt in the minds of this tribunal that they will recall the excitement of the events under discussion here. Senator Seneca, is it your wish that they be summoned here *sub poena?*"

The silence in the room was total. Seneca's face was ashen. Finally, after a lengthy silence, he jerked his head in a negative. "No!" He swallowed visibly and with difficulty. "I will . . . accept the ruling of the tribunal."

"So be it. This tribunal finds the prisoner innocent of any criminality in this matter. The assault he committed was justifiable and provoked. Now, in the matter of the murder of the magistrate Quinctilius Nesca. Legate Titanius?"

My legs almost gave way with relief! As I struggled to keep my breathing normal, the Legate Titanius rose to his feet and detailed the meticulous testimony of the witnesses we had brought from home concerning the affair in Aquae Sulis. When he had finished and sat down again, Stilicho looked around the room and spoke again.

"Bear in mind, everyone here, that this manhunt for the prisoner was unjustifiable . . . No punishable crime had been committed by him. In the year that followed the original assault, however, the prisoner undertook a journey to the west, to be married. In the course of that journey, he survived three attempts upon his life, all made by the same group of hired assassins. On the last of these occasions, the prisoner captured one of these men alive and handed him over to the military authorities in Alchester. The assassin, before he was hanged, made a full confession. He confessed to being in the paid employ of Quinctilius Nesca, who had offered a large reward in gold for the head of a man—any man—fitting the prisoner's description. The officer who took that confession is stationed now in the north of the province, at Arboricum. Senator Seneca, do you wish this tribunal to order the recall of that officer for questioning before we pass judgment on this matter?"

Again the terrible, afflicted silence before a jerked, negative headshake and a whispered "No."

"So let it be. It is the judgment of this tribunal that the prisoner, Publius Varrus, is innocent of complicity in the murder of Quinctilius Nesca. This tribunal also finds the prisoner justified in taking the lives of Nesca's two employees in the protection of his own."

He paused. "Now, in the matter of armed rebellion and banditry." He looked directly at me. "Senator Caius Britannicus will address this tribunal."

Caius rose to his feet, and my guards made no move to check me as I turned my head to look at him.

"Explain the circumstances of your arrest of this man Varrus on these charges." Stilicho's voice was devoid of emphasis.

Caius looked around at the assembled officers, at me, and then at Seneca, before returning his eyes to Stilicho and his two legates. "The charges are specious, my Lord Regent," he said. "They are totally without substance. I fabricated them an hour before the arrival of Claudius Seneca." I knew that Caius had purposely avoided the use of Seneca's senatorial rank. "I had received warning of his imminent arrival, and I knew all the circumstances relating to his hatred for this man, my friend, Publius Varrus. I conceived the subterfuge of bringing Varrus to Londinium under guard as the only means at my disposal of guaranteeing his life."

I could feel Seneca's eyes on me, the hatred in his gaze stinging my skin like acid.

Stilicho spoke again. "How long have you known the prisoner, Senator?"

"For almost three decades, my Lord Regent."

"And you have found him honourable in all that time?"

"Completely."

"To what extent?"

Caius looked at me before continuing and then turned back to the rostrum. "Publius Varrus served with me as a centurion before the first attack on the Wall, my Lord Regent. In the aftermath of the Invasion, I elevated him to the rank of tribune for his conduct in the field. He received the wound that crippled him towards the close of the campaign conducted by the Emperor Theodosius against the invaders, and was responsible for saving my life on that occasion, when we were ambushed in the high mountains. In all the time that I have known him, he has consistently behaved with honour, loyalty, integrity and all of the finest attributes of what we are proud to call the Roman Way."

"Thank you, Proconsul." Caius sat down as Stilicho rose to his feet and banged his ivory baton on the rostrum. "Let all men present hear. In the name of Honorius, Emperor, this tribunal declares the accused, Publius Varrus, innocent of all charges and exonerated completely in the eyes of God and man. So let it be. Strike off the prisoner's chains and see that he is fed and bathed and dressed as befits his rank and the injustices done him. This tribunal is adjourned. Tribune Seneca! My quarters, please. Immediately."

As conversations broke out all around, I stood there alone and knew beyond a doubt that all of the enemies Caius had ever made, combined, could not add up to one-tenth of the hatred he had earned that day from Caesarius Claudius Seneca. Until that day, Seneca's obsession with me had, it seemed, been the driving impetus of his life, apart from amassing money. But now he had another focus for his hatred. Caius Britannicus. And I felt heavily in my guts that Claudius Seneca had ample capacity for double hatred.

XIV

Even as the shackles fell away from my wrists and ankles, I was sick and shaking inside. I had lived twenty-one days, I estimated, chained either in a cage or in a cell, and the knowledge that the whole exercise was a ruse had given me no shred of comfort. None at all. It was a soul-shattering experience, and at the end, as I stood in front of that tribunal under guard and heard the charges being read by Stilicho, I really believed that I was doomed. The charges sounded very black, and I was quite convinced that Seneca had succeeded in getting rid of me after fourteen years. When I heard the verdict of exoneration on all counts, I thought that I would swoon, or vomit, or both; there was a roaring in my ears, and afterwards I saw no face nor heard any of the words addressed to me.

They took me to a smithy and struck off my chains, and they took me to a bath house and washed and steamed and scrubbed away the filth of three weeks, and they took me to an officers' dining room and made me eat, and all the time they talked to me and I to them, but nothing registered. In my mind, in my soul, I had been robbed of my humanity.

I found redemption waiting for me, however, when I awoke the following morning. Catharsis, that abstract purging of the soul, is normally effected through the skills of tragedians and dramatists working on the emotions of their listeners. In my case, however, it was embodied by Plautus. I opened my eyes to find him leaning lazily against the doorpost of my sleeping cubicle with his arms folded on his chest as he watched me. I blinked once at him and he said, "You always were an ugly whoreson, Varrus, but now you're getting lazy, too. D'you intend to lie sweating in that pit of fleas all day?" I sat up, swung my legs to the floor and smiled at him with my whole being, and I felt good!

A half hour later we sat together in the refectory, sizing each other up again, oblivious to the comings and goings of the officers all around us.

"So," I asked him, "how are you finding this posting? You are in high company, with all these imperial troops around."

He frowned and spoke in a deep, growling tone. "What d'you mean, in good company? Are you mocking me? What posting? Look at me, for God's sake! I'm a civilian! I'm out!"

"Out?" I had noticed his civilian garb but had presumed him to be merely off duty, knowing he would never voluntarily present himself in staff officers' territory in uniform. "What do you mean, out? You can't be! You've another five to go."

"No." He shook his head. "Thirty-five years. That's maximum. I'm fifty-three years old."

I stared at him in astonishment. "Good God, Plautus, I had no idea! Why didn't you let me know? You knew how to find me. If it hadn't been for that warning you sent me I'd probably be dead now. I would have walked right out to meet that ill-gotten swine Seneca and he'd have had my balls on a platter within moments."

He dismissed that with a wave of his hand. "Forget it." He was saying nothing else, and very obviously.

"You didn't answer me. Why didn't you let me know you were out?"

The bitter tone of his voice told me even more than his words. "What good would that have done? What was there to tell you? That I was finished? Out to pasture? That the army has no further use for me? That I'm too old to contribute any more? No, I just got out and decided to stay here for a while—until it's over."

"Until what's over? Your life?" I gazed at him in disbelief, surprised by a side of him I had never suspected. "Plautus," I said, "I've seen opinions more valid than that floating in the latrines! What are you doing now?"

He sniffed. "Remember the gold you gave me? Well, it came in useful, after all. I used it to buy a tavern here, with another fellow who got out at the same time as me."

"A tavern?" I was surprised, and happy for him. "Is it going well? Are you enjoying it?"

"It's a sewer, like all the others." He threw me a look of disgust. "I used to say if I ever owned a tavern I'd hold it off-limits to civilians. Well, I've discovered you can't do that. You can't exist outside the army without relying on civilians for everything, because the moment you walk out through those gates for the last time, out of uniform, you're one of them. You still talk like a grunt, and you think and act like a grunt, but you're a civilian. End of story, end of the good life."

What I was hearing was really upsetting me. I did not know what to say to him, other than the obvious. "But what about the Colony, Plautus? You belong there. You were there at the start of it, at my wedding."

"Aye, and if I'd gone there five years ago instead of re-enlisting, that would have been fine. It's too late now."

I snapped at him, irritated. "Horse turds, Plautus! What are you talking about?"

He cut me off with a slash of his hand. "There's no point in arguing, Varrus. It's there, isn't it? The army's not stupid! The army knows what it's doing. The army gets every scrap of value out of a man while he's got something to contribute; then, when he's no more use at all, when they've sucked him dry of every bit of value, he's out, finished! That's a fact of military life! If you're useless, you're out, and if you're out, you're useless."

"Well, you stupid . . ." I stopped in exasperation, looking around to make sure we were completely alone and could not be overheard. "Plautus, I've known you for a lot of years and I thought I knew all your faults. I know you're a lecherous, bad-tempered, foul-mouthed son of a whore who'd rather fight than fornicate and who'll say 'drink' instead of 'think' every chance he gets, but I never took you for the fool you sound like now. 'The army's not stupid! The army knows what it's doing.' Since when, in the name of the sweet Christ? What kind of puke is that? The army's the biggest mess in the Empire. You've always known that. There aren't enough brains among the entire High Command to plan a route march from one end of a straight road to the other. If the army ever knew what it was doing there would be no need for half of it! So what's this stuff that you're bleating up like a sick sheep? You're feeling sorry for yourself, that's your whole problem!"

He was gazing at me wide-eyed, taken aback by my vehemence. I charged ahead, allowing him no time to recover his tongue. "You want something worthwhile to do? I'll give you something that's worthwhile!" I cautiously let my voice drop to a confidential tone. "I've got an army of my own at home, crying out for some decent training. It's a small army, but it's getting bigger every day. We're inventing our own techniques, trying out new ideas that have never been tackled before, and we haven't got one piece of dead wood in the entire chain of command! I've got recruits who have never heard of soldiers' *rights*. They're building fortified camps and marching and drilling the way the legions used to do it a thousand years ago, and they think that's what being a soldier is all about! You think I don't need the kind of help you can provide? You think I can't use your experience? You really think you're that old? That far past being useful?" I stopped and glared at him. He stared at me, speechless.

"Here's something for you to think about, Plautus. We'll be leaving for home in a couple of days. We don't use money in the Colony. We don't need it. Neither do you. You don't seem to be too happy as a tavern-keeper, so think about this. Why not give your tavern to your partner and come back with us? I'll put you to work so fast you won't have time to think about feeling old or useless."

He stared at me, and as I watched his eyes, I saw hope starting to glimmer there.

"You mean that, Varrus?"

I shook my head pityingly. "If you even have to ask that, you talking rectum, you're even further gone than I thought. What d'you say? Do we have a *primus pilus*?"

He nodded, very slowly, and then a great grin crept across his face and murdered years. "You can bet your balls on it, Publius Varrus. You have a *primus pilus*." His excitement was growing visibly now with every heartbeat. "By the testicles of Ptolemy! When do we leave?"

I smiled, content. "I don't really know. Tomorrow—the next day. It will be soon. Caius will know. He has some things to arrange with Stilicho's people. I remember him saying something about it last night. As soon as it's done, we'll be leaving. Are you sure, now, that you want to come? No regrets about your tavern?"

He leaned across the table and grasped my wrist, and I was deeply moved to see tears standing in his eyes. "No regrets, my friend, no regrets. Not ever. Life's too short." He stopped, his eyes crinkling. "Dindo, my partner, will get the runs when I tell him. He won't believe me. He'll think I've lost my grip. He loves the business, but the money was mine. He does most of the work. When I tell him it's all his, he'll shit! Come with me now. Let's tell him. I can't wait to see his face."

I grinned and finished my fruit juice. "Fine, I've got nothing else to do. Let's go and tell him."

Later that same afternoon, Caius came to visit me and we talked for hours, mainly about everything that had happened over the previous weeks and my illness. Naturally enough, the talk soon got around to Stilicho, and I wanted to know everything about him, too.

"How did you find him?" I asked Caius. "Was it difficult to gain an audience?"

He grinned. "No," he said, "quite the contrary. He sent for me as soon as he received my first communication."

"And?"

"He made me welcome."

"Is that all you're going to tell me? He made you welcome? How? What did he say to you? What did you say to him?"

Caius affected boredom, drawing his palms languidly down his face. "Well, if you really want to know, I suppose I shall just have to try to remember." He drew his brows together. "But there's no time for that now. He wants to talk to you this afternoon. He has a meeting with his senior officers that is going on right now, and he wants us to meet with him afterwards."

"Meet with him? Where?"

"In his quarters. Where else?"

I felt my eyebrows rise high on my forehead. "Who else will be there?"

"I don't know. Picus, I suppose. Yourself, and me. Perhaps a few others. It is not a formal occasion. You'll like him—Stilicho, I mean."

"I like him now. I loved him when he handed down his verdict yesterday."

Caius smiled. "So did I, I have to admit."

I felt my eyes widening. "You mean it surprised you? You didn't really know what his judgment would be?"

Again the smile. "No, I confess I did not, although I suspected what it would be and would, in fact, have wagered on it. But I did not really know it for a certainty."

I said nothing as Caius went on to tell me about his first meeting with Stilicho, when he had broached the subject of my presence in Londinium and the crimes with which Seneca was charging me. He had received the unmistakable impression, he said, that Stilicho was none too fond of Seneca, although the Regent had said nothing overt on that subject. When he had eventually gone on to tell Stilicho of my true identity, Caius had been astounded to find that Stilicho knew me well by reputation, thanks to Picus, who was, it turned out, Stilicho's closest ally and confidant. Caius had warmed to Stilicho immediately on meeting him, and the attraction had been mutual, primed as it had been by Picus's closeness to the Regent and the mutual respect the two had for each other. Caius had outlined my case in great detail and Stilicho had taken it upon himself to assign his two most trusted assistants to the gathering of information and evidence in preparation for my trial. It was Stilicho who had insisted on maintaining the subterfuge that kept Seneca unaware of my true relationship to the rest of my "accusers." Caius had suspected that Stilicho intended to make Seneca sweat, but he had not thought fit to voice his thought on the matter. He had been heartened by his interview with Stilicho and fully confident, although not convinced, that my fate was well taken care of.

By the time Caius had finished telling me all of this, it was time to make our way to Stilicho's quarters, and again I became conscious of the might and magnificence of Imperial Rome visible even in the security and the pomp and dignity surrounding our simple visit at his own invitation. I had noticed it earlier, when I was taken from my cell to face the tribunal, but now, walking as a free man among Romans, the irony of all I saw about me resonated almost palpably within my awareness.

I was here—we were here—because of Caius's conviction, to which I had subscribed at first reluctantly, but later with total dedication, that all of this incredible wealth and organized intensity and efficiency surrounding us would soon cease to be ... that Rome herself, the eternal Mistress of the Universe, would shortly die. Marching through those corridors at that time, however, hearing the disciplined, exact cadences of iron-nailed military boots crashing on marble floors, observing the blanked, visionless, forward-concentrated vigilance of the ranked guards we passed and knowing that they had assessed and were ignoring us, their attention focused upon identifying and repulsing threats to the Imperial Regent, it seemed unbelievable to me that such a presence, such formidable, inexorable power, could ever fail, or even falter, in its supremacy. I found myself wondering briefly how Britannicus could have ever have been so misguided, so completely mad as to doubt this reality. But then my own perception of reality returned, reminding me that Caius had never talked of *instant* death. The fate he envisioned for the Empire would begin with an inevitable self-protective withdrawal, a convulsion, a fear-engendered retraction of the imperial armies from places like this, and from peaceful Britain most of all, leaving chaos and emptiness in its aftermath. *Therein* lay the true irony of what was happening here. When all of this magnificence was stripped away at the terrified, self-concerned behest of the imperial civil service, all that I was seeing now would be the stuff of dreams and memories, and people like us would have to fend for ourselves, using the tools we had to hand. Brilliant uniforms and serried ranks of guards and sparkling, battle-ready weapons protecting spacious, open, securely held places of safety would remain in Britain only where the people left behind could provide them for themselves. For the time being, I reflected, they were here, both visible and tangible, and should be accepted as they were. Their replacements were in training, in our Colony. I squared my shoulders and marched confidently among our escort.

Our final approach to the inner sanctum of the Imperial Regent and Legate Commanding the Province of Britain was made along a hall floored in marble that echoed my thoughts, along with the sound of our own footsteps and the hobnailed tramp of the trio that escorted us, one ahead of us and one on either side. Twenty-five guards stood at attention on each side of this hallway, spaced three paces apart and resplendent in dress uniforms of imperial scarlet cloaks and plumes, sky-blue tunics and bronzed armour. The massive doors at the end of the hallway were screened by another quintet of sentries, shoulder to shoulder. We were passed through these portals and into the presence of the most powerful man I had ever faced in person.

Inside, the enormous room was bright and opulent, brilliant with fresh-cut flowers, which surprised me greatly, and heavily scented with their mingled fragrances. I immediately sought the reason for the brightness and saw that great windows filled with tinted glass of many hues allowed the sunlight easy access to the rooms. These were first impressions, instantaneously formed and then disregarded as I found myself subjected to the concerted gaze of a group of magnificently dressed officers clustered around a large table close by the windows. I counted seven of them at first glance, but lost awareness of the lesser six immediately as my eyes singled out the man we had come to see: Flavius Stilicho, Commander-in-Chief of the armies of Imperial Rome, Regent to the young Emperor Honorius.

Silence had fallen as Caius and I stepped through the doors. The centurion who had led us in saluted smartly, turned on his heel and left us standing there. Stilicho acknowledged our presence with a courteous nod, held up two fingers asking our indulgence for a few moments more and continued with his officers, asking them quietly if he had made himself clear? As a man, they stiffened to attention and assured him that he had, and he nodded pleasantly again, indicating that their conference was over. They saluted him, turned and trooped past us to the doors, each of them finding occasion to look at me and take his measure of me in his own way.

Before the doors had closed behind them, Stilicho was crossing the floor towards me, his great hawk-like eyes upon me alone. I stood rigid, suddenly wondering what the correct mode of address would be to one who held all the power, but not the name, of Emperor. It had not even occurred to me to ask Caius what to call him, face to face like this. He stopped directly in front of me and stared at me, an expression of—what was it?—it seemed like mockery in his eyes. He said nothing, and apart from his approach he made no move to greet me. Flustered and uncomfortable, I cleared my throat nervously and bowed to him, searching frantically for polite words that would not leave me looking or sounding like a fool.

"Eminence," I said, "I must beg pardon of you, for I have no knowledge of the protocols involved here. I had not expected to be received so personally and, frankly, I had relied upon watching others for example."

His mouth quirked slightly, the merest tic at one corner, and he slowly extended his right hand to me. The imperial seal was enormous on his ring finger. I stooped to kiss it.

"No! It is to shake, not to kiss."

Astonished, I shook with him, feeling the supple strength of his fingers on my wrist. He brought his left hand to my elbow, making the double clasp, and I was even more astounded. Nor did he release me, but instead he leaned close and gazed into my eyes, that same unusual look still in his own.

"I wonder if you can know, Publius Varrus, how rare it is for me to meet a man for the first time and know that I can trust him and his honour unconditionally? Believe me, it is rare indeed. And now I have had the pleasure of doing so twice in as many weeks."

I blinked at him. "Eminence?"

"Eminence!" He smiled and his whole face underwent a total metamorphosis: humour was there, understanding, and an openness I knew instinctively was shown to very few. "Even the term sounds alien on your tongue! Eminence! Call me General. It is what I am, a plain soldier like you and like your friend here, and his son."

"Picus."

"Aye, Picus Britannicus." He switched his gaze to Caius. "He is the sunlight of my stormy days." The dark eyes came back to me. "He has told me much about you."

I felt a glow of pride for Caius, and knew that it was nothing compared to the pride he himself must be feeling for his son. "He serves you well then, General?"

"Serves me well? Aye, I suppose you might say that. I trust him with my life and with the Emperor's. He is my finest commander of horse and my closest friend." He turned and indicated a large, ornately carved folding screen behind him on my left. "Come, we may sit back here in private. I have made time for you because there is much I want to discuss. We can drink some wine while we converse, but I do have calls to make. You can come with me, if you wish, if the time comes for them before we finish talking."

We went behind the screen to a comfortably carpeted and furnished *cubiculum* where he himself poured wine from a silver ewer. As he poured and served us, he continued speaking. "Senator Britannicus, I am being frank with you and I expect no less of you in return. I have had years of frankness from your son, and I've grown used to the oases of refreshment and common sense he serves up to me daily." He seated himself and gestured with his cup in a silent toast before taking a sip. I tasted my own. It was as excellent as one would expect from an imperial ewer. He cocked his head slightly to the side. "I want to talk about your Colony, but you should know before we begin that I know all about it. I have known for years. It is illegal, of course, but I also know the reason behind its existence, and I know the scheduling of its emergence. Or has that changed? Do you still intend to await the evacuation of Britain before you proclaim your independent strength?"

I saw Caius swallow, hard. "Yes, General. We do."

"Good. We will talk more on that subject later. Let me get to the crux of this. Claudius Seneca. How much do you really know about the man?"

Caius considered the question and then answered him truthfully. "Enough to know that he's no credit to the Empire, General. I must admit I was appalled to discover that he was officially in uniform. It seems to me that Rome has troubles enough without burdening herself with such a man in a position of authority."

Stilicho seemed to be chewing on one of his own teeth, musing. He looked at Caius appraisingly. "Flavius Rufinus? What do you know of him?"

Caius shook his head. "Hardly anything. Only that you and he were not the best of friends and you shared the power of government: he in the east, you in the west."

A smile flickered in Stilicho's eyes. "Nicely phrased. They are saying in Rome that I had him killed. I did not. That is not my way. He is dead, however, and I am not displeased. Seneca is, or was, one of his creatures, set by Rufinus to keep an eye on me."

I had to speak, forgetting my awe. I would not have believed it in this man's character to stand for such a thing. "You knew that," I asked, "and yet you still put up with him? Why didn't you get rid of him, General?"

He grinned at me, a flashing of teeth and eyes. "Politics, Publius Varrus. Something you have neither the time nor the need to deal with. I could not remove him easily while Rufinus lived, for a number of reasons. Now I can, and I intend to, but that is incidental here." He paused and looked at both of us. "You must understand completely what has happened with Seneca. He is not the type of man to volunteer for active service. It was Theodosius who decided to make a soldier out of our friend Claudius, and he did it for two reasons: the first was to demonstrate his power over Valentinian, who was Seneca's mentor and protector; but the second was to demonstrate quite clearly to Seneca that Theodosius was far from satisfied with the resolution of the question of Seneca's loyalty during his term as Procurator here in Britain, up to and including the rebellion of the upstart Magnus Maximus. The reports that Seneca had financed the rebel's bid for the Imperial Purple were convincing and their sources were impressive. There was never any convincing argument put forward against their truthfulness . . . other than the ultimately convincing one of Seneca's return from the dead, almost, with his accounts and books in perfect order and all monies accounted for . . ." His voice trailed away, leaving that last thought hanging, and then he resumed.

"Theodosius remained unconvinced and was at no pains to conceal his lack of conviction. He gave Claudius Seneca a choice: active service with the armies for ten years, or confiscation and forfeiture of all his possessions. No choice at all, in other words. Seneca acceded to the Imperial wishes and was assigned to me for disposition. But there was something, some connection, I don't know what and I don't care, between Seneca and Rufinus. Anyway, Seneca is a very powerful man, with many so-called friends. One of these suggested to me that I assign Seneca to Rufinus, and I was happy to do it. Kept him out of my hair. He stayed with Rufinus for five years, more or less, until Theodosius assigned me as guardian of his son Honorius, when suddenly I found myself under pressure to transfer Seneca to my own command. He came as a spy, pure and simple, but because of the political ramifications involved behind the scenes, there was nothing I could do to relieve myself of the nuisance of his presence without causing great grief and pain to several friends of mine. Aware of that, I tolerated him and made sure that he could do no harm to my designs in any area."

He stopped and peered into his cup for a short space before raising it to his lips and draining it. Having done so, he wiped his lips carefully with a folded cloth and replaced the cloth on the table with the empty cup. He looked up again, at me, and his eyes were cool.

"Now Valentinian is gone, Theodosius is gone, and Rufinus is gone. I hold the power now, for the time being at least." He paused again, his eyes on mine, and I found myself being thankful that he wished me no ill. He continued speaking. "I have had words with Claudius Seneca since your appearance in our tribunal, Master Varrus. His demeanour has altered quite dramatically since then. I have found some work for him to do for me on the northern frontier. He should find the experience enlightening. Believe me, even were he inclined to pursue the matter further, he will find little time, in future, to worry about his personal vendetta with you."

I smiled back at him. "Thank you, General. I am relieved to hear that."

He winked at me, so quickly that I wondered afterwards if I had been mistaken, and then turned his attention and the full force of his personality on Caius.

"Proconsul Britannicus, Picus tells me you love this land more than anywhere else in the world. Now that I am here and have seen the place for myself, I can understand why. I don't think I have ever seen greener greens."

Caius smiled gently and obviously felt no need to comment. Stilicho rose again and replenished our glasses, and I wondered at the charm of the man. There were servants everywhere, living only to do his bidding, and yet for this interview he chose to be our servant. As I was thinking this, he changed the subject yet again.

"You are an infantry commander, Proconsul. What do you think of my changeover to cavalry?"

Caius sipped his wine appreciatively, considering his answer before he spoke. Finally he nodded his head. "The time is right for it, I believe. The enemy has taken to horse and smashed one Roman army. They will try it again."

"And?" Stilicho's face was intent. Clearly this answer was important to him.

Caius shrugged his shoulders. "You will be ready for them. Visibly ready. Knowing that, they will be less likely to provoke you."

Stilicho looked at me, although his thoughts were elsewhere. "It is a major undertaking, Proconsul, to change an Empire's ways of waging war."

"Aye, General Stilicho, some might think it impossible, too. But it is far from impossible, and I believe you are right to do it." Caius spoke softly, and Stilicho jerked his eyes back to him, searching his face as though looking for signs of flattery.

"You think so? That surprises me."

Caius smiled. "Why, General? Because I knew the old infantry legions? That doesn't make me blind to changing needs."

Stilicho grunted. "Hmmm! I wish I could say the same of most of your colleagues, Proconsul. Can you guess why I have come to Britain?"

Now Caius laughed outright. "Easily. You are here to train your troops in action against an enemy who can offer them no opposition on land." Stilicho's face broke into a smile as Caius went on. "The Saxons have never seen disciplined cavalry. Neither have the invaders from the north. They can have no possible defences against your forces. You will smash them easily and quickly, blood your troops, and show the world the value of your strategy and tactics."

"By God, Caius Britannicus, I wish you were twenty years younger! I'd recommission you immediately and give you an army group! You think the way I do. If I had fifty commanders like you, I could turn the tides of history around and undo all the damage of the past two hundred years!"

I felt my stomach tighten as I saw Caius decide to gamble. "I already have an army, General Stilicho," he said. "It is a small enough one, but it is fine. It stands at your disposal, now or in the future."

Stilicho frowned. "What do you mean, you have an army? You mean your colonists?"

"Aye, General, our colonists." Caius's concurring nod of the head was slow and proud.

"How many of you are there?"

Caius looked at me and I shrugged. "About a thousand, in uniform," I said.

"In uniform? You mean a *real* army?"

I nodded. "We also have a hundred heavy cavalry like yours."

"Heavy cavalry? Where did you get the horses?"

"Bred them from our own stock, General."

"And the riders?" His face was expressionless.

"We trained them ourselves."

"Who is 'we'?"

I glanced at Caius again before answering, "I am, I suppose. The ideas are mine, trial and error. I pass my instructions on to other instructors."

"How do you train your people? What tactics do you use?"

I shrugged my shoulders again, marvelling at the way this catechism was running with no word of condemnation. "As I said, that was hit or miss, General. However, we did study the campaigns of Alexander of Macedon and tried to reconstruct the way he must have fought. It was the Proconsul's idea."

"Good God! That's where I began. How long have your people been engaged in this?"

"About ten years."

"I can't believe it! You have a breeding program for your horses?"

"Aye, we do. But our horses are not as big as yours. Not yet."

He rose to his feet and began to pace, his hands gripping each other loosely behind his back, and for a space of time there was silence. Then, "Tell me about this western land of yours, Proconsul. What problems concern you out there?"

I could see that Caius sensed a reason behind his question and was taking care with his answer, thinking it through and phrasing it judiciously. "Very few problems, General Stilicho, compared to the rest of the province. Our major difficulties have been arising recently from the removal of the western garrisons for the strengthening of other parts of the province: the Saxon Shore and the northern frontier regions."

Stilicho listened carefully as Caius went on to talk of our alliance with Ullic and his Celts and of the growing need we had found to lend our protection to our neighbours in the area around the Colony. When Caius had finished, Stilicho hummed thoughtfully and sat down again, deep in thought. I caught Caius's eye and he gave me the Britannican eyebrow. Finally Stilicho spoke again.

"This matter of the garrisons—their depletion and abandonment. I regret to have to tell you there is little I can do about it. I need every man I have to contain this invasion from the north and to guard against a repetition of it after I have gone."

Caius blinked at him. "But you have just arrived, General! Are you leaving already?"

"No." He shook his head and nibbled on a piece of bread. "But I cannot remain here long. The world takes a lot of governing. I'll see this campaign launched and on its way to victory, and then I'll leave it in your son's hands to finish properly. I must be back in Rome within the year. I dare not stay away longer. My wife is looking after the Emperor in my absence, and after the Empire, too, incidentally, and while I have no doubts about her competence, she is a woman, with a woman's weaknesses as well as strengths." He smiled with genuine warmth. "Serena is formidable, but she tends to be naive in certain things and tentative in others. She will throw anyone in jail who seems to need jailing, for example, but she also tends to resist making decisions about who has to die for crimes committed. Each time I go home I find my jails are filled to capacity and sometimes beyond." He turned to me with a quick grin. "That, as I am sure you appreciate, can be a very uncomfortable situation demanding immediate redress."

I smiled and said nothing and he turned back to Caius.

"So, Proconsul, as I was saying, I cannot remain long in Britain, nor can I regarrison the western forts. One thing I *can* do, however . . . if you would be willing to accept my notion." He stopped, waiting for a reaction. I wondered what was in his mind. A glance at Caius showed me that he was wondering the same.

Caius cleared his throat. "Try me, General. I will be honoured to consider any suggestions you have, and happy should they improve our security out there."

Stilicho stood up and stepped away from the table, and picked up a rolled parchment from a pile that lay on a side table against the wall. I watched him in silence as he came back to the table and placed one foot on his chair. Deep in thought, he leaned one elbow on his upraised knee and tapped the palm of his other hand with the parchment scroll. Finally he pursed his lips and sucked air audibly between his teeth.

"I am thinking of an agreement between us, Proconsul Britannicus, to our mutual benefit. The idea had occurred to me earlier, but now I like it even more than I did before. I will recognize your Colony, officially and legally, if you will accept my commission to serve as my *Legatus Emeritus* of Irregular Forces in the South-west." He saw the extent of our shock in our eyes and continued. "I told you earlier, there are too few good men around me I can really trust. There are too many Senecas. I need the unquestioning support and loyalty of people like yourselves. And you, in turn, need the absolution I can tender for your transgressions against imperial law. It would mean much to your Colony—legal status, for a beginning, with no need to worry about inspections or investigations in the future. It would also mean that you could legitimately acquire bloodstock for your horse herds through my own administrative people."

I felt my heart beginning to thump loudly in my breast. This was far more than we would ever have dared hope for. There had to be a negative aspect somewhere! I knew that Caius was thinking the same thoughts when he sucked in a deep breath.

"General Stilicho," he said, "I will not lie to you. The idea excites me. I have, nevertheless, a duty to my people to consider. You said a mutually beneficial agreement, and so far everything you have said has been to our advantage. What would you expect of us in return?"

Stilicho smiled, showing his white teeth. It was a pleasant smile, but I had the feeling that, with a very small change, it could be a chilling one. "Protection of my interests, support, loyalty and a total commitment to my plans for Britain."

Caius paused, holding his breath, and then breathed out. "You will forgive my asking, I hope, General Stilicho, but what do your plans for Britain consist of?"

He was still smiling. "Prosperity, peace and an ongoing presence of law and order in the land. I have an invasion to deal with in the north, as you know. I also have to contend with incessant raiding in the east, north-east and south-east. High in the north-west, we have only minor problems. The land seems too inhospitable up there. But in those other areas I need every man in the armies of Britain, and that means I need even more of the garrisons of the west. I am going to have to strip them to a skeletal presence. That is where I would like to be able to rely on you. Your army, as you call it, may be small, but I would venture to guess that it is quite superb. I need it. And I need it where it is. Your side of the agreement would be to continue your activities as they have been, but to enlarge and expand them. I will provide you with horses, if you can provide the men. I will also give you a signed authority by my own hand. What say you?"

Both of us watched Caius closely as he considered his answer. He looked at me for help of some kind, I know not what, but all I could do was grin foolishly and nod. I thought it was a marvellous idea. Caius was gnawing his bottom lip. Finally he shrugged and told Stilicho what was in his mind.

"This is a grave decision, General. It will have far-reaching consequences for our Colony. By rights, it should be discussed in Council. But I know there is no time for that, so the decision devolves on me. I like it. It has the feel of propriety, of correctness. There is no way that I can see the existence of such an agreement compromising our plans for our future, since we are committed only to survival in the event of abandonment. Co-operation can only lessen the possibility of that abandonment. I agree. I will sign an agreement between us."

Stilicho thumped the table. "Excellent! I will have my clerks draw it up. Now, is there anything else you can think of that you might need, apart from the commission itself and horses? I know you do not use money in your Colony. Or do you?"

Caius shook his head. "No, we do not. We try to be self-sufficient. There is nothing more I can think of now. I could not ask for more, General."

Stilicho grinned, briefly. "Yes you could, but being you, you will not. And that is as it should be. I have to leave, but you may stay here. Picus will join you presently. He is off duty now. You three will have much to discuss, I think."

He shook my hand again before he left.

XV

PICUS, AS IT turned out, did not join us that night. Extra duties required him elsewhere. Shortly after the departure of the Imperial Regent, however, a messenger arrived from Caius's son, bearing his apologies and asking us to meet him at the basilica in the town forum the following morning, where he would be presiding over a civil court as Stilicho's deputy. As soon as the proceedings there were over, the messenger informed us, Picus would take us on an inspection tour of his cavalry encampment, five miles south of the town.

We sent word back that we would be there early—they closed and locked the doors after the arrival of the magistrates—and then went together in search of food. But even that was not to be permitted us. An imperial clerk waylaid us as we approached the commissary and informed Caius that he would require several hours of work from him, beginning early in the morning, in order to prepare the paperwork concerned with Stilicho's commission and its ramifications. Caius made a face, asked a few questions, and then turned to me, bidding the clerk wait.

"Forgive me, Publius, but you're going to have to eat alone on your first night as a free man. You know what this nonsense is like. What these people call 'several hours' could easily take days, keeping us here when we'd both rather be headed for home, so I might as well make a start on it right now, while it's all fresh in my mind."

I nodded. "What about tomorrow morning? The meeting with Picus?"

He smiled, ruefully, shaking his head. "Impossible for me. You go alone. Picus will be happy to see you, and to show you his camp. He's very proud of it."

"I'm sure he is. But what about you?"

"What about me? I've spent many hours with Picus in the past week or so. You and he haven't seen each other in twenty years."

Hearing the words spoken suddenly made me feel how quickly time had passed.

"What's he like, Cay? Has he changed much?"

Cay grinned, his face glowing with pride. "He's my son, what should he be like?" He stopped himself and began again. "No, I'll answer you honestly, Publius. He is . . . magnificent. I would not have known him had I seen him in the street, nor would you. But I'll tell you no more. You deserve the same pleasant surprise I had. Mind you, I always used to jest with my wife Heraclita that one of her grandmothers had come overly close to a northern slave . . .

209

My first sight of my son in twenty years convinced me that the jest might have been closer to the truth than I suspected!" He smiled again, and grasped my arm in farewell. "Give him my love, and enjoy your time with him. I'll be here when you get back, and I hope we'll be able to leave for home soon after that."

He nodded again, then left immediately with the waiting clerk to begin the preliminary work of drafting the details of what he and Stilicho had discussed. I went on to dine alone and retired early.

I rolled from my bed two hours before sunrise the next morning, into the wintry chill of a dank blackness filled with the hissing roar of pelting rain. Feeling very sorry for myself for all I had been through recently, I splashed my face with icy water and made my way to the commissary, where many others were beginning their day, few of them looking any happier than I felt. Seated close to the kitchens, however, I began to feel distinctly better. The bakers had been working all night, as usual, and the kitchens were warm from the heat of the stone ovens and filled with the aroma of new-baked bread.

I broke my fast on new, crusty bread and thick, hot oat porridge with fresh, creamy milk and then made my way to the bath house, where I found a press of bodies already in the *sudarium*. All of us were content to ignore each other as we steamed our way communally back towards humanity. The rain stopped just before daybreak, and as I left the bath house, sunbeams began breaking through the cloud masses in the east.

Less than an hour later, I presented myself to the garrison guards on duty at the forum basilica and asked to speak with the Officer of the Day. I was told that he had not yet arrived, and was directed to wait in an anteroom off the main entrance hall. Though I was on the point of drawing myself to my full height and telling them just who I was and who I was there to meet, I decided instead to do as advised. No Imperial Household Troops, these guards were ordinary infantry grunts trying to be pleasant while doing a boring and unsatisfying task. I nodded my thanks and made my way to the doorway the guard had indicated, where I paused on the threshold, looking around before I entered.

The room in front of me was long and narrow and dim—I guessed at twenty paces long by six wide—and the only source of light was a double-arched, unglazed window in the far wall, opposite the doorway. A recessed, double doorway in the wall directly to the left inside the entrance was closed and guarded by two erect, stiff-postured legionaries, and a bored-looking clerk sat to the right of them, at a large, plain table piled with written records. Beyond him, filling the entire room, was what seemed to me a multitude of people, all evidently waiting to see someone, and all, obviously, ahead of me.

The clerk glanced up indolently as I approached his table, asked my name but not my business, and told me to have a seat. I bit my tongue again and turned away to do as he said, but the two long benches against the side walls were filled, as were the two shorter, back-to-back benches in the middle of the floor, and I could see no place to sit. So I walked the length of the room, picking my way carefully between the rows of outstretched feet, and stood with my back to the wall in the small open space in front of the only window, from which point I counted heads and examined the room's occupants.

There was nothing unusual about them, except that it seemed to me as though they all wished they could be somewhere else. I did, too, but at least I knew I would, in fact, be going somewhere else as soon as Picus appeared. Had that not been the case, I reckoned idly that I would have been twenty-fourth in line. I revised that, however, by examining the crowd more closely. I identified several people who were evidently alone, wrapped in their own concerns, but the majority, I could see now, were in pairs, and there were two groups of three. I wondered what kinds of confrontations and disputes there were to be resolved here, and what kind of a judge Picus would seem to those who sought justice from him as the Regent's deputy.

They were silent, for the most part, and unaware of my scrutiny, avoiding each other's eyes and biding their time stoically. When any of them did speak among themselves, they did so in whispers, and I realized that most of them, if not all of them, were afraid and ill at ease—which was not surprising, when I considered where they were and the probable nature of their business with the military administration and civic authorities in Londinium. I classified most of them as ordinary townsfolk, their drab, muted dress ranging through various shades of plain browns and greys. Three men grouped together at the far end of the room were obviously farmers, and two others, huddled close together on the bench to my right and arguing in fierce whispers, appeared, from the slightly better quality of their robes, to be merchants of some description. None of them even glanced at me and I soon grew bored.

I had been aware for some time of a ragged nail, on the little finger of my left hand, snagging annoyingly on the wool of my cape. Now, to pass the time, I settled my back against the wall, unsheathed my skystone knife and began to pare the rough edge. As I was doing so, I became aware of someone coming towards me and glanced up. It was one of the men who had been seated alone, just inside the room, close to the two guards. He was a big, burly fellow with close-set eyes and a bad squint, and his nose had been flattened at some time in the distant past. His feet were encased in heavy, felt boots and he was wrapped entirely in a thick cloak, its end thrown up over his left shoulder so that his arms were completely covered. His eyes were fixed on my knife, probably because of the amazing brightness of the blade, but as he saw me look at him he looked away, towards the window behind me. His face was expressionless. He came to a stop about a pace from the window, just in front of me and to my right, and the stink of him made me catch my breath. I ignored him, but opened my lips to breathe through my mouth in an attempt to avoid having to smell him. I tested the now-smooth edge of my nail with a fingertip and slipped my knife back into its sheath before glancing at him again. He seemed to be leaning backwards, slightly, so as to keep the shadow of the window's arch across his face. Idly, not really interested, I pushed my back away from the wall, turned and followed his gaze out into the courtyard beyond the window to see what he was looking at, hoping that whatever it was would be boring, so that he would take himself and his smell back to the far end of the room.

Four prisoners sat in the middle of the yard in chains, bound at the wrists, their arms held tightly in place by thick staves thrust between their backs and their bent elbows. They were shackled together by a chain run through metal rings at their ankles and were guarded by a squad of six soldiers. The ten men were motionless. I sensed that the man beside me had known they were there and had approached the window to look at them.

"Who are they?" I asked him. His strange, misaligned eyes flicked to my face and then away again, back to the courtyard, as if I had not spoken. Apart from that, he ignored me and my question completely. Angered, I stepped around him to the other half of the window and leaned out, my hands on the sill, as much for the fresh air as to see what else was to be seen. As I did so, I sensed him stiffen, but he made no move of any kind.

One of the soldiers in the yard saw the movement at my window and looked across at me. My companion drew back slightly further into the room, a mere half-step, but it alerted me. This man did not want to be seen. I waved casually to the soldier and turned back to the room behind me, resting my buttocks on the edge of the window and carefully looking at no one, although I had no reason for such caution, other than the vague stirring of a soldier's instinct. I heard a door open and close in the yard outside, then the measured, heavy tread of nailed boots on cobbles and the raised, unmistakable voice of a centurion. "Right, you people! Get these animals on their feet and unshackle them. Tribune wants them. Bring them along. Come on, get moving!" There was a shuffling and cursing and the sound of metal links being drawn through an iron ring. The man beside me turned and walked back to his original place, and as he did so, I watched the others in the room and saw four sets of eyes follow him, staring at his face. I might not have noticed his tiny nod of the head, had I not been looking for it. Behind me, the sound of hobnailed boots started up again. I didn't know what was happening here, but every instinct I had was screaming at me that there was trouble brewing.

A new sound caught my attention, coming from the main hallway outside the room we were in: more booted feet, approaching rapidly. I turned and glanced over my shoulder again, out into the yard. A smartly turned-out centurion appeared to be marching directly towards my window, followed at a distance by the six guards, who flanked the four prisoners. Presumably they were headed for the door through which the centurion had entered the yard. Hearing a stirring in the room behind me, I turned back. Three officers, the leading one a giant who stretched a full head taller than his companions, were framed in the doorway of the anteroom, gazing blank-faced with surprise at the horde of people awaiting them.

"What in . . .?" The tall officer's voice unleashed a babel of voices from the room's previously silent occupants, and then they all moved towards him in a surging mass. The two merchants started it, standing up and moving quickly towards the door, but in less than a moment everyone in the room was afoot, and the noise was indescribable as each tried to capture the attention of the tall officer.

The scuffle that followed developed almost faster than I can describe. I saw the big, evil-smelling, cross-eyed lout pushing his way towards the tall officer, and in the same glance I realized the officer was Picus. On an impulse, and asking myself even as I did so if I had lost my mind, I turned and jumped up onto the long bench that had been packed with bodies only moments before, my eyes searching urgently for the other four men I had identified as being part of the cross-eyed man's party. Another of them was very close to Picus, on his other side.

"Picus!" I roared above the din. "Assassins—behind you!"

He heard me and his reaction was immediate. He threw himself forward, stiffening his arms and thrusting his two companions ahead of him, but even as they staggered forward, he was twisting and drawing his blade. I had a brief impression of a swiping knife blade sweeping up and across where his neck should have been, and then I became fully conscious of the danger I myself was in. Three of the four men I had noticed earlier were pushing through the crowd towards me, their eyes hungry for me as they scattered the bodies of those unfortunate enough to be in their way. People were shouting now, alarmed, unable to comprehend what was going on, but knowing that they were in mortal danger.

I looked around me, quickly, weighing the odds in my favour. There were none. The guards in the outer vestibule were stuck there, unable to enter the room because of the mass of panic-stricken people jamming the doorway. The guards against the double doors leading into the audience chamber were pinned there, too, unable to move forward against the press of bodies. Only Picus seemed mobile and armed. I saw no sign of his attackers.

The killer closest to me lunged at me with a *gladium*, and I cursed myself for having no sword of my own. His blade came close to catching me as I sucked in my belly and stabbed at his face with my skystone knife—it was all I had time for, and I had no memory of drawing the knife from its sheath. The point went deep into his right eye and he screamed and threw his hands over his face, falling to his knees.

As the first man fell, one of his companions, pushing close behind him, became entangled in the legs of another fallen man, who had been shoved to the floor and was now scrabbling to escape. This second assassin fell, too, cursing loudly and stabbing viciously at the unfortunate fellow who had tripped him. I raised my good leg to the top of the back of the bench I was on, pushed myself up to teeter there for a moment, and then launched myself at the third and last of my assailants. I saw his sword arm sweep up to chop at me, but I was on top of him before he had a chance to swing, and we crashed down together onto a pile of writhing, squirming bodies. In the chaos of the struggle, I lost him completely. Then I heard someone yelling, "Out, out, away!" and when I managed to sit up I saw three of the original five men, including the one I had just leaped on, making their way hurriedly to the open window. I followed them as quickly as I could, vaulting through the window into the yard, landing on my bad leg and sprawling immediately and painfully on the cobblestones.

Before I could even begin to collect myself, I was flat on my back, with the centurion's sword at my throat. The door he had been about to enter was less than three paces from my window. I had a glimpse of the four prisoners being dragged backwards by their guards, realized how quickly events had transpired, and then I had to give all of my attention to the centurion, who was preparing to kill me.

"Not me! Those others," I roared. "The three ahead of me! They're after your judge, the Regent's deputy! Call out the guard!"

He was a quick thinker. His eyes went quickly to the open window above my head and took in the chaos of noise and movement.

"Shit!" he hissed, dragging me bodily, sideways, towards the door in the wall and releasing me immediately. "Who are they?"

"Don't know, I only caught on by accident. But it's not over."

The evil-smelling lout landed beside me as I said the words. He must have seen me jump and it had taken him this long to cross the crowded room and follow me through the window. His long cloak was gone and he held an axe in one hand and a sword in the other, but that was his undoing. He swung the axe high and took the full force of the centurion's lunging sword at the point of his rib-cage. He staggered backwards with a roar as the blade failed to penetrate the mail shirt he wore under his tunic. I spun sideways on my hip and fought to regain my feet, seeing a guard running full tilt towards our attacker then jerking and spinning and falling with an arrow through his neck. I had seen the flashing flight of the missile and I turned to see who had fired, on my feet at last. Two bowmen, in the entrance to the yard, one of them firing at me even as I looked. I threw myself aside and the arrow zipped past me and struck the centurion on the inside point of the left elbow, jerking him violently around and throwing him to the ground. I heard screams coming from the window above me, and then they were drowned out by a roaring, iron clatter as a four-wheeled wagon, drawn by a team of horses, came swerving into the cobbled yard through the now-open gateway, knocking one of the two bowmen flying before the driver regained control of the vehicle's swing and came charging towards me. I turned and ran to the door in the wall, hauling it open. The men guarding the prisoners still held them, their eyes popping from their heads with indecision.

"Get them inside," I screamed at them. "Then bar the door and get some help out here!"

They hustled their charges inside to safety and I slammed the door shut behind them, realizing belatedly that I could have gone with them. The wagon sounded as though it were almost on top of me and I swung back to face it. There were men in the back and two men on the box seat in front, one clutching the reins and the other holding a huge axe as he fought to keep his balance in the swaying vehicle. The lead horses were less than twelve paces from me, and it was obvious the driver intended to crush me against the wall. I snatched up the centurion's sword in my left hand and flipped my skystone knife, holding it by the point and throwing it with all my strength at the driver's throat. I missed. The hilt struck him high on the forehead, and I saw his head snap back as I launched myself into a diving roll away from the wall, almost under the hooves of the panicked horses, narrowly avoiding the massive, crunching wheel of the wagon. I heard a splintering crash as the side of the cart hit the wall, and then I was on my feet and running in my hobbling, lunging fashion towards the gateway and the bowman I had seen sent flying earlier. I had lost my sword when I hit the ground, dodging the cart, and now I was unarmed and an easy target for the surviving bowman.

The bowman was gone; I could see no sign of him. Only his companion lay where he had fallen, and seven arrows lay scattered on the ground around him. I snatched them up and lurched to where the bow lay, about ten paces distant. No one had bothered with me for some time now. I picked up the bow and nocked an arrow, and then I looked around me. Soldiers were beginning to appear from everywhere, leaping from open windows and running at the double in files around the sides of the buildings at the far end of the yard, spreading out as they came. I saw the centurion's body huddled motionless against the wall below the anteroom window, and even from where I was, I could see the blood that covered him. I guessed he had been run over by the cart, and even as I thought it, I saw the cart, now in the middle of the yard, begin to move again. The four would-be assassins were now on board, surrounded by a half dozen others who must have been in the body of the cart all the time. The man at the reins now, a different man from the one at whom I had thrown my knife, was whipping furiously at the horses, dragging them around in a wide circle as they picked up speed, using the wagon itself as a weapon against the foot-soldiers who were now converging from all sides. Javelins arched through the air and fell useless to the ground, and then the arc of the wagon was complete and it came thundering towards me again, headed directly for the still-open gate.

"Close the gates," I yelled, but nobody heard me. A thin-spread line of legionaries had formed across the open gate, but I could see that they were useless and would be annihilated by the oncoming wagon. And then another thought occurred to me, chilling me, and I knew what I had to do.

I drew the bowstring to my ear—it was much lighter than my own great bow—and sighted on the lead horse closest to me, aiming for the soft spot between its neck and shoulders. The shot went straight and true and the animal went directly to its knees in mid-stride, its dead weight pulling its running mate off balance and interfering with the horse directly behind it, so that the wagon slewed violently and several of its occupants went flying.

My second arrow struck the other lead horse moments later and it screamed and tried to rear up. The wagon crashed over onto its side in a ruin and was immediately surrounded by soldiers, who made short work of the surviving passengers. I was too far away to do anything about the slaughter.

I waited until the initial activity was all over and then made my way towards the remains of the wreck. As I drew near, I saw one soldier bend and pick up a bright-bladed knife.

"That's mine," I called. "Thank you."

He looked at me, frowning. "What d'you mean, it's yours?" His voice was truculent.

"Look at the cross hilt," I said. I was close to him now. "It's inscribed with a V. Stands for Varrus. That's me."

The soldier looked, but he was still suspicious. "Then what's it doing here? And who are you?"

"I'm the one who raised the alarm, and it's there because I threw it at the driver. It hit him hilt first and fell back into the wagon. Is the centurion dead?"

"What centurion?"

I sighed and tried again. "Have you ever heard of the Emperor's Regent, Stilicho?"

" 'Course I have. Why? Who wants to know?"

I sighed again. My legs felt weak and there was a strange drumming in my ears. I squeezed my eyes shut then opened them wide, hanging on to my patience with great difficulty.

"I want to know. My name, my full name, is Gaius Publius Varrus and I have business with Stilicho's deputy, Picus Britannicus. Now take me to him, and bring my knife with you."

He looked at me for one more long moment and then apparently decided that he might be well advised to take me at my word. He handed me my skystone knife and beckoned me to accompany him. I tucked the knife into its sheath and followed.

The yard behind the basilica was seething with activity now, soldiers running in every direction. As we approached the door in the courtyard wall, four men were lifting a stretcher holding the body of the centurion. I signalled to my escort and he followed me as I made my way to them. I was surprised to find the centurion not only alive but conscious and *compos mentis*. He recognized me immediately and spoke in a strong voice.

"Who are you?"

"Name's Varrus, Publius Varrus." My voice sounded hollow. "How are you?"

"I'll live." He grunted and his lips twisted in a spasm of pain, but he went on. "Might not fight again, though. Elbow's shot off and my leg's broke. You don't look too good yourself. Is all that blood yours?"

"Blood? What blood?" I raised my hand to my head and brought it away sticky and red. "Hunh," I remember saying, "I suppose it must be." Then the roaring in my ears grew much louder and my knees gave way and I fell across him. I felt myself being picked up and carried, and then I lost consciousness completely.

When I awoke I found myself on a clean cot, my head swathed in bandages, being watched closely by a young soldier who asked me if I could hear him and then left as soon as I'd answered.

I remained flat on my back for a while, then gathered my strength and rose to my feet. I could hear strange noises in my head and the room swayed alarmingly for a few moments, but the dizziness soon passed. I walked cautiously across the room, then rested and prepared to do it again. But before I could begin, I heard footsteps approaching, and then the door swung open and I saw Picus looking down at me.

The boy I remembered was long vanished from this man. Picus was truly enormous! Each of us had now to adjust physically to the changes in the other. He towered more than a full head above me, and the rest of his body was scaled perfectly to his height. I could have fitted twice into his breastplate, and the strength of his arms as he hugged me threatened to crush my ribs. It was a joyous reunion. I knew why Caius was as proud as he was of this towering young giant he had sired.

"Uncle Varrus," he growled, in a great, deep voice. "Thank you, I owe you my life. How do you feel?"

I wrinkled my nose, wondering the same thing myself. "I don't know, Picus. Fine, I think, but not half as good as you look. Can I get out of here?"

Picus looked at the man beside him, a medic, from the looks of him, and said, "Well? Can he?"

The medic pursed his lips and shook his head. "I don't think he should, but he looks determined to go."

"I'm fine," I said. "My head aches, but there's nothing wrong with me, look!" I drew a deep breath and started to touch my toes, but the room started to spin around me and I sank back to sit on the side of the cot. Picus and the medic watched me, neither of them speaking. The room settled down after a few moments and I began to feel better. I raised my hands to the bandages around my head and face. "What happened to me? I wasn't wounded in the fight. No one came near me."

"Scalp wound," the medic said. "Don't know how you got it, but it bled a lot, for all that it's only superficial. I couldn't see any real damage. You have a hard head."

I probed more firmly with my fingertips and found a sore spot high on the thickest part of my skull on the right side, and an immediate vision swept into my head of the thundering, iron-shod wheel of the charging wagon as it swept by me. It had been closer than I thought. The hub must have scraped my head.

The medic left to carry on with his business, and Picus led me to the rooms that had been placed at his disposal, where he poured us both a cup of wine.

"Well," he said, after we had drunk, "what was all that about, do you suppose?"

I put my cup down carefully. "Seneca."

"What?" His eyebrow shot up like his father's.

"Claudius Seneca. You asked me what that was all about. I answered you."

"That's impossible."

I shook my head. "No, it's an absolute certainty, but you'll never prove it, unless your torturers can wring a confession out of the man I wounded."

"Nuh." Picus shook his head. "The big fellow killed him before he fled the room."

I sucked air through my teeth and sniffed loudly. "Now why doesn't that surprise me? No witnesses . . . I thought at first they were after the prisoners out in the yard. . . . I noticed the four of them all watching their leader before you arrived. He'd been standing looking out the window, at the prisoners, I thought. But now I think he was only checking their escape route. It was us they were after. Me and you. And they'd have had us if that whoreson hadn't smelled so foul. I paid more attention to him than I normally would have, just because he was so offensively dirty. I knew they were up to something, but it was only when I saw two of them sidling up to you that I raised the alarm."

He gulped more wine. "Thank the gods you did, too, otherwise he'd have killed me. I hadn't suspected a thing."

"I know. I didn't realize until I was in the thick of it that I was a target, too. So it had to be Seneca. He found out you were going to be here today, and that I was joining you. It was a perfect situation, away from the *praesidium*, and it would have been a perfect revenge—on me, on your father, on you, and on Stilicho. Where's Seneca now?"

"Gone. He left last night, with Stilicho, and won't be back. Stilicho has demoted him, in effect. He'll retain his rank . . . still be a legate entitled to command a legion . . . but he's been assigned to frontier duty in a subservient capacity, up behind the Wall. That should keep him out of mischief. He'll have no more time to be plotting revenge on you or anyone else. He'll ride with Stilicho as far as Pontes, and then Seneca will head north, to the Wall, with the new unit that just arrived from Gaul . . ." He stopped, thinking deeply. "No, by God, he won't. I'll have the whoreson recalled."

I held up my hand to give him pause. "Don't bother, Picus. Leave well enough alone. We're alive, he's gone, and with any blessing from Fortune some northern Pict will soon have his head on a spear. Should he survive, on the other hand, and be foolish enough to come back, *I'll* have his head on a spear. But for now, as I said, there's really nothing we can do, except bring charges against him that we can't substantiate. We can't prove a thing. At least he thinks we're dead."

Picus looked at me and grinned. "It's good to see you again, Uncle Varrus. I had forgotten how cool-headed you always are."

"Don't deceive yourself, Picus. Given half a chance, I'd disembowel that man with my bare hands."

·He rose to his feet. "Come on, let's get out of here. How do you feel?"

"I'm fine, but what about your judiciary?"

"Postponed. I'm free."

"Then let's go."

XVI

A SHORT TIME later, we were leaving Londinium, and five short miles after that, we clattered onto the packed earth of the parade ground outside the gates of a large equine camp the likes of which I had never seen. A military camp for horsemen! There were horses everywhere, thousands of them. I gazed avidly around me, making no move to dismount, and seeing my awe, Picus began to lead me through the lines to where a massive standard of black and white cloth marked his quarters, a large and spacious tent.

I nodded towards the great standard. "That's yours, I take it?"

"It is. What do you think of it?"

I grunted. "It's big enough."

"What is that supposed to mean?" he asked, laughing. "Don't you like it?"

I tried to bluster, to cover up my discomfort with what seemed to me to be a gratuitous overstatement. "Well, now that you ask me, it seems a bit ostentatious."

"Of course it is, it's blatantly ostentatious. That's the whole idea of it, Uncle. It's big enough to be seen and identified from a long way off. Look at the base of it."

I saw that the bottom of the shaft ended in a wide, padded fork. Picus was nodding enthusiastically.

"That padded fork fits over the horse's neck, so the weight doesn't tire the standard-bearer. Stilicho is half Vandal. These new standards were his idea. He adapted them from the kind used by his own people and by the Goths and the Huns." Something else caught his eyes and he nodded to direct my attention towards it. "Look at that."

"That" was formation drill being practised by massed phalanxes of horsemen. We sat our horses and watched them for a while, and then Picus nudged his mount into motion again and this time, when he spoke, neither his voice nor his words bore any relationship to the conversation that had gone before.

"My father's getting old, Uncle."

I looked at him sideways. "Is he? You'd better not tell him that!" I heard surprise and defensiveness in my own tone, and I recognized that I had been lying to myself. I, too, had noticed a change in Britannicus but had chosen to ignore what my eyes were telling me. Caius was no longer young. He had lost weight, muscle, resilience and vitality. All on the physical side, of course. Mentally he was keener than ever. I suddenly felt guilty.

"Well," I admitted reluctantly, "I suppose, now that you bring it up, he is not as young a man as he was when I first met him. Nor even as he was when you left home. But he's not aged, senile or infirm."

"No, I know." Picus's headshake was abrupt. "I didn't mean it that way. God knows, he's strong enough—probably more so than he was when we returned from Africa, twenty years ago—but he looks old, Uncle. I've been carrying a picture of him in my mind for years now, and it's an image of a much, much younger man." There was silence between us for a few moments, until he continued. "Is he happy, Uncle Varrus? Does he enjoy his life?"

I thought for a few moments before answering that, staring at my horse's ears. "What do you want me to say, Picus? Those are two powerful questions. Can any man be happy in this world? What is happiness, anyway? It's different for everyone. A man grows older every day and watches his friends die off. His illusions dry up and blow away in the wind. And every day, it seems, he develops more . . . what's the word I'm looking for? Appreciation? It's as good as any . . . more appreciation of the weakness and stupidities of his fellow men, who are just ordinary people like himself. No recipe for happiness in that, Picus. I can't tell you your father's happy. He's himself. He's busy all day long, his life is good, and he seems satisfied. But happy? I don't know."

"Has he no female friends? Companions?"

I shook my head. "No. None. Except for his sister and the wives of some of his old friends. But those aren't companions. At least, not in the sense I think you mean. If you're asking me if he dallies with women, the answer's no. Never. Your father is the most abstemious man I've ever known, in that regard. He knows no women. I doubt if he even thinks of them. He certainly never speaks of them."

Even as I was speaking the words, I found myself wondering what motivated Picus to ask the question. His own mother, Heraclita, whom Caius had loved and revered, had died with her twin sons and a daughter in a plague in Africa, when Picus was a lad of twelve. Was this the jealous son speaking? Did he believe that Caius should still be faithful to her memory? I knew that was unworthy as the thought occurred to me, and that Picus had asked only out of concern for his father. His next words showed that to be true.

"Then he's lonely?"

"Lonely?" For some reason, the word surprised me and brought me up short, so that I had to repeat it and think about it carefully before responding to him. "Lonely . . . I suppose he is. But then, who isn't?" I laughed aloud. "Picus, we live in a lonely world. Some of us go to great lengths to avoid it, but we can't, because inside his head—inside his soul, if you like—every man is alone. Haven't you ever noticed that? That's why we say 'every single man,' I suppose."

Picus frowned. "Aye, you're right! It's true. I've never really thought about it before, but you're right. Even in battle, every man's alone."

I cocked my head, emphasizing my agreement with that sentiment. "Particularly in battle, son. Ask me about that. I'm the expert on it. In the middle of the wildest fighting, I'm so alone it's as though I were outside myself, looking down at what's going on. And when it's all over and the danger's gone, my world comes back together very slowly. But not until I've been sick. I have to vomit up that loneliness, that insularity, every single time."

Now Picus kneed his big horse closer to me and glanced at me, so that I saw his face, wrinkled with concern. "Are you truly a Christian, Uncle Varrus?"

I blinked at him, caught off-balance by the unexpected question and its modifier. "What does that have to do with anything?"

"A great deal, Uncle." He smiled at me. "I could start preaching at you that a man is never alone if he has God in his heart. But that's not what I meant. I meant are you really a Christian?"

I shrugged, feeling slightly embarrassed by the sudden intimacy of the subject. "I suppose I am." My response was almost sullen, almost an inchoate mumble. "Isn't everybody? I was baptized before I had much time to think about it. I grew up a Christian. I swore my legionary's oath on the Christian cross. Why do you ask me that?"

He was insistent, his tone almost hectoring. "Do you believe in God? That He exists?"

"Of course I do . . . at least, I think I do." Now I was perplexed. "What are you driving at? Don't you believe in God?"

He screwed up his face into a portrait of doubt that might have been comic, but I found myself again admiring the hugeness of him and the picture he made in his magnificent uniform, and saw nothing strange in such a big and obviously competent man agonizing over the existence of God.

"Sometimes I think I do," he said. "Sometimes it's easy. And then there are times when I think I don't. If God were what the priests would have us believe, then this world would have to be a better place to live in. But I have seen things, and have done things as a soldier that God should not allow. Not if He's as good and just and merciful as they say He is."

I sucked on my teeth. "That's what the priests say, Picus. But they say more than their prayers at times, and I've never yet met one of them, even our holy Bishop Alaric, who can prove that he has spoken directly and personally, face to face with God. Mind you," I hurried on, conscious of a sudden feeling of disloyalty to my old friend, "Alaric would never dream of claiming to have any avenue of privileged communication with the Creator. It is too bad that there are few other priests like him." I shifted the grip of my legs and turned further on my horse's back to look more closely at Picus. "How old are you now, Picus? Thirty-six?"

"Yes."

"Well, then, in Christ's name, holy or not, you have better things to be worrying about than that. God is an old man's worry, not a soldier's."

Picus laughed aloud, and then went on to talk fondly of old Alaric, and

I found myself realizing that Alaric was, in the truest sense of the word, quite venerable nowadays. And that, naturally, started me thinking about my own years, something I seldom did. But Picus was talking again.

"He really is holy, isn't he?"

"Who? Alaric?" I cleared my throat and thought about that for several heartbeats before answering. "Yes, Picus, I believe he is. He is probably the most saintly, down-to-earth, true Christian I have ever met. I think our good friend Alaric is genuinely a man of God, a godly man, unlike so many of his fellow priests who assume that rank. Alaric is the only priest I know who lives his beliefs according to the teachings of the Christ."

"Is that your belief?" He was looking at me strangely. "About priests, I mean?"

"Did I state a belief about priests?"

"No"—he was grinning now "—but your praise of them was faint."

Both our horses had stopped moving, and now I kicked mine forward again. "Picus," I said, "I have no time for priests. Never have had." His mount followed mine automatically and we rode knee to knee as I went on. "I've discussed this many times with Alaric, and it is his opinions that have influenced my thoughts, although he would probably die of mortification if he ever thought I could have construed his words the way I have." I spat, for my mouth was suddenly filled with bitterness.

"Priests are men, Picus," I said. "And the majority of men are feeble things, beneath all their bombast. Since the days of the Christ, men have taken His teachings and warped them to their own ways. The Church has usurped the power of God. Its officers—for what is a bishop but an officer of the Church?—have corrupted the teachings of the gentle Saviour and used them to procure power for themselves on earth. Whenever I hear a priest other than Alaric speak, all he does is rant of sin and damnation. There is no joy in priests. And there is no joy in their teachings. They preach subservience and penitence, and it grows worse each time I hear one of them. Haven't you noticed it? Surely you must have?"

Picus merely shrugged his shoulders, unwilling, it seemed, to interrupt me, and so I continued. "It has become fashionable among churchmen to decry women nowadays, and to do it openly. All women! Women like your Aunt Luceiia! That was not always so, Picus. Not when I was a boy. It may have been the fashion in Rome, even then, I don't know about that, but it was not so here in Britain. And Alaric tells me that it is growing worse. Have you heard of the monastics?" He nodded, still wordless, and I pressed him on the point. "So? What have you heard?"

But Picus was not to be drawn out. He shook his head in a negative and asked me, "What do *you* think of them, Uncle?"

"Damnation, Picus, I don't know what to think! It reeks of unwholesomeness. From what I know of it, there are whole colonies of men locking themselves away from life in places they call monasteries, denying themselves the slightest pleasure in life, praying all day and all night long, castigating

themselves, whipping themselves with flails to purge their minds of any
carnal thoughts. They believe women are an abomination. Well, to me, *that's*
abomination! I've talked to Alaric about this many times. He's unwilling to
come right out and condemn the movement, for he believes every man must
find his own route to the life hereafter, and he would like to think that there
are mysterious and divine forces at work in all things, but he doesn't like
what's happening. He tells me it all began in Egypt, about a hundred years
ago, and that the core of the monastic way is a belief in St. Paul's dictum
that if a man cannot abjure his sexual nature, it is better for him to marry
than to burn with lust."

"And what is your response to that?"

"My response is only my own and I'm no scholar."

"But?"

"Yes, but! It seems to my unlettered military simplicity that the blessed
Paul much preferred men to women."

"Sexually, you mean?"

"Can you name me another way?"

"So are you suggesting that monastics are homosexual?"

I laughed, angry though I was. "Of course not, Picus! I'm saying I think
they all seem perverted in what appears to be a hatred of women! There is
no evidence of misogyny in Jesus' life or teaching, is there? The contrary is
true, in fact. But priests today are dealing more and more in hate rather than
love. They deal in fear. They deal in damnation and punishment and guilt
and sin. There is no talk of love, compassion or forgiveness in their doctrine.
They have become bureaucrats, with the pinched and narrow minds and souls
of bureaucrats. They are modelling their Church in Rome, and their entire
hierarchy, on the Imperial Roman Civil Service, in the Christ's name! They
live in palaces and expect their flock to furnish them with everything they
require! Let's talk no more of priests, I may be sick!"

Picus cleared his throat and said nothing more for a few moments, and
we rode in silence, looking at the ongoing life of the camp. Then, "Have you
ever heard of Pelagius, Uncle?" I knew immediately, from the way the question
came so directly out of nowhere, that this casual question was important to
Picus.

"No," I said, keeping my voice deliberately expressionless. "Who is he?"

"He's a lawyer. From Britain. But he has lived in Rome for many years
now. He's very highly thought of there."

"No lawyer is ever highly thought of by anyone with a brain in his head,
Picus," I scoffed, "unless it be another lawyer, and then it's envy."

He refused to be amused. Not a hint of a smile touched his face as he
went on. "What do you know about Original Sin?"

I hauled on my reins and stopped my horse, controlling it with my knees
as I danced it around to follow the progress of a work party that was passing
us, loaded down with armloads of weapons, including a number of short,
two-edged, wicked-looking spears. I watched them until they vanished around

a corner at the crossroads of the camp, and then I returned my attention to Picus, resuming the conversation where I had abandoned it.

"What do I know of Original Sin? Same as everyone else. Nothing. That's too deep for an old soldier, Picus. I was born with it, they told me, and they baptized me to cure me of it, so I don't have it any more. That's enough for any man to know." I kicked my horse into motion and Picus moved with me, talking again.

"Pelagius says it's wrong. He says the whole notion stinks. He believes that the Church has invented Original Sin and is promoting the notion to keep men mired in guilt, believing themselves sinners since before they were born."

I nodded. "Sounds like a clever man. What we used to call a barrack-room lawyer. How old is this fellow?"

"He's young. And he is very clever."

We were still riding along the main thoroughfare of the camp, and as we spoke my eyes were ranging the length and breadth of the place, taking everything in and missing nothing. "So what does your friend recommend? That we abolish sin?"

"No, Uncle Varrus. It's not as simple as that. It all has to do with grace."

I looked at him sharply, feeling a stabbing fear that this young man was becoming too deeply embroiled in the deep and spiritual matters of the religious side of life. "Grace?" I asked scornfully. "You mean divine grace? By the Christ!" I threw up my hands in frustration. "What is grace, in God's name, for any man to understand? I gave up on grace when I was a boy. I saw it as an endless stream of rice grains being poured into the cylinder of my soul whenever some angel pulled a string! Don't try to talk about grace, boy, or to understand it! It's what the priests call a divine mystery. In other words, it's none of your damn business."

Picus seemed to have no trouble with the viewpoint I expounded. "I agree with you, Uncle. But please, will you listen to what I have to say?"

"I'm listening. What do you want to tell me?"

"Just that . . ." He stopped, gathering his thoughts, and then started again. "I spent some days with Pelagius last year and talked with him for hours. He's a fascinating man. But he *is* a man."

"So? Should I be surprised?"

"No, but think of what that says. He is a man, and no more than a man. And so are all the bishops and the priests of the Holy Church. And men can make mistakes. And men can do the most *un*holy things to gain their own ends, if they are convinced that their own way is right and that it is the only way."

I looked hard at him, recognizing the authority he brought to that statement and agreeing with him. "Aye, you're right there, Picus, God knows." I spat over my horse's ears. "Heaven defend me from such good men."

"You and all the rest of us."

We were riding among the paddocks, now; they seemed to stretch endlessly in every direction, packed with beautiful horseflesh. I reined my mount more tightly.

"You intrigue me, Picus. Tell me more of this Pelagius. What did he say to you to upset you this much, so long afterwards?"

He shook his head. "No, Uncle, he did not upset me—at least, not quite, not immediately. It took me a long time and a deal of thought to appreciate what it was that Pelagius said to me . . . Are you familiar with the name of Augustine, the Bishop of Hippo?"

Again, I felt a sense of things of import crossing my horizons. I shook my head. "No, not at all. Tell me about him, too."

"Well," he went on, with a barely discernible hesitation that was emphasized by its briefness, "Augustine is one of the most respected scholars of the Church. A very wise and learned man and a famed interpreter of the Word of God."

"Oh! One of those. That sounds ominous. Go on."

"Augustine, whom most men call a saintly man, has come into conflict with Pelagius—or, rather, it's the other way around. Pelagius has locked horns with Augustine."

"So? What's the problem of the saintly Augustine?"

"Pelagius thinks he is a hypocrite and a liar."

I whistled to myself. "Has he told him so?"

"He has told the entire world."

"Why? For what reasons?" In spite of myself, in spite of the fact that I knew nothing of this Pelagius, I felt dismayed by this last statement of Picus's. "If, as you say, everyone thinks Augustine is a saintly man, your Pelagius runs a very real risk of being thought a madman, or a trouble-maker."

We had almost completed a circuit of the camp by now, and I saw Picus's great standard come into view again in the distance. Picus was still talking very seriously. "Quite so," he said. "But it is bigger than that. Augustine is the champion of the theory of divine grace. He is a man of God. A bishop. But in his youth he was a notorious womanizer."

"A womanizer? Really?" I found that intriguing, but not surprising. "Was he a priest at the time?"

Picus shook his head. "No, I don't think so. Anyway, he has a prayer that has become notorious. He used to pray that God would send him the grace to find chastity . . . but not yet!"

I laughed, but Picus went right on over my laughter.

"Augustine believes that man is incapable of finding or winning redemption without divine help. He believes that man is born damned, in mortal sin. Only baptism will wash away that sin, and only divine grace can enable man to stay away from sin thereafter. He believes that all of life is a temptation and that man should spend his life in prayer, abandoning himself to God's mercy in bestowing grace upon him."

I nodded. "That, my young friend, is the view one tends to get from an ecclesia. That's what all the priests say. There's nothing new in what you've told me, except the saintly bishop's own example . . . And you say Pelagius finds fault with this?" He nodded. "How?"

"Totally. Pelagius believes that the entire concept of grace is a man-made device invented by the Church to keep all men in bondage."

"Hah! Come on now, your friend Pelagius is beginning to sound like one of those old women who sees a rapist behind every bush. How can divine help keep men in bondage?"

"It works by making men forget that they are made in the image of God Himself, and therefore able to determine between right and wrong."

I saw the flaw immediately. "But that's not possible. Your man *is* mad! Men have known the difference between right and wrong since Eve ate the apple. The knowledge of good and evil. Men have always known the difference."

"Exactly, Uncle. That's what Pelagius says." I felt myself frowning in confusion as Picus went on, "Pelagius argues that man, made in the image of God, knows the difference between good and evil, and has the ability to choose between them, and has always done so, even before the time of the Christ. Even barbarians have their moral laws, unwritten though they may be. Pelagius sees this divine grace as an instrument of men, designed to keep all other men in subjugation and reliant on the Church as the only intermediary between God and man. He sees Original Sin as an invention foisted upon men by other men to make all men guilty at birth, and therefore incapable of freedom of choice from the outset. If we are born guilty in sin before we begin to live, how can we live in freedom with free will?"

I was holding my breath by this time, beginning to get an idea of the size of this disagreement.

"Hold on, Picus," I said, holding up my hand to stem the flow of his words and his enthusiasm. "Too much good fodder will founder a bullock! You had better let me think about that for a while, lad." We were approaching his tent. "Can you pour your old uncle a drink?"

We dismounted and moved into the coolness of the tent, and he sent his steward to fetch a jug of wine. When we were seated comfortably he went back at it again, right where he'd finished off.

"Do you see what I mean, Uncle, why I am so concerned with this question? The whole thing goes far beyond the premise of Original Sin and baptism. It digs far deeper. It comes down all the way to personal responsibility. Carried to its logical conclusion, the concept of divine grace destroys the basis of law. Who could punish a criminal, believing that the man only fell from righteousness because God did not provide him with the grace to resist temptation? That's reducing it to the absurd, but that is exactly what it all boils down to. If we accept the wholesome aspects of divine grace, we can paint a beautiful, piteous picture of poor mankind and his all-merciful and bountiful Deity. But if we are to accept that premise at all, we must accept all of it. And that means accepting the fact that law—human law—is folly and predestined to fail, because ultimately, in the absence of grace, the fault for crime can be laid right at God's door."

I shook my head again, sucking nervously on my teeth, knowing that this entire discussion was beyond my scope. "Whoa," I pleaded, "you're getting pretty involved in your thinking there, lad. You're far beyond my grasp."

"No, I'm not, Uncle."

That earned him a snap. "For God's sake stop calling me Uncle. You make me feel like a toothless old man."

"I'm sorry." He did not sound in the least penitent. "But it's not beyond your grasp at all. Pelagius believes, as the Scriptures tell us, that God made man in His own image. If man has the attributes of God, he says, then man must have free will. The majority of men know that society demands certain rules for the governance of property, sanity, decency and dignity. Those rules constitute the law. Pelagius maintains that a man—any man—born with the divine spark is free to choose between good and evil as defined by both Church and society. If he chooses to go against the law, be it divine or human, that choice is his own, and he has to be prepared to accept the responsibility for his choice in the eyes of God and in the eyes of his fellow men."

He stopped talking, and a silence grew between us, broken only by the sound of a man singing nearby. I mulled over all that he had said. He had said a lot. But it made a lot of sense.

"You say this man's a lawyer?" He nodded. "Do you believe him? Or do you believe Augustine and the Church?"

He gnawed at his lower lip. "I believe Pelagius."

I sucked a grape seed caught between my teeth. "It takes a lot of nerve to go against the Church. I'd never heard of this fellow Pelagius before this morning, but he makes sense to me, too. How far has this argument between them gone?"

"A long way. It's the talk of Rome."

"Sounds like it might become the talk of all the world. And you say this bishop is powerful?"

"Extremely. He has powerful friends, great influence. Some say he should be Pope."

"Sounds like your friend Pelagius is spitting into the wind. Will they reach an agreement? Some kind of compromise?"

"How can they? They're like day and night."

"Aye, and darkness is falling quickly, it would seem. Does Pelagius have any support within the Church? Or is everyone convinced he is possessed by evil spirits?"

"He has support. In plenty. Many of the most powerful espouse his cause."

"How many? In terms of odds, I mean. Is there an even match?"

"Perhaps. There could be. If we were dealing only in numbers."

"What d'you mean?"

"Uncle—I'm sorry—Publius, is that better?"

"Much better."

"So be it. The question here is one of basic policy. An army mutineer may have some right on his side in terms of the conditions that drove him to mutiny. But he has to die for his mutiny, no matter how laudable his cause might have been, no matter how understandable and sympathetic his motives. Mutiny cannot be condoned, no matter what the justification. To condone one instance of mutiny would be to invite, and to incite, the eventual and inevitable destruction of all the armies. So it is with Pelagius. He has to lose, or overthrow five hundred years of a Church established by the Christ Himself, with all its rules and methods. Pelagius knows this, Publius; he is not a stupid man. He is not challenging the Christ's Church but men's corruption of it, yet he knows he is too late to alter what others, stronger men than he, have been building for centuries, with a view to making it eternal. You see, Pelagius's doctrine, if you want to call it that, destroys the need for a Church just as surely as Augustine's doctrine destroys the need for the law. Pelagius is saying that every man carries the whole Church within his heart, and that he can commune directly with God by simply meditating! Augustine is saying that man is absolutely nothing without the Christian Church, which has as its symbol the Keys to the Kingdom of Heaven. The Church already speaks for God. Pelagius speaks for man. Therefore, Pelagius *must* be defeated in this struggle."

"And when he is defeated? What will you do then?"

Picus shrugged his enormous shoulders. "I will live my life by the rules he has evolved. I believe he is right, no matter what the evidence against him may be. I will stand before God as I have lived, and if I have been wrong, then at least I will have been wrong honestly, with good will. I will have lived my life according to the rules that I was taught in youth. I'm no great sinner."

I smiled, sensing with great relief that this conversation was drawing to a close. "That I believe." I stood up and clapped him on the shoulder. "Now, enough of this talk of God and man. Let's take a walk together and enjoy this day that God has sent for us to enjoy, whatever way he wants us to believe."

"Done!" He smiled at me, and I saw the boy I once knew in his flashing, bronze-faced grin.

I pointed at the sword hanging by his side. "That looks familiar."

He drew the blade from its bronzed sheath. "It should," he said. "It has never left my side since the day you gave it to me. I found a metalsmith in Iberia who seemed to know what he was about and had him make a gold sheath for me, for full-uniform parade occasions. But gold sheath or bronze, the sword stays with me at all times."

He swung towards the doorway of the tent, but I stopped him, my hand on his arm. "A moment, Picus. You are obviously deeply concerned over this Pelagius thing. But tell me, why did you talk to me about it? I would have thought you'd get more intellectual response from your father."

He grimaced. "It's not the sort of thing I want to argue with my father over yet. I'm afraid I was using you as a sounding board. I'm sorry if I bored you."

"Bored me?" I laughed aloud. "Picus, I've seldom been so far from bored. I may have been out of my depth, but I wasn't bored for one moment. Come on, let's get on our way. There is much that I haven't seen here, and I want to see it all before I leave for home."

He looked at me with a smile.

"Home? You mean the atmosphere of power here in Londinium does not enthrall you? You must run home to your provinces?"

"Aye," I said, "to your Aunt Luceiia, and I care not who knows it or would laugh at me for it."

"Uncle," Picus said, still smiling, "you will hear neither laughter nor criticism from me."

BOOK THREE
GENESIS

XVII

IN SPITE OF the light-heartedness I assumed in speaking of Luceiia to Picus, I was—and had been since the outset of this journey—far from easy in my mind about the prospect of returning home. The truth, quite simply, was that the fear of going home was driving me to distraction. Aware of the old belief that a man can know no finer sensation than arriving home after an arduous and extended absence, I was haunted and hag-ridden by the corollary truth that the pleasure and welcome that man received on his arrival must depend upon the degree to which his absence had been regretted by those awaiting him. My misgivings—my self-flagellating terror—on those grounds had almost brought me to despair at times, when I recalled the betrayal and the pain I had visited upon my undeserving wife and the cold, distant way she had reacted to me afterwards.

Convinced within my soul that I had earned not merely her distrust, but also her dislike, I had found myself terrified, ever since my release from jail, of spending time alone, for solitude invited grim Despair to come and leer and gibber in my mind. Alone with my thoughts, I could not evade my guilt and apprehension, nor could I hide from my deep-seated fear of the prospect of a life of any kind without Luceiia's love. I knew, too, that the greatest part of what I felt sprang from my guilt over what had *not* occurred—that which had been neither suspected nor admitted—the still-fresh, hidden secret of my involvement with Cylla Titens, and it was that knowledge that robbed me of the power to think of my punishment as being anything other than just and merited.

On a rainy afternoon of gusty winds and threatening storms, I knew that this stage of my agony was almost ended, and that the semblance of carefree victory I had maintained so carefully and with such painstaking attention to detail among my fellows was shortly to be exposed for what it was: the posturing of a lost soul. Rather than promising an end, however, that knowledge came close to crushing me. Tomorrow we would come to Camulod.

We had made excellent time on the road back from Londinium, jubilant as the others were with the news of Stilicho's Commission and confident of the triumphal welcome that lay ahead of all of them at the end of our journey. On the last stage, we had a choice of pressing on and arriving at the villa in the middle of the night, or of stopping to sleep under the forest trees for one more night and arriving home with the new day. We chose the latter, my voice among the loudest in support of the idea, and we awoke with the skylarks while the sky itself was still dark, moving on as soon as the light began to penetrate the forest, so that we came in sight of the Colony home farm just as the sun rose fully over it, all signs of the previous night's threatened storm long-vanished. As I looked about me, and for the first time in my adult life, I experienced an almost overwhelming urge to run away and hide myself from the eyes of men, emasculated by the threat of what lay directly ahead of me.

High on the hill to the south-west of us, overlooking the villa and all the lands around, sat the still-unfinished walls of our new fort, picked out clearly and burnished in the light of the new day. Gone was all sign of the forest that had burgeoned there for such a short-lived time, and even I felt good to know that never again would we feel a need to hide our achievements there. Plautus, who had heard about the disguising of the hill and its fort, laid eyes on the site and promptly decided that we had gulled him. Now that he could see it for himself, he said, he refused to believe that we had ever been able to conceal it, and looking at the size of the hill and its crowning fort from this distance, I could appreciate his skepticism. Caius and I merely smiled at each other and left him to believe what he wanted to believe, and Caius nodded to the north, where fresh cloud banks were already rolling in again. "It will be pleasant to rest snug and comfortable by a glowing fire tonight while the rain falls outside on other people," he said, and I smiled and nodded, pretending to agree with him, and then I had no other choice but to keep up with him as we galloped the rest of the way. And suddenly, insanely, considering what I expected to find there, I found myself wild with impatience to be home.

Our welcome was chaotic and overwhelming, but it broke over and about me like crashing waves seen from afar and unheard as I slid down from my horse in an island of silence that surrounded me alone and kept me isolated in the din. But then, to my astounded disbelief, I saw Luceiia flying at me, her face radiant, weeping openly with relief and love as she ran to meet me, uncaring who was watching. The feel of her body as she threw her arms around my neck and leaned into my embrace purged all the frantic virulence of my terrors instantly, as though they had never been, replacing them with vibrant, urgent images of pleasures we had known and shared after even brief separations in the young days of our marriage. So total and insistently demanding was my own unbearable relief at seeing her and holding her again and knowing that she was still mine, that in spite of all the hubbub around us, I managed to spirit her away to our own room, where we tumbled each other hurriedly like a couple of spring foals and yet thoroughly, too, like the well-accustomed partners that we were. No word was spoken of our parting or the quarrel that had prompted it. The only words we spoke were breathless, frantic, tense and urgent, taut, ill-formed, well known and deeply, mutually experienced sounds of pleasure, long denied and fervently devout.

We rejoined the others later, hand in hand, flushed with our renewed knowledge of each other.

Everyone in the Colony had assembled in the grounds of the villa within the hour and rumours of our journey and our adventures were on everybody's tongue, contradicting each other in the telling and breeding variants of themselves in the repetition. Variations on the story abounded so riotously that they reached the point eventually where Caius was forced to call everyone to attention and make an impromptu speech, telling the news of our official recognition as a Colonia and of the designation of our military resources as Irregular Troops. There would be a full meeting of the Council the following day, he said, for the purpose of thorough discussion of the differences our new Commission would make to all aspects of our future life here.

There was little work done on the Colony that day. It was a spontaneous holiday and the midday meal developed into a major celebration that lasted well into the late afternoon, in spite of the rain that fell intermittently throughout the day. When darkness fell, the last, determined celebrants removed themselves indoors and lighted, it seemed, every lamp and candle in the Colony to accommodate their dancing, games and music. By the time Luceiia and I regained our bed, legitimately this time, we were both almost exhausted enough to fall asleep immediately, wrapped in each other's arms. Almost, but fortunately not quite exhausted enough.

I was first into bed and I lay flat on my back listening to the sounds of Luceiia removing her clothing in the darkness. Neither of us had spoken since entering the house and making our way directly to our sleeping chamber, and I lay there wondering what was going through her mind as she disrobed. Moments later, she raised the coverings and slipped in beside me, and I extended my left arm to pillow her head. She moved directly to me, shaping herself to the outline of my side, settling her head into the hollow of my neck and shoulder and laying the silken weight of her left thigh across my front. Her breath was warm against my neck and I bent my arm, allowing my fingertips to rest inert against the pliant muscles of her back, my head swimming once again with abject relief, teeming with ache-filled memories of how I had believed her lost to me.

"Publius—?"

"Sssh! Don't talk. Just let me hold you." I turned slightly towards her, bringing my cheek into contact with her temple and my right hand to rest upon her waist, aware of the swell of her hip and thigh against my arm. Her own arm closed about my neck and she hugged me fiercely, drawing in a sharp, loud breath. I started to ask her what was wrong, but she shook her head and closed my mouth with gentle fingers, and we lay still for a long time in spite of my obvious arousal, which finally began to abate in obedience to my stubborn will.

"My love," I whispered, eventually. "I don't know the proper words to use to tell you how I feel, but I want you to know, now, that I believed we'd never lie like this again."

She said nothing.

"There were times, even in Londinium when I was facing trial by tribunal, and afterwards, when I could think of nothing but the fact that I had lost you . . . and so stupidly! I couldn't bear the thought of that . . . I couldn't bear it, didn't want to live with it . . . I almost didn't come home, so great was my terror of seeing you look at me with empty eyes—"

She jerked away from me, pushing with her arms, and rolled to lie on her back, her body stiff, and all my fears leapt up at me again. Between us, a channel of cold night air swept down to fill the gap her movement had created beneath the coverings, and the feel of it, sudden and ominous, brought the goose-flesh of pure terror out on my skin. I felt my own body stiffen in protest, and lacked the courage to reach out to her again to pull her back to me.

She whispered something, her voice so low that I was unsure what I had heard.

"What did you say? I didn't hear you."

She turned her head towards me and the night was too dark to reveal her face.

"I said I sent you off to die, without a word . . . I was too angry, and too hurt and proud to face you, and yet I knew I was wrong. There was a voice inside me, in my breast, screaming at me that I was wrong, and I was too proud, too stubborn to give heed."

Now I reached for her, sensing this unexpected, different pain in her for the first time, and seeking to comfort her. "No," I whispered, "don't say that."

She ignored my words, holding her body tensed against my pull, and, now that she had begun, the words poured out of her.

"It's true. I went running after you that morning when you left. But you were gone, in chains, and something died in me, and something else was born: a cold and crippling terror, mixed of guilt and shame and despair, and an awareness, stark and pitiless, of my own petty, willful selfishness. I saw you dead a hundred ways in every hour that passed from that time on. I saw you murdered, tortured, flayed alive, beaten and scourged, disemboweled and thrown into a ditch. I saw you slain time and again, each time a different way, and every time, your eyes stared into mine, bewildered, anguished and betrayed by what I had done to you."

Her words, and her grief, were harrowing my soul, and I moved to gather her close and comfort her. "In God's name, my love! You did nothing. It was me! I was the one who caused the rift, by not trusting you with what I knew."

She sat upright, breaking away from me again, the movement abrupt, unaided, almost as though she had released some hidden spring, and her next words were much louder than anything she had said before. "I had no *right* to expect you to. I *have* no right!" Shocked, I lay blinking in the dark as she pressed on. "No sooner were you gone than I saw that. I'd been a fool. And I swore to God, in a hundred thousand prayers for your deliverance thereafter, that I would never again presume to be so bold as to expect, or even think, that I posses your soul, your inmost thoughts."

She stopped, leaving me to consider what she had said, and I tried to comprehend, but finally huffed a sigh.

"My love, I don't know what you're talking about."

Luceiia turned again, to face me now, bringing her knee into contact with my side, and then leant forward to caress my face with her hand, her voice gentle again, addressing me as though I were a little boy.

"You kept a secret from me, Publius. That is what caused all this. You held your peace on something you believed to be important; something from which you sought to protect me. And I, in my arrogance—my stupid, overweening pride and foolishness—chose to believe you had betrayed my trust. Hah!" The self-scorn in that one syllable was scathingly eloquent, but she was speaking again before I could respond. "Well, I had time to see the error of my thinking and to repent at length . . . I have had my own secrets, all my life, but those, I thought, were different; they were mine and mattered not to anyone else. Only God's grace decreed that none of them should have to do with you or us. That was coincidence and nothing more, or less. And my failure to see that in time was madness." She paused, and when she resumed it was with a question.

"Do you remember the first fight we ever had, the first real quarrel? It was over whether or not I would accompany you and Caius to your first meeting with Ullic, at Stonehenge. Do you remember that?"

"Yes, I remember it."

"Well, that fight came from a secret—a nasty, bitter, self-pitying little secret I had nursed inside my breast for weeks. I was afraid of losing you to my own children, do you recall? And I had nursed my fears in secrecy until they hatched like evil goblins. For what? I was angry at my own love of you, for my pregnancy, and afraid of being forever lodged here in my own home, may God forgive me."

"He did," I said, smiling now and reaching for her again, but again she pushed my hand away, her diatribe not yet completed.

"Aye, He did, but not before you did. You were the first. You were the one who understood what I was saying, what I feared. It was you, not God, who took me in your arms and gave me comfort that awful afternoon. It was you who made me know that you loved me—that I *was* loved! You are my husband, the most wonderful thing that has ever occurred in my life, and I know I fill your world as you fill mine. How could I then look for more, knowing that? How could I *do* the sinful thing I did? And yet I did. I did, and God punished me by taking you away and leaving me in silence."

"And forgave you again, my love. I came back."

Her voice faltered. "You said you almost didn't."

"True, but for different reasons. And yet I did come back, to stay, and I am whole and healthy. Feel." I guided her hand with mine and she choked back a laugh, managing to sound angry with herself and with me, too, for being flippant. She flicked dismissively at my rude maleness with the back of her fingers and brought her hand back to cup my cheek again.

"Please, Publius, permit me to finish, to say what I have to say."

I waited.

"This matter of the secrecy that so offended me. It was less than important; it was a nothingness. I was so angered over the seeming loss of your trust in me that I lost sight, completely, of *my* trust in *you*. And yet that trust is absolute . . . Do you understand what I am saying, Publius? My trust in you is absolute. There exists in my mind not the smallest seed of a doubt that you would die to protect me and mine, and I know that death of yours would mean mine, too . . . Can you hear me?" Her voice was tremulous with unshed tears.

"I hear you. I love you. Now come down to me; you're getting cold, sitting up there." She came with a rush, soft and loving, her tears spilling onto my skin, and soon we both were warm again and fell asleep intertwined.

The Council meeting scheduled for the following day did not begin until the tenth hour of the morning and it lasted for five hours. It was not an arduous meeting, for the items to be discussed were all positive and beneficent and the spirit of the Council members was light-hearted, but Caius was looking tired by the time we adjourned. I walked with him to his day-room, where he stopped and ran his hands fondly over one of the codexes that lay on his work-table, where he had left it before we set off to Londinium with Seneca.

"It is good to be home again, Publius," he said. "I think I will write for a while, before the light goes. My eyes are getting bad, you know. It hurts them now whenever I have to write by lamplight, and there was a time not long ago when I could write all night with only one lamp lit and never notice any strain at all."

"That can't be good for anybody's eyes, Caius," I told him. "I think it is a good idea to do it by daylight, if you have the time and the opportunity. Although why anybody would want to write as much as you do mystifies me." He looked at me and smiled, but said nothing. "What do you write, anyway?" I asked. "I mean, you have spent hours and hours writing every day now for years and yet you never show anyone what you've written . . . At least, I don't think you do. Do you?"

His smile became wider. "No, Publius, as a matter of fact, no one has ever seen what I have written. No one has ever expressed any curiosity about it, except Luceiia. She knows what it is, although she has never read it. And she knows that when I die it will pass into her keeping."

"Well, do you mind my asking what it is?"

He smiled at me. "No, not at all, since it was you who inspired it."

I stared at him in amazement. "Me? What did I do?"

Caius laughed. "What, Publius? You do not even remember? You were irate with me for writing my military memoirs! Surely you recall that? You told me I should think of my own descendants and write for their guidance in future years." I vaguely remembered the occasion. "Anyway, that is what I have been writing ever since that day. It is a personal history of the growth of this Colony, set down for the entertainment, and perhaps the guidance, of those descendants of ours who might one day govern this place."

"A history? How do you do that?"

Caius shrugged his shoulders and grinned, in spite of his obvious tiredness. "Very simply," he said softly. "I have disciplined myself to set down, each day, the day's events."

"So it is a chronicle? Like Luscar's log of the Invasion campaign?"

"Mmm." The sound that came from his throat was high-pitched and suggested a negative. "Not quite, Publius, not quite ... More of a journal; less of a legal document. I add my own personal thoughts and observations. There are many of my opinions and thoughts mixed in with the events. As I said, it is a personal history, and sometimes almost embarrassingly egotistical."

"And is that why you have never shown it to anyone? Because it is so personal?"

"Partly." Again he smiled, a faint flicker of amusement, I felt, at his own assumption of importance in this writing endeavour. "Also, the fact remains that no one has ever asked me to show it to him."

I nodded my head slowly. "If I asked, would you let me read it?"

"Certainly. Of course I would. I would be delighted." He was smiling still.

"Then I would like to read it."

He nodded. "Good, Publius. I am glad. That pleases me. You may have the manuscript whenever you want it."

"Then I'll read it tonight."

This time he laughed and shook his head. "You may start it tonight, Publius, but you won't read it tonight. I have found that I can be quite prolix. I tend to enjoy the sound of my own words, if I may say that of an exercise that involves no sound. I've been writing for almost ten years; there is a lot to read."

"Well, then!" I stood up, filled with resolution and enthusiasm. "I will start it tonight, at least. I'm looking forward to reading it. But in the meantime I had better get down to the forge. I haven't been there in weeks. Equus will have forgotten what I look like with my face smudged. Come on, I'll get your fire lit and see that you've got enough wood and ink."

"You will not." He sounded mildly outraged that I should suggest such a thing. "Gallo looks after all of that—you know he does. Go to your forge, Publius."

I ignored him and did what I wanted to do, and only when I had the fire going did I speak again. "Sometimes Gallo, like the rest of us, forgets. Just like us, he's not getting any younger, you know."

I moved his writing table into the afternoon sunlight and settled him comfortably. The iron statue I had named Coventina, the Lady of the Lake, stood close by, on a table by herself. I caressed her, as I always did, running my hand lovingly over her buxom curves.

Caius was watching me. "She is a patient lady, Publius, watching and waiting for you like a virgin bride, wondering what you mean to do with her."

I rested my hand on her head, feeling the bumps of her metal skull against my palm. "I know, Caius," I answered him, my voice almost a whisper. "And she is not alone in that. I'm wondering, too."

I left him to write and walked down to the forge, the sound of ringing hammers in my ears as I approached. I stopped inside the doors to let my eyes adjust to the gloom, and filled my chest with the smoky, iron smells, enjoying the slightly sexual stir I always felt on returning after an absence from this place. Equus was working at the central forge and I joined him, slipping my leather apron over my head.

"What are you working on?"

He gave an exaggerated leap, as though shying away from something that had startled him. "Boudicca's buttocks! Am I seeing ghosts? What are you doing here in a dirty smithy? They told me you were dead, killed copulating with a mare, trying to improve her bloodlines!"

I grinned at him. "No, that was Victorex. I prefer sheep."

"Ah!" He nodded wisely. "Sheep. Well, ram this into the coals, there." He passed me a slender length of iron that looked like a sword blade but was twice the length and more than half again the width.

"What's this?"

"It's what I'm working on."

I hefted it at arm's length, feeling the slight bounce of it against the tongs I held it clasped in. "Looks like a sword blade, but it's much too long and too heavy."

"That's what it is, a too-long and too-heavy sword blade."

I shook my head in mock dismay and thrust the metal into the coals, the feel of the iron tongs welcome and right in my hand.

"I'm serious, Publius," he said, looking straight at me, his eyes crinkling against the smoke from the fire. "That's what it is. I had an idea and I wanted to test it."

I pushed the metal, burying it deeper in the coals. "Well? Tell me about it. Where did it come from?"

"What, the idea? From my head, of course. Where else would it come from?"

"No, Equus, I meant . . . oh, never mind. What is this idea of yours?"

"Just come over here and look. I made some drawings."

"Drawings?" I laughed. "You've been spending too much time with Andros, Equus. One of these days, I'm going to come in here and find you praying on your knees!"

"Hah!" He let out a scornful, roaring guffaw. "Don't you believe it, Publius Varrus! Not unless there's a woman spread on the floor in front of me. Look at this."

Moving to a broad-topped workbench, he seized a large pile of parchments, all of varying sizes, and spread them out in front of him. When he found the one he was looking for, he tapped it with his knuckles and I stepped forward to look. It was a large piece of parchment with drawings of spearheads, javelins, axes and swords. I examined all of them, wondering what was expected of me. I saw nothing that struck me as strange or new.

"Well?" I said, "I'm looking. What do you want me to see?"

"Nothing, yet. There's nothing there to see. But let me talk." He paused. "You wanted a weapon that a man could use from horseback. Well, I've been working on it, but I swear by the balls of Bacchus that I'm starting to doubt if it can be done." I waited, saying nothing, and he continued, nodding towards the drawings. "Every weapon there is for men on foot. Of them all, the sword's the best. Good for both attack and defence. You can stop another man's swing with it and still kill him easily." Another pause, then, "A spear's limited. Lunge with it, or throw it, and it's used up. You'd better have a sword for backup. An axe is even worse. Swing one of those properly and you leave yourself wide open to a sword or a spear. And once you swing, you'd better hit the man you're aiming at, because if he's worth his salt, one swing is all you'll get."

It occurred to me as he was talking that I had never heard Equus say so much at one time on any subject, and he was far from finished. Now, as he talked, his eyes became even more animated than before and his hands moved continuously from one drawing to another, emphasizing his words and directing my thoughts. I listened, fascinated, as he went on.

"Now, when we put our man up on a horse and pack the horses close together the way you want to, we're really mired in shit. An axe is as useless as tits on a boar in a situation like that, because all you're going to do with it if you swing it is hit the man beside you or kill your own horse. A sword's useless, too—it's too damn short. Even if you've got room to swing it, you still couldn't reach a man on the ground if he was kneeling or lying down. So that leaves us with a spear. But spears are only pointed. They're for stabbing. They can't cut. And the *pilum* is made so that the shaft will bend. It's great for throwing into an enemy's shield, to hamper him, but it's useless to us.

"So." He slapped his hand down onto the drawings, covering them with his great paw. "I've been thinking of a new kind of spear. A short, heavy shaft, about three feet long, for weight, and a long, flat blade like a sword, but twice as long—double-edged and sharper than a whore's tongue." He drew it swiftly with a few strokes as he spoke, and I watched it take shape under his charcoal. "A weapon like that might give a mounted man an advantage," he continued. "It could reach down between the horses, with the shaft gripped under the armpit, and it would be manoeuvrable enough to allow some cutting, as well as thrust."

I was impressed. "Hmmm!" I said, as I thought it through. "Equus, you could be right. But it would be usable on the one side only."

"What do you mean?" He was frowning now, not understanding me, but then he caught my meaning and his next words made me realize it was I who had misunderstood. "No, no! Not at all, Publius. Damnation, it's made to use on both sides! The short shaft would let a man swing it over his horse's head and stab with it either way."

"I think you may be on to something. It's certainly worth a try. Make me one and we'll test it."

"Make me one and we'll test it! Christ's Cross, man! Isn't that what I'm doing?"

I looked at the long iron shaft sticking out from the coals. "When will it be ready?"

"If you'll stop interfering and distracting me from my work, I'll have it ready for you in the morning."

"Finished? Complete?"

"Finished, complete and sharpened. Now, would you please allow me to get on with it?"

I spent the next two hours pottering around, checking on our apprentices and taking inventory of what we were producing, from nails to barrel-hoops, checking back every now and then to see how he was doing, finally goading him to the point where he literally chased me, laughing, from the forge.

I was in a frivolous frame of mind that afternoon. I was in no mood to achieve anything useful, and I was thinking quite seriously about trying to take my wife to bed for a daylight romp. I had not felt so full of youthful energy in years, but, as it turned out, a sexual dalliance was not to be, for I heard Victorex calling my name and saw him waving to me from the stables. I strolled over, and he immediately began to get on to me about the need to shoe all of our horses far more often and more regularly while I nodded my head politely. I closed my ears and let him ramble on until eventually he gave up on me and disappeared into the darkness of the stables, muttering to himself and probably calling me nasty names.

Suddenly there was a lethal sound close by my ear, and I dodged down just as I heard the resounding *thwack*! of an arrow pounding into the door beside me. Heedless of dignity, I spun around on all fours, looking for my assailant, but there was no one in sight. I scuttled to the stable door and took shelter behind it, and as I did so another arrow smashed into the wood of the door, piercing its two-inch planks of solid oak.

"Varrus! Come out, Roman!" My stomach lurched as I recognized the deep, rolling voice. "If I were a poorer shot, you would be dead by now!"

"Ullic," I yelled, "you demented Celtic imbecile! Put that thing down before you hurt someone!" Another arrow smashed through the wood, and then another and another. I saw Victorex running towards me through the gloom of the stable and I signalled to him to stop and stay where he was.

"Ullic! Have done! Someone will get hurt!" A sixth arrow slammed home, and then there was silence.

"I have finished, Roman. Come outside and look at the grouping."

I stepped outside. There was still no sign of him, so I did as he had bidden me and looked at the grouping of his arrows in the door. They were perfectly spaced in a circle of six. And they were big. As big as my own arrows. Each of them had completely penetrated the hard wood.

I called out over my shoulder without turning, "Ullic, where would a thick-headed Celt find a bow big enough and strong enough to shoot arrows of this size that hard?"

"He could make one, Roman."

"Not unless he found a way to combine all of the brains of his tribe into one craftsman smart enough to ask a Roman for help."

"Stand aside." I did, and a seventh arrow smacked into the perfect centre of the six.

"Now, you arrogant Latin boor, look on my wondrous weapon and marvel!"

I heard his footsteps approaching me and I turned to face him. His great teeth gleamed his wicked grin, and when he was close enough, he threw me his bow. I caught it in my right hand. It was huge: six feet or more in length and strung with sinew, but made of one piece of wood, not layered, like my own, of wood, horn and sinew. It was circular in section, filling the palm of my hand as I held it by the middle and tapering gently towards the ends. I hefted it and it felt good. I transferred it to my left hand and tested its pull. It was strong—as strong as my own.

Ullic stopped to watch me and didn't move again until I had pulled it and released it gently. Then he reached into the quiver slung over his back and tossed me an arrow. I nocked it, sighted at a fence post and let fly. It was a beautiful weapon.

"Well?" There was a slight smile on his face.

"Not bad." I kept my head down as I examined the great bow, trying not to show too much pleasure. "Where did you steal it from?"

"Pshaw! A Celtic king has no need to steal. His people fight to bring him gifts."

"Who fought whom to bring you this one?" I straightened up and threw him his bow, smiling now in welcome. "Have you eaten yet?"

"How could I have eaten? I've been on the road for three days. I came to impress you with my new toy. But I could eat now, if hospitality were offered. Even Roman hospitality."

"Roman-British, it is. You're looking good, Ullic, your women must be working you hard."

His laugh was enormous and he wrapped his arms around me in a mighty hug. As we began to walk back towards the house, Victorex watched us from the safety of the stables. He never could bring himself to trust Ullic or his people.

"So, my friend," I said as we walked, my arm about his waist, his across my shoulders, "tell me about this bow. Where did it come from?"

"From my own lands. From one of my own trees." His voice was more reverent than I had ever heard it.

"What kind of wood is this?" I asked, peering closely at it.

"We call it yew. It is an evergreen—low and spreading, slow-growing, but strong, springy and perfect for making bows."

"Who made it?"

"Cymric, of course." Ullic held the thing out at arm's length, admiring its lines as we walked. "He has been determined to make something like this for years. He tried to duplicate your great African monster, but the horn defeated him. Since he gave up on that, he has tried wood of every kind, and finally he came up with this one. It took him two years to make it."

"One bow?"

"Aye, Varrus, one bow, but he swears it is the first of thousands. Cymric is very proud of this bow."

"He should be. Why did he give it to you?"

Ullic looked at me in surprise. "He had to. I'm the King."

"Horse turds! Be serious, Ullic! Among your people that doesn't mean a thing. Not when it comes to possessions."

He laughed again. "Poor Cymric! He had to give it to me, for after he had made it, he discovered it was too strong for him. I'm the only one who can pull it."

I grinned and took it from him and pulled it to my ear again. "Not the only one, Ullic."

"Ach!" He waved a hand regally, dismissing my claim to equality with himself. "You don't count. You are a foreigner. A damned Roman."

"True." I grinned at him. "And as such, an exception to your rule . . ." He frowned at me as I continued. "I am glad that at least you can admit we are a superior people."

He came for me and would have wrestled me to the ground if Luceiia had not chosen that moment to notice us and call out a greeting. Ullic was like a big sheep in front of Luceiia, who charmed him completely. In a moment, I was forgotten as he basked in the friendly sunlight of my wife, who was well aware of the effect she had on him. As we approached the house, my daughter Veronica, who was also besotted with the man, came galloping to greet us.

Ullic had heard about our expected visitors and had started out from home with a strong force, prepared to help us fight for our existence, if the need arose. Then, less than half-way here, he had heard that we had left for Londinium, so he turned back, leaving look-outs posted to warn him of our eventual return. These he had left camped now in the hills behind us, and Britannicus sent up a wagon with a keg of ale for them. We heard their shout of appreciation all the way down the hill when it arrived, and soon there were bonfires blazing up there, lighting up the night, and we could hear the sound of Celtic voices raised in song.

Our evening was far more sedate, and it ended early for everyone but me. Instead of going to bed when everyone else did, I borrowed the first two tomes of Caius's journal of the history of the Colony and settled down to read.

That one evening's reading marked a turning point in my life, for what I read excited me so much that I began to think of writing down my own thoughts. The apparent ease with which Britannicus had spilled himself onto the pages of these books made an impression on me, and I made up my mind that I could do the same. I was to learn over the coming months, however, that writing in this fashion was hardly as simple as it looked. There were a thousand times when I would have given up in disgust had it not been for the encouragement I got from Caius himself. He simply would not allow me to stop trying. He made me see that the effort of concentration was worthwhile. He told me of his own troubles in getting started properly and showed me his early efforts, which were not much better than mine. He convinced me that if I tried hard enough, and kept on trying harder, I would one day be able to say what I felt to myself on parchment. And he has been proven right. But those first months of working at it were among the hardest I have ever spent in learning to do anything. It seemed at first that I could do nothing properly, until the day came when I wrote a piece and discovered, to my absolute surprise, that I had said almost what I wanted to say. That was my real starting point. Everything that had gone before was basic training.

It was late, that first night of reading and discovery, when I finally got to bed, my mind seething with excitement. Later still, I had to rise and void my bladder, and I was glad to climb back into bed beside the silky warmth of my wife.

XVIII

THE NEXT DAY did not start off auspiciously. I awoke in the pre-dawn to the sound of torrential rain and decided to start off my day with a hot bath and a massage, only to find that, for the first time anyone could remember, the furnace that heated our hypocausts, our central heating system, had broken. I settled for a cold bath and a stinging massage and drew little comfort from the knowledge that an entire army of workers was busily trying to trace the source of the trouble.

I had intended to ride up to the fort in the course of the morning to check on our operations up there, but the mere exercise of crossing the courtyard to the bath house in the astounding downpour was enough to convince me that a prudent man would look for things to do indoors on such a day. And yet the house was cold because of the broken furnace, or the broken pipes, or whatever else it was that was causing the trouble, so I wrapped myself up in my cloak and made my way down to the forge and its welcome warmth.

Equus had already been there for more than an hour, I reckoned, by the time I arrived, since it was full daylight outside and he still had lamps burning. He looked up from his work as I hung my sodden cloak by the forge to dry.

"Raining outside?"

I thought at first he was jesting, but quickly saw that he was not really interested in my response, whatever it might be.

"Raining? How long have you been here?"

He was concentrating on something on the bench-top in front of him and spoke perfunctorily over his shoulder, his eyes on his work. "All night, I reckon. Wanted to get your spear done." He finished something, tapped metal with a hammer and straightened up, looking out for the first time towards the daylight. "Looks like a whore of a morning out there."

I ran my fingers through my wet hair, flicking them afterward to shake off the rain. "Not pleasant, Equus—but why a whore?"

He grinned down again at what he was doing. "Wet, and available to anyone who wants to get into it, but basically cold, unpleasant and taxing to everyone."

I returned his grin. "Philosophizing this early? You must have had a rough night. What's the matter?"

He straightened up. "Ah, I don't know." He looked disgusted. "I'm not happy with the way this spear thing turned out."

"Why not? What's wrong with it?"

"Split me if I know! But something isn't right about it."

"Where is it? Let's have a look."

"It's over there." He nodded backwards with his head. "Against the back wall."

I saw it from where I was standing. "It looks all right from here—a little strange-looking, but that's what I expected."

I went and picked the new weapon up. It felt heavy and serviceable. The blade was three feet long and double-edged, flaring from the point to a two-inch width within six inches, and then gradually to about four and a half inches at the top. The edges on both sides were wicked. The thickness of the central spine was more than half an inch. He had left the tang the full length of the shaft and had bound strips of wood around it with iron wire, making a solid, two-and-a-half-inch diameter, three-foot-long grip. It was a heavy weapon, but not ungainly.

"What's wrong with this?" I asked over my shoulder. "What don't you like about it?"

Equus shook his head abruptly and dismissively. "I told you, I don't know. I sat on the saw-horse over there and practised with it for a while. There's something not quite right about it, but damn me if I can pinpoint what it is."

"You think it's too heavy?" I raised it shoulder high, springing my arm, testing the weight of the thing.

"No, not for the job it has to do."

"Well, then what about the balance? Are you satisfied with that?" As I spoke, I gripped the shaft in both hands, holding it out straight-armed.

"I think so. Yes, damn it, I am! It balances well for thrust and stab. And it'll cut, too . . ." His voice reflected the frustration he was feeling. "It's just . . . it doesn't *feel* right, Publius. Even though it does what it's supposed to do, it doesn't feel right. Does that make any sense to you?"

"No, my friend, it doesn't." He grunted in disgust. "Well, what do you want me to say? I don't know what *would* feel right to you. It feels fine to me, but I didn't design it or make it."

He sighed and turned back to a piece of iron he had left heating in the coals. I watched him lay it on the anvil and start to hammer it, sending sparks flying with every blow. On the fourth stroke, he stopped, his shoulders slumped in thought, and then turned back to me, the hammer dangling from his huge hand.

"I think what's sticking in my craw is that the thing is neither fish nor fowl. It's a spear, but it has to be used like a sword."

"But it's a new weapon, Equus. It will have to have rules of its own. It *is* different."

"Aye, I suppose it is . . . Well, I hope it works well for you. I'll never use it."

He sounded very despondent, and I put the new weapon down and crossed to where he stood, placing my arm along his shoulders.

"You'll get used to it, old friend. Once you see how well it works for the others, you'll be proud of it."

He grunted. "I doubt that."

"Well I don't. Britannicus charged me with the responsibility of coming up with a new weapon for his new tactics. I passed it on to you. And this is it."

"No, Publius, this isn't 'it'!" He was emphatic, his voice impassioned. "I'm not as clever as you and the Gen'ral, and I don't live well with words. But I know inside myself that thing isn't the answer. It might do for now, but it isn't *right*."

I picked the weapon up again, hefted it in my hand and tested the edge with my thumb. "Well, Equus, we'll see. It's too wet outside to do much in the way of testing today. If the weather dries up tomorrow, we'll see how it performs in the hands of a mounted man."

He punctuated the end of my words with a clanging blow of his hammer on his now-cool iron, cursed and thrust the cold metal back into the coals, and as he did so, Caius himself walked into the forge, his military cloak wrapped tightly around him.

"Ah, Publius, Equus! I was hoping I'd find you both here. It's the only spot in the whole place where there's a chance of escaping the chill today. What's that you have there, Publius?"

I held it out to him. "Your new cavalry weapon. Equus finished it last night."

"Excellent! Well, let's have a look at it." He reached for the weapon, but I hung on to it.

"I will, when you take off that wet cloak. You don't need pneumonia at your age, Caius."

"Hmmm," he grunted. "You're worse than your wife." He removed the wet cloak and I handed him the spear while I hung the garment by the heat with mine, which was already steaming, adding the smell of wet wool to the odours of the forge. By the time I turned back to him, he was feinting with the thing, holding it over his shoulder as if it were a javelin, testing its weight and balance. Equus was watching his face, clearly trying to gauge his thoughts.

"Good. Hmmm, yes. This is good, Varrus. Well done, Equus, I think this is what we have been looking for."

"Do you, Gen'ral? I don't." Equus was at his disconcerting best.

"What? What d'you mean?" Caius looked quite astonished.

"Equus isn't happy with it. It's his own design and he feels he could have done better."

Caius flicked a finger against the edge of the blade as though he had detected a flaw. "Well," he said, looking at no one, "perhaps he could, particularly if he feels that strongly about it. You might indeed be able to do better, Equus, but we won't know until you've tried, will we? In the meantime, I think you've done an excellent job with this experiment." He was peering closely at the blade. "Yes, indeed, this is quite excellent. This will give our men something to master, something to be proud of, something to make them different. No, this is very fine. May I take it with me?"

"Aye, if you want to," said Equus. "Make sure you keep it dry, though. I don't want it rusted before it's been used."

"Don't worry, I'll take care of it. In the meantime, please don't let my enthusiasm interfere with any thoughts you might have about trying to improve upon it."

Equus sniffed audibly and returned to his work with a marked air of finality.

"Publius." Caius turned to me, a smile on his face at Equus's ill humour. "Ullic was looking for you. Did he find you?"

"No. Not yet, anyway."

"Oh, well, if it's important he'll come looking for you, I suppose. He knows you well enough by now to know where to find you. Luceiia asked me to inform you that she would like some of your time today, too. She is preparing a special meal for you at noon, and you will eat in the family room. Were I you, I would make sure not to forget."

"In the *family* room? At *noon*? What's going on, Caius?"

Caius shook his head, a look of genuine innocence on his face.

"Well, there's something up. Something's going on, and I suppose I'll find out when the time comes for me to know about it."

Caius nodded, sagely and solemnly, his face expressionless. "Probably around noon, I would suspect."

"You can wager on it, my friend. The family room is used only for domestic courts martial and important events. If you see her between now and then, please inform my wife that I shall be there."

Luceiia's family room was her holy of holies. It was a large salon furnished with comfortable chairs and couches, and it was the one room in the entire house where entry was restricted to a privileged few. When we were there as a family—and of course Caius was a member of the family—no one, servant or visitor, was allowed to enter or disturb us. The other rooms were all more or less public, with the exception of the bedchambers, but only close friends, intimate friends, were allowed entry to the family room. Luceiia even did all of the cleaning and maintenance of the place herself, and it was uniquely hers in a way that made it different from any other room not only in the house but, I am sure, in the entire land of Britain. Of all the people we knew, Ullic Pendragon was the only one who had the prerogative of casual access to the family room.

The rain dried up about an hour before noon, but the clouds showed no sign of breaking, so I worked on in the forge until it was time for me to make my way back for this intriguing "special meal." "Be careful," muttered Equus as I shrugged into my cloak. "Summonses from women—wives in particular—can be dangerous. You're going to get talked into something. I just hope you're going to be fit to live with afterwards."

I laughed at him and headed for the house, wondering idly what this was all about. I had no real worries. Luceiia had been in a fine humour the night before, and even this morning, with no heating, she had been cheerful. I had become adept at sensing even mild wifely dissatisfaction in its early stages, so I was sure that there were no storms on my personal horizon.

The first thing I noticed on entering the house was that the central heating was working again. There was a noticeable improvement from the early-morning temperature I had left behind when I fled to the forge. Luceiia met me at the door with a kiss and a hug and a smile, took me by the arm and led me into the family room, and I was quite happy to allow her to do so, relieved as I was by her friendliness in spite of my conviction that nothing was amiss. The room was bright and cheerful, as it always was. A fire blazed in the fireplace and warm light flooded the room from the translucent glass windows that were Luceiia's one major extravagance, specially made and brought to the villa from Gaul at outrageous expense. A small table had been moved into the middle of the space in front of the fire and there was fresh fruit, bread, cheese and wine surrounding a covered earthenware pot.

In her travels as a young woman of substance, Luceiia had picked up a number of recipes for exotic dishes. She loved cooking the way I love working with iron. She had made one of these dishes for me before we were married and it had become a ritual "happiness" meal for us, appearing only on special and momentous occasions. I knew that was what was in the pot. I had no idea what made this occasion special or momentous, but I was prepared to take it on trust, for the aroma of pheasant and chicken breasts simmered in wine with herbs, small onions and mushrooms drew the saliva into my mouth as soon as I entered the room. I stopped just inside the door and looked around, taking notice of the vases of flowers on every table, the light aroma of some eastern incense from Constantinople, and Ullic standing against the wall to my right.

"Luceiia? What are you up to?" My eyes went from her to Ullic and back to her again. "What is going on here?"

Her eyes sparkled as she smiled at me, full of love and mischief. "Going on? There's nothing going on, my love. Ullic came all the way from his mountains to welcome you home, and it has been so long since he was last here, it seemed a shame not to celebrate his visit in some way. We see him far too seldom."

"Seldom?" I growled. "Two or three times a year is too often for an untutored savage to see the inside of a civilized home. It will make him dissatisfied with his own rude hut. Next thing you know, he'll be getting ideas above his station, thinking he can mix with real people all the time."

She punched me playfully on the shoulder. "Come now, behave yourself and stop growling like an ill-natured bear. I saw the rain this morning and I knew you would be staying close to home, so I decided to brighten up your day. And ours, too."

I kissed her, squeezing her waist with my arm. "About time, too. I swear that the only time I seem to get decently fed nowadays is when this great Celtic boor comes by."

She tossed her head and crossed to the table, moving like a young girl still, in spite of the fact that she was a matron who had now borne five children.

Ullic had not responded to any of my jibes, which was more than unusual. I looked at him more closely. "What's the matter with you?" He grinned foolishly and shrugged his big shoulders, saying nothing. The foolish grin was his normal expression around Luceiia, but his silence was strange. I followed it up.

"Are you feeling unwell, King? I've never known you so quiet and well behaved." Again, no response. I turned to Luceiia. "Where are the children?"

"They're eating in the kitchens today. I decided they were too boisterous this morning so I banished them."

"Good. They'll love that."

"That they will. Sometimes I wonder if they think more of Gallo and the servants than they do of us."

"When it comes to eating they do, my love. They are pampered, fussed over and spoiled when they eat in the kitchens. We discipline them when they eat with us."

"Come and sit, both of you."

The meal was delicious and the wine, a light yellow nectar made by the Burgundians, matched it perfectly. Ullic found his tongue shortly after we sat down and we chatted pleasantly throughout the entire meal. Finally, I finished the last of my goat's cheese and fresh-baked bread and pushed myself slightly away from the table.

"Very well, my friends . . . Luceiia, that was a beautiful meal—magnificent. All the more so for being unexpected. I am well fed and mellowed by wine, and warmed by the light, the fire, the flowers and the scent of incense. So. What is it that you two have in store for me?"

Ullic immediately looked as apprehensive as a sneak-thief caught in the act. He glanced wide-eyed at Luceiia.

"Nothing outrageous, my love," she said. "Ullic wanted to speak to you, but was unsure about how to approach you. You two speak so ill-manneredly to each other all the time that he was afraid you might not take him seriously enough and so he asked me for my advice."

"And you devised this scheme to loosen me up! It must be quite a favour you are looking for, Pendragon."

"You see what I mean?" Luceiia's tone was sharp. "You have proved him right already. Ullic has no favour to ask of you, and he needs no irony."

"Not fair, wife. There was no irony there!"

"It certainly sounded like it."

I raised my hands, palms outward in surrender. "Forgive me, then. Ullic, I beg your pardon. I am impressed, honestly, with the way you have approached this problem, as you call it, even though I have no idea of what's involved.

But I must confess to being a little hurt that you would think that after all this time I would be insensitive to anything you asked of me, or said to me, that obviously means so much to you."

He cleared his throat. "Don't be hurt, Publius." That shocked me. He *never* called me Publius! "You will understand in a moment why I had to come about it this way, when you hear what I have to say."

I waited. He was obviously thinking hard. Luceiia had a strange half-smile on her face.

"It's about your eldest daughter."

"My daughter? Veronica?" I was puzzled. "What about her?"

"I want to marry her to my son, Uric."

"You *what*?" I was dumbfounded.

"I want my son Uric to be married to your daughter, Veronica."

Even hearing it the second time, I still could not believe my ears. "Veronica?" I said. "She's just a child! An infant!"

There was total silence. Ullic sat looking uncomfortable, his eyes lowered to his hands, which were clasped on the table in front of him. My thoughts were chaos, so great was my surprise. Veronica? The Magpie? It was unthinkable! I fastened on that aspect of my outrage and put it into words, hearing the harsh tone of my own voice.

"It's absolutely unthinkable! We will not speak of it!" As soon as I had said it, of course, I knew I was being too abrupt, for I knew she would have to marry some day. "There will be time enough in years to come for talk of marriage, once the child has grown."

Luceiia spoke, her voice gently chiding. "Publius, that is unfair. Where are your eyes? The child *is* almost grown."

I swung around to face her. "Don't interfere, woman. This is none of your affair."

She flinched as though I had slapped her, and in a way I had. When she spoke again, there was an implacable quality to her voice that I had never heard before.

"I am sorry, husband, but this *is* my affair. Veronica is my daughter, too, and I love her no less than you do. Your responses to me and to Ullic are both emotional and inconsiderate." I made to interrupt her, but she overrode me. "Let me finish!" I subsided and she continued. "Veronica is twelve years old and already, physically, a woman. Ullic is our best friend outside of the family. He is not suggesting that we ship the child off today, before supper. His thought was only to *arrange* a marriage, a marriage that would not take place until the girl is fully grown and ready to be a wife."

I was almost appeased, but not quite. The first stirrings of guilt at my harsh reaction made me sound surly, even to myself. "Then why all this secrecy?"

"What secrecy? Ullic was worried that you might behave exactly as you have. He knows how great your love for Veronica is. She is your sun, moon and stars."

I had to smile, and the surliness was gone. "No, wife," I said. "You are my moon and stars."

"Well, anyway, poor Ullic came to me, hoping I might be able to help him blunt your wrath. Look at the man. He is your dearest friend, your guest and a king, and he sits squirming at your table!"

I turned to Ullic, my guilt running at full flood now and tinged with shame. I reached across and grasped his left wrist. "Ullic, my friend, forgive me. My reaction was overstrong, I can see that now. But you hit me in a tender spot. We almost lost Veronica once . . . She is very precious to me. In my eyes, she must always be a little girl . . . my little girl. The thought of losing her, even to a fine husband, is repugnant to me, even though, deep down, I know I'm being foolish. She is growing up. I've noticed it, and I've been resenting it. Your proposal surfaced unexpectedly. It hurt. I reacted violently. Pardon me."

He shrugged, his face breaking into a smile. "Publius, we are friends. There is nothing else in the world that I would have hesitated to ask you for. But I know how you treasure her, and I knew that everything would be in the asking, so I approached your wife, instead. And I was right, was I not? So was she."

I picked up a piece of bread and tore off a pinch of it, kneading it between my thumb and forefinger, seeing my daughter's lovely, smiling, innocent face in my mind. "So," I said, "tell me about this son of yours, whom you would have as husband to my Veronica."

"You met him when you visited me the time before last, two years ago. He was the age then that Veronica is now."

"So that makes him, what? Fifteen?"

"Almost. He has not quite filled his fifteenth year."

"So, when would you want them to be wed?"

"On his eighteenth birthday." This was better. Veronica would be a woman by then. Fifteen, almost sixteen.

"And why Veronica?"

"Why Veronica? Are you serious?" His smile was broad and easy now. "She is her mother's daughter! And yours, of course, although that's a misfortune she has learned to live with. I know my son could do no better."

"But she's a Roman."

His grin was all teeth and crinkled eyes. "Not so. She's a Briton, Publius. Don't you remember? The Britons were reborn at Stonehenge the night we met."

"So, you believe a Celtic–Briton match would be a good one, do you?"

His smile vanished instantly, to be replaced with an expression that contained no levity.

"Aye, my friend, I do. It would be good for the young ones and good for us. We are both kings, Publius, each in his own way, for you are Britannicus's heir, his spiritual heir if you like, in spite of Picus's return and in spite of your Roman fears of kingship. For I swear I never saw two more kingly men than you and he."

"You flatter me, Ullic." I was pleased. "I would not have expected that from you."

"I flatter no man, friend. It is the truth. No more than that."

We spoke no more for some time, each of us absorbed in his own thoughts. It was Luceiia who broke the silence, placing her hand gently over mine as she asked me, "My love, are we agreed? You seem to be in favour of the match, but you have not yet said so."

I looked from one to the other of them. "Is there any more wine?"

"Plenty."

"Then pour us all a draught to seal our bargain, woman. If we are to mix our blood with Celts, we might as well get drunk."

Ullic threw back his head and laughed a great laugh of relief and pleasure, and then he jumped to his feet and embraced each of us, and we drank a toast to our children and to their children whose own children would join our two peoples long after we were gone.

XIX

WE WERE FORTUNATE enough to be able to see Picus often during the two years of Stilicho's campaign in Britain, in spite of the fact that the fighting was intense and hectic all during that time. It was he who told us that the major problem facing Stilicho's forces was one of deployment, since the enemy they were fighting was seaborne and undisciplined and there was no master plan behind the Saxon incursions. Picus insisted that it was inaccurate to speak of invasion for that single reason: lacking a master plan, or even a recognizable leader, these attacks, significant and consistent though they were, nevertheless consisted simply of massive numbers of Saxons, Hibernian Scots, Caledonian Picts, and Franks from south Gaul striking without warning wherever they made landfall, so that Stilicho's armies were constantly reacting instead of initiating. This was a new form of war; there was never any question of military confrontation, of meeting and defeating a static enemy in a fixed battle.

In the course of those two years, Stilicho's greatest weapon, his supreme advantage, was his new heavy cavalry. It became clear very early in the campaign that the speed and manoeuvrability they possessed demanded augmentation and encouragement, and Stilicho was a brilliant commander who believed in making the most of every advantage at his disposal. Within months, boatloads of prime horseflesh began arriving regularly at the Saxon Shore forts along the south coast—the very finest horses the Empire could provide.

Young Quintus Flavius, one of Picus's close friends, was promoted to general and given the responsibility for overseeing the breeding farms of the armies of Britain. It was far from coincidental that every time one of these two visited the Colony, he came mounted on a fine stallion, and our own stock improved with every foaling.

Late in the autumn of 398, Picus arrived one night accompanied only by a small, armed escort. He saw to the quartering of his horses and his men and then he drew his father and me aside into Caius's study. We could tell that something important was in the wind, but we had no idea what it was, or how it might affect us. Picus let us know the answer to those questions just as soon as Gallo had brought us wine and honeyed wheat-cakes and had built up the fire in the great brazier so that it was now a roaring blaze. As the door closed behind the old man, Picus opened his pouch and produced a rolled parchment, which he handed to his father. The imperial seal that held it closed was dazzling in its import.

"Read it aloud, Father."

Caius broke the seal and scanned the parchment quickly, then cleared his throat and began to read aloud:

"'Caius Britannicus, Proconsul of Rome, from Flavius Stilicho, Commander-in-Chief, Imperial Armies.

"'In the name of His Imperial Majesty, Honorius, Emperor of all Rome, the time has come for me to remind you of the terms of the commission issued to you by my hand in the year of my arrival in Britain.

"'Now, in the second year of our campaigning, it appears that our armies have turned the tide of invasion and re-established the supremacy of Roman arms in this province. I am commanded by His Imperial Highness to withdraw my legions to the marshalling of his affairs elsewhere in the Empire; departure will be immediate upon conclusion of military arrangements in Britain to my satisfaction.

"'The Legate Picus Britannicus will remain in Britain with his cavalry, as my deputy, until such time as the Empire shall have need of him elsewhere or until he has established a cavalry command to his own standards within Britain and can feel confident in delegating his own authority to a subordinate, freeing himself in conscience to return to my command.

"'With this letter, to be delivered to you by the Legate Britannicus, I am enclosing a plenary warrant of authorization confirming you in the rank of *Legatus Emeritus* of the Irregular Armies of South-west Britain, in the name of Honorius, Emperor of the West. In this capacity, you will use all the powers at your command to defend the territories delineated on the accompanying chart signed by my hand and sealed with the seal of Honorius.

"'Stilicho, Commander-in-Chief. Pro persona: Honorius, Imperator.'"

When he had stopped reading, we both stood staring at Picus.

"So," said Caius, "what does this really mean? Apart from the obvious. Stilicho is leaving and you are to remain, for the time being. How long will you remain in Britain?"

Picus shrugged, smiling. "Who knows, Father? He may send for me next month, although I doubt it. My guess is that I am here for a long time. Stilicho has three commanders of cavalry here in Britain with him now, not counting Flavius. I am senior of the three. He has chosen to leave me behind to organize Britain. It could be a big undertaking."

"Could be?" Caius's tone was sharp. "Could be? Are you unsure?"

Picus shook his head, chastened. "No. Let me rephrase that without false modesty. It is a major responsibility. Stilicho does me great honour."

"That's better."

I caught Picus's eye, feeling the half-smile on my face at hearing the meticulous father critical, although only mildly so, of the favoured son. Picus, however, was unaware of me. His expression was thoughtful, and he stared intently into the fire of the brazier for a long time before he spoke again.

"It's not going to be an easy matter to build a permanent cavalry garrison here, or to staff it with a self-sufficient command that I can leave behind. There is too much entrenched resentment among the regular army command."

"How so?" The look on Cay's face was measuring, his eyes intent on his son as the young man laid out before us the problems facing him.

"They're jealous, I suppose," Picus muttered, finally. This was accompanied by another shrug of his shoulders. "After four hundred years of Roman occupation in Britain, their authority, as they see it, is being usurped by an upstart body of elitist troops under the command of a chain of staff officers most of whom are not yet twenty-five years old."

"Damn it," I said, "that's the way it has always been. All the brilliant soldiers of history have been babes in arms!"

He glanced in my direction, noticing me, I felt, as one would notice a passing wasp. "Aye, but most of them fought on foot, Varrus."

Caius interrupted. "Invalid, my son. After that same four hundred years of occupation, Roman military intelligence has finally come up with a new way to re-establish Roman supremacy. Surely the army commanders can see that?"

Picus half twisted his head, an incomplete gesture suggesting that his father's suggestion was an unconvincing one. "Perhaps they can, Father, but that doesn't mean they have to like it."

"True, absolutely not. But Stilicho's imperial authority means they have to accept it."

"No argument." Picus held up his helmet and brushed at its crest with the sleeve of his tunic, preening the stiff, scarlet-dyed horsehair. "But any acceptance, Father, can be qualified by willingness. Resistance to change is an intrinsic human failing. I remember, as a boy, hearing you say time and again that true change, lasting change, comes very slowly. The military command in Britain has had radical change thrust down its throat in the space of two years. My cavalry has no tradition. It has no history, and you, of all people, Father, know what tradition and history mean to the officer corps of the Roman army."

He held out his helmet to his father at arm's length. A full face-mask of heavy metal hung from the brow of it, peaked in a crease so that the sides of the mask swept in to the cheekbones and then flared out. It was obvious that its prime purpose was to deflect missiles.

"Take this, for example. I have insisted that all of my men have face-masks like this one fitted to their helmets." Cay took the proffered helmet and examined it closely, raising and lowering the face-guard on its intricately hinged flaps as his son continued. "Our speed brings us too quickly within bowshot of our enemies, and our faces are unprotected. It is a new circumstance, but I have lost too many men to this kind of injury. Now my men's faces are protected, but their pride is taking a battering from the jeers of the old infantry sweats and their officers, who have never had a need for face-masks."

Britannicus chewed on that for a long time before answering. "You know, my son," he finally said, "you have just made a point that I have to acknowledge and emphasize. One of the advantages of growing old is the growth of the astonishing ability to accept that one can be, and frequently has been, wrong in one's deepest beliefs. I have been wrong in many things in my lifetime, but the paradox has been that much of the time, at the time, I was correct." He paused and looked down at the imperial letter he was still holding. "We are living in a time of changes—changes that would have been inconceivable fifty or a hundred years ago when the world was still set in its ways. Nowadays we have to accept and accommodate the need for such changes—sudden, radical changes, wholesale adaptations to new and abrupt circumstances. And when I say 'we' I mean we colonists in this tiny corner of the Empire. The rest of the Empire cannot, will not adapt to such changes. That is why the Empire's days are numbered. That is why we are here. Your cavalry corps is an adaptation to changing circumstances. If the inertia of the military chain of command, the hidebound military intellect, will not accept the need for it, that is tragic."

I had been pouring wine and sampling the honeyed wheat-cakes while this last exchange was going on, and now I spoke through a mouthful of food. "Tragic it may be, but it's not unusual." I handed each of them a cup of wine. Caius sipped at his before answering me.

"No, Varrus, it's not unusual. We are unusual. We are determined to adapt, and so we shall survive. Your daughter's wedding next spring to young Uric Pendragon will mark an official bonding of two peoples. The fruit of that bond will mark a new beginning in the history of this island of Britain. Your grandchildren, Publius, my great-nephews and great-nieces, will be set apart by their blood."

I demurred. "I don't often argue with you, Cay, but this time I think you're exaggerating a little. Romans have been marrying the women of Britain for as long as there have been Romans in Britain."

He shook his head, dismissing the validity of my comment while apparently agreeing with what I said.

"Of course they have, my friend. We all know that. But it has never happened at this level before. This is a monumental step, don't you see that?"

"No, Caius," I said. "I don't. What 'level' are you talking about?"

"The highest level."

"What's so different about it, in God's name? They're just two young people who are being wed by their parents. They're no different from any of the other young people who have done the same thing, gone the same way."

"Publius Varrus!" He shook his head impatiently, a frown of annoyance on his face. "Have you no sense at all of the order of things? There is no Celtic blood in my family that I am aware of, nor is there any in yours. Is there?"

I shook my head, twisting my lips into a grimace of unconcern to show it was matter of complete indifference to me. "No, not as far as I know, although I haven't made an issue of investigating it."

He pounced on that. "There you are, then! We have been bred in Britain, it is true, but our blood is pure Roman. Unsullied Roman blood, Publius. Republican blood. And it is a matter of great pride in our friend Ullic that his own blood is, as he would put it, untainted by Roman impurities. His race is regal, Varrus. He is pure Celt. His people have ruled this part of the world for centuries, long before the Caesars came to power. And you say you can't see what this means?

"When your daughter weds Ullic's son, it will be the start of a new bloodline—the same thing that excites Victorex in his breeding of horses. And breeding is what we are talking about here, let us not lose sight of that. We are causing the creation of a new breed of man by mingling Veronica's pure Roman blood with Uric's pure Celtic blood. Forget the others that have gone before. That was miscegenation. Roman legionaries have not been pure Roman for hundreds of years. They are a mongrel creation of the Empire, romanized, perhaps, but never Roman."

He swung on his son, whose face was as blank as mine. "Picus, don't tell me that you had failed to mark the significance of this match?"

Picus shook his head slightly in bewilderment. "No, Father, I'm afraid that had not even occurred to me. I hadn't thought much about it at all, and certainly not from that perspective."

"Then think about it now! And think about it from this time on. Your cousins by this union will be the progenitors of a noble house of unique qualification."

Picus's lip quirked upwards. "Yes, I suppose they will, when you put it like that."

"No suppositions! They *will* be!" Caius looked from Picus to me and then raised his cup. "Now! Join me in a toast to the unborn. To the sons of Veronica and Uric, the future rulers of this Colony and this whole land, for we will raise them to a legacy of strength and freedom that has not been seen by men for centuries. To our heirs!"

It was a fine toast and a stirring thought, and we drank to it gladly, although I had to resist shaking my head in wonder at my own lack of perception. There were times when Caius Britannicus could make me feel like an absolute bumpkin. But then another thought occurred to me, and its occurrence chilled me so that I swung my eyes to look at Picus, who was watching his father's face and smiling. Caius saw my look and his expression changed immediately to one of concern.

"What's wrong, Publius?"

I shook my head in stupefaction, unable to articulate the thought in my mind, and now Picus, too, was looking curiously at me.

"Varrus? What is it?"

I knew I had to answer, and I expelled my breath in puff of exasperation. "Well," I began, "it seems to me that, in drinking to the children of this coming union as the heirs to Camulod and all this land, we've neatly dispossessed your own heir, Picus."

Both men were gaping at me, the significance of what I had said sinking home only slowly, and the silence stretched and held as they grappled with the ramifications of my words. Finally Caius spoke.

"Damn me, Publius, but you have a Draconian way of getting to the meat of things! That had not once occurred to me."

"Nor should it have, Father," Picus said, his voice calm. "For I had missed it, too, and it's my patrimony we're discussing. I heard nothing of dispossession."

Caius turned his eyes to look directly at his son. "But then Publius had not yet said what he has said."

Picus shrugged, apparently unperturbed. "No, true enough, but even now, nothing has changed. Or had you thought to do such a thing?"

His father answered with a question of his own. "What do you think? I mean that; please, tell us."

Picus's eyes moved from his father's face to mine, then back again, and then he screwed up his face, scratching the end of his nose with the tip of one finger.

"What do I think? Well, let's start with what I thought, at first, and then we'll see what has changed since then, shall we? I caught the fire of your enthusiasm. These children, if they're born at all, will spring of noble blood from both sides of their line. If your ambitions, and this dream of yours, should come to pass, they could wield power—strength and power—here in Britain, from a solid base within this Colony. But that will be in thirty years, at least, from now. In the interim, someone has to govern here, and for the time being it is you two who bear that responsibility. But this Colony, if that's what we're discussing, is not my patrimony, and I am a soldier. I might die as a soldier. I might, on the other hand, survive to retire someday, as you did, Father, and come home. If that occurs, I'll do as you have done, and contribute my time and what abilities I have to governing the Colony as a Councillor. But my patrimony is this villa . . . the Villa Britannicus. If I ever marry, which seems unlikely at this time, at least, since I have not the slightest urge, nor do I know any suitable women, then my own heirs would inherit what I leave to them. The Villa Britannicus. Not the Colony, and certainly not Britain! So I see no threat to me in what you have proposed, unless, as I said, you intend to take the Villa . . . If that is the case, then I shall merely adjust my expectations and acquire another villa." He was smiling now, clearly confident that he was right. Caius stepped to him and embraced him.

"Your patrimony is safe, my son, as well you know. You read my mind *exactly*. I spoke of the Colony meaning exactly that: the community of combined properties that make up our territory. The Villa Britannicus will always be the Villa Britannicus, not the Villa Celtic." He smiled at me and moved towards me, embracing me in turn, and then he looked about him. "Why are we all still standing like idlers on a street corner?" Caius finally asked. "Let's sit and enjoy the fire. There is a nip in the air tonight that reminds me of my multiplying years." He sat by the fireplace and we joined him, pulling our chairs closer to the flames as he spoke again to Picus. "So, let's talk of strategy. *Is* the invasion turned?"

Picus nodded. "Yes. We believe so. The indications are all there. Reported raids have decreased greatly in the last few months."

"How significant is that?" I asked him.

"Highly significant. No raids at all in the last two weeks. Prior to that, only three in three weeks. In the three months before that only twelve, and six of those occurred in the first month of the three."

"That is still a lot of raids," said his father. "You really feel justified in claiming that to be a significant decrease?"

Picus leaned forward and toasted his palms in front of the glowing coals for a few moments before answering. Finally he said, "Yes, Father, I do. Very definitely. In the same period last year, there were more than forty raids. In any man's language that has to be a significant difference."

"Yes, I suppose it is." There was silence for a time and then Britannicus went on. "Your technique, here in Britain—how has it developed?"

"I'm not sure of your meaning, Father. From what viewpoint?"

"How has it improved over the past two years? What have you learned? What have you done? What have you initiated?"

Picus smiled. "Much. A great deal on all three points, Father. I think perhaps the first thing we learned is that, faced with an enemy whose strikes are unforeseeable, the last thing one can hope to do is operate under the normal conditions of warfare. No, let me rephrase that." His speech slowed perceptibly as he enunciated his thoughts with much greater precision. "The last thing one can hope to do is operate as though the accepted traditional ways and methods have any application. They do not." He paused and drank deeply before going on. "We were forced to accept, right from the outset of our campaign in Britain, that we could never hope to react in time to have any preventive effect upon this type of enemy incursion. We had to evolve new tactics to deal with new conditions, and so we split our forces, our cavalry forces, regionally, into five central bases: one in Eboracum, one in Glevum, one in Verulamium, one in Dubris and one in Noviomagus. Using each of these bases as the hub of a wheel, we set up lines of observation—outposts of infantry—tending signal-fires along lines radiating from the centre. Once these lines were established and in place, the news of raiders passed as quickly as the visibility of the fires. Sometimes the ancient methods are still the best—we simply adapted the signal-fires to our own needs, and used more of them. And while we were setting up these beacons, we also set up relay stations along the same lines, fully staffed and equipped with fresh horses. We split our active troops into self-sufficient squadrons with one centurion in overall charge of each, two decurions and forty troopers. Our reasoning in this was that one long-boat could contain anywhere from thirty to fifty men. Two boatloads would double that potential, and so on. Our arithmetic considered one squadron of disciplined cavalry to be at least the equal of two boatloads of raiders, so each relay station was stocked with eighty-eight horses, kept in a constant state of readiness.

"Each outpost was responsible for the building and the maintenance of groups of five signal-fires, set up side by side in a straight line and far enough apart to avoid any confusion. One fire meant one boat. Four fires set alight simultaneously meant more than three boatloads—a heavy raid. Five simultaneous fires means more than six boats—a major invasion fleet. It works very well, for our whole operation is predicated upon the advantage held by a double squadron of heavily armed, well-mounted, disciplined troops over a body of men on foot numbering twice their strength or even more. When four signal-fires are lit at once, for example, three squadrons are dispatched in response. Two of these ride at speed to catch the enemy on land, at work, and keep him from retreating to his boats. The third proceeds more slowly, in reserve, backed up by a full cohort of infantry moving at a forced march."

"It sounds good," said his father. "How well does it work?"

"As well as we can hope for. Our major weakness, at the start, was that we did not have enough good horses. It takes a lot of horseflesh to implement a plan like that. In the beginning we were operating at half strength in every area. We had to. We could not simply neglect some areas in favour of others, since we had no idea where the next spate of landings might occur. But the signal-fires passed the word quickly and our response time was very fast. As the rightness of our method began to prove itself, Stilicho moved heaven and earth to appropriate more and better horses for us. He used to joke that he was stripping the Empire clean of horse-flesh to feed the people of Britain, and there were times when it looked as though it might be true. It seemed that every second Roman galley arriving in Britain was loaded with prime horseflesh."

"Impressive," I said. "How soon after your arrival did you start to put all this in place?"

"A matter of months. As soon as we grew tired of looking foolish every time we arrived on the scene of a raid to find all the damage done and the enemy gone."

"Which was often?"

"Always would be more accurate."

"I see. And since you switched over to these new tactics all of that has changed? Whose idea was it to set up these regional bases?"

He shook his head. "No one's, and everybody's. The idea came out of a staff meeting. I mentioned the possibility of splitting our forces to gain manoeuvrability, and the idea grew from there. By the time that meeting had ended, the rudiments of the plan were in place and the logistics were under consideration. From that point onward, it was just a matter of time until we had our units positioned and ready to move at the sight of a beacon. Once the troops were distributed, it became a matter of tightening up our procedures, learning from our mistakes and adapting to conditions as they arose."

He stood up, stretching himself. "I can give you an example of what I mean by that, too. One of the first things we learned was that, almost invariably, when there was only one boat involved in a raid, the enemy was gone by the time we arrived, no matter how fast our response was. They hit, cleaned up and got away in a hurry. As soon as a raid involved two or more boats, however, their operations time slowed down very considerably. We really don't know why this should be, but we suspect it was because of their numerical strength. It seemed to give them the confidence to move further inland. Of course, with twice the men, they needed twice as much booty to be equally successful. Anyway, a pattern began to emerge very quickly and it indicated that it simply was not worthwhile dispatching troops against a single-boat raiding party.

"There are people, I know, who think that was a callous decision. But it was the only one we could make, the only one that made any sense. At the height of the raiding activity in the early summer of the first year we were in action, there were four occasions when we were short of men to tackle major raiding parties because troops had already been dispatched to minor raids, and on none of these four occasions did our squadrons make contact with the small raiding parties. They were gone, back out to sea before our people ever came near them. Standing orders were changed to alert troops to one-boat raids but to respond only to raids involving two or more boats."

"Makes sense," I said. "If what you say is true, and I don't doubt a word of it, the people in the farms and villages along the coastline who were being hit by these small raids were beyond help in any case."

"Exactly. But a strange thing has happened in the course of two years. Do you know that there is now an almost uninhabited belt, ten or twelve, sometimes fifteen miles wide, around the entire coastline of southern Britain?"

I shook my head. "No. You mean the people have just moved out?"

"Most of them. Moved inland. A few stayed, too stubborn to move away from their homes and their living—mainly fisher-folk who live right on the coast—but the majority, the farmers and farm workers, just abandoned everything and moved inland to safety."

"How has this affected the raiders and their methods?" Britannicus was watching his son closely, a tiny frown ticking between his brows.

Picus shook his head decisively. "It's too early to say with any kind of certainty, but we are pretty well convinced that it has had an effect—and a positive one—on the number and the nature of the raids. Single-boat raids are almost non-existent now. It takes a lot of guts for one boatload of thirty-odd men to travel inland for ten or fifteen miles in the hope of finding a village, hitting it and getting out again before our people arrive. It puts a lot of distance between them and their boat."

"But your people don't respond to one-boat raids, you said."

"They would now, knowing that the enemy is going to be on foot for fifteen miles inland and back. But it simply doesn't happen any more."

"So raiding parties are getting bigger?"

"Yes. That's absolutely correct. And fewer, too."

"So how much thought have you given to future developments in this pattern?"

Picus flashed a grin at his stern-faced parent. "We hope it develops to the point where all of them land together and we can smash them once and for all, but that's a dream. If the trend continues, and at this time it is only a suspected trend which time will prove or disprove, but if, as I say, it continues to develop, then we could see numerically stronger parties raiding more systematically next year."

"And how will that affect the deployment of your cavalry?"

"It won't. Not adversely, at any rate. We're already prepared for it. Plans are in place to consolidate our lines of communication. We'll simply strengthen our reserves and be prepared to move in greater strength."

"You obviously think that this is going to happen?" Cay's inflection made this more of a question than a statement.

"No, I *hope* it's going to happen. I've just dismissed it as a dream, but it is true that the more men they use, the bigger the fleets they assemble, the greater will be our advantage. Just let me get an army of them in one place at one time, and I'll smash them beyond recovery."

"Hmmm." Cay sounded mildly sceptical. "Dream as it may be, have you the strength to do that?"

"Aye. And more, I have the speed and the weight. You know yourself, Father, how wild these people are. They have no concept of concerted discipline. They operate, all of them, as independent units. Each boat's crew is devoted to itself. Land a large number of boats together and you have a fearsome band of savages. But they are a rabble. I can destroy them easily if they do that, and in their pride and ignorance, they can't admit it." He snapped his hand in front of his face as though snatching a fly out of the air, holding his clenched fist high in front of his face. "Just let me have one chance to catch them on land, in strength. I don't need a whole army of them. Just a mob big enough to grapple with at leisure."

His father sucked at his front teeth. "And how do you see our role here in the Colony shaping up, now that I am *Legatus Emeritus* of the Irregulars of South-west Britain? And, by the way, you still have not delivered my warrant into my hands. Is that a deliberate oversight?"

"Oh! Pardon me, I have it here." He delved again into his scrip and produced a second scroll, this one much bigger than the first. His father took it from him, broke the seal and scanned the contents quickly before passing it across to me. It was a clear, clean and specific document bearing the signature and the personal seal of Stilicho and the imperial seal of Honorius. I read it with appreciation and handed it back.

"Well, General," I said. "I can call you General again."

"Again? You never stopped." He eyed his son. "You haven't answered my question, Picus."

"What answer would you have, Father? You read your warrant. It's unique. You have autonomy under imperial seal. I can't tell you what to do, nor can any other."

"You can make suggestions if I ask for them."

Picus nodded, smiling. "True, I can."

"Well then. I have already asked you. How do you see our role here developing?"

"I would like to see it develop considerably, Father, if you are willing. How many horses do you have now?"

"You mean trained cavalry mounts?" Picus nodded and Caius shook his head. "I don't know with certainty. Victorex will have the exact number, but I suspect it will be around a hundred and fifty, perhaps a hundred and seventy-five. No more."

"Hmmm! Not enough." Picus sat in deep thought, flicking his thumbnail against his teeth. "I can let you have a hundred more now, and the same again, later, say in six months to a year."

"Can you, by God?" I jumped into the conversation again. "And how will you justify that to your superiors?"

He grinned at me in boyish delight. "What superiors, Uncle? I have none in Britain, once Stilicho is gone. No, that's not strictly true. Marcus Tella, Military Commander of the Province of South Britain, is my nominal superior, but he has been well briefed by Stilicho on the real extent of his jurisdiction over me. He is to forward my reports to Stilicho regularly, assist me in any way he can in the strengthening of my command, preserve my autonomy in terms of allowing no interference with my performance of my duties and otherwise leave me strictly alone. I don't have to *justify* anything to anyone. I have decided to supply you with the horseflesh you need, so that you in turn can be useful to me in the prosecution of my mandate. If your men are well enough mounted, they can patrol this whole region and set up watching-posts and cavalry depots along the entire coastline of the territories given into your charge by Stilicho."

"To the north or to the south?"

"Both, eventually. For the moment, to the north, guarding the estuary leading to Glevum and freeing my men there for duty in the south-east. And there, if I needed any, is my justification."

Britannicus jumped to his feet and clapped his hands loudly together. "Excellent! So be it! We will work together." The door opened in answer to his summons and old Gallo came back into the room. "Gallo, is General Picus's room ready for him?"

"Of course, Master." There was just the barest hint of reproach in the old man's voice.

"Good. Excellent. When will dinner be ready?"

"Whenever you are, Master. The ladies are waiting."

"Then we are ready now. Come, Publius, Picus, let's dine. Your aunt will be glad to see you, lad."

"I hope so, and I will be glad to see her. It has been months now since I was last here."

We began walking towards the dining room, and as we went, Picus began quizzing me on weapons, asking how we were solving the problem of arming our men.

"Oh," I told him, "we are making some headway, but nothing revolutionary. We've had no major design breakthroughs. I'll show you what we have tomorrow, if you're still here. Will you be still here?"

He grinned and raked his spread fingers across his close-cropped scalp. "I'll be here. I have had a rough couple of weeks and could use a day off. I'll get back on the road before dawn the following day."

"Fine." I clapped him on the shoulder. "Now, no more talk of weapons or of war. Your aunt and your niece are completely tied up in their arrangements for the wedding next spring. Since Veronica has 'become a woman,' as she likes to phrase it, she and her mother have formed a conspiracy to domesticate the men in this household. We are actively discouraged from discussing business at table. Your father and I have decided that, until the wedding is over, we will humour them. We talk of generalities and social affairs at table now, all of which means that we listen to the latest developments in planning the nuptials."

He laughed aloud. "It sounds as though this is going to be a major celebration."

"Depend upon it. It is," his father answered him. "And I for one am not unhappy about it. Bear in mind what I said earlier about the underlying connotations of this match. The more moment we accord to it, the better it will suit itself to our purposes."

"You mean it really is political? A dynastic marriage?" He was still half joking.

"Yes, I do. The young people like each other, which is a valuable bonus. But this marriage is, nevertheless, political above and beyond all else. Had I planned it myself, I could not have arranged a better match. As it turned out, I did not have to. Varrus and Ullic between them arranged the contract, Varrus in total innocence of its portent. Ullic, I know, knew what he was doing."

I interrupted. "By the way, Picus, what of Seneca? Is he still in Britain?"

He barked a laugh. "Oh, yes, he's still in Britain. He's my commander in the north and I keep a close eye on him. He knows I do, and he takes great care to keep his nose clean."

"What will happen when Stilicho leaves? Do you expect any trouble from him?"

"From Seneca, you mean? The only way he can cause me trouble is to mutiny, and if he tries that, I'll crucify him, and he knows it. No, he'll cause no trouble. He has two more years to serve, according to imperial decree. When he gets out, then he might try to cause trouble for me, but the prospect holds no terror."

We arrived at the doors of the dining room just as he concluded this last sentence, and Britannicus placed his finger to his lips in a silent "Shhh," his right eyebrow quirked high in his own particular way, and led Picus and me, both grinning, into the company of the ladies.

XX

I SLEPT POORLY that night and rose long before dawn had even begun to register in the east. So I was surprised to find Picus up and about ahead of me, finding himself some breakfast. We ate together and talked for a while, and he suggested going for a ride. I was happy to go, but I made a joke out of slipping away quickly before Luceiia noticed us and found some work for me to do. We were soon mounted and heading out into the open fields behind the villa, where we gave our horses their head and let them gallop until they became tired and slowed of their own volition. My mount, Germanicus, was four hands shorter than the big black Picus was riding, and yet he was the biggest horse we had in our entire stable. I was eyeing the big black with my new appreciation for horseflesh when Picus broke in on my thoughts.

"Would Aunt Luceiia really have stopped you from coming, Uncle?"

I looked at him in amazement. "Of course not, it was a joke! She'd never even think of such a thing. Why would you ask that . . . you find it credible?"

He was frowning slightly, perplexed. "I don't know. Women are a mystery to me . . . I never feel at ease in their company, never know what to think or do . . . I can't imagine being married to one."

I grinned. "Welcome to the world most men inhabit! When you're safely married, you learn to appear to *think* and to *do* what you're told to think and do, if you want a quiet, peaceful life . . . and in return, you're allowed to complain long-sufferingly about how hard it is to be so blessed . . . And that was another joke!" It earned me an uncertain, not-quite-convinced kind of smile.

By this time we were more than three miles from the villa, at the upswell of a range of low hills that held one of my favourite spots for being alone, by myself or with Luceiia.

"Swing left, over that way." I pointed with my chin and Picus kneed his big horse gently towards the hillside on the left, asking no questions. We swung into the rise and crested the hill to find a wooded depression that was hidden from below.

"Here, let me lead the way. I've been here before." I guided Germanicus down into the bushes, following a trail he knew as well as I did. As we descended, the bushes grew taller and closer around us, brushing against us as we wound down into the centre of the hilltop. Picus was right behind me as Germanicus turned to the right, and suddenly we were in a tiny jewel of a valley, a natural amphitheatre ringed by rock face on three sides and by the dense growth we had come through on the fourth. The whole place was less than fifty paces wide in any direction. Straight in front of the path by which we had entered, a deep pool was fed by a silent cascade of water that glided down moss-covered rocks from the cliff above and fell free the last three feet to splash on a large, upthrust rock shelf so that the sunlight made rainbows in the spray. Along to the right of where we were, a bank of mossy turf looked as inviting as a down-filled couch.

"How did you find this place, Uncle Varrus?"

"By accident. You like it?"

"I've always liked it. It used to be mine." He smiled widely at my open-mouthed consternation. "I grew up here. I had my first girl there, right on that bank. And several others after."

I felt my eyebrows go up in shock. "You did, did you? And here I thought it virgin. Not to speak of you!"

He laughed, a great, booming sound. "I was sixteen! And before that I'd been—aware?—for six whole years. It was a soldier I wanted to be, remember, not a priest."

"Well, then, welcome home. Again. Let's take a rest."

We dismounted and threw ourselves on the grass. I noticed Picus looking around him as though searching for something along the small beach at the side of the pool.

"What are you looking for?"

"Ashes. Can't see any. It looks as though no one's been here for years."

"No one has. Except for myself and my family. Why would you look for ashes?"

He looked at me in surprise. "You've never fished here?"

It was my turn to be surprised. "Fished? No, I haven't. Why should I fish? I come here to escape, not to eat."

"Oh, Uncle Varrus." He shook his head in mock regret. "You have missed one of life's greatest pleasures. When I was a boy I would come here for whole days at a time. I pitched my leather legionary's tent here, where we're sitting. I'd have my bow and arrows, my sling, some fishhooks and a line, my salt and bread and my fire-starting box. I was totally self-sufficient. I caught my food right here and cooked it on my own fire."

"What kind of fish?"

"Trout. Succulent, beautiful trout."

"Are they hard to catch?"

"Sometimes. But they are never impossible to catch."

"Really? What else did you catch? Fish would be a monotonous diet."

Picus shook his head gravely and with total conviction before lying back on the grass and crossing his hands behind his head. "Not trout, Uncle Varrus! Trout is never boring. But sometimes I'd catch a rabbit, and sometimes a pheasant, or maybe a duck. But mostly rabbits."

"You shot them how? With arrows, or with your sling?"

"It depended on how far away they were when I found them. Arrow or stone, it all depended on distance."

"Ever miss?"

"Most times, at first." He laughed and sat up, remembering. "But hunger can do wonders for improving the aim."

I lay back, flat on the grass. "I found this place one day because my horse brought me here. He seemed to know where he was going, so I just let him take me. It was a pleasant surprise."

"Was it a grey horse? Old?"

"Yes. Was he yours?"

He nodded, smiling. "We came here often, he and I. His name was Cupid. Silly name for a horse. He must be dead by now."

"Yes. Five or six years ago. During the winter. I remember, because I found him one morning dead in the paddock."

He grunted, a note of regret in the sound. "He was an old horse even when I was a youngster. It seems a shame that horses have to die. They're often worth more than men, in terms of their nature."

"Aye, it can seem that way sometimes, I suppose." I nodded at his own mount, which stood cropping the grass beside us. "That's a fine horse you have there. I noticed all your men were mounted well. Where do such horses come from? He must be four good hands bigger than mine, and mine is a big horse."

He eyed Germanicus with a horseman's eyes, then looked back at his own horse. "Aye, he comes from Gaul and he has good lines—I would even say beautiful lines. The Gauls breed big horses, Germanic forest horses. They use them as draft animals on their farms. I don't think there are any bigger in the world. Of course, they're shaggy brutes, with long, rough hair that is almost impossible to groom, but they are phenomenally strong and surprisingly gentle, considering that they run wild in the forests. We're breeding horses now all over the Empire." He paused, considering a question that had obviously just occurred to him, before turning to me. "When did you start your program here in the Colony exactly?"

I sat upright. "Exactly? I don't remember. It was about ten years ago, I think. The idea was your father's, naturally. We had been talking about the Adrianople slaughter and about Alexander's Companions, and we were always talking of the Saxon pirates. Your father thought it might be worth our while to train some men to fight the way you do, as heavy cavalry and not merely mounted bowmen. It worked, as you know."

A wood-pigeon exploded out of the trees across from us, disturbed by something prowling below it. I looked at the sky. "Well, it looks as though the rain is going to stay away today, at least. We'd better be heading back to the villa. It's almost mid-morning."

An hour or so later we were all assembled in the forge, examining the results of the most recent experiments in weaponry carried out by myself and Equus.

Picus had picked up the very first of Equus's efforts and was swinging it around, testing its weight and balance, when he noticed some specks of rust on the blade and drew my attention to them.

"This is unusual, Uncle Varrus. A rusty blade, here in the temple of metallic perfection?"

I grunted. "Blame Equus. He'd rather not have to look at that one at all, let alone keep it in good condition."

"He doesn't like it? This? Why not, in God's name?"

"I don't know, lad. He made it. Ask him. He took a dislike to it before it was even finished and he has done nothing like it since then."

"But it's the best of the lot! Look at it. It's versatile—cut *and* stab! The long blade . . . I've seen nothing like it before. Uncle Varrus, this thing *works*!"

"Tell that to Equus. He thinks it's a disaster."

"But why? It's cumbersome, but it has something that none of the other spears have. This shaft is solid. Heavy. I think it's just too long. If it were shorter, so that it could clear the chest and let a man swing it across his body all the way, it would be formidable. A horseman could change hands at will, with no awkwardness. No, I like this." He turned to Equus. "Equus, I think you had a fine idea here and let yourself lose it."

"Don't talk crazy," growled Equus. "I changed my mind because I saw how stupid the idea was. How can a rider shift his spear from hand to hand? What's he going to do with his shield in the meantime? Hang it from his bottom lip?"

Picus, however, was not to be so easily discouraged. He held the weapon aloft and looked at it, moving it around so that the light played upon the blade. "Equus, if I could have something like this, with the weight and the balance this has, that I could use in either hand, on either side of me, I'd be tempted to throw my shield away."

"Hah!" Equus's voice was filled with disgust. "And then where would you be? You'd get skewered like a rabbit on a spit by the first pikeman you came up against."

"No, I don't think so. I'm serious. I would wear a heavier breastplate, and the added advantage of being able to swing this thing would offset not having a shield. Father? What do you think?" He was feinting with it as he spoke, holding it straight out at arm's length, the strength of his arm muscles making a mockery of the weight of the thing.

Britannicus looked at it, his eye running the full length of Picus's outstretched arms and the seven-foot length of the spear. "I have no idea at all, my son. It might work, I suppose. How much of the shaft would you remove?"

"About half the length."

"You're both mad," Equus was growling to himself. "Cut off half the length—any of the length, for that matter—and you foul up both the balance and the weight. Weapons are designed in proportion, you know. We don't just leave an extra length on there for decoration."

I was listening closely, although I was taking no part in the conversation, and something was beginning to tickle at the back of my mind.

"That's a spear you're talking about," Equus went on. "Boudicca's buttocks! You're swinging it around there as if it were an axe."

"But it almost is an axe, Equus. I think it's because of the shape and weight of the blade."

Equus slapped the top of his bench in his frustration. "That's right, man! It's neither one thing nor the other. It's a bastard thing, bred in a moment of unwisdom. The weight distribution in the blade's all wrong, so you can't use it for a hard swing. All the weight is concentrated at the top, too close to the shaft. Hit anything hard with that thing and it'll crumple like a piece of parchment. Believe me, Picus."

Picus screwed his face up in a wry expression of regret. "Well, if you really feel that strongly about it, and you designed it, I'll have to take your word for it. But it seems a shame, for no matter what you say, I *know* there's something about it that's *right!*" He looked at me. "Varrus, you're saying nothing. How do you feel about it?"

I reached out my hand and he passed the spear to me. It was very heavy.

"Equus is right," I said. "It's too cumbersome. You can handle it, but you're almost a giant. No ordinary soldier could use the thing the way you suggest, and I suspect it would tire even you in a short space of time if you were swinging it in a fight. The weight *is* wrongly distributed for that, and by shortening the shaft you'd only aggravate the imbalance." I tossed it back to him, smiling at his crestfallen look. "But you're right, there is something good about it. I just wish I could define what it is. I'll work on it."

"Good! When you've solved the problem, I'll buy them from you by the hundred."

The conversation moved on then to other topics, but I paid little heed to what was being said from that time on. There was something bothering me, something that had almost formed in my mind in the course of the conversation between Picus and Equus. Of course, the more I tried to pin down what it was, the more it eluded me.

There are few things more frustrating than trying to recall a fleeting, half-formed thought. I even found myself trying to tell myself that it was not important, but I knew it had to be, or it would not have been worrying me. Eventually, however, when the others had gone and left me on my own for a while, the elusive memory I had been seeking suddenly sprang into my mind and I cursed myself for having been so intense about it. They had been talking about weight and balance and Picus had said that the spear was almost like an axe, because of the shape and the weight of the blade. And now I remembered seeing, as a young soldier, a child in some remote African village splitting wood with an ancient bronze sword that had a heavy, leaf-shaped blade. The thing had been really old and battered, and what edge it once had had been lost long in the past. But the boy was using it to split wood, and the lover of arms in me was saddened by this menial use of a weapon that must at some time have been someone's proudest possession. I tried to buy it, but the boy fled, taking his sword with him.

So that was what had been driving me mad, and now I was irritated because I could not see the significance of it. Why should it have flashed up into my memory after more than thirty years of oblivion? What possible connection could my mind have formed between today's conversation about a spear and an axe and that encounter in a dirty north African village street so long ago? Obviously, the shape of the blade was the connection, but why? It made no sense to think of Equus's spear with a leaf-shaped blade—that would be worse than useless—so what was it? I was becoming angry at myself—I recognized the symptoms—so I forced myself to empty my mind as much as I was able to and began to walk back towards the house, nodding to those I met along the way and trying to keep my mind bare of thought. I knew the answer would come to me. I simply hated having to sit around and wait for it.

Four of Picus's escort were squatting by a corner of the wall that surrounded the house. They saw me coming and put away the dice they had been using to pass their time, standing erect as I approached. I nodded to them in response to their salutes and asked them where their legate was. One of them, the oldest of the four, appointed himself spokesman.

"We're waiting for him, sir. He went into the house with the Proconsul and told us to wait here for him."

"Good, then I shall wait here with you, if you have no objection." Naturally, they had none. I had not been there long, talking of trivial things, before Picus appeared. They were like soldiers everywhere, cocky, confident and proud of their elite unit, and slightly awed by the fact that a senior officer, even a retired one, would stop and talk to them as people.

"Here comes the Legate now, sir."

I looked up and saw Picus striding towards us through the gateway. He saw me at the same time and smiled.

"Commander Varrus, you have a nose for secrets that always leads you to the right place. Pecula, show the Commander your sword." The youngest of the four flushed to hear his general address him by his nickname, which meant thief or pickpocket, and grinned in embarrassment as he drew his sword and offered it to me, hilt first. It was an ordinary Roman *gladium*, or short-sword, with one abrupt difference that I felt as soon as my fingers closed over the hilt. I immediately tightened my grip, looking the young man in the eye.

"What is it? Where did you get it?"

"What, sir?"

"The covering on this hilt. What is it?"

I was answered by Picus himself, who waved to the soldier to say nothing. "What do you think it is, Commander Varrus? Without looking at it."

I turned to him, gripping the hilt of the sword tightly and flexing my wrist hard, testing the grip. "I have no idea what it is," I said. "But I want to know."

"What does it feel like in your hand? Think hard."

I concentrated on what I felt, fighting the temptation to look down and see what it was. "It feels unlike anything I've ever felt before. It's not leather—too rough for that. It's not metal, not bone, not wood. It feels like . . ." I squeezed my grip again, feeling the texture against my palm. "Like leather covered with fine sand."

"You're nowhere close, and you never would be if you tried all day. Look at it."

I looked. The hilt was covered with a material that was neither black, nor grey, nor silver, but a mixture of all of them. The texture was as rough as a file. This thing would never slip from a sweaty or a bloody palm. Whatever it was, it had been wrapped tightly around the hilt and then bound there with tightly criss-crossed metal wire.

"I give up. What is it?"

"It's fish skin."

"It's *what*?"

"Fish skin."

I remembered his teasing about the joys of trout fishing earlier in the day and I looked closely at him to see if he was joking with me, but his face was serious. I returned my gaze to the young trooper, Pecula.

"What kind of fish skin?"

The young man shrugged, his open face apologetic. "I don't know, sir. I won it in a dice game. The man I won it from said it was fish skin. Said his father made it. Told me his father was a fisherman."

"Who was this man?"

"Don't know, sir. Just one of the garrison soldiers in Londinium."

"How long ago since you got this?"

"About a month ago, sir."

"Have you seen the man since then? Would you know him again?"

"Yes, sir, I'd know him, but I haven't seen him since that night."

I looked more closely at the hilt of this sword and I knew that I was looking at a thing of great value. This was a milestone discovery. I looked again at Picus, and then back at the soldier.

"I have never seen anything to equal this, and I am a collector of weapons. Would you be willing to part with it? For a good price? And a new sword?"

His eyes flickered to his general and back to me. "Well, sir, I don't know. I didn't know it was valuable."

"It's not, lad, except to me. The blade is a poor thing, nothing out of the ordinary. It's the fish skin that's valuable, but only if we can find out what kind of fish it is and whether or not we can get it here in Britain. How much is it worth to *you*?"

He was looking uncomfortable, knowing he could name his own price, but hesitant to offend his general by appearing to take advantage of the general's friend. I decided to help him out.

"I'll give you two months' wages and the pick of my own swords in exchange for this."

His eyes flew wide in shock. "Done, sir."

"Good man! Go to the house there and ask for Gallo. He's my major-domo. Tell him Commander Varrus would be pleased if he would show you to the weapons room. You'll find enough of these there to make your day. Take your pick of them. I made all of them with my own hands, so you should find something there to suit you."

Picus spoke up at this point, unsheathing his own sword. "Commander Varrus is one of the finest swordmakers in the Empire, Pecula. He made this one for me, when I first joined the legions. Go, now, and see if you can find one better. But I don't want to see you flashing a sword that looks as though it should belong to an Emperor. Pick a plain one."

"Yes, General!" Pecula snapped a salute and began to turn away, and then he hesitated. "Commander Varrus? You want the sheath as well?"

I smiled. "Yes, Pecula, you'd better leave that with me, too. Your new sword will have a sheath of its own."

He fumbled excitedly at his belt and handed me the scabbard. It was a plain, old scabbard, but well kept.

"Thank you," I said as I took it from him. "By the way, Gallo will also give you your two months' wages, so don't forget to ask him for them."

"Yes, Commander!" He saluted again, turned, and marched away, followed by the envious eyes of his three friends.

I slipped the sword into its scabbard. "General Picus, I'd like a word with you. Will you walk with me?"

As soon as we were out of earshot of the others, he spoke. "I thought that might appeal to you, Varrus, but two months' wages and a Varrus sword? Don't you think you overpaid him?"

"Picus, you know me. I'm an enthusiast, but I never let my enthusiasm get the better of my judgment, if I can help it. If I can discover what this fish skin is, there will probably not be enough wealth in the Colony to pay for its real worth. Believe me. I want to know what this fish is. Where it comes from. If I can find that out, I'll import it all the way across the Empire if I have to. So, I need your help. Find this soldier for me, the one young Pecula won this thing from. Question him. Find out about his father—who he is, where he lives and how he discovered this skin. As soon as you do find out, assuming that he knows at all, get the word back to me. Will you do that?"

"Of course I will."

"Good. Some day I'll make you a sword with a fishy grip."

"Sounds disgusting, but I'll look forward to having it. By the way, can you smell that stuff on your hand?"

I grinned and sniffed my palm. "No. Nothing there at all."

"That's a relief. It must be trout."

As we approached the house again, Pecula came out, bearing his new sword proudly, his face wreathed in a smile. We stopped and admired it, for he had chosen well, picking one of my best. I wished him well in the use of it, and Picus took all four of them off with him in the direction of the stables, leaving me alone. I carried my new sword into the house and made a place for it in my weapons room, then stayed there for an hour, playing with my treasures and letting the atmosphere of weaponry absorb me.

Two hours later, I was back in the forge fiddling with a piece of charcoal and a scrap of Andros's parchment. I had filled every inch of it with sketches of swords, spears, axes and Equus's new spear. Some of the swords I had drawn had leaf-shaped blades, but most of them were straight-edged. Equus was watching me; I could feel his eyes on my back. Finally, he spoke.

"You having problems with something?"

"No more than usual. I can't stop thinking about what Picus said. About shortening the shaft of that spear. He's right, it should work."

"Boudicca's belly, Varrus, I'm surprised at you! You've worked with weapons all your life and you know it can't be done! Make him a long-handled club like the ones the barbarians use, or an axe—something with all the weight at one end, so that he can swing it. But you can't shorten that spear shaft and keep it balanced, any more than you can lengthen a sword blade and keep it balanced!"

"I know, Equus, I know! But still, if there was a way . . ."

"Horse turds! If there was a way to turn horse turds into apples, no one would ever be hungry! It can't be done."

So I sat there and fiddled, eventually turning the parchment over to use the other side of it. I drew a *gladium,* the finest, most efficient weapon ever designed. And then I took my charcoal and doubled the length of the blade. What a pity that wouldn't work! With a sword that length, even Picus could reach a man on the ground. But the whole shape was wrong. The straight *gladium* blade, extended to twice its length, would lose its rigidity and would have too much weight. And then, quite suddenly, I saw what my mind had been trying to tell me with the memory of the leaf-bladed sword. It was not the shape of the boy's old sword that had been important, it was the principle underlying it! Picus had been talking of combining a spear and an axe—rigidity with impetus. It wouldn't work; it was apples and horse turds, as Equus so eloquently put it. But a sword with the length of Equus's new spear . . .!

Excited without really knowing why, I got to my feet and fetched the weapon, laying it on the bench in front of me and focusing my attention on the blade. It was spear-shaped, tapering from a sharp point to a broad, flared base before plunging back down to the width of the shaft, like a diamond with two sides extended to the point of being ludicrous. The thing was fully three feet in length to its broadest point. I looked closely at the way Equus had reinforced it. In section, it was diamond-shaped again. Now my charcoal began to work again in earnest, sketching the lines of the blade, the proportions of the taper on its width, and finally I had what I was looking for. I couldn't have told anyone what it was, but I knew it was almost right.

"Equus, come here a moment, will you?" I heard him put down whatever it was he was working on and then I felt his presence beside me.

"Aye," he said. "What've you got?"

I didn't raise my head, for I was concentrating so hard on what I was thinking about that I could feel the tension of a frown between my brows. "I want you to look at this and then do what I ask you to do, without any comments or any argument, understand?"

"I hear you."

"Good. Now think of the elements of a sword: blade, tang, hilt, grip and pommel. The hilt fits over the tang to add weight to the fulcrum and support the grip. The grip fits against that and the pommel holds the whole assembly together."

"What's this? A lesson in elementary armoury?"

"Be quiet and listen. Look at this spear of yours. A heavy, strong blade, shaped like a spearhead, but three-feet long, with a three-foot tang, the shaft, bound with strips of wood, fitted and bound together. We've been arguing about the balance because we've been looking at it as a spear."

"So? That's what it is. It's a spear."

"I know it is, but listen. I want you to try something else for me— something different—and the last thing I need right now is a list of a thousand reasons why it can't be done. I want it done, even if the end result is something I'm not strong enough to pick up off the floor. Do you still hear me?"

"Aye. What's in your mind?"

"This," I said. "I want you to make me a blade one-fourth as long again as this one is. I want you to reduce the width of it by one-fourth again, at its widest point. You follow me?"

He nodded, his eyes glowing with interest now that I was improvising. "The most difficult part, technically, will be the taper," I went on. "I want you to keep this blade double-edged and as near to straight as you can get it, and yet I want you to taper it from its point of greatest width to half that width about a hand's breadth from the point." I could see that he was holding himself in check with difficulty, bursting to speak. "Can you do that?"

He surprised me by not bursting out with a response immediately. He bit his lower lip between his teeth, staring at the blade, and then he picked up my stub of charcoal and began to draw with rapid, sure strokes, weighing the changes he would have to make.

"Aye," he nodded, at last. "I can do it. But that narrowing worries me. It could be a waste of time." At least he hadn't said it *would* be a waste of time!

"How so?"

"You know as well as I do. The width, combined with the length." He laid his hand on the spear blade. "This thing is as strong as I could make it, but beyond the midway point from the shaft, it's too thin for the job it has to do, and at its widest, up here, it doesn't get enough support along its edges from the central spine. The metal becomes too thin. It's like a scythe—wonderful for cutting grass, but we've got thicker, tougher things to chop."

"So? Have you a better suggestion?"

"Perhaps. Let's say, for the sake of argument, that we do what you suggest. We lengthen the blade by a quarter of its length, but we taper it by a third of its width only, instead of half. Say then we extended the taper so that the full third was narrowed from the base all the way to within a thumb-length of the point, which would be sharp and abrupt. That way, the reinforcement would be greater all along the blade, although it would still bend under the leverage from the shaft."

"What shaft? I want no shaft on this." He looked at me as if I had lost my wits. "In any case," I went on, giving him no chance to argue, "the shaft is not important right now. Let's get the blade fixed up, first. I like your idea. It obviously adds strength. But we still have to reinforce the thing. How do we do that?"

"Same way I reinforced this spearhead. Make the spine an iron bar."

"No, I don't think so. You said yourself, that doesn't give enough support to the edges. What if we merely thicken the blade?"

"How? Like what?"

I drew him a quick sketch. "Like this. Start it oblong in section and then round it."

He looked at my drawing. "Boudicca's belly, Varrus, that's just like a *gladium!*"

I grinned. "It is, when you draw it like that, and it will be when you make it. Except that it will be far longer and totally different. I'm serious, Equus. The proportions are different. One-third along the length from the shaft, this blade will be thinner in section than the *gladium*. Two-thirds along, it will be thinner still."

His eyes narrowed. "You mean a two-way taper?"

I nodded. "Yes. I told you it would be technically difficult."

"Aye, you did. You were right, too. But it's not impossible. What about the thick end of the blade? How steep a plunge there?"

"Vertical. I want it flat-ended, just like a *gladium,* with a tang two hands-breadths long."

"A tang!" His voice was leaden. "So, we've designed a sword! Now, can you tell me how we're going to engineer a fulcrum point that will balance this thing?"

"I think I can, Equus, but I won't know until I've tried it. I have a thought in mind, though, that might work. When can you start on this?"

He never got the chance to answer me, for the door was flung open and one of the household servants stumbled in.

"Commander Varrus! We're being attacked!"

XXI

I KNEW HOW long it usually took me to stroll from the forge to the house. Today, at my fastest speed, it seemed to take twice as long. Men were running in every direction, but there seemed to be no panic. I could hear trumpets blaring in the distance and I recognized one of our centurions as he strode past me in the gathering dark. I grabbed his arm as he swept past, oblivious to my presence, and asked him what was going on. He blinked at me in surprise.

"Commander? I'm sorry, sir, I didn't see you. It's Vegetius Sulla, sir. His place is under attack."

"Under attack? By whom?"

"I'm sorry, sir, I don't know. Don't think anyone does."

Vegetius Sulla's place! This caught me totally off guard. Of all our villas in the Colony, his was the one generally thought to be the safest from attack, since it was the most south-westerly of all, guarded by high, hostile hills at its back, with nothing to the south and east for thirty miles except the high, rolling plains that led to Stonehenge.

"Who raised the alarm?"

"A patrol of our own men, sir. They saw smoke and went to investigate, and turned up a nest of snakes. Wiped out, except for one fellow who managed to get away and bring the word back, and it doesn't look as though he'll live."

"How many raiders? Did he say?"

"They couldn't tell, Commander. They didn't get close enough to see them. They were ambushed on the way in."

"How do you know so much and so little, man?"

"I was on duty at the gate when he came in, sir. Took him up to the main villa."

"All right. Get about your business." I limped on at top speed, cursing my lame leg for the first time in years.

The courtyard and the house were ablaze with lights as men with torches scurried everywhere. Stablemen were gathering horses and the cobbled yard was a madhouse. The same four members of Picus's escort were standing at the main entrance to the house itself, a four-man island of immobility in a sea of chaos. I went right to them.

"Is Legate Picus here?"

"Inside, Commander."

I passed them and made my way through the crush and into the house, where the first person I saw was my wife, white-faced but calm, although her eyes were full of apprehension. This was the first time real danger had ever come close to her. I crossed to meet her as she came towards me and took her in my arms. She was trembling. I kissed her, hugging her hard, heedless of who was watching.

"Don't look so worried," I whispered. "They'll never even threaten to come here. This place is in no danger. Where is everyone?"

"In Caius's day-room. What will you need?"

"My armour, and some food. There may not be much time to eat in the next few days, so I'd like some bread and cheese and some wine to take with me."

"Gallo has all of that in hand. He set the kitchen staff to work as soon as the news arrived. He's laying out your armour now, personally."

"Good. I'll go and put it on while he's still there. It'll be quicker if he helps me. Then I'll join the others. Where are the children?"

"With their nurse, Annika. She will keep them safe and out of the way."

"Fine. I have to go." I kissed her again and headed for my rooms.

"Publius?" I turned back to her. "Be careful. Don't get hurt, will you?"

I winked at her. "No, I won't get hurt. I'll take my bow and arrows. That way, nobody will even get close to me."

With Gallo's help on the buckles, I was able to get into my armour quickly, conscious of the thickness of my waist and hips inside the unyielding harness. Moments later, my helmet tucked under my left arm, I joined the war council. As I entered Caius's day-room, all talk stopped abruptly.

"Excuse me for being so late. I came as quickly as I could when I heard the news. What's going on?" My eyes swept the room. There was Caius himself, Picus, some of our senior officers—and Vegetius Sulla. My eyebrows shot up in surprise to see him there.

"Varrus," he nodded, a strained smile on his face. "I stopped by here on my way home from Aquae Sulis this afternoon. I was just preparing to go on my way when the news arrived. Caius Britannicus would not allow me to leave alone then."

"Quite right. There's nothing you could do alone, and if you ride with us, you'll get there in one piece, at least. Is your wife with you?"

"No. I left her at home. With my sons."

"Well, let us hope we find them alive and well. What's happened so far?"

It was Picus who answered me. "We don't know for certain. One of our patrols was ambushed . . ."

I interrupted him. "I've already heard that. They were probably careless, not looking for danger there. So we don't know how many raiders there are?"

"No. We have to assume they're in strength. They could only have come up from the south coast, overland. By any other route, they would have been seen and reported. And to have the confidence to come so far inland, they must be strong in numbers."

"That's a long march. You're right. There must be an army of them. So what steps are we taking?"

"General assembly call's gone out." This was Plautus. "If the response is as good as it's been in training, our men should be assembled at the training ground in half an hour."

"Half an hour from now?"

"No. From when the call went out."

"And then?"

"Sulla's place is to the south and west of here, about three hours away by forced march at night."

"Picus?"

As I spoke his name, he turned to me. "You're in command, Varrus."

"Nonsense. You are the serving legate. I fought long enough beside your father to have confidence in his son. Will you lead our cavalry?"

"Gladly!" He looked at his father who nodded his approval.

"General? Any suggestions as to how we might best tackle this?"

He shook his head. "No, Publius. Our men have trained for this for years. Now we can gauge the value of our methods. Picus, the infantry will follow your cavalry at the forced march. They should not be far behind you by the time you arrive. How do you want them deployed?"

Picus was deep in thought, his eyes on Vegetius Sulla, who was rubbing his hands together as though washing them, plainly beside himself in his anxiety to be gone from here. "Vegetius," he said. "I have not seen your home since boyhood, but I remember an open field to the north-east of the main buildings. Is it still there?" Vegetius nodded. "Bounded by that little wood to the north? And by the river?" Sulla nodded again. "Good." Picus turned back to us. "Varrus and I will take the cavalry and swing south, cutting off the road back to where these people came from. We will then turn and attack at first light, driving the enemy north, away from the farm.

"Vegetius, you will take us to your home by the shortest route. We will leave you there to wait for Plautus and his infantry. See to it that they are concealed among the woods and that they stay there, hidden, until we start to drive these people into their arms. Then when the time comes, form your battle lines in the open field and we'll crush these lice between the hammer and the anvil."

In spite of the seriousness of the situation, I found myself wanting to smile at the reference. It brought back memories. Picus, meanwhile, was still talking.

"We have to improvise with what we have, gentlemen. Until we know the enemy's strength, we will be unable to make a sound military disposition of our troops, but we do have our cavalry hammer and we have our infantry anvil, and the enemy, no matter how strong he is, doesn't know we exist. So let's go and introduce ourselves."

Britannicus stopped me on my way out of the room. "A word with you, Varrus."

"General?"

He smiled at me, a sad smile. "No more, my friend. In spite of Stilicho's warrant, I am grown old, quite suddenly. Too old to go to war."

"But not to plan."

"No, never too old for that. Observe my son for me, Publius. I believe he is as good as they say he is. You will be my judge."

"Don't worry, Caius. You have bred an imperator. It shines through his eyes. He's just as you were, thirty years ago." I saluted him and left him standing there, my heart heavy at the parting.

The ride to the south-west was hellish. The land was heavily treed, and had Vegetius Sulla himself not been there to lead us, we would have had to take the long route in the black of night. As it was, he led us across country by some fairly open ways he knew of. It was a cloudy night with a brisk, warm wind and a full moon. When we were in the open, the moon's light showed the fields clearly, when it was not obscured by clouds, but in the darkness of the woods the going was the stuff of nightmares, with men being knocked from their mounts continually by unseen branches. It took us just over two hours to reach Sulla's lands. A sullen, red glow flickered in the distance. Vegetius raised his arm to call a halt and turned to Picus and me.

"We're about two miles from the home farm. That's it there, burning. The big blaze on the left." His voice sounded dead, and I found myself admiring his calm self-discipline in not demanding that we charge the place immediately. But his next words showed me the true mettle of the man. "I have it in my mind that my wife and sons are dead. If I am right, I want to be avenged on those that killed them. All of them, not just the few we would catch if we were to charge up on them now. If, on the other hand, my family are being held, then they are safe enough for now and probably asleep. Any damage done to them will have been done long since. I'll be avenged for that, too, if it is so." He paused, sitting his horse in silence for a time before going on.

"There's a road, a farm track, directly ahead of us here, running from right to left, west to east. If you take your men east, you will come to a fork about two miles along. Take the south road. It leads up through the hills to pasture. The road ends at the entrance to the pasture, but if you hold to the right and follow the line of the trees, you'll come again to open fields on your right about three miles further on. You can muster there. You'll be just less than two miles from the buildings with nothing to impede your advance.

"I will take Plautus's infantry along this road here to the west when they arrive. It will take us about an hour to get into position from this point, and they should be about an hour behind us, little more. That should put us in place about an hour before dawn, by which time you should be ready, your men and horses rested. Start your attack any time you want to. We'll be waiting for you."

Picus's horse bridled and jigged nervously, jostling mine, which reared, almost unseating me. I pulled him back down savagely. Vegetius looked at both horses.

"One more thing. I don't sleep well at night. I often walk outside alone when everyone else is asleep, and I've noticed that if a fox barks or an owl hoots up on those hills to the east where you are going, it sounds as though he's just beyond the buildings. I don't know why it should be so, but sound really travels from up there, so be careful."

"Thanks for the warning," Picus said. "We will take care to make no noise."

"Nobody would hear us tonight, anyway," I said, and I immediately wanted to bite my tongue out.

"No," said Vegetius, his face expressionless. "The sounds of the burning should cover everything, but there's no point in taking chances."

"No, you're right. We'll take none." I felt awful, mentally cursing my big mouth. "Vegetius, I wish there were something I could say or do about this."

"What could you say? What's to be done, Varrus? What could you do to change anything?" He smiled bitterly, his face ghostly in the moonlight. "What could I have done, even if I had been at home? I would be dead now, with my family. At least this way, I'll have some vengeance."

I reached out and squeezed his shoulder and then I turned to Picus. "We'd better be going."

"Yes, you're right. Sulla, my friend, there is nothing I can say to ease your pain, but we can offer retribution, for what it is worth, on the heads of your enemies. Farewell."

I passed the word back through the ranks and we moved out. Within a quarter mile we found the farm track and followed it until we reached the fork. There we swung to the south, following the wheel ruts in the chalky ground until we began to climb. As we rode higher the wind died away. Picus stopped me and signalled to one of his men who rode directly behind us. The man came up to where we waited.

"General?"

"The wind is gone. It was blowing from our right, taking our noise away from the enemy. Any moment now, we are going to start smelling smoke from the burning buildings. It won't be pleasant. Pass the word back to bind the horses' nostrils. We don't want to wake anyone below with the noise of their whinnying. And tell the men to take it slowly. I want no noise, is that clear?"

"Yes, General."

"Good. Then make sure it is equally clear to everyone you tell it to, and tell it to *everyone!*"

We started moving again, riding two abreast, slowly enough that our horses took the gradient easily. I had bound a kerchief over Germanicus's muzzle and Picus had bound his mount's with a scarf. We rode in silence until Picus spoke in a low voice.

"My heart cries out for poor Sulla. It must be purgatory to wait as he does, within two short miles of home, not knowing if your loved ones are alive or dead."

"Aye," I responded. "I don't know if I could bear up as stoically as he under the same circumstances. It's ripping me up inside just trying to imagine it. God only knows what he's going through, knowing that it's real."

We rode on again in silence for a distance, and again it was Picus who spoke.

"Where *do* you think they came from, Varrus?"

"I've been racking my brains on that one. They *have* to have come up from the south."

"But that's what? Thirty miles? Forty?"

"Easily. Perhaps more."

"*Inland*, Varrus? It doesn't make sense. Why so far? On almost any other stretch of coast on the island, they'd have come across a town or a village within twenty miles. Their leader must have iron balls. Forty miles into hostile territory is a lot of risk."

"They may not be from the sea."

He jerked his head around to look at me. "What do you mean?"

"They could be outlaws."

"Rebels? Where from, in God's name?"

I shrugged. "I have no idea, Picus, but I know there are small groups of outlaws around. I ran foul of one group the first time I came out to your father's villa, before it became the Colony. That was a long time ago. Perhaps they are growing stronger, organizing themselves."

"But where would they come from?"

"Where do desperate men ever come from? They might be deserters. They could be farmers who have lost their farms, or villagers whose own homes have been destroyed—who knows?"

"By the living Christ! If these are deserters I'll crucify every one of them, living or dead!"

"Then again, they might have come down from the north-west, through the hills from the estuary, but that's even more unlikely. That's Ullic's territory, and his people watch those shorelines like eagles. I just can't imagine them getting through Ullic's country unseen, even though much of it is brush and heavy woodland."

"Well, we'll know in a couple of hours."

We had reached the pasture at the top of the hill and we could see the burning ruins quite plainly now in the valley below us. We looked down at the smoke-wreathed scene in grim silence.

"Sulla said to hold to the right and follow the line of the trees." Picus pulled his mount around and led us downhill until the tree line loomed up out of the darkness ahead of us, blocking the burning farm from our view.

The smoke was heavy now, oily and sour-smelling. As we rode on along the line of trees, each man among us began to prepare himself for what lay ahead of us. We were coming very close now to battle.

Less than an hour later we rounded the end of the trees and found ourselves in open fields. We had ridden clear of the drifting smoke some time previously and the glowing buildings now lay to our right. Picus led us out into the open until we were directly abreast of the burning villa, where he signalled a halt and summoned his man again.

"Tell the men to dismount and stretch their legs. Water the horses. It will be dawn in less than an hour. That will be when we attack. I want no sound before then. Nothing. No talking. These people may have sentries out, so we can take no chances. Clear? Spread the word and then come back to me."

The man's silver wristlet slapped against his breastplate in salute. "Yes, General!"

"Fine. Next time, salute me quietly."

"Yes, General."

As soon as the man had gone, Picus swung his leg over his horse's head and dropped to the ground. I did the same, but backwards, taking my good leg over Germanicus's rump and holding his mane, favouring my bad leg as I lowered myself, rather than dropped, to the ground. It was good to be off his back. My buttocks ached.

"We have a hundred and fourteen men, counting ourselves, Varrus. How do we use them best?"

"Any way you want to." I was pleased to see that he, too, was kneading his buttocks. "But we have open ground ahead of us and a two-mile advance to the villa. I think we should make the most of our numbers, letting them see how many of us there are. It should scare them to death before we ever reach them. Our objective is to run them into the infantry. I suggest that we attack either in two lines of sixty or in three lines of forty. Three lines might be better. Ten paces between each two men and the same distance between each two lines. That way, to anyone seeing us coming, it'll look as though there are hundreds of us."

"I think you're right. That's the tactic we talked about last time I visited the Colony. I've had my men working on it, but we've never tested it."

"Neither have we. But it should work. There's enough room."

"So, three lines converging into three arrowheads. Can your men do this?"

I smiled at him. "Can crows fly?"

"Who will lead the third line?"

"Bassus. He's my strongest leader."

"Let's get him up here."

Within the quarter-hour we were ready, instructions having been passed among the men. This was a brand-new tactic designed one cold winter night by Picus, Titus Harmen and myself, expressly for situations like this one:

open ground, room to manoeuvre, surprise on our side and an enemy who had never encountered cavalry before.

We would start our attack in three extended lines of forty men each. Each line would be staggered, so the enemy could see the troops in the second and third lines. As we moved forward, walking at first, then cantering, then loping before breaking into the charge, our manoeuvre would begin. The front rank would begin to converge on the man on the far left of the line: in this instance Bassus. At the same time, the second rank would begin converging on the man on the far right of their line: me. Two lateral motions, one from left to right, the other from right to left, and simultaneously with these moves, the rear rank would converge upon its centre man, Picus.

By the time the troops were cantering, the leaders would be moving slowly in again from the left and right, timing their movements so that as they rode, each had two men behind him, and three behind them, and four behind them, and so on; only the rear rank, led by Picus, would form up in its wedge directly behind its leader in a straight advance.

A watching enemy would see broad lines of mounted men moving across each other and finally solidifying into three wedge-shaped formations of heavy cavalry, each one capable of ploughing through any mass of men on foot.

We knew it would work. Our only concern was that it was untested in battle. Everything depended on the timing of the manoeuvre, with Picus's rear line becoming the pivot of the whole attack. He had to bring his squadron into line within moments of the completion of squadron formation, to show the enemy a solid line of horsemen coming at the charge, with three armed points extended towards them.

Once this had been accomplished, the arrowhead formation should, we believed, be almost infinitely versatile against infantry. It was easy to maintain. A man on the outside of a squadron only had to know that the man ahead of him was to his right, if he himself rode on the left side of the formation; vice versa if his place was on the right side of the arrowhead. Those on the inside of the formation moved ahead and then either right or left to replace any on the outside ranks who went down. Each man had enough room to fight and enough protection inside the formation to be safe. We had simply quadrupled the traditional Roman fighting space per man, to accommodate the horses.

As I said, we knew it *should* work. I wondered how many of the men behind me suspected that this was the first time I had ever *ridden* into battle as a bona fide mounted trooper?

In the next quarter of an hour the night grew pitch-black. We could see nothing. Then I heard Picus say, "Varrus, I can see you," and I opened my eyes and saw the dim shapes of men and horses again. As the light grew stronger, Picus issued the order to mount up and form three ranks. Someone gave me a leg up on to Germanicus and I took my place at the far right of the second rank. And then we waited, watching the dawn come up and waiting for Picus to give the signal to advance—waiting for the killing to begin. Somewhere to my left a horse nickered softly and was answered by another from in front. Germanicus was restless, and I stroked his neck, gentling him. Somewhere up ahead a lark starting singing in the dawn sky and was joined by another and then another until the sky was filled with birdsong.

XXII

I T SEEMED TO take hours for the light to grow full, but eventually we were able to see the buildings of the villa standing out clearly in the morning light less than two miles away across the open fields. Our force sat motionless. I heard the sound of a horse approaching me, and I swung around on Germanicus's back to see Picus coming towards me at a walk along the line behind me. He looked magnificent in his black and white and silver on his great, black horse, and I suddenly became aware of the colours of our group. The six men on either side of the space in the rear line where Picus had been were dressed in his colours, black armour and white tunics, and all six were mounted on blacks. My own men were mounted on unmatched horses but looked superb in their scarlet and bronze and brown leather.

Picus drew rein beside me. "Your men look good, Varrus. I don't want to waste this first charge. I want those animals ahead of us to get their first good look at a charge of Roman cavalry, so we'll wait a little longer until they can't fail to see us."

"It's Roman-British cavalry, Picus, but I see your point."

"Roman-British, of course. Anyway, I think it's light enough now. I'll walk back to my place and sound the advance. Where are your trumpets?"

"One beside me here on my left. One with Bassus at the far end of the front rank."

"Excellent. Will your men take up my call?"

"They will, they're waiting for it."

I watched him walk his horse slowly back to his position in the centre of the rear rank, passing the time of day with the troopers as he passed, and as he regained his place I returned my gaze to the villa, straining to see signs of movement.

Then the trumpet call rang out, harsh and brassy, to be taken up by our own trumpets. I watched the man in the line in front of me kick his horse to a walk and I gauged the gap between us until it was about fifty paces, then I kicked Germanicus and felt him move forward beneath me as I looked left to make sure that my own line was in order, with no one out in front of me. The space between the lines was crucial; too close together and the lines crossing into formation could be completely fouled up. My men were fine.

We walked for about a furlong and then I squeezed Germanicus into a trot, seeing the man ahead of me beginning to move to his left, angling towards his own formation point. The sound of hooves was growing louder now as the tempo of our pace increased. I glanced over my right shoulder and saw my trumpeter, who had been on my left, riding close behind me, just where he should be, and even as I looked, another man emerged behind him to his right. So far, so good. Our arrowhead was forming according to plan, just as we had rehearsed it on the parade ground so many times. Once again I looked ahead. The rank ahead of me had pulled far to the left, performing nicely. I checked over my left shoulder, resisting the urge to pick up the pace. The tail-end of my rank was now clearing the centre of our line of advance, heading obliquely towards me, and I saw the black and white of Picus's point coming forward. Now was the time to pick up speed again. I loosened the reins slightly and Germanicus surged into a canter.

The villa was less than a mile away now, and I could see men running back and forth in what I hoped was panic. I swallowed hard, my mouth dry, and checked over my shoulder once again. My formation was complete; a solid wedge of men and horses surged behind me. Bassus, over on my left, was formed up, too. The noise of hooves was very loud now, and then I heard a thundering on my left as Picus brought his wedge up to mine at the gallop. I squeezed hard with my knees, flicked my reins loosely and felt Germanicus surge forward, matching Picus's big black pace for pace until we were abreast of Bassus's column on the far left and all three wedges were charging flat out. I gripped the handhold on my shield tightly, pulling my elbow close in to my chest to hold the shield against me, making a mental note to change the shape of it to make it less cumbersome. I was riding easily, exulting in the surging power of the horse between my thighs, loving the thunderous sound of our advance, noticing the lightness of the leather helmet on my head, wishing I held the spear that Equus hated as I felt the quiver full of arrows slapping against my back.

Ahead of us, I could see men running in every direction, but mainly away from us. And then, totally unexpectedly, I saw a group of horsemen break from one of the buildings that had not been fired. There must have been ten of them, galloping flat out, away from us to my right, to the east. I glanced over at Picus to see if he had seen them. He had, and was already waving me away after them. I raised my spear arm above my head and angled my horse to the right. I could hear the noise of my squadron coming with me as I swung east to try to head off the fleeing enemy. They had about a quarter of a mile lead on us and their horses were fully rested, whereas ours had been moving all night and had already run a mile and a half, and yet we overtook them steadily, closing the gap between the two groups to less than a hundred paces before we had covered another mile.

I glanced over my shoulder then to see, to my great dismay, that my squadron had strung out far behind me, and when I looked ahead again, the fugitives had vanished beneath the brow of a hill. Then I felt my great Germanicus falter, and I knew he had reached the end of his endurance. Raging inwardly, I released the pressure on him and let him slow down in his own good time. By the time I crested the brow of the hill, he was walking, his breath coming in great, shuddering snorts, his flanks heaving like mighty bellows. Then, as the crest of the hill dropped below my line of sight, I could see our raiders still galloping for the safety of the forest in the distance, and I nearly wept with fury and frustration.

I heard a noise from below and looked down to see a riderless horse, rearing and flailing as it tried to free itself from its reins, which were tangled in the branches of a fallen tree. There was no sign of its rider. I heard the sound of my own men coming up behind me and waved them away. They stopped. I scanned the hillside below me. Nothing moved, except the snared horse. I guessed at first that it had stumbled and thrown its rider, but then I noticed an oddity about its appearance and decided that it must be a pack-horse, for it had a pack-saddle of some kind strapped to its back. That was why I could see no rider. It had none.

I waved for the men behind me to come forward, and when they had approached I sent one of them down the hillside on foot to bring back the trapped animal. He stopped some distance from the horse and bent over something in the long grass, and his voice came back up the hill to where we sat watching him.

"There's a dead man here, Commander."

I sent two more men down to bring up the body. They picked up the corpse with surprising ease and carried it back up, while the first man gentled the frightened horse, freed it and began to lead it back up the hill.

The corpse was dumped unceremoniously on the ground at my horse's feet and he sidled away from it, nervously.

"It's just a boy."

"Aye, Commander. A rich boy, whoever he was. Look at his clothes."

"I'm looking. Here, take these." I handed him my shield and spear and unslung my bow from around my shoulders, handing it down, too. Unencumbered now, I swung my leg over Germanicus's rump and lowered myself to the ground, where I knelt by the side of the dead boy. His face was badly scraped, but there was little blood, and his head sagged unnaturally sideways.

"Broken neck."

"Aye, Commander. Broken back, too, by the way he flopped when we tried to pick him up the first time. He landed among some fair-sized, solid rocks down there."

The boy was blond and wore a tunic of some rich, blue material. There was a gold collar round his neck and strong leather boots on his feet. Over his tunic he wore what looked like a metal shirt that laced right up to his neck, made of thousands of tiny, overlapping metal rings. I reached out and undid the thong binding it at his throat and slipped my fingers inside the shirt. It was lined with soft, supple leather onto which the rings were sewn. It was impressive, much finer than the one left me by my Grandfather Varrus with his treasures so many years before. The art of crafting them was improving. I straightened up.

"He can't be any more than fourteen, but he was old enough to ride to

war, and old enough to die for it. Strip that tunic and shirt off and throw
the body back where you found it. He was no Christian, whoever he might
have been, and I have a feeling we'll have all the burying we can handle when
we reach Sulla's place." I looked at the horse that had been brought up from
below. "Bring that horse over here."

It was a fine-boned animal, small and suited to a stripling lad, but it was
the contraption on its back that held my attention. I looked around me.
Everyone was staring at the thing. I stepped forward and laid hold of it,
pulling it towards me. It was some kind of saddle, as I had guessed, for it
was solidly anchored, fastened firmly around the horse's belly. It didn't budge
when I pulled at it.

"Does anybody know what this is for?" No answer. "Has anyone ever
seen anything like it before?" No one had.

"Some kind of saddle, but it looks more like a chair, set sideways, doesn't
it?" someone said, obviously referring to the thing's high back.

"Then it's a damn small chair," said another voice.

"Aye, Brutus, too small for your fat arse!" There was a roar of laughter
which I silenced with an abrupt motion of my arm.

"That's enough! We have little to laugh about this morning. Someone
leg me up onto my horse. And bring that with us." I pointed at the horse.
"I'll examine it more closely later. Have you got those clothes safe? Don't
lose that shirt, or I'll have your hide." They had just finished stripping the
torso, which looked white and pathetic on the cold ground, but I had no
sympathy to squander on raiders merely for being young. As I had already
said, if they were big enough to go to war, they were old enough to die. "Get
rid of that," I said, nodding towards the corpse. "Let's go."

I stepped into the cupped hands of the soldier who was waiting to help
me up, and he hoisted me to where I could throw my leg across Germanicus.
I swung him around, hard, and headed back in the direction of Vegetius's
villa. Just before we reached it, I looked back. My men were all behind me,
riding two abreast. "All right, there, smarten up! We didn't catch the enemy,
but that doesn't mean we should ride in looking like failures! Form up on
me!" I flicked the reins and brought Germanicus to a trot and we arrived at
the villa looking like a military unit.

We found the place deserted, except for a few scattered corpses, and the
stink of charred wood was appalling. I looked all around, but I could see no
female bodies and no children. Then I saw Vegetius. I had looked at him
and past him already, not recognizing him, for his face was completely masked
in blood, but now I recognized his armour. He lay huddled on a pile of straw
bits at the base of a stone wall. I flung myself from my horse and went to
him, thinking he was dead, but as soon as I touched him I knew he was alive.
He had taken a bad blow from something that had torn the skin from his
forehead, leaving a bloody flap dangling down over his eyes. I lifted it clear
and pressed it back into place on his brow with the palm of my hand and

he immediately looked far better. There was hardly any blood in his eyes at all, but he was unconscious.

"Cato!" I yelled. "Bring me that boy's blue tunic!" He brought it at a run. "Rip me a strip off that and bind it round Vegetius's brow. Be quick." He did as I ordered. "That's better. Now help me to move him up onto this pile of straw." As we moved him, I wondered idly why the straw had not burned, and then I really looked around me for the first time. Most of the buildings were intact. Only three had burned: the villa itself and two others. It made sense that the stables would have survived, since the raiders had ridden horses. As I looked around me, Cato spoke.

"Here come the others, Commander."

I turned to see Picus and Bassus emerge with their troops from the edge of the trees that surrounded the rear of the yard. They saw us and cantered towards me ahead of their men.

"Is that Vegetius?" Picus nodded towards the activity by the wall.

"Yes. Not dead, just unconscious."

"Where was he? Where did you find him?"

"Right here, against the wall, but don't ask me how he got here."

"I don't have to. He came alone, ahead of everyone else. He led the infantry into place and then disappeared. He must have been trying to reach his family."

"Aye. Well, he didn't find them."

"How did you make out? Did you catch them?"

I grunted my disgust. "No. We lost them. Their mounts were fresh. They outran us. What about you? Much trouble?"

He grinned, totally without humour. "Worked like a sorcerer's spell. They ran like cattle, out through the trees at the back there, where they thought we couldn't follow, and smack into the spears of our infantry. It was slaughter, and we didn't lose a man. A few of the foot-soldiers were wounded, but none of them seriously."

"Any prisoners?"

"Seventeen."

"How many were there, altogether?"

"About ninety."

"Any idea who they were?"

"Aye. Apparently they're Franks."

"Franks?" I was astonished.

"Aye, Franks, or Burgundians."

"But what about the horses?"

"What about them? They brought them with them."

"In boats?"

"Apparently, unless they swam behind." Picus dropped down from his horse and began to knead his buttocks. "God, I could eat my weight in something."

"How in Hades can you be hungry with so much blood around? I wonder where Vegetius's family went to? They're not here. Did you leave orders with the infantry about the bodies?"

"The prisoners are digging a pit to bury them."

"It'll take a deep pit to hold ninety corpses."

"That's their problem. They've nothing better to do."

I turned to Bassus. "I want you to pick twenty of your best men and follow the horsemen who escaped. They left a plain trail. Find them and destroy them, then return to the Villa as quickly as you can."

He saluted and left, moving quickly, and I left Picus, still massaging his buttocks, and went about the disposition of my men. It is always the same after every action—reaction, then inaction. By the time I had organized the preparation of a meal and set my men to clearing up the shambles of the farm, Picus was busy with his own six men, and I went back to where Vegetius Sulla was now being tended by one of our medics. As I approached, his eyes opened and I saw him look at me and recognize me, his lips forming my name as I knelt at his side.

"Vegetius. How are you feeling?" Stupid damn question, but what else can you ask, even though you know the truth?

His eyelids fluttered, closed, fluttered again and opened. He was looking directly at me. I watched his eyes focus on me, brighten and then start to glaze. It was the strangest thing I had ever seen. Then he spoke my name, his lips barely framing the syllables. I leaned in to him.

"What is it?"

"The stable cellar. Tried to get them . . ." His voice trailed off into a slur, but he had solved the mystery of his family's whereabouts.

I took one of his hands in mine. "Don't worry, Vegetius. They're safe enough. We'll get them out."

His fingers tightened suddenly, convulsively, on mine and he arched in agony. I leaned forward to squeeze his shoulder, but my hand never reached him, for suddenly blood ran from his ears and from his mouth and the life went from him in a rush. I froze there in mid-action, stunned by the speed of it. The medic kneeling on the other side of him leaned over and closed his staring, agonized eyes.

"What happened?" I asked him. "He wasn't that badly hurt."

"Something must have burst inside his head, Commander. I've seen the like before with bad head blows."

I lowered Vegetius Sulla's hand gently onto his chest and tried to find a prayer for him, but I had none; my soul was empty. Feeling very old quite suddenly, I rose to my feet with a sigh and looked towards the entrance to the stables. Stella and her children would emerge from the blackness of that cellar into a lightless world. "Cato," I said. "Bring two of your men and come with me." I led them into the stable and started kicking at the straw on the floor.

"What are you looking for, Commander?"

"A trapdoor in the floor."

"Over here, sir." The words had barely left my lips before the answer came, and I felt my stomach lurch in awful anticipation at the speed of the response. I turned to see one of my young troopers pointing at a rectangular area of the floor that was free of straw. I walked towards it slowly.

"Open it."

They were all dead. Almost twenty of them, women and children. All of the females had obviously been raped, irrespective of age. The male children were all at the bottom of the pile. They had been killed and thrown into the hole and then the women and girls had been used, finished and thrown in on top of them. Sulla's wife, Stella, lay sprawled on the top of the pile, naked, bloody, battered, yet still easily recognizable. Her staring, dead eyes glared accusingly into my own. A vision of the face of the dead boy we had found on the hillside sprang into my mind and I wondered if he had taken any part in this.

I backed away from the horror of the sight, fighting the vomit rising in my throat until the edge of the trapdoor cut off my vision and I was no longer looking into Hades. My mind was recreating what must have happened here. Perhaps they had not thought to leave someone outside to cover up the trapdoor with straw. Or it could have been that one of the children made a noise and was overheard. Or had some late arrival been seen and followed? No one would ever know, now, but they had been found, and their sanctuary had become their grave.

I heard the wet noise of one of my men being sick and realized that it had been going on for some time, but instead of triggering me into a similar upheaval, the sound hardened everything inside me. I spun on my heel and marched out of the charnel-house, blinking hard as I emerged into the brightness of the morning. I called to the first trooper I saw and told him to fetch the Legate Picus at the double, and then I stood there, looking around the yard, my eyes squinting fiercely, unaccustomed yet to the bright sunshine after the gloom of the stable. I lost track of time, standing there so deep in thought that I didn't see Picus approach, and his voice startled me.

"What's the problem, Varrus?"

I pointed with my thumb, over my shoulder towards the stable entrance. "Take a look for yourself, but be ready for it. It's not pleasant." When he came back out his face was pasty white.

"Is Sulla's wife among them?"

"She's the one on the top of the heap. She must have been the last to die."

He was visibly shaken, and for some time neither of us spoke again. A party of soldiers approached the stable doors, carrying buckets. Picus stopped them in their tracks.

"Where are you men going?"

"Centurion sent us to get some oats from the stable, General."

"You!" Picus pointed to the one who had spoken. "Go back and tell your centurion that your squad has been commandeered by me for special duty.

The rest of you put down those buckets and split into two parties, one to guard this door and the other to guard the doors at the back. No one is to enter this building without direct permission from either myself or Commander Varrus. Move!" He turned back to me. "Let's walk."

We crossed the yard side by side and our presence had a visible effect on the men who saw us. One after another they all became very diligent about whatever it was they happened to be involved in. We ignored them and walked in silence until Picus spoke.

"We'll have to bury them, I suppose. We can't take them back with us."

"Why would we even want to do that, Picus? They're dead."

He shook his head. "This is going to cause a lot of shock in the Colony. Is this the first time you've ever been attacked directly?"

"No," I answered him. "The second. But it's the first time we've been hit so hard. And from this direction."

"What's to be done?" There was a strange tone in his voice that made me turn my head to look directly at him. He noticed my expression and went on. "It's the novelty of the situation that's throwing me, Uncle. This isn't military. Not in the regular sense. These people are civilians. And they're my own people, at least my father's and yours. I'm used to dealing with casualties impersonally, but these were friends of my Aunt Luceiia. War has come a lot closer to home, quite suddenly."

"Aye, lad, I know what you mean. But don't let that blind you to the facts here, which *are* military, whether you accept that right now or not. This is the most outlying of our properties, and it's too far from the home farm. That's a fact that's been tragically proven today. As a farm it is now useless to us. That's another fact, a proven extension of the first one. We're going to have to redefine our borders, cut down our properties and redeploy our forces to defend the ones we intend to hold. That's another fact.

"The animals who did this had cavalry cover. That's a fact, and it alters our whole concept of the forces that are coming against us. It means that the enemy, or part of them at least, are just as mobile as we are. From this time on we have to make allowances for that. That's a lot of facts, Picus, all military realities and none of them wholesome. We've got to get back to the Colony just as fast as we can and alert the Council. We have to define some new priorities for our growth and for our defence."

"What about burial for the victims here?" His face was bleak.

"They're already in their grave, lad. We'll lay Vegetius out beside his wife and sons and burn the place over them. As martyrs of the Colony, it will be a fitting end."

"You're right, Uncle, as usual. I'll see to it."

"Wait. Summon all of our men, infantry and cavalry, to stand as a funeral honour guard. They should know what we are doing and why it's being done. And bring the prisoners, too. They will be confronted with their atrocity and executed." He opened his mouth to speak, but I cut him off. "No arguments, Picus. They die."

He nodded, after considering the look of me for a few moments. "How do they die?"

"I ought to crucify the swine, and if I had the time, I would. But I don't."

"How, then?"

"In the fire. They burn. They seem to worship a fire god. Now they can meet him, face to face." He gazed at my face for the space of ten heartbeats, and when he spoke, his voice was low.

"You are a harder man than I thought you, Publius Varrus."

I spoke through my anger. "Vegetius Sulla was my friend. His wife was a gentle, kindly woman, full of dignity and peace. You saw how they used her. They burn."

"So be it. They burn."

"You still sound unsure. Does your conscience bother you on this?"

"I don't know, Uncle. Perhaps it does. They deserve to die, but burning them alive seems unchristian."

"Remember your friend Pelagius, Picus. Freedom of choice and personal responsibility. As I see it, that's the only route available now to men of true conscience. We're not dealing with Christians here. Turn the other cheek to such as these, as the priests would have us do, and we'll all be dead within the year. The old God of the Hebrew testaments suits me far better, now, with his eye for an eye, than the gentle Christ does. I choose His way and I'm ready to stand responsible for the survival of our people."

"Aye. You're right." There was conviction in his voice now. "I'll see to it. But what about the pit they're digging now, for the others?"

"Leave it. Let them rot in the open. None of our people will be around to smell the stink. Assemble the men. We'll march them past the pit and show them what has been done here, then we'll let them see justice done in the execution of the criminals in the pyre of their victims."

And so it was done.

XXIII

IT WAS A long, quiet ride back to the Colony. Every man among us had plenty to occupy his thoughts, and the black smoke of the Sulla family's pyre hung all around us, although we had left it far behind. When we arrived, Picus and I went directly to meet with Caius. He was waiting for us in his day-room with Bishop Alaric, who had arrived on one of his regular visits. As we entered the room both men rose to their feet, scanning our faces. I nodded to both of them and spoke to the old bishop first.

"You should have been with us, Alaric. We could have used you."

"For what?" Caius's voice was tense.

"Funeral services."

"It was bad?"

"Worse than you could imagine." I told them what had happened and what we had found in the cellar. Picus did not attempt to add anything or to interrupt me in any way. By the time I had done, both of my listeners were as whitefaced as Picus had been when he emerged from the stables.

"You executed the prisoners?" This was Caius.

"I did."

He looked into my eyes, and if he had any difficulty accepting my actions I saw no sign of it. He turned and walked away from his chair a few steps, his shoulders hunched over. "This changes everything," he said. "We had not expected an enemy with cavalry. Now we have to plan our defences differently in every way."

"Not cavalry, Caius, horses." He turned and looked at me, frowning. "I made the same mistake, at first, but the people we chased were not cavalry. They were just mounted men. But that alone makes a difference in terms of the mobility of the enemy. It was obviously the strength afforded by a band of horsemen that encouraged the others to venture so far inland."

Bishop Alaric had so far said nothing. He had merely subsided into his chair and sat looking from face to face among the three of us. Now he spoke.

"But where would these people—Franks you say they were?—where would they find horses here?"

"They didn't, Alaric. They brought them with them."

"From Gaul? How?"

"By boat, the same way Picus brought his."

"No comparison," Caius broke in. "Picus used imperial galleys for transportation. Large ships. The Franks have none of those."

"No, Caius, you're right, they don't," I said. "But they don't need them. We saw only ten or a dozen mounted men. That number of horses could be accommodated easily on two or three longboats. But it's not the numbers that matter, it's the fact that they're doing it at all. We have to find out where they landed and make sure that none of their friends follow them, and if that means constant patrols of the entire south-west shore-line, then that is what we are going to have to be prepared to live with. Picus agrees with me. We discussed it this morning on the ride back."

Caius grimaced. "Then you do think they came up from the south coast? All that way?"

Picus nodded. "Thirty, forty, perhaps fifty miles overland, depending on the route they followed. Yes, we do. The horses would give them the added protection they felt they needed—speed and mobility in scouting the land ahead of them. We estimate that this was a three-boat party, with about thirty-three men and three or four horses to a boat."

"I see." The tone of his voice confirmed it. "So what do we do now?"

I told him. "We call a Council meeting for tomorrow morning to define some new priorities."

"Such as?"

"Such as deciding how much of our land we should give up as untenable under these new circumstances. We absolutely have to abandon some of the villas, even if we continue to farm the land. We have to pull our most outlying people back to where we can defend them properly. And from now on, every party working our fields has to have an armed guard."

He nodded wordlessly, agreeing with each point as I made it.

"What else?"

"Well, I was thinking about our defences all the way back. It seems to me that as soon as we have our harvest safely in, we have to concentrate all of our efforts on finishing the fort on the hill. We should build a permanent headquarters there and be prepared to move all of our people in to shelter at a moment's notice."

"That makes sense. Picus, you agree with Publius?"

"Yes, Father, I do. But remember that you're going to need easy ingress and egress. You're going to need a road, even if it runs no further than from the bottom of the hill to the top."

"Yes, I suppose we are, we have to have some way of getting our people in and out quickly."

Picus hammered the point. "Your people, yes, but mainly your soldiers, both mounted and on foot."

Caius turned back to me. "Varrus, you are correct, this is a Council matter. I'll summon an emergency session tonight."

"No, Caius," I interrupted him. "Not tonight. Tomorrow morning will be soon enough. Let everyone get some sleep. In the meantime, I have some things I have to see to, so if you'll pardon me, I'll go and look after them now." I bowed and left the three of them together as I went to find Luceiia and tell her the sad news of her friends.

She was waiting for me in the family room of our quarters and she took it far better than I had expected, though I ought to have known better than to have such expectations of my wife. Knowing how close she had become to Stella Sulla and her children, I had been racking my brains all the way home, to find the kindest, most gentle way of breaking the brutal news to her, but as it turned out, I did not have to say a word. The mere look of me, despite the fact that I had tried to school my face to blankness, or perhaps because of that very blankness, told her the worst, and her eyes filled up with tears before I had the chance to speak.

"You were too late. Was it awful?"

I nodded, miserable with the admission yet seeing no advantage in lying. She would soon know the truth from others.

"Was she . . . Did they . . .?"

"Aye. We were too late to help. I saw her body. She had been violated, but not mutilated—" I broke off, realizing the inanity of what I was saying. "Anyway," I went on, hearing the roughness of my words, "it must have been short-lived, for I had the . . . the impression, and it was very strong, that she had died quickly."

"And what about the children?"

"They are all dead, love, Vegetius, too; killed in attempting rescue."

The breath went out of her in a rush and then she straightened, breathing deeply again. "Poor Stella," she murmured, almost to herself, remembering. "She was such a gentle woman, and so bright, like sunlight in springtime." Luceiia turned her head away; then her shoulders slumped and she moved to me, leaning her face against my chest as she sobbed several times, and I wished I had thought to remove my armour before coming to her. And yet, for all her grief, it was obvious to me that she had prepared herself for just this outcome and was determined not to let it affect her too visibly. I held her close until she had composed herself and then she forced herself to become the mistress of the household once again, straightening her shoulders and leaning back to look me in the eye.

"And the attackers? What of them?"

"We caught them. Franks, we think, or Gauls. They came from the south, and they were strangers, alien. But wherever they came from, they will not be going home."

Her forehead wrinkled. "What did you do with them?"

I looked at her, stone-faced. "Killed most of them. Those left alive, I burned alive in the Sullas' funeral pyre."

Her eyes widened, scanning my face, and then she nodded, accepting my judgment without question. "Good," she said, then stepped away from me, looking down at her hand as she fumbled in a pocket of her gown and produced a kerchief.

"You must be famished," she said, wiping her nose. "When did you last eat?"

"Last night, before dawn. I gnawed on some of the bread and cheese I had with me. I haven't had much stomach for food since. Picus is in with Caius and Alaric. He must be starved, too."

"Will you eat now?"

"No, my love, I can't. I have to see to Germanicus and talk to Equus first. If I leave now, I can be back in an hour."

She reached up and kissed me. "Go, then, and hurry back. I'll have Gallo prepare the bath-house attendants for your return, and there will be a hot dinner waiting for you by the time you have bathed and dressed."

A short time later, I found Victorex in the stables, gazing in perplexity at the device he had removed from the small Frankish horse. The thing lay on the ground at his feet, and he was crouched beside it, running the palm of his hand across its smooth leather. I slid down from Germanicus and handed his reins to a groom,who led him away to one of the stalls.

"What is it, Victorex? Ever seen anything like it before?"

He shook his head. "No. Damn me if I know what it is, although it's a saddle of some kind." He paused, then ran his fingers over the device again, hooking them under its lower edge and hefting the weight of it. "Nothing like any Roman saddle I've ever seen . . . as you well know, they're made of leather stretched over bronze plates, for strength. They're light, but they're awkward things. That's why so few of our men ever use them. But this . . ." He turned the device over to expose its underside. "Look at this! This thing's built on a wood frame . . . And look here . . ." He flipped it right-side-up again. "Look at the back of it, the way it's shaped, and this weird-looking thing on the front . . . This was never designed to carry a pack! It's shaped for a man's arse! But once a man put his crotch over this, with his backside jammed up against the back piece there, he'd be useless. There's no way he'd ever be able to sway with his mount, or control it, and there's no way even to grip a horse's barrel through the thing. It's too thick! Too heavy and too solid. A rider would bounce right off the horse's back . . ." His voice faded away in perplexity, then resumed. "Anyway, that's all beside the point, isn't it? It's too small for a man."

"A boy," I said. "The rider was a boy, and I think, in spite of your doubts, that it is some kind of saddle, though why on earth anyone would want or need such a thing . . ." My attention was caught then by two appendages, one attached to either side of the device, and I nodded at them. "What about those two things hanging down, there? What do those look like?"

He picked one of them up, pulling it towards him as far as he could. It was no more than a broad strip of leather, fastened at the top to the main apparatus, and ending in a loop. A flat piece of wood, carved with a niche at each end, had been inserted across the bottom of the loop, stretching it into a delta shape.

Victorex gazed at it wonderingly for some time, then, "No idea . . ." he muttered. "Unless . . ." His voice trailed away and then came back as he tapped the wood-stretched loop against the back of the saddle. "Look, Commander, if this *is* for sitting on—if it is a saddle of some kind, which is what its shape would suggest in spite of common sense—then there's no way a man could vault into it. The back's too high."

I nodded. "So?"

"So, how does he get up on the horse? I've seen you get many a leg-up onto Germanicus. I've cupped my own hands for you a few times." He waved the loop end under my nose. "This thing could serve the same purpose: a mounting step."

I stared at it. "By God, you're right at that, Victorex! But why would anyone go to all that trouble? Unless the boy had a crippled leg."

"Did he?"

I shrugged my shoulders. "I don't know. He was dead when we found him. I didn't even look. His neck was broken, and so was his back. No one paid any attention to his legs."

"Then that could be it? Because this could have been a harness for a crippled boy. It had to be. He was probably unstable in it, and that's why he fell off in the first place."

It was my turn to be bemused. Why would any man take a crippled boy on campaign? Even a favourite son? A chief's son, as the gold collar and shirt of mail suggested he was? But I had other, more important things on my mind.

"I haven't got time to ponder mysteries. Have one of your people take it up to Gallo at the house and tell him to place it on a saw-horse in my armoury. It will make a memento of a savage occasion."

I left Victorex still looking at the Frankish harness and found Equus at the forge, working outside in the late afternoon sunshine. He had already heard the news of the Sullas and wanted to ask me all about it, but I was in no mood to discuss it yet.

"How are you making out with that new sword design?" I asked him.

He led me inside the forge and showed me the length of metal that lay there on his work-bench. Beside it, on a scrap of papyrus, he had drawn a sword—a sword with a blade twice the length of the *gladium*, and a handle to match, with a heavy weight at the pommel.

"I haven't had much time to work on it, and I won't guarantee that it will work the way you want it to." He shook his head dubiously. "I knew what the problem would be. I've got to get enough weight into the pommel to counterbalance that bastardly long blade. The thing sticks out there like Rhea's teats, but Rhea's got the buttocks to balance her, and this thing doesn't."

I laughed at that. Rhea was one of the Colony's most outstandingly endowed young women, and Equus had been quietly lusting after her for some time.

He laughed with me, shaking his head. "Ah, that Rhea! Now there's balance! She's so well balanced, may all the gods bless her, that she can fall on her back as lightly as a feather, anytime she wants to, which is most of the time, except when she's around me." He laughed again, a great, raucous laugh directed at himself.

I reached out and clapped him on the shoulder. "You've made a start, anyway. Keep at it, Equus. By the day after tomorrow, I'll be able to work on it with you."

"All right, but you'd better be prepared to spend a lot of time on it. This whore is not going to give in to us just because we smile nicely."

"I'm prepared for that, my friend. And now I'm going to bathe, shave and eat. Council meets tomorrow and I want to be in good shape for the session."

I left him as I had found him, hard at work, puzzling over the weighting of the new weapon.

XXIV

I WAS LATE for the Council meeting the following day, in spite of all my good intentions, so I don't really know how the argument started. All I do know is that by the time I arrived, the session was about half an hour old and a great storm had blown in during the opening moments. I heard the hullabaloo as I approached the doors of the chamber, and the volume amazed me. I stopped outside and remembered Vegetius and his whistling stone, and then, on an impulse, I went looking for a trumpeter, or a trumpet. Typically, there was not a soldier to be seen anywhere, so I ended up getting a brass horn from my armoury.

Back once again at the doors of the Council chamber, where the racket was still going on, I tucked the horn under my arm, pulled the door open and stepped inside. The noise in the great room was unbelievable—complete pandemonium, with everybody shouting and screaming at the same time. I scanned the room looking for Caius and quickly located him at the front. He stood erect, watching the scene going on around him, and at his side stood Bishop Alaric. They were the only two people in the room, apart from myself, who were not making a sound.

I had served with Caius Britannicus for a very long time and thought I had seen all of his moods. On occasion, I had seen him angry, and on a very few memorable occasions I had seen him furious. I took one look at him that morning and I knew that I had never seen him this angry before. His face was pallid and the skin was drawn tight over his cheekbones, and his lips were so compressed that he seemed to have no mouth at all. But it was his eyes that gave me pause. They were like stones: hard, cold, unyielding and pitiless. I whipped the horn up to my lips and let its brazen scream smash everyone into silence.

They all turned to face me, stunned a little by the suddenness of the interruption. Then somebody said my name, and from the tone of the voice I could guess that its owner was about to try to solicit my support. I silenced him with another blast, holding this one until I ran out of breath. Nobody moved until I did, but then, as I started to walk, they began to talk again, and I silenced them again with a third blast. This time, as I removed the mouthpiece from my lips, I pointed to the front of the room and said, "Caius Britannicus!"

All eyes went to him. He remained rigid for a few moments and then he said, "Let us be seated."

Again a voice was raised, and in an instant, Caius had drawn his sword

303

from its scabbard and smashed the flat of it on the table in front of him with a clang. "SILENCE!" he roared. The silence he received was absolute and awestruck. Utter stillness.

"I said, let us be seated." This was almost a whisper. Now all the anger in the room had turned into embarrassment in the face of his wrath, and everyone sat down.

Caius picked up his sword again from the table, reversed his grip on it and hammered the point deep into the wood, so that the sword stood erect in front of him. When he spoke again, his voice was low, intense and sibilant with disgust.

"I have *never* in my life, *never*, been subjected to such a disgraceful display of spleen! How dare you subject me—and yourselves—to such debased behaviour! You people are the *Council* of this Colony. The elders! Collectively, yours is supposed to be the voice of wisdom!" His eyes raked every man in the room, and there were many who squirmed. Finally, after what seemed like an age, he spoke again.

"Now. I want you all to listen very carefully to what I have to say. I want each of you to make a supreme effort to forget about your own personal demands, or requirements, or interpretations of what you may or may not have heard before coming here." He bit his upper lip and glowered at them, commanding their attention, stretching the silence he had achieved. "Listen for your lives. It is I, Caius Britannicus, who speak to you!" His eyes moved from face to face and again he stretched the pause, making them wait for his next words.

"This is my house. You are here at my invitation. I brought this Council into being!" An expectant hush stilled the room. Finally, when he was convinced that no one was going to break the silence in defiance of him, he continued, and the clarity and conviction in his voice rang throughout the room, even though he spoke with no great volume. No one doubted by this time that they had given grave offence to the presence, the power, that was Caius Britannicus, and his gaze moved from face to face, singling no one out but leaving no one exempt from the import of his words.

"I will tolerate no more outrages of this kind in my house! Is that clear? If you wish to behave like animals, or like hucksters in the street, then go and fight among yourselves in the stables or in the marketplace! Not here!" He was overwrought, brittle, and therefore fragile, in his anger. Struggling to calm himself, he lowered his head, pinching the bridge of his nose between the thumb and fingers of his right hand.

I began to move towards the front of the room just as Lars Nepos, a skilled leather-craftsman who was standing in front of me and to my right, leaned over to make a comment to his neighbour.

"Nepos!" I roared, slapping him hard on the shoulder. "Hold your peace! The man hasn't finished yet."

He subsided immediately, looking abashed, and I continued my walk to the front, coming to a stop just behind and to the right of Caius, where I turned and faced the Council, looking at their faces, searching for anger, resentment, hubris. All I saw was shame, mingled with concern for Caius.

He raised his head and squared his shoulders, and when he spoke again his voice had returned to its normal pitch though it was oratorical in its cadences.

"When we founded this Colony, we dedicated it to the cause of survival in the face of Armageddon, and we dedicated it to the preservation of all that was originally great in Rome.

"When we formed this Council, for the governance of the Colony, we spoke with pride of solving our problems nobly, in regulated session dedicated to the common good, as did our republican forefathers in the Senate. *This Council is our Senate!*" He stopped again, to allow that comment to penetrate the minds of his listeners, and again his gaze swept the assembly, missing no one.

"This Council is our Senate. That is the truth, but it has never been stated before, because it sounds overly grand and intimidating, and it reeks of affectation and unearned and inappropriate powers." Another all-encompassing, ranging look around, without breaking his tempo. "Nevertheless, it is the truth." His audience was spellbound.

"You men are this Colony's senators. We have not used the term, as such, until this time and this regrettable circumstance, but that is what you are, and this is the perfect time to point it out and engrave it in your minds and your souls . . . You are this Colony's senators."

He drew a deep, shuddering breath.

"Here, in this Council chamber, every man is equal. Each has his part to play. Each has his value, which is his alone and never better used than when it is dedicated to the solving of our common problems. No man's voice should be more important here than any other's, including my own. My function is that of moderator only, or has been until today. Now, like Julius Caesar, I stand here as dictator, laying down the law, because you have *forced* me to speak thus! I am not grateful for this distinction." He stopped yet again, deliberately moving his eyes from man to man in sequence, missing none in his scrutiny.

"I will not accept this role you thrust upon me." There was utter stillness in the room. "I will not play the father to your childishness." He drew a long breath. "My son Picus is much concerned these days with personal responsibility. Each one among you should seek him out when next he visits us and spend some time talking with him about it, *because like it or not, each one of you has accepted personal responsibility for the welfare of this Colony.*

"This debacle today has absolved me of a responsibility I never really had . . . yet thought was my duty . . . a personal responsibility for you, for your actions and behaviour, and for the Colony. From this time forth, I will no longer stand as moderator of this Council." He raised his hand quickly, trying to forestall the spontaneous murmur that these words caused, and to which I myself contributed an involuntary grunt of surprise and apprehension.

"Hear me! I am not being dramatic. I mean this. I am growing too old for this and have been thinking for some time now that my task is done. Today I see that I was wrong. My task is far from complete. But it will be completed now, finally, for better or for worse.

"In spite of the way you have behaved this morning, you are all grown men. It is time that you took responsibility for your own course. This session will be my last as moderator. The Senate of Republican Rome had no permanent moderator, nor will this Council.

"I have suspected for several sessions now the emergence of a spirit of elitism among us. I had accused myself of being cynical and suspicious, but I can see now that this was not so. This morning's fiasco has, at its roots, exactly the spirit I have feared: elitism! It must not be allowed to grow, to continue, for if it does then this Council, and this Colony, are doomed." He paused again, and once again no one sought to interrupt him.

"We have newly lost our first Council member in war. We have gained our first martyr. Vegetius Sulla held his place among us with honour. Now he is dead, and he must be replaced. I find it tragic that it should be the question of replacing such a man, the occasion of his death, that should precipitate such a pitiful scene as the one we have just witnessed here." His voice soared again to a shout, booming in the stillness of the room.

"How dare any man here seek to advance himself in such circumstances! How can any among you be so petty as to squabble over who should sit where?

"What does it matter if you are young or old? Why does it matter whether you sit at the rear of this assembly or at the front? Shame be on any man who thinks it does! Are there those among you who think that by sitting close to me you might gain import? Well, if so, that has been taken care of. I shall be here at the front no more!

"Or are there those among you who think that you will not be listened to if your voice comes from the rear? Such thoughts impugn the honour of this body! They are unworthy! In this assembly, all voices are equal and every man among us is assured his right to speak and vote! This is a Council chamber!" His voice fell again, almost to a whisper. "Not, as I have said, a marketplace."

He stopped again, always mindful of the need to permit enough time for his words to register in the minds of his listeners; then he raised his right hand, his index finger extended.

"We have had only one rule governing our sessions in this room in all the years we have been meeting here. Now, I believe, the time has come to initiate more rules, not for governance, but for simple, honest guidance, to serve as a reminder of who we are and what our true function must remain. We are the members of a Council appointed to serve the best interests of the people we represent: the Colonists who share our lives and our destiny. With only two exceptions, myself and Publius Varrus, each man among you is here because all the others feel that man has a contribution to make.

Vegetius Sulla was a prime example. In our time of utmost need, it was his insight that enabled us to take the only steps that could have protected us, steps that no man among us but he would ever have dreamed of. And when he spoke that time, as those of you who were here might remember, he did so from the far corner of this room, before moving forward!"

He raised his hand to the hilt of his sword, still imbedded in the table-top, and worked the blade from side to side until it came free. Then he slipped it quietly back into its scabbard.

"I have been railing at you. I have accused some of you of wanting to advance your own designs by taking prominent places in the Council here. It occurs to me now that this can be simply circumvented." He stopped abruptly, obviously waiting for a response this time, and someone, I didn't see who it was, asked the question in everyone's mind.

"How, Caius?"

"How? By our adoption of a rule, here, at this time, that all future Councils will be seated in a circle. Let us place all of our chairs in a ring around the room, and let the rule entail that no man shall sit beside the same person twice within seven meetings." This time he made no move to quell the outburst of speculation that his words gave rise to. Instead, he raised his voice and spoke into the noise.

"Think of it, my friends! Think what that would mean! Each time this Council gathered we would have cause to recall the reasons for this rule!" The voices died away and the room was silent again, listening as he went on. "We could go even further. Inside the door of the chamber could be a bag of stones, with twenty white stones and one black. As each man entered, he would draw a stone, and he who drew the black would moderate the day's proceedings. Thus, a single man might draw the black stone more regularly than his fellows, but each time it would be by random chance only, and by no other means."

Again the swelling murmur of comment, but this time a hand was raised and waved in the air by Quintus Seco.

"Yes, Seco?"

Seco rose to his feet and looked around him, his face flushing red. He coughed and cleared his throat and then spoke out.

"Caius Britannicus, you have given us—deservedly—the rough edge of your tongue and more than good reason to feel shame. I have listened closely to your words and I believe all you have said is true." He cleared his throat again. "But I believe that what I liked least is the truest part of all. We have begun to forget why we are here. We *do* feel self-important. I am proud to be a member of this Council. But you have made me think that I might be *too* proud. This notion of a circular Council makes much sense to me. So does the notion of a randomly chosen moderator for every session, although I have no wish to offend you by seeming to suggest that we are ungrateful for your past contributions."

Caius dismissed that with a wave of his hand. "You do not offend me, Quintus. Go on."

"Well, I think we should adopt the suggestions you have made. I think we should do it now. I think we should vote on both together, without debate."

Seco sat down, still red in the face, and for a time no one responded. Then Varo, Caius's brother-in-law, raised his voice.

"By God's blood, Quintus, I'm with you! I say let's vote on it, right now!"

Caius once again took the floor. "Before you put it to the vote, is there anyone here who wishes to speak against the idea?"

Everyone began to look around, and at the back of the room a solitary hand was raised. Caius looked at the man, his face expressionless. "Totius, you wish to speak against it?"

Totius got to his feet, red-faced and almost surly-looking. "No, Caius, I don't, but it seems to me that the room is too small for a circle of twenty-two chairs."

Caius smiled. "I think not, Totius. When we have cleared the floor there should be room enough. But you are right, in one sense. The chamber could be larger."

Totius seemed to be the only one with any comment to add to what had gone before, and so the vote was taken and the changes approved unanimously, Caius alone abstaining, as moderator.

Immediately, Varo was back on his feet again. "I say let's change the seating now!" There was a spontaneous cheer, and then the scene degenerated again into chaos as people wrestled with their chairs until they had formed a circle in the centre of the room and order was gradually restored. Caius's chair rested haphazardly on the circumference of the circle, as did my own. No man moved to be seated, for there was an air of momentousness about this occasion.

Caius looked all around the circle and smiled. "As moderator of the Council for the last time, I declare this first session of the Round Council to be officially open."

Everyone sat then, amidst a great shout of approval. I sucked in a great breath and got back onto my feet at once, to be recognized immediately by Caius. I looked to my left and then to my right, and out across the body of the circle, surprised to see how easy it was to address everyone in this format.

"My friends," I began, "this is good. When it comes your turn to stand and speak, you will see how good it is. I came here today to speak to you about the events that have happened over the past two days, and of the effect I see them having on all of our lives from this time on. I came late and was prepared to offer my apologies for that, but no one seemed to notice." There was a burst of laughter at that. I waited for it to die down and continued. "I came late for several reasons, the first of which is that I was awaiting a report from the group we dispatched in pursuit of the horsemen who escaped from Sulla's farm. There is no report. It hasn't arrived, yet. The second reason for my late arrival was that I had a long talk with Legate Picus who, as most of you know, returned to his affairs this morning. We had said our farewells last night, but he decided he had more to say to me before he left, in order that I could pass his words on to you."

I stopped and fumbled in my scrip for the notes I had scribbled on a piece of papyrus, and the Council waited in silence for me to continue. I glanced at what I had written and, my memory refreshed, I resumed speaking. "The gist of them is this. The Legate believes, and I do, too, that our Colony is no longer as safe as we once thought it to be. Sulla's villa fell to a surprise attack from an unexpected direction. But from any direction, Sulla's villa would have been indefensible against the attack it suffered. And we suspect that the same would be the case with all the other villas we own, including this one where we are now. These villas are farms only. They were never intended to be strongholds against the kind of attacks we are undergoing nowadays. That is Picus's opinion, and it is also my own, and it is the opinion of Caius Britannicus. All of us are soldiers and all of us are charged, in differing degrees, with the safety of this Colony. Times have changed more quickly than we thought they would. Our entire system of defences is now inadequate." I paused for a moment to let them digest that and then I continued.

"If we hope to offer safety to all our people, we have to do one of two things: we either have to turn each villa into a permanent armed camp, which is impossible, or we have to finish our fortifications on the hill behind us here to such an extent that every person in the Colony can shelter there in reasonable comfort if and when the threat of direct attack ever comes to be." There was a buzz of comment and I spoke over it. "Another thing: the Franks who raided Sulla's farm had horses."

That brought silence again. Every eye was on me. I waited three heartbeats before continuing.

"Yes, you heard correctly. They had horses, and that gave them a speed and a mobility that we can only match, not better, since we cannot know where they will come from next. They had only a small band of horsemen, but those were able to escort a large band of raiders. And we did not even know they were in Britain.

"So there you have it. Faced with mounted enemies, we have to defend ourselves more thoroughly, and that means finishing the fort at the greatest possible speed. We have the manpower, and the harvest is almost in, which means we have the time if we do it now, before winter comes."

I sat down amid a rumble of comments and listened carefully to the tenor of what I could pick out. Men talked among themselves. There was no one man who rose to make an individual comment. I looked at Caius, who was also listening to the talk around him. He turned to me at length and raised the old sardonic eyebrow, and I got to my feet again.

"My friends!" I waited until every eye in the room was on me. "We need agreement on this matter now. Tomorrow will not do. There is too much planning to be done, too many details to be resolved, for us to run the risk of wasting one day. The most important element is time. Time is the one thing we have little of." I waited for a count of ten, forcing my voice and posture to reveal no hint of my impatience. "Let me suggest this to you. Since we have made a new beginning here today, I propose that we continue with the same intent. We have our walls, up there on the hill. They're still unfinished, but they are high enough to give us shelter now, should need arise. I propose that we erect a building there, within the walls, to house our Council sessions. It would give us a focus for our efforts, and could have many other functions when not in use as a Council Hall."

This was well received; I could tell by the buzz of comment. And then Bishop Alaric rose to his feet and all noise stopped as the Council members became aware of his presence. The bishop was a guest without official status here, not a member of the Council. Caius, however, masked any surprise he might have felt and nodded courteously to the old man, who looked around the circle and began to speak.

"Caius Britannicus, and members of this Council: I have no right, I know, to raise my voice here in this session, but I have felt for many years now that I belong in my heart within your Colony. I was here at its founding and I knew its founders before its conception. It pleases me profoundly that you have acted as you have in the course of the past few moments." He paused, seeking the right words. "It is that pleasure that makes me bold enough to speak out now." He indicated me with a nod of his head. "Publius Varrus has made a fine suggestion. The building that he suggests would indeed give focus to your work and to your lives. If you adopt his notion, and I pray you will, then I hope you will adopt this one of mine. Let this building be erected with all speed—a Council chamber and a centre for your lives. But let it also be a home to the Christ, a focus for your spiritual needs as well. Let the Christ Himself live among you."

There was a different quality to the silence this brought—almost a hostility. I sensed it in the posture of his listeners. Alaric himself, however, seemed unaware of it as he continued with a gentle smile, "I know that there are those among you who are thinking that you could not talk and act as freely in your chamber if that chamber were also a temple to the Christ, but you are wrong, my friends. I am not speaking of a temple, nor even an ecclesia. I have no wish to turn your hall into a permanent place of worship. My suggestion is that the place would be a place of worship only at the times set apart for worship. At other times it would be as it had to be: secular. Not consecrated to God's use alone." He nodded to himself, as though acknowledging some secret, inner thought.

"I am an old man now, and I must die soon. Before I do, I would like to consecrate a special altar-stone for you and for your Colony. A stone that could remain here to be used by any bishop who may have need of it. It is not the altar that is sacred, friends. It is the altar-stone—the stone that sits upon the altar-table—that is sanctified with the blessing of God and houses the sacred relics of His saints and martyrs. It is the altar-stone that, brought into a room and laid upon a table, converts that room into a house of God. It is the altar stone I wish to give you, to keep in a place of safety and to use, whenever need arises, to dedicate your Council Hall to God's holy use." The tension in the room had now dissipated.

"If you will honour me, an aged man, by permitting me to make this contribution to your lives, I will travel from wherever I might be to sanctify your new home and to celebrate the first service to the Christ in your new building." He bowed, moved his hand in a slight benediction and resumed his seat.

Caius rose and thanked him on behalf of all of us and of the Colony, continuing, with a smile, "Forgive me, Bishop Alaric, for labouring the point, but did I hear you right? That the Council chamber will become a House of God only when this altar-stone you speak of is brought into it? And when the stone has been removed again, back to its place of safety, the chamber will revert to being what it was before?"

Alaric stood up again, nodding solemnly as he reiterated this all-important point. "That is correct, Caius Britannicus. That is the way of the Church. Graced by the presence of the altar-stone, the meanest slave's hut becomes an ecclesia for as long as the stone remains there. When the stone is removed, the hut is but a hut again."

"And men can shout therein?"

"Shout, and rant and even blaspheme, as all men do from time to time, being men."

Caius sighed aloud, dramatically, and turned to face the circle. "So be it. Councillors, how do you vote on this? Shall we take up the Bishop's offer?"

"Aye!" Unanimous.

"Then, Publius, you have your answer, too." He cocked his head, smiling still, towards the centre of the ring. "Is that not so?"

"Aye!" Unanimous again.

I was on my feet in an instant. "Then I need only two more mandates. I need your permission to conscript Tigellinus Corax here, our famous architect, to set about the planning of the fort's interior and the construction of its main building."

"Aye!" There was much laughter in that shout, for Tigellinus was not noted for his tendency to volunteer anything, ever.

"And I need your approval to have Marcus Leo and his engineers make a start on building a road up from the plains to our new gates. We have no need of a fully engineered highway, but we will very soon need a practicable road. Leo's men are capable of building one and he himself is a full-fledged engineer. Have I your blessing?"

"Aye!" The enthusiasm of this day would brook no objections.

I was more than satisfied. I turned and nodded to Caius. "Caius Britannicus, I ask permission to leave this Council and initiate the work immediately."

Caius smiled at me. "Thank you, Publius. We will continue without you."

It was an hour before noon, and the courtyard was deserted. I started to walk across the yard in the direction of the stables, and then I heard a shout and the clatter of hooves from beyond the main gates. I stopped where I was and watched Bassus and his men ride in. They looked discouraged.

Bassus saw me immediately and rode his horse over to where I stood, saluting and then slipping wearily from the animal's back to stand looking at me.

"Well?" I asked him.

He shook his head slightly. "We lost them. I am sorry, Commander."

I restrained an impulse to shout at him. Instead, I kept my voice low. "Explain that. How could you lose ten mounted, galloping men?"

Bassus shrugged. "Hard ground, Commander. They rode into a stream to cover their tracks, and stayed in it for a long time. I had to split my squadron to go both ways. Then they crossed about a mile of open fields and found the main road running north and south to the east of here. By the time we reached the road, there was no way of telling which way the raiders had gone."

"Did you try to follow them?"

"Yes, Commander, and found their sign. They headed up into the hills. The Mendips. That's where we finally lost them. There were just no tracks to follow on the stones."

"Damnation!" I swallowed my frustration and accepted the unacceptable. "Very well, Bassus. You did all that you could do, I suppose. Get your horses stabled and dismiss your men."

He saluted me and walked away. I cursed.

BOOK FOUR

THE SWORD

XXV

WE HEARD NO more of the Frankish horsemen, and, since the following months were filled with frantic activity, we eventually forgot about them. The harvest was brought in successfully before the weather broke, with every field protected by armed men. Then, as winter approached, Marcus Leo finished his planning of the road up to the fort and Plautus set his men to building it, taking full advantage of both the peace and an unusually mild winter. His soldiers worked hard through rain, wind and snow so that, by the approach of spring, their task was done and a brand-new road stretched up the contours of the hill to the main gate of the fort. This gate itself was constructed of heavy logs and was mounted on massive iron hinges that Equus and I had forged together. Our masons had built the circular walls so that the two ends overlapped, instead of meeting to close the circle, creating a lateral, curtained passageway some fifty paces long and fifteen paces wide that could be defended easily against direct attack, since any attacker would have to enter the passageway and be exposed to the defenders on top of the walls on both sides. The huge gates hung at the inner end of the passageway and would not be easily stormed.

Meanwhile, inside the walls, the building of our new home was progressing rapidly. Every carpenter, builder and owner of a free pair of hands had been put to work building the new Council Hall, which was serviceable already, an enormous rectangular hut with stout log-and-plaster walls, two entrances and a thick, although still incomplete, roof of thatched sedge and rushes. A number of other buildings were in various stages of completion as well. Our new granaries were finished and filled with grain, and I already had a forge in place against the western wall.

Tigellinus Corax, our architect, had ensured his fame forever among our colonists by designing a huge cistern to collect the water run-off at the back of the hill, and he and Marcus Leo had devised a system of pumps, based on the screw technique of Archimedes, to raise this salvaged water back up to the top of the hill. We were lucky that the acquisition of lead to line the pipes was a simple matter; the land directly to the north of us was full of it, and there is no metal easier to smelt. Our army engineers made short work of building that entire system.

Our building plan was based on the classic, standardized Roman military camp, except that there was only one major and one minor exit, instead of the usual four. To accommodate our growing need for stables, we simply

315

extended the area normally dedicated for that purpose, giving ourselves ample room for upwards of four hundred animals.

I remember realizing quite suddenly one bleak, blustery autumn afternoon that I was fifty-five years old that year, and the realization shook me. All my life I had considered anyone over fifty to be an old man, and now here I was, half a decade older than that and still, in my mind at least, in my prime! My muscles, thanks to the life I led smithing and soldiering, were as hard and strong as those of a healthy man twenty years my junior, and that was no idle conceit. I knew it to be true because I worked with such men every day in the smithy and on the parade ground. I had become aware in recent months, most usually when putting on my armour, of a consistent thickening about my waist and hips, but it was a solid thickening and my belly was still flat and hard. Sexually, too, I was still active and interested. I was no longer a rutting stallion, of course, but I was far from being an impotent old man. Yet still the fact was inescapable: I was fifty-five!

It was the statue I had named the Lady of the Lake that brought the passing of the years to my attention. I had been sitting staring at her, wondering about the age and origins of metals and thinking about the draining of the lake and the finding of my skystone, when I suddenly realized that these events had taken place twenty years earlier! I had spent more than seven whole years trying to smelt the stones, and the Lady herself had stood here serenely on her table in Caius's day-room for twelve more years since her birth. As I have said, the realization shook me and made me see all at once that I could not afford to let any more time drift by. I rose immediately and crossed to the open window, where I saw two soldiers standing talking in the yard outside. I summoned them and told them to pick up the statue and follow me, and then I stuck the skystone dagger in my belt and went to find Equus.

He was sitting on a high stool by his work-bench, holding his right forearm in his left hand while he stared intently at the fingers of his right one, wriggling and clenching them. There was blood crusted on and between his fingers, and from wrist to elbow his forearm was swathed in blood-stained bandages. I pointed to a place where the soldiers could leave the statue and then dismissed them, crossing to Equus.

"What happened to you? What's the matter with your arm?"

The look he threw at me in response was eloquent. "You did! You happened to me! You and your bright ideas!"

I blinked at him, mystified, and looked again at his bandaged arm. "Are you saying I am responsible for that? What are you talking about?"

He turned and shouted over his shoulder. "Joseph! Bring those things over here!" One of our young apprentices approached, carrying two long swords. Equus jerked his head towards his work-bench. "Put them down here." The boy did so and left again.

"Well," Equus said, "there's your new sword. Two of 'em. What do you think?"

I picked one up in each hand. They were beautifully made, their blades long and lethal, their hilts heavy, elongated and weighted at the ends by large pommels. They balanced perfectly.

"Equus, they're superb," I whispered. "How did you weight the hilts? They don't look like *gladia* at all, now that they're made. There's no resemblance."

"The pommels are lead," he muttered. "And you're right. There's no resemblance. Those whoreson things are like ungrateful dogs. They bite their masters."

I looked from the swords I was holding to his bandaged arm. "One of these did that? How? I've never known you to be careless with weapons."

He grunted again and got to his feet. "Come with me," he said. "I'll show you."

I followed him outside, still carrying both swords, to the sword-practice post that stood in front of the smithy. As we passed through the doorway, he picked up a heavy infantry shield that leaned against the wall. Outside, he turned to me.

"Give me a sword. Take the shield. Standard sword practice. Go ahead."

Wondering what this was all about, I took the shield from him and lined myself up in front of the practice post in the normal manner. I rested the base of the shield on the ground and crouched behind it, brandishing the sword, and then I straightened up, looking at him and feeling foolish. I did not even attempt a swing.

He was watching me, an expression of wry amusement on his face. "Aye, that's about as far as I got, too," he said. "We have just destroyed a thousand years of technique and training. You can't use those things like a *gladium*. They're too damn big, too long. You get within *gladium*-reach of an enemy with that thing in your hand and you're a dead man. He'll cut you in two before you can get your arm back far enough to defend yourself, let alone attack him." I started to speak, but he pressed right on, overriding me. "Oh, I know what you're going to say. It's a cavalry sword, not meant for a man on foot. That's all very well, as long as you're on a horse. But what happens if you fall off? Or when your horse is killed and you find yourself on foot?"

I stood there, mute.

"And that's not the worst of it." He held up his bandaged arm. "This is the worst of it. At least, it's the worst I've discovered so far. How d'you think I got this? Can you guess?" I shook my head. "Well, I'm not going to tell you. I'm going to show you. Wait there." He went back into the forge and came out carrying a leather apron. "Here, hold one side of this. It's an old one." I held it and he cut it lengthwise down the middle.

"Now wrap that around your sword arm." It went around four times and he tied it in place with two thongs. Then he gestured with his head towards the practice post. "Now show me the standard block, parry and slash. You're going to have to step away from the post."

I stepped back and carried out the basic manoeuvre. I had to straighten my arm completely to finish it and the whole thing felt utterly alien.

"See what I mean? Your whole balance has to be different. You can't chop with that thing and you can't even try the infighting stab. It's impossible. You have to swing straight-armed, and the arc of the blade's about four times as long as the *gladium* swing."

I was staring at the sword in wonder. "But, Equus," I said, "that's marvellous! That's what we've been looking for. The force of this thing's swing is unbelievable!"

He hawked up phlegm and spat off to one side. "Aye, I'll grant that. And you could carve a *gladium*-wielder into pieces with it from beyond his reach. But what happens when you're facing someone who's swinging one of these things too? That's what happened to me."

I looked again at his arm. "How?"

In answer he grinned and fell into a crouch. "That's what I'm going to show you. I'm going to attack you. Straight attack, no tricks. You defend yourself. Don't try to attack me."

We squared off and he came for me with a round-armed, overhead swing. I brought my own blade up to block it easily, marvelling again at the easy balance in the thing. Then his blade crashed against mine with a ringing clang and the shock of the impact flung my arm away, out and around, almost ripping the sword hilt from my grasp. He carried his swing through and poised at the top of the upswing, ready to disembowel me with a backhand slash. He would have killed me easily, for I had no chance of recovering in time to block him.

"Different, isn't it?" He lowered his sword. "Now you're prepared for it, let's try that again."

We repeated the move, and this time I was prepared for the shock and better braced to block his first swing and throw his backhanded slash down to my left off my horizontal blade, finding that I was gripping my sword two-handed for better support against his backhand. His blade swooped down, then up and around again, and I released the hilt with my left hand and met his swing, hearing the clash of tempered blades and then losing everything as the world erupted in a sheet of blinding, flaming pain. I did not feel the sword go flying from my hand, but I felt my knees hitting the stones of the yard, and then I felt rough ground against my face and hands tugging at me, pulling me up.

I opened my eyes, fighting the waves of pain-filled nausea that swirled over me, and eventually regained my senses. My right arm was devoid of feeling except at the shoulder, where the socket felt as though it had been wrenched apart. I was sitting on the ground, my back against the practice post, and Equus was on his knees in front of me, his face concerned.

"What happened?" I asked him.

He spat off to the side again, seeming to savour the time it took him to respond. "Same as happened to me, except I hit you harder. If Joseph had hit me that hard, he'd have taken my arm off."

"My arm?" I looked down. The layers of leather apron around my forearm were still there, but three thicknesses of the stiff, grease-coated hide had been sliced open. I had an immediate vision of what my arm would have looked like had that toughened leather not been there, and my stomach heaved. It took me several more moments to recover. Equus watched me retch, making no move to aid or succour me. Finally I swallowed the taste of bile one last time and got myself under control.

"I think my arm is broken."

He shook his head. "No, it's not, but you won't use it too easily for the next few days. I caught you just below the elbow. Hammered the big muscles there. You'll bruise badly, I expect, but there's nothing broken."

"What caused it, Equus? What did you do?"

He shook his head again, abruptly this time. "Nothing. It's the swords themselves. They're different. They behave strangely. The blades bounce away from each other uncontrollably. Bounce right over the boss of the hilt and hit the arm or the wrist."

I moved to get up, but I still couldn't feel my right arm. He pulled my to my feet by my left, still talking.

"It must be a combination of the temper of the metal and the force and angle of the swing, Publius. Whatever causes it, it's damn dangerous. I can't see our people using these for a while yet. Not until we can figure out a way to stop them losing arms and hands in practice."

I took one of the new weapons in my left hand and examined it with a new awareness. It still felt good to hold. I examined the edge of the blade. There was a nick in it.

"Equus? What's this? It looks like a nick."

"It *is* a nick." Equus's voice sounded reflective. "That's my finest iron, but it's too soft. Look." He held the other blade towards me. It, too, was nicked. He brought it close to his own eyes. "I don't know how hard these two blades were going when they met, Publius, but I'm glad my fingers weren't between them when they did. I've never see a new sword of ours take a nick before."

"Neither have I." I turned away and moved back into the smithy, trying to flex my fingers. They responded, but my whole arm was still numb. "My God, Equus, that thing bounced before it hit my arm! Imagine what a full-strength swing would have done!"

"Aye, imagine if it had hit you in the neck."

I nodded to the statue, which still stood where the soldiers had left it. "I brought the Lady down. I think it's time she went to work for us."

He looked at her and then back at me. "You mean you're going to use her to make one of these?"

"Why not? If she's of the stuff of my skystone dagger, she won't nick."

He shrugged and patted her on the rump. "I wonder if she'll shine."

"God, my arm hurts! Let's go and have a cup of wine, and then I'm going to find the hottest steam room in the place. As soon as I regain the use of my arm, if I ever do, we'll find out whether she can shine or not."

He caught hold of the statue's faceless head and tilted the whole thing sideways. "Does Caius know you're going to melt her down? He's had her for a long time."

"Too long," I said. "No, he doesn't know yet, but he's always dropping hints about using her for something." I grimaced with pain, feeling the sensation starting to flow back into my hand. "Anyway, he can have her back later, part of her at least. I'll only need about half of her the first time."

That night I frightened my wife half out of her wits by shouting aloud and jerking upright in bed, wide awake, during the blackest part of the night. The shout was one of pain, for my injured arm had somehow become tangled in the bedclothes, but the vision in my head when I awoke was bright and clear. I had been dreaming of Claudius Seneca, seeing him leap at me, his eyes glazed in fury, his sword flashing down to end my life, and then had come a jarring blow that sent lances of pain up my arm as the edge of his blade slammed into the arm of Alaric's silver cross.

The vision kept me awake for the rest of the night, and when Equus arrived at the forge next morning, I had already been there for hours, alternately heating the Lady statue and hammering it into a rough, rectangular ingot, ignoring the pained protests of my outraged arm.

From that time on, I worked on the new sword every day for four months, giving it every moment I could spare and much time that I really could not. Equus was content to leave me alone for the greater part of that period, but he helped me considerably with the delicate, time-consuming, meticulous job of fashioning and extending the double taper of the blade. This sword, right from the outset, was to be perfect. I burned a forest of charcoal over those months, heating and reheating the metal as it changed from a rough ingot to an elongated bar, and from that to a recognizable, blade-shaped length of blackened iron. And then, almost unnoticeably, it was almost finished, waiting only for the final temper to be added to it.

"Equus," I said to him one day, "go out and find me a virgin."

"A virgin? Here?" He shook his head in mock dismay. "There's your daughters, that's it. And when Veronica gets wed there'll be one less. Virgins are scarce in armed camps. I'll go and look for one, but don't stay awake waiting for me to come back. What's an old goat like you want with a virgin, anyway?"

I was squinting along the edge of my new blade, admiring it. "Blood. Don't you remember? The ancient smiths used to quench their new blades in virgin blood, for purity."

"I didn't know that! Are you serious?"

I looked at him. "That's what the legends say. They believed that blood-quenching—virgin blood, of course—would impart the secret essence of the white iron."

"Horse turds!" His voice was rich with scorn. "Anybody with a brain knows it's the charcoal that makes the difference."

I put the blade down. "You know that, Equus, and I know it, but the ancients didn't. Not for centuries."

He came to my side and picked the blade up, squinting at it critically, looking for flaws that weren't there. "Looks good, Publius. How are you going to hilt it?"

I hadn't told him about the cross-hilt idea in my mind. "Oh, I've got a few ideas. First I have to temper it. I wonder if it will have a shine?"

"It has already, look! You can see it, can't you?" He angled the blade into the light.

I nodded. "There's something there, all right, but I'd hardly call it a shine, Equus."

"Then don't! But I'm telling you, that's what your dagger looked like at this stage, and I've never seen another piece of metal look like this, have you?"

I shook my head. "No, I have to admit I haven't."

He dropped it with a clang. "Well then, get on with edging it. It won't temper itself."

He walked away and I picked the blade up again and started to scale it with a file, whistling under my breath and feeling good about life in general. We had been untroubled by raiders of any kind throughout the autumn. The walls of our fort were completely finished in some places, and the new Council Hall was nearly completed, too, lacking only the thatching of a portion of the roof. The new year coming would be the eleven hundred and fifty-fourth year of Rome, but it would be the four hundredth year of the Christian era, and the usage of the latter method of marking time was increasing rapidly. This new year, then, would mark either the close of a century or the beginning of a new one. I had heard arguments over which was which: was 400 the last of the old or the first of the new? Personally, I did not care; the year ahead looked good for the Colony.

I suddenly remembered something—I've no idea what prompted the memory—and reached into my scrip for the shell I had picked up from the dining table the night before. My fingers found it and I placed it delicately on the work-bench in front of me, squeezing it gently shut. It was a mature cockle-shell, one of a basketful brought to us by the young priest who accompanied Bishop Alaric everywhere nowadays. They had arrived the day before and would remain with us for several more days before moving on.

I smiled to myself as I realized that even Alaric had brought us no bad news for months. Last night at dinner he had pointed out to us God's great concern with detail in fashioning the perfection of even the humble cockle-shell. I had picked this one up and examined it minutely, and a voice had said clearly in my head, out of nowhere, "pommel." The thing was exquisitely crafted and perfect in its symmetry, the tracery of its ribs immaculately fine as each one swept out from the full thickness of the shell's base to the indented point of one of the tiny scallops around the serrated edge.

I had seen in my mind's eye a duplicate of this shell I held, crafted in solid gold, adding its weight to the counterbalance of my new sword. Now I looked at it again in daylight and knew that my intuition had been correct. A gold pommel. Solid gold. I smiled at the idea. But a gold hilt? A gold cross-hilt? No, I decided, that would be too vulgar and probably too heavy. Besides, gold was too soft for a cross-hilt such as the one I envisioned. I looked again at the shell, bringing it close to my eyes. It was a large one, as wide as the full length of my thumb across its base, and half as thick in section, front to back. It would make a fine, solid pommel. But how would I mount it? That, I had discovered, was a major problem, for the extreme length of the new blade set up vibrations that had never existed in the shorter *gladium*, and these vibrations threatened to destroy any joint in the metal that was not perfectly solid. I was plagued with the problem of how to attach a cross-guard firmly to a straight blade and then fix a hilt with a comfortable handle between that cross-guard and a pommel. These vibrations alone could destroy every idea I might come up with.

I dropped the cockle-shell back in my scrip and left the blade lying on the work-bench as I strolled back to the villa in search of Grandfather Varrus's old scroll on the ancient art of pouring moulds.

Luceiia sat in the family room talking earnestly with Veronica and her younger sisters, Lucilla and Dora, both of whom were awed and overcome by their older sister's imminent transition from girlhood to womanhood. In their eyes, Veronica had already passed into adulthood, leaving them far behind her. Not that they were in any way jealous of her—slightly envious, perhaps, but only in that wide-eyed, wonder-filled, breathy manner that seems unique to very young adolescent girls.

The four women of my family enjoyed an easy, close and warmly intimate companionship. They were discussing the wedding, of course, which would take place in the spring, and I am sure they completely failed to notice me as I apologized for disturbing them and passed on through, taking away with me the image of my daughter Veronica's bright eyes and high, proud breasts. She was a beauty, my Magpie. I was still whistling under my breath as I searched for the scroll, wondering idly, for the hundredth time at least, about the magical process that could so abruptly transform a beautiful, trusting little daughter into a ravishingly self-possessed young woman. I found the scroll right where I had left it and took it back to the smithy to study it, and it did not take me long to arrive at the conclusion that I was going to need help from Father Andros.

XXVI

By the time the hawthorn blossomed in March that year, there was a steady stream of two-way traffic on the new road every day from dawn until dusk. Everyone in the Colony was completely absorbed in the task of preparing our new quarters, with the exception of my own womenfolk, who had a wedding to worry over, too. There was an air of buzzing activity everywhere, and even the absence of the soldiers withdrawn from the fort for active patrol duty—about two-thirds of our forces—seemed to make no great difference to the tempo of the work.

The extra horses Picus had promised us, including two magnificent and unlooked-for stallions, provided purely for breeding purposes, arrived early in March and were put into service immediately, making a major difference to our capabilities.

One of our colonists, a white-bearded veteran of many wars, had approached Caius in January with the idea of starting our young men's training early. He was prepared, he said, to take on that responsibility and Caius was happy to allow him to do so. Now he commanded a body of forty-five young men between the ages of fourteen and sixteen who spent their days marching and countermarching, learning the use of weapons and studying the new cavalry tactics.

It was a warm spring, full of promise. We were moving into a new, safe home, facing a new century, according to the Christian calendar, and we felt sure of our destiny. All around us, where we had been prepared for threats and danger, there was only tranquility. We were ready, however, for anything that might occur. Our farmers ploughed their fields under the gaze of watchful soldiers and the wagon train we sent to Glevum that spring went under heavy escort. We were determined that no raider would find any sign of weakness among us.

The wedding was to be in April, the feast time sacred to both Celtic Druid and Christian alike, and by the end of March, Ullic's people began to arrive. They set up their camps in the open fields around the villa, mainly along the new road to the fort, and Ullic and his main party arrived in pomp and savage Celtic splendour on the first day of Eastertide. His arrival coincided with the far less ostentatious arrival of Bishop Alaric, who had come, as promised, to conduct the wedding services and to celebrate the completion of our Council Hall with a special Mass.

Ullic brought gifts and barbaric excitement; Alaric brought our new, hand-dressed altar-stone. Ullic brought love, laughter and song; Alaric brought love, laughter and piety. Ullic brought Druids in his train; Alaric brought one priest, a gentle giant of a man called Phonos who was barely out of his teens. The scene was set for war or peace the first time the Druids and the Christian priests came face to face on that first day. That, at least, was the way I saw it, but as it turned out, I had no cause for concern; there was no sign of any hostility between the two groups then or later.

At dinner that night, a festive gathering, the talk was all about the prospects of the bride and groom and of the great hunt I had arranged for the following day. Caius was at his mercurial best that night, and the conversation around the table sparkled with wit and humour.

I am not normally a superstitious man, but I remember feeling that night that everything had been going too smoothly. It suddenly seemed to me, looking around the table and feeling the warmth and love there, that our lives, for the past eight months, had been too easy. I felt as though somewhere, out there in the night, forces were gathering to annul our gaiety, so that all during dinner I half expected to hear the slap of leather soles on the floor outside as someone came running with news of catastrophe. But no one did, and the evening passed with no alarums, as did the week that followed. The wedding was set for the day of Easter, the festival of spring and resurrection, the emergence of new life. It seemed appropriate and correct and approved by Heaven. Our hunting was successful every day and we enjoyed a plethora of fresh meats of every kind and fresh fish, both salt-water and fresh-water.

There was one young woman there, with Ullic's group, who turned the head of every man who saw her, including me. Her name was Enid and she was Ullic's youngest sister. Her skin was golden and her teeth were fine, snow-white against the amazing redness of her lips. Even my gentle Luceiia showed her claws the first time she saw Enid, warning me almost, but not quite, playfully to keep my attentions to that one casual. This surprised me, for it was the first time that my wife had ever made such a comment. I mentioned it jokingly to Caius later that first evening and he was wise enough to observe immediately that Luceiia probably felt she was no longer young enough to compete with such an animal as Enid.

And an animal she was, although I say so with not the slightest hint of malice. She was wild in the way a deer is wild: sleek and clean-lined, apparently timid and easily startled, giving one the impression that a too-sudden movement would cause her to disappear from sight immediately. And yet she was savage-looking, with all the allure and grace of the great cats of Africa. Her eyes were green-blue and her hair was startling in its tawniness among the black-haired, blue-eyed Celts. She was high-breasted, and her breasts were large and firm, and even though I was innocent of any lustful feelings towards her, I was tempted more than once, finding her close beside me, to attempt to span her tiny-looking waist in my big hands. Of course, her waist could not have been that small, but placed as it was between the lushness of her breasts and the sweeping swell of her hips, it *looked* that small. And I looked, as did every other man there who was not related to her directly. My own admiration of the young woman, conducted from a distance and modified by a need to give no offence to my wife, was avuncular—a combination of "I wonder . . . ," "What if . . . ?" and "There was a time . . . ." There were others in our gathering, however, who were unhampered by the twin constraints of age and marriage, and among them they managed to keep Enid from becoming bored. She was the undisputed centre of attraction for every single young male in the Colony, and for a fair number of others who were neither young nor single. My youngest apprentice, Joseph, at not quite sixteen years, was sore smitten with first love and followed her around like a pup, sitting as close to her as he could get, and sometimes forgetting even to eat.

Luceiia had made a point of getting to know the beautiful newcomer, and had now decided that she liked her. It was she who told me Enid's history. The woman was beautiful, headstrong, stubborn, thoroughly likeable and quite prepared to go to her grave unwed. Her one, true love had died saving her life from a giant bear and she had found no man to compare with him in the years that followed. She was almost thirty now, in reality a half-sister to Ullic, sired by his aged father upon a second wife, and Ullic had despaired of matching her years ago. Enid, Luceiia told me, was quite happy with that state of affairs and wanted nothing to change it.

The day before the wedding was a day I tried hard to avoid. The entire household was a madhouse. I attempted to slip away to the smithy to spend some time with Equus, but it was not to be. Luceiia called my name as I was setting out and sent me on an errand to the fort, and from that moment on I was caught up in the general insanity. Not until we were preparing for bed did I have another moment to myself that day.

Bishop Alaric was to consecrate the altar-stone here in the villa the next morning and bear it in procession to the hilltop. It would be a long walk for the old man, but he was adamant in his determination to do it. The journey, he said, would be symbolic in several ways: symbolic of the Christ's walk to Calvary, and of our own struggle upwards as a Colony towards a better, more Christian life. I was not sure what he meant by that, but I had no wish to argue with him.

The bride, my own Magpie, Veronica . . . I had to shake myself hard to realize what that really meant . . . would be carried uphill on a litter specially built for her by one of our carpenters. An honour-guard of sixty infantry would provide ample muscle for the long haul up the hill. Luceiia and her friends would ride in chairs upon the shoulders of more infantry. I myself, as father of the bride, would lead the way, mounted, with Caius and ten other friends constituting a formal vanguard to the entire procession. The weather had been perfect so far. If it rained tomorrow, the result would be a fiasco. I preferred not to think about that. It was going to be a long day.

Luceiia's voice broke into my tired thoughts. "Picus didn't come."

"No. He said he would try to get here, but he is at the mercy of the Saxons, love. When they invade, he moves. I would have been very surprised to see him here at this time of the year." I fell onto the bed, pulling the fur robes back, and crawled beneath them like an animal crawling into its den. Luceiia blew out the lamp and there was silence between us for so long that I was almost asleep when she spoke.

"Do you realize, Publius, that this time tomorrow our little daughter Veronica will be a woman? She will belong to her husband, not to us."

"Aye," I answered, turning to face her. "I'm aware of that. She will be wife and woman, and if she's half as good at being either as her mother has been, she'll do well by herself and by her man." I reached out and slipped my arm about her waist, which was still slim enough to belie her years.

"You don't sound upset at all!"

I was surprised. "Why should I feel upset?"

"Less than three years ago you almost went to war with Ullic when he mentioned this marriage."

"Ahh!" I said, thinking rapidly about the impossibility of attempting to explain any of that. "I see what's bothering you . . ." I allowed my voice to fade away and then said, "Shh, woman! That *was* almost three years ago. Veronica was a child then. Now it is time for her to be a woman and to enjoy the pleasures you enjoyed as one."

"Do I hear a past tense? I still enjoy them, husband."

"Aye, but not so often."

"No, not quite as often. That is true . . . and sad."

"Why sad?"

"Because I do not want my man to grow old, leaving me with my lusts unsated."

I raised myself on one elbow, looking down at her in the darkness, knowing she would hear the smile in my voice. "Unsated? Woman, I hold myself back only because of *your* advancing age. Yours are the bones growing fragile. I would hate to break any of them in the name of love."

Her hand came behind my neck. "Come here, you old goat, and break me. I defy you."

The following morning dawned golden and perfect. I heard the noises of preparation begin while I was still steaming in the bath house, and I took an unusual degree of care with my ablutions and dressing, to the point where Luceiia herself was ready before I was.

I wore my official uniform for this occasion, something I seldom did. I had spent so much of my life in military harness that the finery of my commander's regalia gave me little pleasure; I was far more comfortable and felt far better dressed in the leathers that Luceiia had made specially for me. Today, however, for my daughter's wedding, I was cordially prepared to suffer. I wore helmet, breastplate, backplate and leg-greaves of solid bronze. The helmet and breastplate were magnificently worked, if I do say so myself, in some of the finest Celtic ornamentation that Father Andros had unearthed in his far-ranging travels. The outsized crest on my helmet was of tufted horsehair, dyed the same scarlet as my cloak, the shoulders of which were so crusted with finely worked bronze and silver wire that the garment itself resembled a piece of armour. My dress tunic was of white linen, edged with scarlet, and the straps of my armoured kilt were of bronze plates wired loosely, end to end. I wore my finest sword, with its bronze hilt and scabbard, and when I had everything finally strapped and buckled on I paced the room a few times, distributing the weight of all of this regalia comfortably about my body and wishing I could have worn my good old boots instead of the stiff new sandals and leggings that went with the outfit. Finally I could put the moment off no longer; I went out to join my wife and my daughter.

The sight of them took me aback. I had never seen my daughter looking so beautiful. On this, her bridal morning, she was radiant, dressed all in white so that she shimmered from head to foot. Ten years earlier, Luceiia had bought the material for that gown, knowing exactly what she was buying and the use it would one day be put to. The fabric, whatever it was, had come from Africa, and its fineness and purity were astounding. When I had first seen the gown made from this fabric, it had seemed to be the simple *stola* that the young women of republican Rome wore every day. That, however, was only at first glance. A second look had shown me that this was far from being a simple *stola* or a simple anything. The material, and I know Luceiia had a name for it although it eludes me now, had been piled layer upon layer, finely stitched together and worked with thousands of tiny, opalescent sea-shells. Whenever Veronica moved, these tiny shells clicked and rattled together, but their noise was muffled in the layers of the cloth. It was a marvellous creation.

My daughter smiled at me and came forward to take my arm, and as I felt her fingers touch the skin of my forearm I sucked in my breath and swelled with pride and fierce paternity, finding myself swearing a silent oath that I would flay this new husband of hers if he did not lay the moon and the stars at her feet. I had a large lump in my throat as we moved together to the doorway of the house, her mother and her sisters close behind us. As we stepped into the sunlit morning a spontaneous cheer broke from the crowd of more than three hundred who waited for us, already formed in line for the procession to the hilltop. I handed my daughter into her litter, and her mother and her sisters into their chairs, then marched my finest, limping march to the head of the column, where my horse was waiting. Equus himself helped me up onto Germanicus's back and, once seated, I turned my horse and inspected the honour-guard minutely. Finally satisfied that they could have looked no better, I gave the signal to proceed and nudged Germanicus forward.

It was a slow progress, but I felt peaceful and well content with my post in the vanguard. Caius rode on my right and ten more of our close friends accompanied us, but no one spoke. Everyone seemed to appreciate my unspoken need for silence in which to enjoy this occasion.

We had gone about one-third of the way to the hill along the new road when I saw a sudden flash of light in the distance off to my left and my heart

gave a sickening lurch in my breast. No one else had noticed it, but I had
and I knew what it was. The early morning sunlight had reflected off metal
where no metal should be this day. I raised my arm immediately to stop the
column behind me, my mind racing as I tried to decide whether to run for
the fort or break back to the villa; I was more than aware of the number of
women in the train. And then I remembered that we had our soldiers deployed
in force behind the home farm, and I knew there was no danger to our
column.

Caius asked me why I stopped and I merely nodded in answer, pointing
my head in the direction of the reflection I had seen, and presently we were
able to make out the swift-moving column of mounted men and the great
black-and-white standard of Picus Britannicus.

He came in splendour, to the cheering welcome of the crowd behind me
and the blaring of horns from the hilltop fort, where Ullic's people watched.
And Picus, too, came dressed for a grand occasion, in his finest, gilded armour,
his men, in spite of having ridden far and hard, turned out as for an imperial
parade. As his column approached ours, his standard-bearers formed up behind
him, the SPQR standard of the Senate and the People of Rome taking pride
of place beside Picus's own, directly behind Picus himself. Each bearer took
a position some twenty paces behind and forty paces to the side of him. The
three lesser-formation or squadron standards formed up behind them, again
with some forty paces between each. Together, including Picus at the forefront, these standards formed a small arrowhead of six mounted men at the
head of three great forty-man arrowhead formations.

The people behind me in the wedding train were cheering even louder
as this proud cavalcade thundered towards us and slid to a halt in perfect
formation with Picus at its head, less than four paces from me. Picus snapped
me his clenched-fist salute.

"Hail, Publius Varrus. We were detained, but here we are now as honour-
guard for a beautiful bride on a beautiful day."

A silence had fallen as he had clattered to a halt, so that all heard his
shouted greeting clearly. Now the cheering broke out again as I answered
him.

"Well met, Picus Britannicus. When you have paid your tribute to your
father, Caius Britannicus, and to our bride today, I shall be glad of your
company."

His troops remained motionless as Picus danced his horse from his father,
beside me, to Veronica's litter and his Aunt Luceiia's chair. His respects paid,
he returned to my side at the head of the column, smiling broadly.

"Uncle Varrus, I am impressed! This is not just a wedding—it is a gala
of epic proportions!"

"Aye, Picus." I smiled back at him. "It is. It is the beginning of the
coming-true of all our dreams, your father's first among all, and it is the first
major celebration we have indulged in since the Colony's founding. How do
you want to dispose your men?"

He looked over at his troops and then glanced up the hill to where the new road wound upwards to the fort.

"I was thinking of that as we approached. Your train is formed and under way and to attempt to change it now would cause confusion. Why don't I send my troopers on ahead to line the road on both sides up the hill? Ten paces between each two men would give you better than a quarter-mile of guards."

"Splendid," I said, laughing. "That's a fine idea. Do it. And when you are no longer a soldier you can grow rich arranging spectacles in the Circus Maximus."

He turned and approached his standard-bearer, signalled to his squadron commanders and pointed up the hill. The result had obviously been prearranged, but it made a wonderful spectacle. His men wheeled smartly, changing formation as they kicked their horses to the gallop, and then took the road before us in columns of four, quickly leaving us far behind. I gave the order to resume our procession, raising my hand to the train behind me, and we followed Picus's men at a pace far more sedate and dignified.

As soon as I was satisfied that we were all safely under way again without incident, I turned back to Picus, who rode at my left.

"So, lad! What's been happening out there in the world? I must admit I had not expected to see you here today."

"No more had I, Uncle." His voice was unexpectedly low and serious, and I glanced immediately to Caius, seeing his own gaze sharpen as he nudged his horse closer to hear what was coming. Picus waited until his father was within easy hearing before continuing. "All Hades has broken loose in the north. We'll never be able to hold the Wall if things continue the way they are at present."

"How so?" Cay's voice was urgent. "What do you mean?"

"Just what I say, Father. It is sheer, absolute chaos up there. We've been under constant, escalating attack ever since last October. Never a let-up. We've been hit at every point along the eighty-five miles of the Wall— usually in three or four places at once, miles apart. There's just no way to defend against them. And our cavalry is useless, except as back-up to the regular garrison. If there's a breakthrough, we can clean up the people who come through the gap, but only if we are close enough to hit them instantly do we stand a chance of driving them back."

There was silence for a few moments as Caius and I digested this disquieting news, and then, as usual, it was Caius who spoke up.

"I had no idea things were so bad up there. We heard some rumours, of course, but we thought the enemy in the north was being held, by and large, in abeyance."

"They are. For now." Picus sounded sceptical. "But that won't last long. They're too well co-ordinated. They have some first-class military minds directing them."

A female shriek rang out behind us and then a booming roar of laughter.

I swung around to look back, but I could see no sign of the source of the hilarity, nor the cause of it.

"Anyway," Picus continued, paying no attention to the noise, "that's talk for later, when the ladies are abed. This morning should be for pleasure alone."

We rode in companionable silence for a time, enjoying the beauty of the day and listening to the tinkling of the Celtic musicians entertaining the ladies behind us. The first of Picus's troopers sat his horse on the left side of the road about half a mile ahead of us, right at the bottom of the hill.

"Look," Picus observed, "Janus has staggered the men, ten paces apart on opposite sides of the hill. That's good. I like a man with initiative. Now you have almost half a mile of mounted guards."

"Aye," Caius grunted, good-naturedly, "that will please the ladies." He paused, as if reflecting, before he observed, "Do you know that yours are the only imperial troops some of our people have ever seen? Especially the young ones."

Picus's voice showed his surprise. "I suppose they are, now that you mention it. You are a bit off the beaten track."

"Aye," I added, "and, please God, we'll stay off it. By the way, what news of your young friend with the wild ideas? What was his name? Pelidorus?"

"Who? Pelidorus?" There was bafflement in Picus's voice, then, "Oh, you mean Pelagius!"

"Aye, Pelagius, that was it. The theologian. What of him?"

Picus shook his head. "Nothing. No news. I haven't heard his name mentioned in ages. Not since we spoke of him that day, in fact."

"Do you think he's still alive?"

"Why not?" Picus laughed aloud. "It was a bishop he offended, Uncle, not the Emperor. And speaking of bishops, when did you last see Bishop Alaric?"

"Alaric? About an hour ago. He's right behind you, about the middle of the column. He will consecrate the wedding and our new altar-stone at the same time."

"Altar-stone? What's this?"

"You'll see. The good bishop has talked the Council into establishing a meeting-place for priests and prayers alike, in the Council Hall."

"Has he, by Mithras?" There was ungrudging admiration in Picus's tone. "How did he do that?"

"Cleverly," I answered him, smiling. "And at a time when it had most effect: It got the chamber finished."

Picus pursed his lips and glanced from me to his father and then back to me.

"You said this morning marks the start of all my father's dreams coming true. The marriage I understand, but what else is there?"

"Well, there's the new Council chamber, as I said, and our new quarters. The fort itself is coming into full use today for the first time as well. This is the first procession of our people as a group along this new road, too. And this is the first springtime of a new century in the year of our Lord the Christ. Think about that, Picus. What you will witness today is, in its own small way, the birthing of a new society, in a new place, surrounded by new walls at the opening of a new age. And all of it—the people and their dreams, the place, the soldiers and their weaponry, and all the hope for the future—has sprung from the mind and from the dreams of your father."

Caius coughed and cleared his throat in embarrassment and would have demurred, had I not cut him short in midcough.

"No, Caius, you may not interrupt and you may not dismiss my words. Everything I say is true and there is no way you can escape retribution for your plannings and machinations, so you might as well not try."

Picus spoke for his father and for himself. "Publius Varrus," he said, "your words make me both proud and humble that I should be my father's son."

"Good. That is as it should be. In both instances. Pride is a strong man's sword, and a little humility does no man harm."

We had drawn abreast of Picus's first man who sat stiffly at attention, reining his horse in hard, his naked blade shining in the sun as he stared straight ahead, his motionless eyes fixed on infinity as his Legate rode past. Both Picus and I had drawn ourselves up into our formal stance as we approached him and we remained that way, our bearing a reciprocal tribute to the guards themselves, until we reached the gates at the top of the hill.

The noise there was unbelievable—a cacophony of horns, whistles and cheers of welcome for the bride and her escort. The inside of the fort was brightly and appropriately decorated for the day's festivities. Long bolts of brightly coloured cloth hung from the walls, and Ullic's Celts, brightly clothed at the best of times, were all bedecked in their gaudiest finery. The entire scene was a maelstrom of colours. My ears picked out several sources of music of one kind or another, and off to my left I saw the gigantic brown awesomeness of a dancing bear. Then, as the lead party started to enter through the gates, someone began to beat out a slow, welcoming cadence on the Celtic war-drum, and others took up the beat, the tempo increasing gradually and steadily until the very air throbbed with the rhythm of the percussion. These were the drums that had frightened the lights out of Caesar's men four hundred years earlier, and their effect had lost nothing in power over the centuries. Yet they looked deceptively flimsy, being light, easily carried affairs, nothing more than a dried skin stretched over a wooden hoop a handsbreadth deep, reinforced by two cross-braces that formed a handhold at their junction in the centre of the drum. Struck with either end of a short wooden stick, which these people wielded with amazing dexterity, these devices produced an inordinate amount of fierce, martial, reverberant and threatening noise.

Ullic, grand showman that he was, stood waiting to greet us, surrounded by his family, his chiefs and his Druids, the latter dressed in either all-black or all-white robes, depending on their function. Ullic himself was something to behold, blazing with colour, crusted with jewellery and wearing on his head the symbol of his kingship, the huge eagle helmet I had last seen at our first meeting at Stonehenge. His men had built a platform for him and for his party so that they stood head and shoulders above the surrounding crowds. Uric stood on his father's right, a proud young man wearing a simple tunic of blue cloth tied with a crimson sash and trimmed with a Greek pattern of golden squares. His legs and feet were encased in fur-lined boots with golden studs, and on his head he wore a ceremonial helmet adorned with the horns of what must have been a mighty ram, for they curled downward to rest on his shoulders.

Caius, Picus and I kneed our horses directly to the space left clear for the approach of the bridal party and halted directly in front of Ullic's dais, leaving enough room between Caius and me for Veronica's litter, and between Caius and Picus for Luceiia's chair. The remainder of our people spread out on both sides of us in good order, so that when the bride and her party entered the enclosure of the fort they were able to make their way unhampered to their proper place.

It took about one-third of an hour for our entire group to wend its way into position, but at last everyone was in place and Ullic raised his right arm high, commanding an instant silence, since all eyes were already upon him. He allowed the silence to grow to a point just short of discomfort before he began to speak, and then he welcomed everyone, singling out Caius Britannicus as the prime reason for the wedding being celebrated here in this place and enumerating the achievements of the man that everyone present there had grown to admire, if not to love. Amid a growing tide of approbation, Caius raised his own hand in protest and Ullic stopped.

"You wish to speak, my friend?"

It is amazing how dense a silence a thousand or more people can generate from time to time. Cay's voice rang into the stillness clearly.

"King Ullic, we are here this day to witness the joining of your son in marriage to my niece. These two young people are the celebrants. Eulogies are appropriate for them only, today. May we not come to the ceremonies directly?"

Ullic barked a single roar of laughter. "Hah! So be it! You have the right of it, old friend, we are here for a wedding. Then, by all the gods at once, let us have one. Sound the horns!"

Amid a roar of approval from everyone assembled, a party of Celtic hornsmen began to blow in what was obviously a carefully rehearsed series of calls involving some six or seven different sizes and sounds of horns. I had never heard the like of it; the sounds lacked the brazen clarity of our Roman trumpets and *cornua*, but the effect was stirring. As soon as the last notes had sounded in the sequence, another party—of drummers this time—beat out an intricate rhythm, which was followed by the same horn sequence, played this time at double the tempo, and followed again by the drummers. At the climax of this second, exciting drum sequence, Bishop Alaric entered the courtyard from the direction of the new Council chamber, whose great, thatched roof dominated everything else in the place. He was accompanied by his acolytes, Father Phonos and our own Father Andros, and by a group of Ullic's Druids, one of whom was robed entirely, from head to foot, in a cowled garment of royal red.

This procession approached the dais and stopped directly at the centre, between Ullic and Uric and Caius and Veronica, and Alaric himself and the red-robed Druid mounted the dais and turned to face the assembly. The silence was complete, and it held more than a little tension mixed with the anticipation. There was a sense of great occasion here, a feeling of portent, for as Caius Britannicus had pointed out to everyone and anyone willing to listen, this was no ordinary marriage.

Alaric looked around him and began to speak in the voice of a trained orator, which surprised me, although it should not have, since he was Roman-born and educated well. I found myself realizing that I really knew little of the man, longtime friend though he was, outside of his life as a bishop. I resolved to find out more about him as he began to speak in the grand, oratorical voice, his words ringing strong and clear, betraying little sign of his age.

"People of Britain," he began, "Celts and Romans alike. We are here together this day in preparation for the coming of a new age: an age of opportunity, but also an age of fear and uncertainty in many places.

"We stand today in communal assembly before the eyes of God, and neither He nor I care what name you give to Him, each in your own heart, so long as you believe that you stand here with us, each one among you, alone in His sight. He is the One God who embodies all the gods men thought to appease when they had no thought of any god being as powerful as He. He is Mithras, the soldier's god; He is Amon-Ra, the sun god of Egypt, for He made the sun itself; and He is the pantheon of the Celts, whose mystical presence fills the sacred groves." He stopped abruptly and glanced sideways to the Druid beside him, who immediately began declaiming in the rippling, liquid language of Ullic's Celts, obviously repeating and translating Alaric's words for the benefit of the Celtic-speakers. When he had done, Alaric began again.

"Today, we make a new beginning, a complete departure from the ways of old, and yet we will do it in a way that keeps the best of the old ways— the best of the Celtic ways and the best of the Roman ways.

"These two young people represent the best of both our bloods. Uric is your king's son and will be king some day in his own right. His blood is pure, his ancestors known for twenty generations back and more. Uric's fathers ruled their own people in their own hills long years before Caesar's eye beheld the shores of this, their land. He is a Celt, unsullied and unstained by foreign blood." Alaric stopped and his red-robed consort again repeated what he had said. Alaric waited patiently, allowing the surge of comment from the listening Celts to subside before he spoke again.

"Veronica, whom Uric will take to wife here in your sight this day, is no less nobly fathered. Her veins are rich with the patrician blood that made Rome mighty in the days of old. And her blood is pure. Pure Roman, from the hills of Rome itself, unmixed with that of any other race . . ." He paused and allowed the echoes of his words to die away as people absorbed what he had said. Then, when the silence was barely beginning to vibrate with tension, he continued, his timing perfect.

"Until today. Until this union . . . this marriage. This bonding of two people, each unto each, that is more than a simple bonding, far, far more. For this joining of two people that we, together, will witness here today shall mark the bonding of two peoples!" Alaric's voice was ringing now, vibrant and strong. "Two peoples! Roman and Celt together!" He held up his hand to still a noise of speculation that did not come, and then he nodded to the Druid, who repeated his words, right to the final gesture, after which Alaric took up the cadence again.

"Here in this land the Romans have named Britain, there have been many tribes, many peoples. Before the Romans came, you called yourselves 'the People.' They called you *Durotriges* and *Belgae*. They named your neighbours to the west of you *Dumnonii*; and across the river's mouth to the north-west, the Romans named the people the *Silures*. And we all know that this was foolishness. You were, and are, the people of this land, holding it in strength long before the Romans found its shores . . .

"Now, it appears the Romans may withdraw. This is the word of reason that has come from Caius Britannicus and has convinced all his friends. From that belief has sprung the existence of this Colony. Rome today, the Empire, is like a bubble that has grown in a tarn of pitch. The winds of time have dried the surface of the bubble, taking away its power to stretch and grow, or even to burst. The bubble is collapsing, falling slowly in upon itself, losing its shape, its substance and its life. And as it falls . . ." His voice rose to a shout again, bringing the image he had created into the forefront of each listener's mind. "As it falls, my friends, its edges will sink back beneath the surface of the tarn, melting again, shrinking the bubble's very girth until, in time, only the wrinkled, dried-out centre will be left for men to look at and wonder." He had thrown his hands high in the air, holding them far apart, and now he brought them slowly down and in, towards his breast, until they formed a cup in front of him. Every eye in the crowd followed the gesture.

"This lovely land of Britain that we hold so dear lies at the outermost edge of the Empire's bubble. It will be among the first imperial territories to be neglected. Rome has problems close to the heartland of her Empire. She has no problems here. Our land is rich, and though our wars seem great to us, they are as nothing to the Empire, which contends with barbarian hordes far greater than can be mustered against us. So Rome will leave us, perhaps one day soon, to see to our own defences."

As the Druid took up the recitation again, rolling the Celtic syllables out for Ullic's people, Alaric watched the faces of the crowd, noting the fascination on the faces of Celt and non-Celt alike as they all hung on the words and sounds of the Druid. When the red-robed priest's voice fell silent, Alaric was prepared and raised his voice high again in the grand manner of the accomplished orator.

"There is reason for great joy here today, my friends! For our joy today will be our strength tomorrow! United, our two peoples will withstand invasion and we will win! We will survive! For the children of this marriage will be ours, the best of all of us, combined in strength! The start of a new people— named by us, and not by foreigners! Their children—our children!—will be the people of Britain. Not Romans, not Celts, not *Belgae* or *Dumnonii* but BRITONS!" He stopped, for the space of three heartbeats. "BRITONS! You have all heard the word before. The Romans talk of Britons, meaning the folk who live in this land. But the children of this union, our children, will be Britons of a new and different kind! Their pride in the name of Britons will become *legend*!"

This time, when he stopped, his listeners broke into spontaneous cheers and whistles of approval, even those who would have to wait for the Druid's translation to truly understand. My own heart was thumping violently in my chest and the small hairs on my neck and arms were bristling with excitement. Finally, when the tumult began to die down, the old bishop, timing his moment again to perfection, raised his hands and silenced everyone.

"Let the bride come forward."

I dropped down from Germanicus—almost nimbly, for once—as the drums started up again, and stepped across to help my daughter down from her litter. She was weeping and smiling and one teardrop hung sparkling on the lashes of her left eye. I kissed her hand as she stepped to my side, and then I led her up on to the dais to stand before her husband.

As Uric stepped forward to claim her, his father leaned across and whispered in my ear. "Well, Roman, you outpeacock me today! I did not know you had such finery." I smiled and said nothing. "Come on," he continued, "it's our turn now."

We stepped forward, to the front of the dais, where we faced each other, about a pace apart, placing the crowd on one side of each of us and the bridal party on the other.

"Publius Varrus," Ullic addressed me in a stentorian voice. "Here, on this starting day, do I render unto you the bridal price agreed upon between yourself and me. Into your hand, as purchase of your daughter, I submit the wealth of all my family and my land, giving your grandson and my own, as yet unborn, the right and title to my name as King, after his father."

The crowd was thunderstruck. This was unheard of. What if the union should not produce an heir? Such must have been the thought of every person there to hear those words. And never before in history, to anyone's knowledge, had there been a marriage at which the bridal price did not change hands in physical form: cattle, gold and treasures. Quickly, before this stunned reaction could wear off, leaving doubters free to voice their doubts, I answered him in the terms we had worked out with Caius.

"Ullic Pendragon," I responded, my voice as strong and clear as his, "I accept this price, and, in fair token of good will between our peoples, here on this starting day, in full view of all people, I likewise submit the riches of all my family and my lands, together with the riches and the lands of Caius Britannicus, to your grandson and my own, as yet unborn, granting to him also the right and title to the rank of Duke, Leader, Commander and Ruler of all our estates and, in the fullness of time and by the voted and sworn oath of all the Council of this Colony, the right and title to the name of King in these lands of South Britain."

There! It was out: the news of Caius Britannicus's greatest triumph; the admission of the greatness of his vision; the proof of his persuasiveness and of the power of his personality. For one man—any man—to have convinced the Council of our Colony to endorse a king was contrary to all the mores and the history of Rome. I held my breath and waited for the inevitable reaction, prepared for anything. But the time was right and the people primed.

"Long live the Britons! And their King! Hip, hip, hip, hurrah!"

I have no idea which brawny throat that first cry sprang from, but it brought instant and enthusiastic response from the huge crowd and the cheers went on and on. Four hundred years earlier, when Caesar first landed here, the sound of that strange chant, "Hip, hip, hip, hurrah," the battle-cry of the fierce, woad-daubed clansmen, chilled his battle-hardened men because, unlike most of the battle-cries they had encountered, the nature of this cry—one voice calling for response and receiving it from everyone, instantly—suggested an inborn, savage discipline and a united will to win.

Today, the enthusiasm of the cry and the criers was unmistakable. I smiled at Ullic and we threw our arms around each other, to the approving cheers of the crowd. Then we stepped back and away, allowing the bridal couple to be wed.

Apart from my euphoria, I have almost no recollection of the ceremony itself. The bride was lovely and the groom was young and strong and fine. At one point they were wrapped together in a single, finely spun robe and tied with a golden cord; then the robe was peeled down from their heads and left hanging over the cord as they stood revealed from the waist up, concealed from the waist down and still bound, face to face, breast to breast, man to wife. It was done. Ullic stepped forward and announced that a feast was prepared on the hillside outside the walls and, still cheering, the crowd began to disperse.

XXVII

THE NEWLY WEDDED pair were escorted in the direction of the Council Hall, and I saw Luceiia's chair being carried there, too. I was surrounded by congratulatory friends, as were Ullic and Caius, but eventually Ullic and I were able to come together again, with Caius only a pace away, talking to one of his friends.

"Well, Roman, it was well done, I think?"

"Aye, Ullic, it was. It was well done."

"Your bishop friend spoke well. I was glad he was here."

"I was, too. He summed it up better than even Caius could have. And he surprised me, I have to admit. I have known Alaric for many years, but I don't think I have ever heard him speak in public before. I didn't know he was an orator. He played with the crowd, and with me too, the way your Druids play their instruments."

"How do you feel, now that you own my lands?" There was a slight smile on his face.

"Responsible," I replied with a matching smile. "I wonder what will result from this start."

Ullic heaved a great, sharp sigh. "Who knows, my friend? We have sown the seeds, that's all. There is no more we can do. Now it all depends on how the wind blows, and on how well young Uric sows his own seeds."

I nodded my head gravely, teasing him. "Aye, that's true. The last thing needed here is a great crop of daughters."

"Hah! No fear of that! We Pendragons are famed sirers of strong sons. Only effete Romans produce daughters with regularity."

"Then thank your gods, pagan, that they do!" I turned and reached my hand to Caius, breaking him away from his conversation and talking back across my shoulder to Ullic. "They'll give your stallion sons plenty of fields to plough in years to come."

I winked at the man whose conversation with Caius I had interrupted and drew Caius towards me. "Pardon us, my friend," I said to the man, unable to recall his name. "I must interrupt you and steal your listener, for it is almost time for us to go to the festive hall and join our ladies, and we have to drink, we three, to years to come."

Ullic was looking around at the almost-empty courtyard. "Everybody has gone in. They'll be waiting for us. Are you ready?"

"No," I said, "I am not. It will be crowded in there and I am already stifling in this ridiculous outfit. I think what I would like to do is shed this heavy cloak, dump all this armour and be comfortable. In fact, the more I think of it, the more I'm sure that it's exactly the most sensible thing to do. Where did Picus go? I see his horse there."

Caius spoke. "He is probably inside the hall." As he said the words, one of his household servants emerged from the festivities, saw us and came straight towards me.

"Lord Varrus, the Lady Luceiia sent me to find you. She asks that you join her in the Council Hall."

I made a wry face at Ullic and Cay. "Well, it seemed like a good idea." I returned my attention to the messenger. "Please inform the Lady Luceiia that King Ullic, Caius Britannicus and I will join the party shortly. In the meantime, please ask that they proceed as though we were already there. We will not be long." He turned to leave and I stopped him. "Wait. Is General Picus there?"

His face went blank. "I don't know, sir. I didn't see him, but I was not looking for him."

"No matter. I will find him later." The fellow went on his way and I turned back to my companions. "We had better go in to the proceedings, I suppose, but before we do I think we should set aside a time while we are all three here—four, if we count Picus—to talk of planning, of strategy. We have set some things in motion here today that should not be left untended. Uric should join us, too. When would be a good time?"

"When would you like it to be?" said Ullic. "I have nothing else to do while I am here."

Caius raised his eyebrow. "Tomorrow?"

I nodded. "Aye, in the afternoon. Alaric has the morning set aside for prayer."

Ullic blinked his eyes at that and stared at me strangely. "Prayer? Is that what you said? Why? What's going on?"

"Merely a Christian service, Ullic. In the Council Hall. Alaric has dedicated a special altar-stone to the Colony's use. He will use it for the first time tomorrow. Would you like to attend?"

"Aye, I might. A sacred stone, you say? Like ours?"

"Almost," I said with a smile, and Cay added, "But not as big, and not as phallic."

"What do you mean?"

I grinned at him. "Phallic, he said. You know what that means, don't you? Like a phallus. Your people, in your olden days, were very fond of raising great erections everywhere."

"Erections? You mean temples? Like Stonehenge?"

"No, Ullic, I mean erections, as in penises. Stonehenge has lintels across the top of its uprights, forming a circle, but the other stones I have seen are just like great stone penises, thrust into the air all over Britain."

Ullic was suddenly looking around him, almost furtively. "Watch what you say, Publius," he muttered hoarsely. "Priests are not famous for their tolerance when mocked."

His comment surprised me and made me feel slightly ashamed, as though he had caught me doing something beneath my dignity. I cleared my throat to cover the sudden confusion he had stirred in me and made amends immediately.

"Come, Ullic, I would not mock your priests, nor your beliefs, I merely said what I have often thought, in the hope that it might amuse you. I can see that it was thoughtless of me. Forgive me."

Cay spoke up. "Where will we meet tomorrow? Must it be in private?"

"No," I replied, "not necessarily, although I would rather keep the content of our talk among ourselves at this stage."

"Well then, why don't we all ride down to the villa? We can talk on the way, have a cup of wine there and then ride back."

"Sounds fine to me," Ullic said. "But why go to the villa? We could take a wineskin with us and ride overland."

"True, we could," I agreed. "But it suits me that Cay would want to go to the villa. While we are down there, I have something I would like to show both of you. Don't ask me what it is, for I won't tell you. I'll show you what it is tomorrow. Now, let's go and do our duty as fathers of the father and mother yet to be."

"That leaves me out!" Cay sounded aggrieved.

I laughed and threw my arm around his shoulders. "Don't be silly, Cay, you're an honorary father for the day."

As we approached the entrance to the Council Hall, someone called Ullic by name. He glanced over his shoulder and stopped. When Cay and I stopped too, he waved us on.

"You two go ahead, I'll join you presently. I have to talk to Cymric here."

We continued walking, and I found myself shrugging mightily in a vain attempt to get my cloak to hang more comfortably. I felt like a walking anvil, so great was the weight of metal I was carrying, and I was looking forward now to getting into the shade of the Council Hall, out of the hot, strong sun.

Cay and I stepped through the main entrance and stopped there, blinking our eyes to adjust to the gloom after the brightness of the sunshine outside. There was a false wall, or partition, just inside the entrance, creating the semblance of an entrance vestibule and serving also to shield the interior from outside when the main doors were open. Picus was standing there, one arm outstretched, leaning his weight on the partition, and between him and the wall was Ullic's sister, Enid. Picus still wore his helmet and his cloak and both he and Enid were oblivious to our entry, having eyes only for each other. The tension between them was almost tangible, an aura of taut sexuality apparent in their very stance. I looked at Caius and found he was already looking at me, his eyebrow riding high on his forehead. Wordlessly, we made our way around to the other side of the partition without disturbing the couple. I am not normally perceptive of subtleties, my wife has often told me, but even I could pick up on the situation between Picus and Enid. It was as subtle as a kick in the groin.

As I was passing out of their sight, however, it occurred to me quite forcibly that if Ullic stepped through that door as we had done, and received the same impressions that had come immediately to me, he might be moved to react in a way that could be regretted by everyone concerned. The sexual force these two were generating by just standing together was that strong. I started to turn back, but then stopped myself. These two were full-grown, old enough to do whatever they wished to do. He was an imperial legate and a commander of cavalry, and she was a princess and a ripe, mature woman. What they did was no business of mine. I left them to their own devices.

Caius and I joined the revelry; Picus joined us shortly after, showing no sign of anything unusual, but every now and then I could see him looking off across the hall, and there she would be, looking straight back at him. The thing that amazed me most about this was that I seemed to be the only person present who was aware of the sparks flying back and forth across the gathering. I passed a remark to Luceiia about it and completely failed to stir a spark of interest in her. She looked around cursorily to find Enid seated some tables away, engaged in conversation, as chance would have it, with the fellow next to her. Picus was likewise talking at the time with someone else and looking nowhere in Enid's direction. Luceiia frowned at me in some perplexity and started to say something, then changed her mind and gave my hand a squeeze and launched into a retelling of the conversation she had had with two of the Council members' wives after the wedding ceremony. I sat there feeling foolish and let her words pour over me, in one unlistening ear and out the other, thinking that women, even the best of them, could be unutterably blind, even when telling us how blind we are.

My other recollections of that day's proceedings are like my memories of a fight; fragmented, frozen images: the bride, my daughter, radiant with joy, holding her husband's arm tight to her side, laughing into my eyes; the great, brown hill bear I had seen outside, dancing and beating on a tambourine; some of Ullic's men tumbling and spinning, turning somersaults in the air; a roasted swan, its flawless feathers back in place, surrounded by a flock of roasted ducks and geese, passing before me on a massive board carried by several men; and my own owlish eyes peering back at me from the surface of the wine in the goblet I was peering into. It was a grand feast, I gather; for perhaps the third time in my life, I was carried senseless to my bed. But then, I was the father of the bride.

I awoke in pitch-darkness, with no idea of where I was; I knew I was abed, but that was all. I could hear people singing drunkenly, off in the distance, and my memory came back to me slowly. I was in our tent, outside the walls of the new fort. I reached out slowly for Luceiia, but she was not there, and that left me wondering what hour of the night it was. I struggled upright to a sitting position and immediately wished I hadn't done so; my head felt as though all the smiths of Vulcan's forge were pounding inside it.

I was groaning unashamedly, in a fine stew of self-pity, by the time I got to the opening of the tent, and there I stopped, stung by the cool night air into realizing that I was wearing nothing more than my tunic. I wondered who had taken off my armour and my clothes. And then I wondered how.

Going back to the pile of furs that was my bed, I fumbled about in the darkness and finally found the cedar chest that contained my clothes. Luceiia had insisted I bring my sheepskin tunic, knowing that the nights would still be cool up here on the hill. It took some ill-natured groping and fumbling in the dark before I located the heavy sheepskin, but then I pulled it over my head and went back to the entrance of the tent, throwing the leather flaps wide to admit the moonlight. The improvement was great and immediate. I then found my sandals and took down a woolen cloak from a peg on the tent pole before going outside to sit on the ground and lace up my sandals, realizing that even the light from the crescent moon was painful to my eyes. I was not happy; in fact, I could not remember ever having felt quite so awful as the result of what were supposed to be pleasurable activities. The ground felt cold against my backside, too, so I struggled back to my feet, groaning again, and re-entered the tent to pull a couple of skins from the sleeping pile. There was a tree of some kind no more than a few paces from the front of my tent. I threw the skins down at its base and seated myself carefully upon them with my back to the trunk, my cloak wrapped tightly around my shoulders as I breathed very deeply, gulping great draughts of the cool night air and squeezing my eyes tight shut.

A dog began to howl quite close by and my mind cringed at the sound. I swore if the cur came any closer I would find it and choke it to profound, permanent silence. And then I heard footsteps approaching me, and someone began to sing in a loud, drunken voice, to be joined immediately by his equally drunken companions. I scrambled to my feet and fled into the night, clutching the fur I had been sitting on.

I must have walked a good half-mile along the hillside, paralleling the walls that loomed above me, tilting my body upwards against the steep slope that fell away downhill on my right. I could still hear an occasional shout of laughter from late revellers within the walls, but I was soon far enough away from the level tent area to leave all noise there completely behind and my head was thankful.

Eventually I found myself another tree to lean on and sat down, bracing myself slightly against the fall of the slope with my heels, resting my elbows on my upraised knees and pressing the heels of my palms against my pounding temples. I felt as sick and miserable as I had when, as a green recruit, I had first drunk too much of our thin, sour legionaries' wine.

I have no idea how long I sat there. It might have been an hour—perhaps more, perhaps less—but I eventually dozed off and scared myself back to wakefulness when my head slipped from the crutch of my hands. I blinked and growled and muttered and peered around me at the darkness on all sides. In front of me, low on the horizon, the moon was almost gone from sight. I was chilled to the bone, but I felt decidedly better than I had earlier. I cursed, knowing that my bad knee was going to cause me agonies when I tried to stand up, and hugged my cloak closer, seeking warmth that wasn't there. I had been sitting too long. Grimly, I pulled myself to my feet, gritting my teeth against the fierce pain now in my knee. It felt as though all the bones in the joint were brazed together, but I forced myself to walk, limping outrageously, staggering and at one point almost crawling, supporting my weight on one hand against the hillside where the slope was particularly steep.

With movement, as the exercise restored the flow of circulation, the pain began to lessen and I began to make better progress, although the going was still much harder than it had been on the way there because the slope of the hill was now against my bad leg. It was no use berating myself for not having thought of that earlier, for then I had been too sick to think or even care. I simply bit down on my teeth the harder and took advantage of every tree I came to, stopping to lean against each one and rest my aching leg.

I was perhaps half-way back to my tent when I paused to rest against a large tree and my bladder let me know that it was under pressure. Fumbling at the binding of my breech-clout, I was noticing the silence now from the walls above me when an unearthly moan seemed to issue from the ground at my feet and the hairs on my neck and arms stirred in horror. I am not a superstitious man, but that sound, on a bare, empty, dark hillside, turned my guts to water. I froze, my bladder forgotten, my ears straining in the absolute stillness that followed the shocking sound. Nothing stirred, anywhere, and then it came again, a long-drawn, sighing moan, less loud this time and much, much less unearthly. This time I recognized it as coming from a human throat, and I also placed the direction of its source. There was a dip in the ground in front of me, down to my left. Whoever had made that noise was down there in the hollow. I was highly aware of feeling much better now that I had found relief and identified both sound and location. I moved out from my tree slowly, approaching the lip of the hollow with great caution, and there I stopped, feeling my flesh crawl again.

There was no one there. No one at all. It was an empty, grassy bowl, inky dark and empty. And then I saw a pale flash and realized what I was looking at: two people lying hidden, covered and totally concealed by a dark blanket. The darkness of the night had blended it into invisibility until one leg had come briefly into view before being withdrawn again. And then I heard whispering and the man laughed and my stomach turned over.

The dark blanket was a black cloak, the cloak of Picus Britannicus, for it was he who had laughed, and I had no need to guess who the other person under that cloak with him might be. I backed away from there with a feeling akin to panic in my breast. What would they think if they found me there, spying on them like this? And then my heel caught on a tussock and I overbalanced, unable to catch myself on my bad leg, and I fell heavily on my backside. It seemed to me that I came down with the noise of a landslide, loud enough to wake the dead, but the two people below me were too caught up in being alive to hear me.

I got to my feet again slowly and with caution and hobbled away, hearing the noises of their coupling growing louder and more passionate behind me until the distance I gained was great enough to permit them their privacy. Sweet Christ on His Cross! This could be a pretty mess, I thought, if Picus handled it wrongly. I had no idea what I should do, or how I might proceed in order to make the seriousness of his conduct clear to Picus. Enid was Ullic's sister, and one of his favourite people. An insult to her might be unforgivable; that would not surprise me at all. Though it was as little Ullic's affair as it was mine, that meant little. I suspected that he might be more than simply angry.

And yet there was nothing wrong or unnatural about the attraction or the natural lust that Enid and Picus had sparked in each other, nor was there anything unusual in their gratification of their feelings. So why was I feeling so apprehensive? I did not know, but my mind kept feeding me images of their two bodies grappling with each other, uncovered by the cloak. I visualized Enid's face twisting with the pleasure of what she was feeling and then suddenly it was I, not Picus, who was above her. The realization of what I was thinking brought me up short, and only then did I perceive the reason for my state of mind. It was caused by envy! I was jealous!

I stopped again, this time by an outcrop of rock, and tried to take stock of this new discovery. It was a novel one, for I could not remember ever having dedicated a thought to any other woman, apart from Cylla Titens, since I had wedded Luceiia. Not a serious thought, at any rate. I had remarked the occasional voluptuous breast or swelling hip from time to time, but only in passing. And now, all of a sudden, I was jealous? From somewhere, I found the strength to laugh at myself and recognize both the humour and the truth of the situation. This beautiful, ripe woman had simply reminded me of my lost young-manhood. That is why no one else had noticed their mutual attraction; it was so normal, so natural, that it had gone unremarked. Only I had seen it because, without my knowing it, I had been looking for it and resenting it.

All at once, I felt much better. My aching head had been forgotten, and now my aching leg stopped hurting as if by magic and my swollen bladder reasserted itself. I relieved it and made my way back to my tent, where I found my wife asleep and a lamp burning to light my way to bed. I put out the lamp and climbed in beside Luceiia, snuggling close to her welcoming warmth and hardly even sparing another thought for Picus and Enid and their coupling before I fell asleep.

XXVIII

PICUS LOOKED FRESH as a daisy the next day.

We were all astir at dawn, and the smells of cooking and wood-smoke were everywhere. Bishop Alaric unveiled the altar-stone to open admiration and celebrated his mass, calling the benediction of God and His heavenly saints upon this place new-built upon an ancient site.

Ullic, his family and his Druids were there in attendance, the latter watching with grave, impassive interest, and when the mass was over Alaric allowed everyone to examine the stone before placing it for safe-keeping in the beautiful case that had been made for it. I had not known what to expect, never having seen an altar-stone up close before, and I was frank in my admiration of the care and workmanship that had been lavished upon it.

It was a solid block of marble, three-fourths as long as it was wide, and it was about as wide as my shoulders. In thickness it was about a handsbreadth deep, slightly more than the width of a sword blade, and the two shorter sides were carved to look like the hempen cables used to secure naval vessels to the shore. The top surface had been scrolled with a border of Celtic design, and in its centre was the *Chi Rho* symbol of the Christians. Directly above this symbol, a rectangular hole had been chiselled into the stone to allow a cross to be slotted into place, and below the *Chi Rho* was a single rectangle, grooved into the smoothness of the marble.

"What does this signify?" I asked Alaric, pointing at the rectangle.

"It *signifies* nothing, Publius. It is the lid of a hollow chamber which contains a precious relic from the land of Christ; a finger-bone of blessed John the Evangelist."

That silenced me.

"It is a beautifully worked gift, Alaric," said Caius. "We will make good use of it."

"I know you will, my friend." Alaric picked the stone up as though it were made of air and fitted it into its wooden case. "One thing only would I ask of you: the stone is portable, but your Colony is now permanent. It would be good and most pleasing to our Master the Christ if, some day when there is the time and the opportunity, your people could construct a permanent home to house the stone. A house that would be God's house only."

"You mean an ecclesia?"

"An ecclesia. In Germany, in Gaul and in Italia itself there are many

344

ecclesia being built today. Permanent houses of prayer. I would die happy if
I knew one would be built here, some day."

"Then rest easy, old friend." Caius smiled. "I promise you there will be
a house here for God."

One of the Druids, who had been standing back observing us, asked then,
"What is the significance of this stone?"

The old bishop looked at him with a smile.

"It has the same significance as those your people erected in bygone days.
It is to the glory of God. It is sanctified—blessed—and contains, as I have
said, a relic of a wise and holy man. When this stone is taken into a room
for prayerful use, that room itself is blessed by the stone's presence, and any
table upon which the stone is set becomes an altar sanctified to commemorate
the Body and the Blood of the Christ, both given in sacrifice to free mankind
from sin."

The Druid frowned slightly but made no further comment, and Alaric
closed the wooden case, hiding the stone from profane eyes, after which he
and Father Phonos carried it between them to the small enclosure at the far
side of the Council Hall that had been specially built to hold the stone.

Later that day, after the midday meal, we met as we had planned and rode
together down to the villa—myself, Caius, Picus, Ullic, Uric and Equus. Picus
and I were ready first, and as we sat waiting for the others to join us, he
tweaked my nose verbally about my having drunk too much the day before,
telling me that I'd missed the most interesting part of the day. I smiled to
myself as I imagined what his expression would be were I to tell him of what
I had seen and heard in the night on the hillside. Of course, I said nothing,
and the others soon joined us so that he left off his teasing.

When we arrived at the villa I led them past the house and directly to
the forge itself, a move that occasioned some comment, since we had been
talking on the way down from the fort about cracking a jug of wine as soon
as we arrived. The inside of the forge was dark and the fires were all out. We
threw open the doors at the front and back of the forge and opened the
window-shutters, letting in enough of the bright spring sun to lighten all but
the darkest corners.

Picus perched himself on the edge of a bench, first taking care to clean
the dust from it. Ullic leaned against a pillar, oblivious to dirt, smacking his
lips and clearing what was obviously supposed to be a parched throat, with
much spluttering and dumb show. Young Uric stood quietly beside his father,
saying nothing. He had barely spoken six words since leaving the fort, this
being his first outing as a man among men. He had taken unmerciful teasing
all the way down here from all of us, myself included, and had not been a
bridegroom long enough to develop the confidence that was needed to cope
with such banter without embarrassment. And that, naturally, provided more
fuel for the fires on which we roasted him.

I seated myself on one of our three-legged stools and nodded to Equus, who walked to a chest at the back of the forge and produced a long, cloth-wrapped bundle.

"Equus has something to show you," I said.

He brought the bundle back, dropped it with a clank onto the floor and unwrapped four long swords, one matched pair and two others. Wordlessly, he passed them around, giving Picus one with a long blade that was slightly curved, with a flared end just behind its point. Ullic took the other singleton, and Caius and Uric each held one of the pair of long, tapering, straight-bladed swords with the heavy, leaden pommels and long, two-handed grips.

"We've all been looking for a new kind of weapon to suit the needs of our horsemen," I began. "The standard sword we've always used is too short, now that we're up on big horses. These are some of the results we've come up with. Picus? What do you think?"

Picus was holding up the sword he had been given in his two hands, his right gripping the hilt and his left supporting the flat blade as he ran his eyes along the sweep of its length, which gleamed dully in the dim light. He removed his left hand from the blade and swung the sword tentatively, testing it gently and grimacing slightly with satisfaction before standing up from his bench and stepping forward to give himself room to swing the sword in earnest, stabbing it downward to touch the floor, point first, while his elbow was still bent.

"I like this, Uncle!" He flipped it up into the air and caught it just below the hilt, examining the hilt itself and the pommel counterweight. "How did you make this? What is it? Lead?"

"For now, yes," I told him. "Lead over iron."

"How did you get the weight right?"

"Strung lead discs over the iron tang like beads and then heated them." This was Equus who spoke.

"Will it remain solid?" Picus gripped the hilt purposefully, flexing his fingers and splaying them to wrap tightly around the grip.

"Aye, it'll stay solid," Equus continued. "It *is* solid."

Picus returned now to his inspection of the blade, extending his left hand and laying the pointed tip on the upturned palm.

"Why the flair above the point?" he asked next. "It looks familiar, but I know I've never seen it before."

"Yes you have, Picus," I told him. "Africa, and Asia Minor. The desert peoples there use similar blades, curved, with a slightly flared tip to add impetus to the swing."

"Of course, that's it! But this is different again—this blade is not so deeply curved."

"No, nor so deeply flared, for that matter. Remember, Picus, our men are mounted. We are attempting to create something here that will stab like a spear yet chop like an axe, something that can be used effectively without being swung too hard."

He nodded towards the sword I was holding. "That one is different. Why?"

I shrugged. "They are all different. The one Ullic has is much broader in the blade close to the tip than yours is. That one we have already rejected as being too heavy, too unwieldy. Try it."

Picus exchanged swords with Ullic and one swing of the new sword was enough to show him that I was right.

"I agree. Too heavy. Clumsy. The first one's far superior."

"Yes, but also no. It's better, but it's far too light in construction. It will bend in battle. It is the prettiest, the most aesthetically pleasing, but it is the least practical of all the prototypes we have tested." I held up the one I was holding. "This is the winner. The best we have come up with to date." I threw it to him hilt first and he dropped the one he was holding to catch the one in the air. He caught it, arm extended, and held it there at arm's length, his eye sweeping from the boss out to its distant point. Long moments he held it there, unmoving, and then, as though its point were anchored at the centre of a circle, he began to walk around it, watching the light change on the blade as he made the turn. Then he flexed his elbow, bringing the weapon close up to his face until the iron touched his cheek before tilting his head back to look up at the point held vertically above him. This done, he took a slow step forward on his left foot and swung the sword, feeling its weight and balance at every point on its arc.

"There is nothing wrong with this one, Uncle. Much that is right, but nothing wrong."

"Let me try it." Ullic's face was rapt, and Picus handed the weapon over to him and then turned back to me.

"I think you have solved the problem, Uncle."

"So do we," I smiled at him. "Even Equus likes it."

"With the exception of one raw imperfection." Equus's voice was heavy with irony, and I tried to quiet him before he said any more, waving a minatory finger and frowning in reproof as I shook my head sharply, hoping Picus would not see. Naturally, he picked up on it immediately.

"What's wrong? What imperfection?"

I grunted and accepted the inevitable. "A minor imperfection, Picus, far from insoluble," I said. "The iron of the blades is difficult to control, because of its temper and the length of the swords. They bounce off each other and are dangerous to the unwary. But it is not a matter that is insoluble. We're working on it now."

"Then why is Equus so disgusted?"

I smiled at him. "For the same reason as always. He is a perfectionist and refuses to countenance imperfection. In the meantime, the problem I am working with Equus to solve should have no effect on you. I would like you to start immediately training your people to fight with the sword from horseback. By the time you have enough of the swords to begin the training, I should have solved the problem of the cross-hilt."

"The what?"

"The cross-hilt. I'll show it to you when it's done. Far simpler than trying to explain it. Just remember not to let your men even attempt to train against each other with these prototype weapons."

"As you wish, Uncle." Picus's acquiescence was unconditional, but his face betrayed his incomprehension. Nevertheless, he covered himself very well. He turned immediately to Ullic. "What do you think of this sword?"

"I think it is a good sword, as swords go, Picus, but I'll stick to my new bow, my short-sword and my axe."

"You don't like it?"

"Oh, I like it well enough." Ullic's shrug showed his disdain of the new weapon as clearly as his next words. "But what need would I have of a great thing like that? I don't fight on horseback. I walk to fight, and sometimes I run. A long sword like that, I'd be forever tripping over it and falling down. My kingly dignity would suffer sadly."

"Now there's a point, Uncle Varrus." Picus was grinning now, acknowledging Ullic's humour but holding the sword point-down by his waist, where Romans always wore their swords. "A man won't be able to wear this in the traditional way. It touches the ground."

"Aye, so it does," I agreed. "Nor would he be able to draw it right-handed from his right side. Our men will wear their new swords hanging from their necks, across their backs."

"How? In a scabbard?"

"I don't know yet, Picus, but probably through a metal ring attached to a cross-belt. We have plenty of time to work that out. First we have to make the swords. We can decide later how we will carry them."

"How long will it take you to make two hundred of them?"

I looked at Equus with a smile. "How long, Equus? Two years?"

"About that."

"Two *years*?" There was pain and anguish in Picus's voice. "Two years? Why? Why so long?"

"Because, my impetuous friend, we have just begun working on this thing, this problem. Even this iron is not tempered properly. We have been more concerned with weight, shape and balance, than with quality at this stage. This weapon has a long, long way to go before it's ready for use in mock combat, let alone in battle."

"Then would you mind if I set my own armourers to work on the design?"

The question surprised me, and I looked at Equus to see his reaction before I spoke again.

"Don't ask me," I said then. "It was Equus who came up with the design. If he has no objections, how can I?"

"Equus?"

My big friend shrugged his shoulders and shook his head. "I don't mind," he responded. "It's a simple extension of the Roman short-sword in the first place. I'm surprised your Roman armourers haven't come up with it already."

"They have not come up with it, Equus, because they lack what you and Publius Varrus have between you: the genius to look at something that has been unchanged for centuries and see how it can be improved to meet new needs." Picus stopped short and then looked at Equus, and from him to me. "And I have just told myself why I am going to say nothing about this to anyone."

"No, Picus." My interruption was quick and sincere, for I knew what he was going to say next and I knew also that he was wrong. "You cannot do that. You have a duty to Stilicho, if not to your Emperor, and above all that you have a duty to your troops. If this new long-sword can improve their battle strength, you have to get it for them as quickly as you can."

Picus nodded and then glanced from Ullic to Uric. "What do you two think? Is Varrus right?"

Ullic held up his hands, palms outward, his expression one of entreaty and mingled fear and anger, and although it was clear that he was jesting it was equally clear that he was not speaking completely out of mockery.

"Leave me out of this, I want nothing to do with it! Why should I vote in favour of arming Romans better than ourselves? It might come back like a ghost to haunt me someday."

Uric watched his father in some awe, a smile in his eyes, but ventured nothing.

Picus turned back to me. "I will say nothing more on this now, Uncle, but I believe you are correct: this is a better weapon than anything we have, or are likely to have in the near future. I think I am duty-bound to give it to my armourers to play with. My men need this weapon in large numbers."

"So be it, Picus," I answered him. "You have talked yourself right into it, answered your own doubts. Now, let's get over to the house and try that jug of wine."

The wine was excellent, and by the time we saw the bottom of the jug, we had prepared a plan of action for the future that would see our combined forces—Ullic's, Picus's and our own colonists—working closely together in the coming months.

Ullic told us that he now had Cymric and four other bowyers working full-time at fabricating more of his great bows: a lighter, modified version of his original giant weapon, but still a mighty bow. He believed that the time would come when the Long Bow of Ullic, as he grandiloquently termed it, would become commonplace among his people. In the meantime, Uric, he had decided, would spend half of the year with us in the Colony, learning our tactics and the way we made war, and the other half teaching what he had learnt to his own people. Uric, however, was quick to point out that his mountain people were not the type that great cavalry troops were made from, nor were their horses. The Celts' mountain-ponies were admirably suited for their own terrain, but they offered little hope of organized weight of the kind we were developing in the Colony. And by the same token, he pointed out, our own great horses were simply too big and cumbersome to function satisfactorily in the mountains.

It was agreed, therefore, that Uric would study with us from a new viewpoint, that of a liaison officer who could combine the two methods of warfare, theirs and ours, to make the best use of both when both were needed together. But we all agreed, in a spirit that was only half jocular, that his first priority should be to sire a son—a living symbol of the bonds between our two peoples from this time on. Uric blushed crimson, but smiled and found the confidence to say shyly that he had already begun to work on the matter.

Picus was the one among us with the greatest problems. He was intensely frustrated by the role his troops were being forced to play in the north, along Hadrian's Wall. Picus felt, and correctly so, I believed, that he and his forces were being exploited, used as morale-builders for the garrisons up there in that inhospitable country. His troops were part of the forces of South Britain, headquartered in Londinium. He had been placed in a political crucible by requests from the military commander at Arboricum in North Britain for the specialized help of his mobile forces in dealing with marauding bands of infiltrators from above the Wall. These requests had come, in a highly concentrated form, at a time of relative quiet in the south, and against his own better judgment Picus had agreed to a temporary secondment to northern duty. He had then spent the ensuing three months gnashing his teeth in fury, galloping his men across the northern expanses of rock and moorland chasing small bands of marauding, fleet-footed Picts, while the solid barrier of the Wall itself prevented him from making what might have been a decisive impact by attacking into the enemy's territories.

He had been recalled, eventually, when the Saxons began making their annual springtime raids in the south, but it was his belief that the Wall in the north was doomed as a frontier. There were not enough men stationed up there to handle the kind of pressure the garrisons were being subjected to, and morale was lower than it had ever been. The soldiers on duty there knew that the Wall was far from impregnable; it had fallen back in '67 and had been breached to a lesser extent several times since then in several places. The garrison troops on the Wall felt they had been handed a useless and thankless task in defending it, and they knew that the seaborne raids to the south would continue to guarantee that they would receive no permanent reinforcements.

Even Stilicho's consular army of ten thousand men was of no help to them, for it was employed in strengthening the coastal areas, mainly along the Saxon Shore in the south-east, and in the east itself.

Picus would be returning to duty the following day, he informed us. He would go straight to Londinium and from there he expected to be dispatched directly to the south-east.

"Dispatched?" I asked him. "I thought you were your own commander?"

"I am, but where the raids are coming heaviest, there I go, most of the time at the request of military headquarters. It's a formality, Uncle Varrus. I'd be going there anyway."

"I have no doubt of that, but aren't you concerned that they might grow accustomed to *directing* you through these requests?"

He smiled at me, a very pleasing smile.

"Not really. If conflict ever should arise, I shall do what my mind—and my prime directive from my commander—tells me is correct, based upon the best input I can accumulate. After that they can all complain to Stilicho."

"I see," I said. "And you have no plans to return to the north?"

"None at all, unless the fates play me truly foul. You know, Uncle, it seems very strange, but the only person I ever knew who enjoyed northern Wall duty was Claudius Seneca."

"Seneca?" I could hear my own astonishment. "You jest, surely?"

But Picus was shaking his head. "I swear, Uncle, Seneca was like a different man up there. Even his soldiers noticed it. They would do anything he called on them to do, and he called on them to do things that he had never done before. Things I would never have expected him to do."

"Such as? Give me an instance."

"Well," he paused, but only for a fraction of a heartbeat, "he volunteered his troops and himself for nightpursuit duty, in foul weather, on several occasions. Believe that if you can. I had difficulty with it myself, and I was there."

I was gazing at him, open-mouthed.

"It is true, Uncle, I swear. Seneca behaved like a man. Like a professional soldier. Like a leader."

"Why, I wonder?"

"What?" Picus was blinking at me, not understanding my question.

"Why, I asked. Why would Seneca suddenly start acting like a responsible officer after so long?"

That, of course, was a question to which two honest, unimaginative soldiers like Picus and me could provide no answer, lacking the subtleties and insight of politically minded men. We pursued it no further, but each of us tucked it away in his head to study further at a later time.

Picus soon bade us farewell to return to the fort and check up on his men. His father walked with him to find his horse, and Ullic watched them both leave the villa with a curious expression on his face that I would have quizzed him about at any other time. The memory of what I had seen the day and the night before, however, was fresh enough in my mind to make me watch my tongue, and so I said nothing. Ullic, however, was under no constraints.

"He's a good man, that one."

"Who? Caius?"

"No, not Caius! Picus."

"Ah, Picus! Yes, he's one of the best. His father's son. Have you just realized that?"

Ullic threw me a look of disgust and spoke to me in the tones one reserves for dull children.

"No, Publius, I have known it for a long time. I have simply never remarked on it aloud before now."

"I see. And what makes you notice it now?"

"My sister. Uric, would you bring us some more wine?" He watched Uric walk away and then turned back to me, signalling with his head for me to get up and follow him to the furthest end of the big room, out of earshot of the others.

"I have this sister, Enid," he went on. I made no comment, merely waited. "It occurs to me she should have wed long since. She is overripe." I bit my tongue to distract myself from the thought that sprang into my mind as he went on. "But she's a headstrong wench whose one, true man was killed by a marauding bear eight or nine years ago, just before we met, you and I. He died saving her life. She watched him being mauled and then held him in her arms until he died." Ullic sighed. "He was a good man. Too good to go like that. Anyway, Enid has weighed every other man she ever met against him, the one who died. And they've all lost. It occurred to me that Picus might be man enough to tame her. Why has he never wed?"

"The army. He's a soldier, remember?"

"So was his father, but he sired a son."

"Not before he was Picus's age!"

That gave Ullic pause. He chewed on it for a while, then: "No, I suppose you are right. Caius must have been Picus's age at least when the boy was born."

"He was. What is your point, Ullic?"

Young Uric approached us and filled his father's cup and then mine. Ullic stared into his wine as the young man moved away again.

"How can I get Picus to wed my sister?"

"Mention it to him." I tried to keep my voice expressionless and non-committal. "He might not be averse to the idea."

Ullic now looked me straight in the eye. "You think not? Even though she is not of Roman stock?"

"That is unjust, Ullic, even in jest. Especially now, when he is here at his own urging, on his own time, to celebrate the joining of our bloods."

Ullic pursed his lips and leaned against the wall. "I know it seems that way, my friend, but Legate Picus Britannicus is still a Roman officer, in spite of all that is happening here. He wears their uniform and he fights their wars. He is *very* Roman."

"No, Ullic." My interruption was firm and instantaneous. "This time you are wrong. Picus is Cay's son. He is one of us. His loyalty is first to Stilicho, his best friend and his commander while he is still in uniform. But after that, I'll swear his loyalty is to us first and then, only then, to Rome. I would stake my life on that."

"You already have, Publius Varrus. And you are correct, I know it. This question of Enid is a thorny one that plagues me badly from time to time. I see my son wed now, and am reminded that my duty is to find a husband for my youngest sister. She does nothing, either, to make my task easier."

"She is very beautiful, Ullic."

"Aye, she is, and very stubborn, wilful, obstinate, infuriating and intransigent. She drives me mad. Now if, as you suggest, I approach Picus and he laughs at me, what would my reaction be? I really don't know, Publius, how I might react."

"Then try it and see, my friend. I have a feeling that he might not turn you down." I could feel a slight smile growing on my face.

"Why?" Ullic was looking at me closely. "Why are you smiling? Have you seen something? Has he said something to you?"

"No, Ullic, not at all." I was laughing at his earnestness. "But I saw Picus *see* Enid yesterday, if you know what I mean . . . He was highly conscious of the fact that she was there in the same hall as him. And Enid saw him, too."

"When? I didn't notice."

"Of course you didn't. Why should you? I only noticed myself by accident." That was almost true, I told myself.

"By God, Publius, that's encouraging! I'll watch them tonight and see how they behave towards each other. If they look interested, I'll bring the matter up with Cay."

"With Cay? Why would you do that? Why not approach Picus directly? He's a man full-grown."

"Aye, so he is. But Cay is still his father." Ullic was sounding stubborn, so I shrugged my shoulders and let the matter rest, telling myself that I was no one to balk at the proper way of doing things.

As it turned out, however, Picus had bypassed both of us and spoken directly of it to his father when the two of them went out together to the horses, telling Caius bluntly that he wished to take Enid to wife as soon as possible. It was probably one of the shortest marriage negotiations on record, wrapped up and agreed to by all concerned within the hour, celebrated that evening by firelight because everyone necessary was already present and the groom had to go to war the following day. And once again, everyone had a drunken night. Uric and Picus, early abed naturally enough, were probably the only two men in the assembly who did not have thick heads the following morning.

I know Picus was tempted to steal one extra day of love before going back, but the spirit of duty was bred too strong in him, and before noon he led his files of men off, down the winding road on the hillside and out of his new bride's life again. She watched with us from the top of the walls until they entered the distant forest and were lost from sight, and then, dry-eyed, she went to join the other women. I watched her leave and spoke to Ullic.

"We are binding ourselves closely, my friend."

"What do you mean?"

"Your sister. Now she is my niece, since my wife is aunt to her new husband. Any child of theirs will be great-niece or nephew to me. And your son is now my son, and his son will be our grandson, yours and mine."

"True, Publius." Ullic laid his great paw on my shoulder. "Their blood will not be to blame should they not prosper. I only hope Picus comes back soon to plant his crop."

"You jest, of course! He is a Britannicus, Ullic! They are not noted for standing idly by and getting nothing done. He planted it last night." Or the night before, I thought with a smile.

XXIX

 THE PRIEST, ANDROS, sat across from me, shaking his head sadly. "I am sorry, Publius," he said, "but that is my only suggestion. I see no other way to do what you want."

I was still stunned. We had been over this problem time and time again, for months now, and we kept coming back to this one, inescapable point. There seemed to be no way to go around it. I had asked Andros to help me with the design of a cross hilt for the new sword. I wanted to pour the hilt, using a mould, so that it would be one solid piece, and he understood my needs perfectly. Now he was asking me to accept and acknowledge *his* needs and my own hitherto unrecognized requirements before we could make the thing work. I had made a basic error in the design of my new sword, a very basic error, considering what I now wanted to do with it. I looked down again at his drawings. They were very simple: three small sketches side by side.

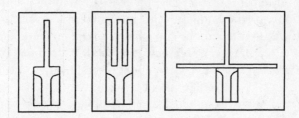

The first sketch showed what I had given him; the second showed what I should have given him; and the third showed how the second must be adapted to serve as a skeleton for the moulded hilt. I squeezed my temples between the heels of my hands.

"Damnation, Andros! This means I have to start all over again, from the beginning, every step of the way!"

He nodded, his honest face untroubled. "Yes, if you want to do this correctly. Is it that important? The cross-hilt, I mean?"

I thought about the plans I had been making for this new sword, the hands that would some day wield it. I nodded, resignedly. "Yes, Andros, it's that important. But it's going to take months, all over again."

He smiled. "Well, you have them. Now that the wedding is over, you have time on your hands. The fort is completed. So is the Council Hall. The road is built, and your big stables up on the hilltop, inside the walls, are all but completed, too. You have plenty of time, Publius." I glared at him, balefully, but he continued, unperturbed. "Besides, you have already done it once. It will be easier the second time, and if you pray to God for help, He may even make it turn out better this time."

"It was *perfect* this time!"

Andros shook his head gently, a sad little smile of human understanding on his lips. "No it wasn't, Publius. That is why you now have to do it again."

I gritted my teeth in the face of his naive honesty. "Thank you, Andros. You can go now."

As soon as he had gone, I crossed to my work-bench and unwrapped the long bundle that lay there. It gleamed at me, liquid silver in the gloom of the smithy. It had a shine, to be sure. Shine and to spare. It was the finest blade I had ever made. But it was wrong, flawed, and the fault was mine; it had nothing to do with the skystone metal. I took it in my hands, looked one last, long look into its mirrored surface, and then I thrust it into the fire, deep into the glowing coals, and reached for the bellows. Now I had to untemper it, melt it again to a shapeless mass of metal and recreate it with a triple tang.

The smithy was deserted, save for myself. Equus and the other smiths worked up in the new smithy in the fort most of the time now, and the villa proper was strangely silent nowadays. The staff of servants was being removed little by little to tend to the new quarters up above as they were built. The villa would remain in use, but only as spare quarters. The new living accommodations for the family up in the fort were less spacious, and less gracious, but they were luxurious enough and would grow more comfortable with use. They were far safer, too, now that the fort itself was impregnable, with walls that were twenty-five feet high in places, rising vertically from the steep hillside.

I moved back to the work-bench again and found a scrap of papyrus and a stick of charcoal. I knew I would have few distractions in my second struggle with the skystone metal, so I set myself to thinking of the difference the triple tang would make to the weight, proportions and temper of the blade. I would not again deprive Caius of a portion of his goddess; I would make do with the piece of her I had already, and that thought led me to a consideration of my own women at home in the fort on the hill.

Veronica's departure with her new husband had not been as cruel a deprivation as I had expected, mainly due to the fact that her place in the household had been taken immediately by Enid, who would live with us while Picus was away campaigning. Luceiia had defined the situation succinctly, as usual, telling me that I had lost a daughter but gained a niece. I smiled as I thought of the two of them together. Luceiia had gained more of a friend than a niece. I supposed that the main reason for Enid's closeness to Luceiia was that they were two of a kind, both cut from the same cloth. Each of them was stubborn, wilful, intelligent, implacable and yet almost paradoxically serene, self-sufficient and dignified. And each was a beauty in her own right.

I was surprised to find myself whistling tunelessly as I waited for the sword blade to grow red-hot.

In the weeks and months that followed, I worked diligently, almost religiously, at my forge, discovering to my pleasure and surprise that Andros was right, the task was much easier the second time, and I had come to know better the properties of the metal I was working with. The second blade emerged from its shapeless mass as a longer, more slender and altogether finer entity than its predecessor, so that by the time I set out to refine it and temper it and create its cutting edges, I found myself in the grip of an intense, almost mystical excitement, a sense of awe that inspired me to conceal my work from everyone, including even Equus, until I had completed it. Only then, when I was convinced I could not improve upon what my hands and mind had wrought, did I call him into the forge and show him the long, cloth-wrapped shape lying on the bench. He looked from me to it and then back to me again, and his big face broke into a slow, ungrudging smile that held no trace of rancour over the long time I had kept this piece of work from his sight.

"So, you finally finished it. Am I allowed to look now?"

I nodded and he unwrapped the blade. For a long time he simply stood there, staring down at it with his back to me, saying nothing. I waited. Eventually he brought his hands abstractedly to his buttocks, wiping his fingertips clean on the material of his breeches before fumbling a cloth out of his apron pocket and using it to pick up the blade, protecting it from finger-marks. When he turned to me at last, holding the blade reverently in his hands, there were tears in his eyes. He shook his head savagely, trying to clear his vision, and uttered half a laugh.

"Varrus!" he said. "It's a Varrus blade." He shook his head again. "I'm weeping, thinking of your grandfather. He would have wept to see this, too. I think there has . . ." His voice choked up and he had to clear his throat. When he spoke again, he was making a determined effort to sound strong. "There has never, *ever*, been anything like this made in iron by a man before, Publius. This is perfection."

I had to swallow hard to overcome the emotions that his tone brought out in me. I fought to sound casual. "No, Equus. Not perfection. Not yet. I still have to hilt it."

He shook his head, dismissing any possible difficulty. "Oh, you'll hilt it. That's what the triple tang's for, isn't it? You're going to pour it like the dagger's hilt?"

I nodded. "Aye, in a cruciform. That way, no blade will skip across the boss. The outside tangs will be twisted at right angles, and I'll pour the mould around them."

He shook his head again, his eyes still fixed on the blade. "God, Publius, this is superb." There was real awe in his voice, matching the awe I had felt in helping the blade emerge from the raw metal. "It's longer than the first one, and narrower, by a good inch." He turned it sideways. "Thicker in section, too. And look at this." He was fingering the reinforcing spine that ran centrally the length of the blade between two thumb-wide channels. "God! Look at this thing!" He raised his eyes eventually and looked at me. "Have you designed the hilt yet?"

"Aye, I have the drawings here, and the finished mould. I couldn't have done it without Andros. He's a true artist. Come and see."

I led him to the back of the smithy and lit two lamps by the light of which I showed him the open halves of the finished mould and how the triple tang would fit inside it. He asked me how long it would take me to finish the hilt and complete the sword, and I looked at him and shook my head and told him that it would take as long as it had to take. We had just blown out the lamps and were on our way out of the smithy when Ullic's big shape blocked the light from the doorway.

"Roman," he yelled. "Are you in there?" We were within two paces of him almost, but he was sun-blinded.

"I'm here, Ullic," I answered him. "What brings you back so soon?"

"News, my old friend!" He stepped inside the door and grasped me by the shoulders. "We are to be grandfathers, you and I! Veronica is with child! Didn't I tell you we Pendragons are potent sires?"

"Hah!" I flung my arms around him. "Fertile mares, too, you Celtic lout! We are to be uncles, too! Your sister Enid has the same affliction."

I felt him rear back from me and saw his eyes light up. "Enid? Already? By the great sun god! When is she due?"

I laughed. "By the new year. Picus wasted no seed."

"Nor did Uric, by God! The two of them will whelp together. This demands celebration, Varrus!"

We celebrated, and within the week Picus came home on a flying visit and we celebrated again. The women watched our drunken antics and smiled knowingly among themselves.

Picus remained with us for only one day. He had no real right to be here at all, he told us, but had seized an opportunity to come one last time before all Hades was loosed on the land. Things were going rapidly downhill in every direction. His spies reported major trouble brewing in the north again, behind the Wall, and he doubted that the northern garrisons could any longer withstand an all-out attack from the strength that threatened them. The Picts, he believed, had amassed an enormous army reinforced with Scots from Hibernia and the wild men from the Germanic lands across the water to the east. These were not Saxons, he told us, but a different race altogether, bigger and more savage than the Saxons. I had heard of these Northmen, as they called themselves. I said nothing, and his father asked him about his cavalry. How was Seneca doing?

Picus thought for a few moments, and when he replied, his answer was not encouraging. His cavalry was virtually useless, he said, because of the Wall itself. We had known that from previous reports. All his people could do was ride east or west in front of it. Theodosius had walled up the gateways after the Invasion back in '67, so Picus's cavalry could not use their strategic advantages against an enemy who could not be reached. The Wall, built to defend Britain from the Picts, was now defending the Picts from Roman cavalry. But Seneca, he said, was still doing a noble job up there, which would have been more surprising had Picus himself not recently sent Seneca some of his own finest officers to keep the sullen legate on his toes. Their presence, and their unimpeachable loyalty to Picus, were effective and ongoing safeguards against either sloth, guile or treachery on the part of Claudius Seneca— safeguards that Seneca bore with scant grace and less liking, although he put up with them nevertheless, lacking any alternative. Seneca, therefore, was continuing to soldier and making the best of it, now and again showing those surprising flashes of leadership and genuine military ability that were forced to the surface, Picus had no doubt, by the rigid confines of the life he was forced to live. In spite of that, however, Picus still watched him carefully and constantly. Seneca's hatred of the Britannicus family was pathological, and vigilance, Picus knew instinctively, could never be relaxed where he was involved. I listened to all of this without comment, thanking my private gods that Seneca was well out of my life, and thinking that he, too, must now be showing the ravaging effect of passing years.

The following day, when the time of Picus's departure came, I could see that he was reluctant to leave his bride, and I sympathized with him. He dallied with her, procrastinating until the time he had set himself for leaving was past and gone, and when he did come to say farewell to Caius, Ullic and myself, he made us promise to look after her for him when her time came.

His father slapped him hard on the shoulder. "Come, Legate! That's seven months away. We'll see you long before then."

Picus was sombre. "I hope so, Father, but I doubt it. I have a bad feeling in my guts about this one. The raids are heavy already, all along the eastern and southern coasts, as if the troubles in the north were not enough. All the signs and auguries are ominous. I'll be writing to Enid often." He smiled a small, embarrassed smile. "She made me promise. I'll keep you up-to-date on what's developing. If anything threatens you here in the west, I'll do my best to make sure that you know as soon as I do." He saluted us and spun on his heel.

As he rode away, Enid stood once more on the walls between Caius and me, her eyes following his every move until the distant forest swallowed him up. She was a beautiful and healthy woman in her early thirties, and all her attributes were enhanced as her belly grew with the child she bore.

But the months passed in unbroken train and Picus did not return to soothe his bride, although he maintained a steady stream of news to her, and so to all of us. From these dispatches we learned of the final fall of the great Wall of Hadrian. The garrisons that had manned it were withdrawn to Arboricum, and all the lands between there and the north were left abandoned. We learned also of a great invading force hammering inland from the Saxon

Shore, and of the desperate countermeasures being taken to push them back into the sea again. And then the news stopped coming.

We had become accustomed to receiving dispatches every week, and then came a week when none arrived. It was followed by another, and by the third week, we were all alarmed. Three more weeks passed, and one of Alaric's priests brought us the news that Picus was alive but had been sorely wounded, struck down in battle by an arrow that had pierced his face, entering his open mouth and striking sideways through his head to emerge behind his right ear. No one knew whether he would survive, but according to the priest, he had been lodged in a villa to the north of Lindum, with the family of one Marcus Aurelius Ambrosianus, a Roman magistrate. He was receiving the finest medical attention, and his fate was in the hands of God.

Enid wanted to go to him immediately and was restrained only with difficulty. Logic had little effect on her, but we finally made her see that her journey would be a wasted one, and possibly highly dangerous to the child she carried. The priest who brought us the news had been long on the road, and by now anything could have happened. Picus might be already dead and buried, a terrible thought but one that had to be voiced, since the report was that his wound was grievous. Or he could have been moved. He might even have recovered enough to go back to duty, at least administratively. On top of all of this, the world outside our own small Colony was too chaotic with marauding armies for us to permit a woman, especially a pregnant woman, to go riding off by herself, even with a well-armed escort.

Alone with my thoughts, I tried to visualize the wound he must have taken, and I did not like the thought of it. I even took an arrow in my mouth and prodded the back of my throat with it. Not pleasant! When I tried to imagine the effect of a hard-shot arrow finding the same soft spot, my mind rebelled. I determined to find a way to protect a horseman's face from such a shot, which must have been angled upwards from beneath.

Some time later, we received information that Picus had indeed survived, but the story was such that we could only wonder at it. Again, the news was brought to us by a visiting priest. Marcus Aurelius Ambrosianus, Picus's host, had apparently lost his senses and attacked the Legate one night while he lay sleeping. Picus, whose face was swathed in bandages, had not known his attacker and had strangled the man to death before help arrived. There was no question of premeditated murder, or of anything else except a mindless tragedy. The attacker's sword was bloody where he had stabbed the sleeping Picus in the side, and when the guards arrived they had found Picus, still wrapped in his tangled bedclothes, with his hands locked in a death-grip round the dead man's throat. It was impossible that Picus could have known who his attacker was. The room had been in darkness and Picus himself was blinded by the bandages that swathed his head. Here was a mystery that would remain unsolved, at least until Picus himself came back to explain it to us. We hoped that would be soon, for it was apparent to all of us that the nature of his wounds must be serious enough to preclude, temporarily at least, his further fighting.

In spite of all our hopes and prayers, however, Picus had not yet returned when Enid was brought to childbed and delivered of a healthy, bawling, leather-lunged brat of a boy at the fourth hour of the morning of the second day of January.

Only three nights before, Caius, Enid, Luceiia and I had sat around the fire discussing the impending births of our grandchildren. There was no news of Veronica from Ullic's kingdom, but no news was good news.

"What will you call him, if he is a boy?" Caius had asked Enid.

She smiled into the fire. "Picus and I talked about that. He will be Picus Caius Britannicus."

"Another Caius Britannicus. Why?"

She turned to squint up at him, for he sat above her, perched on the arm of her couch. "Why? To honour you, of course. Does that displease you? Or surprise you?"

He smiled and caressed her high-piled hair. "No, my dear, of course not. But you could please me more by changing it."

Enid hitched around in her seat to face him completely. "Changing it? The child's name? To what?"

He shook his head slightly. "I have no idea, child, but think of this place and what we have done here. This place is *British*. Its people are, too. We are a new breed here. It seems to me that the full name you would give your child is too Roman—too old-fashioned—for this time and place." He stroked her cheek with the back of his fingers. "Your son will have the blood of Celtic kings in his veins, Enid. Kings of Britain. So give him a British name, one of your own." He grinned broadly. "But none of your Celtic jaw-breakers. Make it a simple name, one that men will hear and know and remember. A name for this land. That would please me greatly."

She stared at him for long moments and then reached out and took his hand. "Thank you, Father Cay," she said. "I like that. I will think carefully about it and try to find something that will please all of us."

She named the baby Merlyn, after the blackbird whose magical songs filled the long spring and summer days throughout the length and breadth of Britain. Caius Merlyn Britannicus.

XXX

THE NEWS OF my own grandson's birth arrived from Ullic's people a short time later. No Roman nonsense there; the child, a boy, had been named Uther, Uther Pendragon. Mother and child were both well and would come to visit us in the spring, as soon as the snow, heavy in the hills this year, had melted.

I was content with the news of the children, but I was far from happy with the results of my attempts to pour a hilt for the new sword. Nine times I had tried it by the beginning of spring thaw, and nine times the result had been failure. Andros and I were convinced the technique must work eventually, once we had mastered the knack of pouring the metal in the correct volume, at the right speed and at the proper temperature, but our early efforts had been ludicrous, and I had often thanked God and my stars that the metal of the sword was as hard as it was, because I had been constrained to melt nine messes of bronze and gold from the adamantine tangs, cleaning them completely after each failed attempt. It was starting to prove expensive, too, for we were never able to reclaim all of the gold from the abortive attempts, and each time we tried again I had to melt a few more coins of Grandfather's hoard.

Perhaps it was because I had so much on my mind at that time that the significance of what Luceiia was saying escaped me when she told me that the two children, Uther and Merlyn, had been born at the same time, the fourth hour of the morning of the second day of January. Later, when I thought about it, I laughed to myself at the old wives' mutterings that would give the baby boys power over each other's lives in the years to come because of the coincidence of their birth. As I have said before, I never was a superstitious man, and although I was prepared to grant the strangeness of the timing, I well knew the cause of it. Had they been born together, under the same roof, I might have given the matter some more thought, but that is useless conjecture; they were born sixty miles apart, and they were as different as day and night from the time of their birth. Caius Merlyn Britannicus and Uther Pendragon would live their separate destinies. The cousins would grow up knowing each other well, but as individuals, with but little influence each on the other. I put the matter out of my mind and concentrated upon my own immediate problems.

And so it was that dawn of the Ides of March that year found me sitting alone in the smithy, waiting for my tenth mould to be cool enough to crack open, and looking admiringly at the silver blade of the sword that projected from the great cubic mass of the mould like a tongue of liquid light. I remember wondering then if I would ever be able to hold it properly in my hand as a finished sword. I touched the mould tentatively. It was still too hot. I hissed with frustration and impatience and made my way across to the villa in search of something to break my night's fast. I had not slept at all that night, but I had little awareness of that at the time. I was too tightly wound, like an overstressed spring, to think about sleep.

I heard my great-nephew Merlyn howling as I entered the villa. His mother had made her permanent home there since his birth, living in one small section of the house and refusing to have servants wait upon her. She was a Celt, never comfortable with having other people do the work she considered to be hers by right. As she put it, she could not enjoy having other people live for her. Because she was so obviously sincere in this, we humoured her, leaving her alone to look after her section of the big house, and the servants came down from the hill on two days each week to maintain the rest of the building. We made sure, however, that someone from the household stayed with her each night. Caius and I had both been there the previous night, so I had felt no guilt about spending the entire night in the smithy.

I followed the sound of infant wails to the kitchen, where I found Enid heating food in a pan over the fire. I greeted her and picked up the boy, soothing him into silence.

"Is he hungry, Enid? Is that why he's crying?"

"No, he is a pig," she smiled. "That's why he's crying." The baby was quiet now, staring up at me with great, brown eyes. She came and pinched his fat cheek gently. "A greedy little pig, aren't you? He's sucked me dry this morning, so he'll have to wait. Even a cow runs dry, you know!" This last was to her son, who ignored her.

"What are you heating there? Is there enough for me?"

She nodded, stirring the contents of the pan. "There's enough for all of us, but Father Cay hasn't stirred yet." She paused for a heartbeat and then asked, "How old is Caius, Publius?"

"Cay? Let's see . . ." I had to think about it for a few moments. "Well, he's about five years older than me, I think, so that would make him sixty-two or sixty-three, something like that. Might even be a little older. Why do you ask?"

She frowned slightly. "I don't know. He seems to me to be ageing quickly, that's all."

"Ageing quickly? You think so?" I was surprised. "I haven't noticed anything. Not recently, I mean. There was a time, back a few years ago, when I really worried about him, but he came through that, and he's been in excellent fettle ever since . . . At least, I haven't noticed anything to indicate otherwise. You evidently have. What is it?"

She shook her head. "I don't know, Publius. It's nothing obvious, but it is there. He seems to tire quickly nowadays and he sleeps more than he used to."

I laughed at that, tossing the baby gently into the air and catching him before he really lifted out of my hands. "That's because this fellow here has made him a grandfather. I mean, Cay is over sixty, Enid. Most men never see that age. The few who do tend to slow down afterward, particularly if they are spending most of their time playing with babies."

"Hmmm, I suppose they do." She tilted her head to one side in a gesture I had become familiar with and accepted my opinion. "I am probably imagining things. Put tomorrow's emperor down and come and eat. I'm famished even if you are not."

Caius joined us as we were finishing our meal, and he and I chatted together as Enid moved around preparing food for him, and then I left again to resume my vigil at the smithy. As I was leaving the house, I met Plautus coming in to visit and so I stopped to talk with him, too. It was one of those brilliant early mornings that presage a glorious spring day. He asked me where I was going and I told him that I was about to crack the mould for the tenth time. As soon as he heard that, he wanted to come with me and watch the operation.

"Are you quite sure about that, Plautus?" My question was only half in jest. "I am not the most pleasant or courteous person when my moulds do not turn out correctly."

"What's new? You've been an unpleasant whoreson ever since I first met you."

I grinned. "Well, don't say I didn't warn you. Andros should be here any time now, so we may have to wait for him. He has worked as hard as I have on this thing."

Half an hour later Andros had still not appeared and I decided not to wait for him. Plautus had been rooting among the shelves at the back of the smithy and I called him over. He came towards me clutching something in his hand.

"What's this?" he asked me.

I looked at the hardened roll of material he was holding and smiled. "You'll never guess what it is, Plautus, but it's the same as this." I picked up a square piece of supple, silvery material with the softness of fine leather and the paradoxical texture of fine sand and held it out to him. He took it from me, rubbed it between finger and thumb and then looked disbelievingly from it to the hard roll of stuff in his other hand.

"What is it?"

"It's shark skin. Belly skin."

He blinked at me, confusion in his eyes. "From a shark's belly, you mean? The big fish? What's it for?"

I grinned at him. "It holds the shark together, idiot!" I pointed at the sword sticking from the mould. "And it's for that. It will wrap the hilt of my new sword, so it will never slip in anyone's grasp."

"Hmmm!" That was his only comment. "I wonder what happened to Andros?"

I stood up. "I don't know, but I'm not waiting any longer. Come on, you'll have to help me. I'll tell you what to do."

It took another half hour before all the tight-twisted binding wires around the mould had been loosened, and I stood shaking with anticipation, my hands on opposed top corners of the mould, ready to crack it open. Plautus held two bottom corners.

"Well," I sighed, tensely, "we'll never know if we don't look, Plautus, so here we go!" I twisted and jerked upwards, and the mould came apart with a soft crack. Slowly, hardly daring to hope any more, I looked down in silence.

"Well?" Plautus's voice was filled with anxiety. I relaxed slightly.

"It seems to be fine on this side. I hope the other one is as good." I levered upwards on the blade and peeled the hilt audibly from its bed, turning it over as I did so. It was flawless. I slumped back onto my stool, overwhelmed with relief, my long-held breath whistling out forcibly.

"What's the matter?" Plautus was almost sick with worry. "What's wrong with it?"

I raised my hand to soothe him and spoke quietly. "Nothing is wrong with it. It looks exactly right."

Plautus let go his breath in a long rush and slumped down, too, onto a bench. "Thank God! I thought for a moment there you'd fouled it up again!"

We sat in silence for a time, staring at the hilt. It was dusty, covered with a waxy film, and tiny knobs of metal projected from it in a number of places where the molten metal had filled the air holes in the mould. These I would file off in a few moments, once I had recaptured my breath completely. I was beginning to feel a mighty exaltation. The gold cockle-shell of the pommel was perfect, as was the junction where the second pour, the gold, had knitted to the bronze of the first pour.

"Now what, Publius?"

I smiled at him again, feeling weary and yet triumphant. "Now I clean it, polish it and add the shark-skin grip."

"How long will that take?"

I shrugged. "An hour, perhaps less, to clean it and polish it. A day to add the grip, I would guess."

"May I hold it?"

I shook my head. "No, not yet. It's not ready yet. Give me an hour to clean it, then you can hold it."

"May I watch while you clean it?"

I laughed at his little-boy eagerness, but I was pleased. "You can watch." I reached for a small file on the bench.

Less than an hour later the job was done and the effect was breath-taking. The golden cockle-shell pommel was superb, every line cleanly etched, and the Celtic scrollwork on the thick cross-guard was crystalline in its purity. I had avoided grasping the hilt in all this time, and I had not used the file on the gritty texture of the hand-grip itself. As I applied one final flourish with the polishing cloth, Plautus was fiddling with the shark-skin square.

"You know," he said, "I don't want to sound critical, but this stuff is almost as silver as the blade, and the pommel's gold. Your cross-guard is going to look dull by comparison. It's just plain bronze. Had you thought about that?"

"I've thought about it." I stood up and eased a kink out of my back. "I'm going to coat the cross-guard with silver leaf."

"With what?"

I pointed to a box close by his hand. "Sheet silver, beaten so fine that it's almost weightless and transparent. There's some in that box there."

While he was looking at the silver leaf, I released the sword from the clamps that held it and closed my fist firmly around the hilt for the first time. "Now!" I swung it into the air and my heart almost broke with joy to feel the beauty of it in my hand. All the worry, all the fears, had been for nothing. Our agonizing calculations of the weight and balance had been accurate. *Now* I was holding perfection!

"Excalibur," I said.

"What?"

"Excalibur. That's its name. That's what I've called the sword. That's what it is."

Plautus blinked at me. "Excalibur? I must be stupid. I've never heard it before."

"No, Plautus," I said, "you're not stupid. It's never been said before. Calibur—*qalibr*—is the north African desert people's word for a mould. This came out of a mould . . . Excalibur." I handed it to him. "Don't touch the edges, if you want to keep your fingers." Minutely graduated lines rippled like water-marks along each side of the long blade, flowing outward from the thick central spine to edges sharper than any I had ever known, reflecting the light in their patterns and showing where the metal had been folded upon itself and beaten times without number during the tempering process.

He grasped the hilt and swung the sword and his eyes grew wide. "My God! What a weapon! Excalibur." He swung again and ended up with the point towards the open door just as Andros appeared in the opening.

Andros crouched in the doorway, squinting with sundazzled eyes into the blackness of the smithy. "Publius? Are you in there? Picus is home."

"Picus?" I swung to Plautus in pleased surprise. "He's here? That's wonderful! Have you seen him?"

Andros had come into the forge now and he was gazing at the sword in Plautus's hand as his eyes adjusted to the darkness. "You opened it! Did it work? Is it right?"

Plautus held the sword out to him. "It's perfect," I said. "We have made a masterwork, you and Equus and I. Where is Equus, by the way? And when did Picus arrive?"

He was gazing at the hilt from a distance of about a handsbreadth, peering closely at the details of the scrollwork and the cockle-shell as he answered me. "Equus is up on the hill at the other forge. I was there with him for a while, working on some drawings he has need of." His voice was barely audible, so intent was he on examining the hilt.

"And Picus? When did he come?"

"Hmmm? Oh, Picus. Just now," he muttered. "I saw his big standard above the hedge along the lane, headed to the villa."

"You mean just now? This very moment?"

He threw me an uncharacteristically impatient glance, irritated at being distracted from his examination. "Yes, that's what I said—just moments ago. I saw him just as I turned in through the gate to come here."

"How does he look?"

He frowned slightly, still peering at the gold cockle-shell. "I don't know. I didn't really see Picus, just his standard, above the hedge. I told you that."

"So you did. I'm sorry. I'm distracting you from your triumph. What do you think of it?"

"It looks good. Very good. I'm pleased. Does it work?" He reversed his grip and held the sword properly, looking around him as though searching for something to test it on. The look on his face made me apprehensive.

"Andros, have you ever swung a sword before?"

He threw me a preoccupied look. "No, I haven't. What difference does that make? I've never made a successful mould before, either." He walked quickly across to an anvil and slapped the flat of the sword against the tongue of it. The sound of the impact rang as clearly as the note of a bird. I looked at Plautus and shrugged my shoulders in bewilderment as Andros looked around again and fastened his eyes on my work-bench. He stepped determinedly to the side of the bench, whacked the sword blade against one of the legs, whipped the blade upright and pressed the end of the pommel to the table-top. The effect was magical. The whole room suddenly reverberated with a deep, musical hum that emanated from the sword itself. Plautus actually blessed himself with the sign of the cross and I raised my own hands to my ears, so intense was the sound. Gradually, over a lengthy period of time, it lessened and faded away entirely. The silence stretched and stretched.

"What was that?" I asked Andros.

He smiled his familiar, modest smile. "I don't know what it was, Publius, but I remember hearing somewhere, a long time ago, that the old smiths used to test their iron blades that way. The better the quality of the metal, the purer the sound it would produce when you did that."

"I've never heard of that," I said. "Let me try it." I did what he had done and again the vibrant, clean note filled the smithy. "That is astonishing. What do you think, Plautus?"

Plautus merely shook his head, his eyes on the sword. "Excalibur," he said. "The singing sword. I've never seen or heard of anything to match it."

I swung it, hissing, around my head. "There never has been anything to match it, that's why! Come on, let's go and show it to Caius and Picus, and to Equus. He is going to be angry to have missed its emergence from the womb."

We walked out into the sunlight, squinting against its brightness, and as I went I swung Excalibur from side to side, revelling in the apparent weightlessness of it. As we entered the lane leading to the main courtyard of the villa, I swung at a young sapling growing in the hedgerow and sheared through it completely without effort. I was wiping the sap from the blade with the hem of my tunic when I heard Plautus say, "That's peculiar!" Something in his tone alerted me even before he gripped me by the elbow, pulling me to a halt.

I looked up in some confusion. "What is? What's peculiar?"

He was standing motionless, staring towards the villa in an attitude that immediately set my nerves on edge. I hadn't seen that look in years, but I responded to it immediately.

"What's wrong?"

He nodded towards the portico. "You tell me!"

I could sense him withdrawing into his inimical, soldierly persona and I followed the direction of his look. Eight horses stood outside the main doors of the villa. Eight horses, all riderless. No guards. No one left outside. No one left waiting. All eight men had gone into the house. I felt goose-flesh stirring the small hairs on the nape of my neck at the wrongness of the sight before my eyes picked up another signal that was wholly out of place: a patch of black and white on the ground. It was Picus's great black and white standard! The one he had said was meant to be recognized from a great distance. It had been discarded casually, thrown aside on the ground as though its bearer had no further use for it. All my defensive instincts were now aroused, alarm-signals jangling. I heard Plautus say, "Shit and corruption! I haven't got a sword!"

His mind was far ahead of mine, but those words galvanized me. I rounded on him, a thousand thoughts jamming into my mind all at once.

"The smithy," I told him. "Against the left wall, where the mould was—there are two long-swords leaning there, and daggers and *gladia* on the table-top. I'll wait for you." He was gone almost before I had finished speaking. I dug my fingers into Andros's arm. "Andros, can you ride a horse?"

"If I have to, I can."

"You have to! Get back to the smithy and get your arse up onto my horse." I looked along the valley floor towards the bottom of the new road. Something was badly wrong, but I did not yet know what it was.

"Look, Andros," I said urgently, "something stinks here. I don't know what it is, but I want you to get up to the fort as fast as you can, by the back way, up the rear of the hill, out of sight of the plain, to the postern door. Do you hear me?"

He nodded. He had not read the same signs Plautus and I had, but he had read our reactions to them accurately. "Then what?" he asked.

"Find Tribune Bassus. Tell him I sent you, and where we are. Tell him I smell something rotten. If there are any of Picus's troops in the valley below the gates, I want them contained. In any event, I want a squadron of cavalry down here at the villa as fast as he can get them here. Have you got that?"

He nodded again. "What's happening, Publius?"

"I don't know, Andros," I said. "But something stinks. Get up there fast, and make sure nobody sees you. I don't care if you have to tie yourself to the horse, just get there as fast as you can. Will you do that?"

"I'm on my way, Publius." He was as good as his word, disappearing backwards towards the smithy just as Plautus showed up again, one of the new long-swords in one hand and a wicked-looking dagger in the other.

"Right," he said. "What's the plan?"

I stood there, hesitating for a heartbeat, staring towards the deserted portico, vainly hoping I was mistaken. "You really think there is something wrong, Plautus?"

"Horse turds, Varrus. Does shit stink? What now?"

That was enough. I sucked a deep breath. "What else? We have to go in. But carefully."

He threw me a look eloquent with unstated scorn. "You think I want to get my arse in a grinder for fun? At my age?"

Side by side, we ran across the empty space separating us from the main wall of the villa and flattened ourselves against the stone façade. We were about ten paces from the main entrance. He looked at me.

"What if they've left a guard inside the doors? We're dead. There's eight of the whoresons."

I grimaced. "Let's hope they haven't. If they'd meant to leave a guard, they would have left him outside to guard their horses, at least."

He nodded to me, formally. "You know, I've been wondering for years why Britannicus promoted you all those years ago. Now I know. You think. I suppose that's the final difference between an officer and a grunt like me." He was talking purely for effect, attempting to bring us both to the correct frame of mind, but as he said the words Enid screamed, loud and long, from inside the house. The sound made my blood curdle.

"Oh, shit!" he said. "That proves it. *Now!*"

Together we launched ourselves towards the entrance, diving through the open doors and separating just inside, throwing ourselves one to each side of the hallway. The place was deserted. Another scream rang out, agonized and harrowing, undistorted by distance and walls this time, from the back of the building.

Plautus waved me forward and we ran together again through the main atrium of the villa towards the living quarters at the rear, trying to make our sandals slide silently over the marble flooring of the hallways. In spite of my limp, I was slightly ahead of him as we reached the double doorway leading into the small, tessellated courtyard in front of Caius's day-room. I knew this was where they were and I waved him frantically to the side before he could charge through the doorway and betray our presence. We ended up staring at each other, holding our breath, one on each side of the open doors. He wiggled an index finger at me, indicating that I should take a peek. I inched my head forward, straining to hear and see without making myself visible, and heard an indistinct babble of sound coming from the room. The small courtyard beyond the doors where we stood seemed to be empty. I gritted my teeth and leaned out to look. It was. The doors of Caius's day-room were partially open. I bit my lip. But they were also partially closed—enough, I hoped, to cover our next move.

Plautus was watching me intently. I held up my open hand towards him, fingers extended, and mouthed, "In five!" He nodded, and I began to count, flexing my fingers with every beat. "Five—four—three—two—go!" Together, we eased ourselves around the doors in front of us and slipped sideways, each against the wall on his side, moving swiftly and silently, sidling towards the partly open doors that screened us from the people inside the room. As I came to rest with my back against the wall, my eyes fixed on Plautus's own, the voice of the speaker came clearly to my ears and I recognized it with a chill of horror. Plautus knew it too; I could tell from the way his eyebrows shot upwards. Caesarius Claudius Seneca was speaking.

". . . would want me to look after his poor old father and his only son, knowing that he had been so badly wounded. I wish I could tell you how distraught I felt when I heard the news. Claudius, I said to myself, your duty is clear. You must attend to the family, the poor afflicted kin of the Legate Britannicus. He is the son of a senator, after all is said and done. Under these tragic circumstances, his family should be cared for. How will his noble father feel, I asked myself? And his beloved wife? And, I said to myself, if it should happen that the unfortunate Legate should be recalled by Heaven from this place of earthly sorrows before he has the chance to repay his debts to you, Claudius Seneca, it should be your right, your *pleasure* and your *honour* to ensure that his much-lauded first-born son, his only heir, should be absolved of all his father's debts and should earn his father's honours and his rewards from your hands. So here I am, come at all speed to remind all of you that the ways of God are great and strange."

My stomach was heaving with disgust and revulsion but I could not move, and Caius answered him. His voice sounded placid and normal, almost relaxed, although disgusted.

"I once heard Publius Varrus call you a sorry pederast, among other things, Seneca. You disgusted me then and you disgust me now, although I believe you are now degenerating even beyond description. Your voice grates on my nerves. It reeks of that unmistakable femininity that marks the true degenerate. It sickens me to know you are a senator of Rome. Let's get this over with and have done with it. I am no play-actor. You came here for me, to be revenged on me for the defeat you suffered at my hands in front of Flavius Stilicho. So be it. But let the woman and the child go free. They have not harmed you and they do not even know who you are."

"Now!" Seneca's voice was almost strident, and he was obviously speaking to his minions. "There speaks the voice of Rome! Do you hear that clarity?

That ringing tone? That is the voice that made Rome great! The voice of Cicero! Of Marcus Antonius! The cultured notes that made the mob forget they hated Caesar! That is the voice of Reason! Now you must all forgive me, while I peer aside, into my heart of hearts, and find my human goodness. And when I have done so, we will stand aside and let this poor, mute, heart-broken widow and her son depart, to nurture hatred in their hearts for us!" The tone of his voice changed again, abruptly and drastically, and I realized with a chill, although I had known it from the start, that I was listening to the ravings of a madman.

"Publius Varrus! Where is he? The guest of honour at our little gathering! Publius Varrus? Here? Never! you say. But I, who know so little of the fine things of your life here in your petty Colony, know more than that. My people have told me. If the famed Publius Varrus be not there within the villa, they have said, then search for him among the ashes of his forge, where you will find him labouring, his manly brow bedewed with sweat from his honest labours!"

Seneca fell silent and I glanced at Plautus. His face was grim. He jerked his head in a negative. Not yet. We might be listening to a mad dog raving, but there were seven others in there with him who were sane. Slowly, hardly daring to move at all, I put my eye to the crack of the door.

Caius stood over to my left, his back against the table that held his books. He was being held close by two men, one of whom, the one closer to me, held a *gladium* pressed against his neck. Enid knelt in the middle of the floor, her back to me, her head hanging. She, too, was being held by a pair of men. On the far left of my restricted view I could just make out a part of another man standing close to the doors. He was standing at parade rest, as far as I could see, so I assumed another man to be standing across from him where I could not see.

Claudius Seneca was seated at Caius's work-table, but because Enid and her guards were between him and me I could only see one, outstretched, sandalled leg. The eighth man was the only one I could see clearly, and I knew him. I had not seen him in more than sixteen years, not since that first confrontation at the *mansio*, but I recognized him immediately. He was the beautiful catamite who had worn the kohl on his eyes. Now he was older and no longer beautiful, and he wore the uniform of a military tribune, but his face still wore that petulant, feminine sneer. He stood with his back against the farthest wall, facing me, his arms folded on his chest, his eyes moving ceaselessly from Caius, to Enid, to Seneca and back to Caius.

Seneca had fallen silent, and no one else felt compelled to speak. Now he gathered his legs beneath him and stood up, looking directly at me. I thought for one panic-stricken moment that he could see me there, behind the door, but he spoke to the man I had correctly assumed to be there, out of my line of sight. His voice this time sounded normal—the clipped, professional tones of a soldier.

"You, Marius, and you, Dedalus. Somewhere in the grounds here you will find a smith's forge. The occupant will be Publius Varrus. Bring him here to me." The two men began to move but his next words stopped them. "Listen to me! I do not want him alarmed, or harmed. Make sure he has no suspicions. Be pleasant to him, and courteous. Salute him, and tell him the Legate Picus has come home and that he is here in the villa with his wife and his father. Say that the Legate is still convalescent and would like to see him. I don't care what you tell him after that, but bring him here without arousing his suspicions. I want to see his face when he sees me. If you disappoint me you will answer for it. Now go."

I heard the sound of two punctilious salutes and then two men marching in step towards the half-open doors. Plautus and I tensed, prepared to be discovered then and there, but the men marched out looking neither to left nor right and kept on going. That made the odds a little better, although they would soon be back.

I heard a scuffle and another scream and spun back to the crack in the door. Seneca had moved to the crib that held the baby and Enid must have moved to try to prevent him. Now she lay whimpering face down on the floor. Seneca was looking down at her, his nostrils wrinkled in disgust.

"I would have liked a son, you know," he said to no one in particular. "But I could not defile myself by stooping to such filth as has to be to get one. Ugh!" He shuddered. "Get the evil-smelling sow away from me. Get rid of her. Shut her mouth once and for all time. Not here, you fool!" This last was a shout at one of his men who had brought up his sword. The man hesitated, wondering what he was supposed to do, as Seneca leaned over the baby's crib and appeared to be tickling the child under the chin. Seneca spoke without looking again at either Enid or her captors, using that silly tone of voice people use when making noises at babies. "We don't want her filthy, evil-smelling female blood all over the floor, do we? Take her somewhere else, and do what you have to do. Just be sure to keep her silent." He straightened and turned to face them, his voice again the crisp professional's. "You may find you want to use her." He sniffed. "If you do, be quick about it and get back here immediately afterwards. But keep her quiet and make sure that she is dead. Hold her upright!"

They hauled Enid to her feet, side-on to my gaze. Her lips were split and blood dripped from her nose. Seneca drew his sword and cut the clothes from her fastidiously while Caius struggled futilely against the men who held him. When she was naked, Seneca looked her up and down, his features twisted in disgust. Her beauty was magnificent, but it held no allure for him.

"Look at this!" Enid's breasts, heavy with suck, were oozing milk around the nipples. He prodded one of them with the point of his sword, drawing blood, and turned towards his friend who still leaned against the wall. "A cow," he said. "A great, ungainly, unhygienic cow! Ugh!" He shivered with loathing and Enid spat on him. He turned back to her and punched her brutally in the stomach, and she grunted with pain and would have collapsed had she not been held.

"Whoreson," I thought. "For that alone, you'll die."

"Get the bitch out of here. She defiles my sight!"

As the two men began to turn her around, I leaned backwards and looked across at Plautus, who nodded, holding up two fingers. We pressed our backs to the wall and waited. Enid was a big girl and she fought hard, in spite of the pain she was in. It took long moments for them to wrestle her to the doors. I heard Seneca say, "Close those doors behind them," and I hoped Plautus had heard it too and would wait. They came through the doors, both men giving their full strength and attention to controlling Enid, who was struggling like a demented thing. As they left the room, somebody pulled the doors closed behind them. Plautus and I both sprang at the same time and the two men died before they even knew they had been taken. They died quietly, too, but before we could lower their bodies to the floor, Enid fell heavily, and the two men who had gone to search for me came back into the atrium. There was no point in silence now. We dropped both corpses with a clatter and a voice inside the room said, "What was that?"

"See to Caius. I'll take these whoresons." Plautus had already dropped into a crouch and was moving forward. Enid lay motionless where she had fallen. I swung back towards the closed doors just as they were flung open and I slashed Excalibur sideways in a hissing sweep at the first man who came charging through. Its tip sliced through the front of his neck as though it had encountered nothing. His eyes and his mouth went wide in disbelief and his momentum kept him coming. I side-stepped onto my bad leg, following the direction of my swing, and whipped a backhanded slash at the second man in the doorway, who had not had time to recover from his surprise. Again, it was the tip, the last six inches of the blade, that caught him. He was still almost seven feet from me and had just drawn his *gladium,* so his arm was bent upwards in the slashing position. My blade took him on the wrist, severing his hand completely before clanging against his helmet. From behind me came a clash of blades as Plautus met the others, and I threw myself forward into the day-room, slamming my skystone dagger to the hilt beneath the handless man's still upraised arm in passing, and jerking it out again with the weight of my forward momentum.

The scene that confronted me stays stuck in my mind like a memory of a mosaic picture. Seneca still stood beside the crib, frozen in consternation, his eyes and mouth wide open in anger and surprise, his hands raised in front of him, fingers pointing towards me. Caius had launched himself across the floor in a stumbling run, either to attack Seneca or to try to save the child, I do not know which. The Catamite, as I thought of him, was leaping towards Caius on an intercepting course, a dagger in his right hand, his left reaching for Cay. As I absorbed this, the two men met and the weight of the younger man took Caius over backwards, off-balance and falling. The Catamite, however, had more strength than I would have thought. His left elbow hooked around Cay's neck and held him up until they crashed together against the wall. Before I could react the Catamite had Caius pinned firmly in front of

him, his back arched against the pressure of the stranglehold, the point of
the dagger pressing into Caius's neck below the ear.

I hesitated and lost the initiative. I heard the slither of Seneca's sword
come hissing from its sheath and his voice filled the room: "Kill the old man!
This is the one we want!" And then Caius gave me back the initiative. He
brought up his knees and let his whole weight jerk his captor forward, away
from the wall. As the Catamite stumbled towards me off balance, I went for
him, swinging my new sword high and bringing it down like an axe across
his back. It caught him across the shoulders, slicing clean through the leather
cuirass that he wore, but it lodged there, caught in the toughened armour
for the space of two heartbeats.

I saw a flash of whiteness and jerked the blade free, whirling towards the
movement. Seneca was snatching the baby from its crib, holding it by its
bunched swaddling clothes, and Enid, beautiful, naked Enid, was throwing
herself on him. Their bodies came together and my insides screamed as I
saw the blade in his hand strike upwards. She convulsed, her whole body
seeming to hunch around the point of impact, and then he pushed her away
violently and stood there wild-eyed, like a demon straight from Hades, the
blood-stained blade in one hand and the screaming child, soaked with its
mother's blood, in the other. Enid fell heavily on her back, her arms across
her bloodied belly, her legs scissoring convulsively. Nearby, almost unnoticed
by me, the Catamite began to crawl away from the huddled shape that was
Caius.

"Stand away!" Seneca's eyes were glaring with that same sickening, empty
intensity I remembered. "Back! Stand back or the brat dies now."

"If the baby dies now, you will take months to die, Seneca, I swear to
you on his mother's blood."

"Then save him! Save the little bastard!" He hoisted the child high in
the air above his head so that it dangled, red-faced and screaming. His other
hand, raised high beside it, pressed the bloody blade to the child's gut. "Save
him, Varrus, you son of a raddled whore! Throw that thing down. That sword.
Now. Over here, by me. Throw it!" He was screaming at the top of his voice
and I was terrified that he would kill the child in spite of everything.

I had no choice. I looked at Enid's body, now grown still and odd-looking
in the strangeness of death. I looked at Caius and saw blood bubbling slowly
from his neck, around the hilt of the Catamite's blade. The Catamite himself
was about two paces behind me, crawling painfully, scrabbling at the marble-
tiled floor. I thought of all the blood and all the carnage and the misery and
pain that had spilled down from that one day so many years ago, and my
anger and grief overwhelmed me. My dear friend Phoebe had died for that,
and now Enid, and Caius. All the innocents. I turned my back on Seneca
and raised my new sword high. The skystone dagger fell at my feet as I grasped
the cross-hilt in both hands and drove the point downward, like a spear,
between the Catamite's shoulders and into his evil heart.

"Varrus!" The voice was an insane scream. "I gave you an order! Didn't you hear me? I gave you an order!"

I turned my head slowly, incredulous, to look at him, and at the sight of him I closed my eyes.

"That thing! That sword! I want it over here. Now!"

I gripped the hilt firmly and began to work it slowly back and forth, loosening it until I could pull it from the corpse, and then I flung it to him, beyond caring any more. The baby had to live. If I gave in to him, surely not even as demented a thing as he could kill a baby ...? The sword clanged loudly on the marble floor and slid to his feet. Still holding the infant high, he stretched with one foot and kicked it away from him, behind him.

"Now down! On your knees, you crippled pig!"

I felt every one of my fifty-seven years, and I felt my spirit give way inside me. A small, surprised and clear-toned voice inside my head was saying that I had never seen so much blood in one room before. It was everywhere, and none of it was mine, and none of it was Seneca's, but it was everyone else's. Even the baby was bleeding now, where Seneca had nicked his tiny cheek with his blade. I could see Cay's blood, and Enid's blood, and the Catamite's blood, and the blood of the other men I had killed. Soon now, I knew, I would see my own blood, too, for I had lost the will to fight any more. I wanted it to be over. My eyes blurred with tears and I sobbed aloud, not caring I was beaten, for I knew he would kill the child. I fell to my knees. I had lost track of time and place and reason. I saw only blood and I wanted an end to it. And then I saw Seneca straighten up even more and step back a pace.

"Get away!" he screamed. "Back, or I kill the brat!"

Bemused, I looked around me and saw Plautus framed in the doorway behind me, and my own sanity returned in a rush. I put one hand on the bloody floor and pushed myself to my feet.

Plautus still held the long-sword in his right hand. His left was clutched around the hilt of a *gladium* that protruded from his chest. His face was deathly pale and his eyes seemed to burn in their sunken sockets. He walked like a drunken man, one slow, staggering step at a time. There was death in his face—death for Claudius Seneca. Seneca side-stepped, moving crabwise away from him, screaming again that he would kill the child.

Plautus swayed to a halt. "Go ahead," he said, in a clear, small voice. "It's not mine. I don't care. All I care about is killing you, you stinking vomit."

I saw my skystone dagger lying on the floor at my feet; I saw Plautus take another lurching step; and then I saw Caius move, just as Plautus fell to his knees, blood gouting from his mouth.

Seneca, unbelievably, began to laugh, a high-pitched, gibbering giggle that chilled me. He took two more sideways steps away from Plautus, still holding the baby and his own blade high above his head, and then he shook them both, blade and baby, staring at Plautus, who was trying to regain his feet. At this point, Seneca's own right heel came to rest in the angle of the cross-guard of Excalibur. He glanced quickly down, saw what it was, and kicked it away from him again. It slid across the marble floor, this time to stop in front of the open eyes of Caius Britannicus.

Somehow, incredibly, Plautus staggered erect again and took another stumbling, implacable step towards Seneca. As he did so I stooped and snatched up my dagger. Seneca whimpered like a child, took another skipping step backwards and then rose to his tiptoes, stretching high in the air, his eyes darting from one to the other of us as Caius Britannicus somehow swung Excalibur from where he lay, flat on the floor. The edge of the shining blade sliced into the back of Seneca's bare knees, cutting the stretched tendons, dropping him immediately and flopping him backwards so that his shoulders hit the floor. The baby Merlyn landed on his dying grandfather. Seneca screamed like a woman, squirming frantically, trying to get up, but crippled far worse than I had ever been. The baby's screams were tiny, lost in his.

I walked across to where he lay, and it seemed to take hours for me to reach him. He scrabbled for me with clawed fingers, shrieking and spitting. I grasped the sword's hilt and pulled it free from where it was trapped in the fold of his legs, feeling it cut through more meat as I dragged it away. My face felt frozen. Caius lay behind Seneca, his screaming grandson clutched protectively in his left arm. The blood had ceased to pump from the wound in his neck. He was very still. I looked at his face, so pale, and time slowed down once more as I flexed my fingers around the hilt of the great sword. Then, ignoring the screams and sounds he was hurling at me, I raised Excalibur high above my head and swung it down with all my strength, striking Caesarius Claudius Seneca's head from his body. Plautus said, "Good man!" in a blood-choked voice, and I heard one last crash from behind me. I did not need to look to know that he had fallen on his face, onto the hilt of the sword that protruded from his chest.

Moving slowly, I crossed the room to the pile of garments that had been stripped from Enid earlier and draped them across her ravaged, nude body. Then I picked up my great-nephew and carried him out of that slaughterhouse.

The baby quieted as we walked through the warm, sunlit afternoon. I carried him in the crook of my left arm, the way his Grandfather Caius had carried him, and in my right I clutched Excalibur. Somewhere in the distance I could hear the sounds of battle, but I did not care. There was a lark singing in the sky high above me and a blackbird trilling close by. I heard my name being called and heard hoofbeats coming towards me at the gallop, but I didn't care. The forge would be quiet and safe for the baby, and it would be dark and warm. That was all I cared about.

I, too, had to find a dark, safe place, dark enough to hide me from the horrors tearing at my mind.

EPILOGUE: SUMMER, 401 A.D.

ULLIC CLAPPED ME on the shoulder, got up from his stool and went out into the bright, hot day, leaving his heavy, ceremonial helmet on the bench beside me. It crossed my mind to call him back for it, but then I thought that, eagle helmet though it might be, it was not going to fly away and he would come back for it later. I smiled at the thought and reached for the pot of polishing oil I had been using, but my outstretched fingers caught the rim of it and the pot overturned, spilling the thin oil over my work-bench. I cursed and scrambled to pick up the odds and ends threatened by the spill, and felt a lance of remembered pain pierce me as my hand closed over a rolled scroll that had lain forgotten there at the back of my bench for months. I stood as though petrified for a few moments clutching the thing, and then I sat back on my stool, leaving the spilt oil to do what it would and unrolling the parchment for the second time since I had received it.

Greetings, Father,
You have been proven prophetic. Stilicho has recalled me to Rome. The barbarian King Alaric—how unlike our own dear friend—and his Visigoths stand poised to attack the Motherland itself. My preparations are being made in haste, for I must move with all possible speed. Stilicho's word is peremptory. "Come at once," he bids me. "Bring your men and leave all else behind." That, in this case, means horses, since I have no way of shipping out all my stock at such short notice. Your commission from Stilicho entitles you to have what I cannot take with me.

I have dispatched word to my depots in Glevum, Durovernum and Londinium itself to expect your men, who will take the horses I have left for you. In all, there will be six hundred and eighty head. Collect them quickly. I proceed in haste, but there may be others who must follow later. I know you will use the horses well. I shall return for them some day.

I must rely on you to use your powers of explanation and persuasion with Enid. I have tried to write to her, but find I am unable to write the words I ought to. My wounds have healed, but they have left me speechless and unlovely, so she is encumbered with a husband who is

*both ugly and absent. Explain to her, if you will, that these cancel each
other out. I will return, some day. My love to Publius Varrus and his
family. Look after my wife and my son while I am gone.*

Farewell,

Picus.

*Addendum: I hear nothing of Seneca since I received my wound.
He may have died in the fighting in the north. I hope so. If he still
lives, however, he will sail with me to Stilicho's command.*

Even now, months later, the words still had power to hurt.

The soldier who brought the missive had disturbed me at my work.
Luceiia had sent him to me with his message and I had read it and sent him
to the kitchens at the fort, thinking he would have to return quickly. But he
had asked my pardon and informed me that he was Gwynn, and had been
Master of the Stables for Picus here in Britain. Picus had left him behind to
work with Victorex, who was now a very old man. Surprised, and still in a
state of shock from receipt of the letter, I had welcomed him to our Colony
and failed to understand the blankness of his look when I called it by name.
I had thought then to explain, but had not had the patience at the time.
Instead, I told him that he would learn the whole story later.

He had smiled at me and saluted crisply, saying he was sure he would,
and I stood there and watched him march briskly away, thinking how incredibly
young he looked to have already retired from being Master of the Stables of
the Imperial Armies of Britain, and thinking also that the story I could have
told him was not really long at all.

Caius Britannicus, who had built this Colony, had been born in the oldest
Roman town in Britain, a town built on the site of a settlement already
honoured for centuries as the home of Lod, war god of the Trinovantes of
the east. Over the four hundred years since then, men had gradually changed
its name to Colchester, meaning "the fort on the hill," but Caius had always
called it by its real name, its ancient name, Camulodunum, deploring as
usual the way men changed things for the sake of change, with no thought
of tradition or the ancient value of the thing thus changed.

Here in his beloved west, on another hill, he had built another fort, this
one without a name. It was his mausoleum, standing above his grave. His
sister, my wife Luceiia, had named it in his honour, recalling his own words.
"None of your Celtic jaw-breakers," she had said. "Give it a new name, this
fort on a hill—a British name, not Roman or Celtic. Not Camulodunum,
but a name of this land. And make it a simple name, a name that men will
hear and know and remember."

We called it Camulod, in honour of Caius Britannicus, the last of the
great Roman Eagles of Britain. When we are dead and gone, men may make
of it what they wish.

I released the scroll; it rewound itself with a parchment rustle, and I wondered if I would ever see Picus Britannicus again. Then I became aware once more of the smoothness of polished wood under the ball of my thumb and looked down at the surface of the case I had spent so much time making. I was not a worker in wood by choice, but I had had no other option than to make this case myself, using as a model the much smaller one left me by my grandfather to hold the skystone dagger, many years before. This case was of planed and polished oak, and set into the lustrous surface of the top was a silver star, trailing a comet-tail of gold. I picked it up and carried it to the back of the forge, where I opened it up and ran my hand once more over the fitted doeskin that lined the interior. It would suffice.

The sword lay where I had left it, wrapped in a silken cloth that Luceiia would have skinned me alive for taking, had she known. I undid the silk and lifted the weapon that it caressed. Excalibur! The name was right for it. Lightning flickered along its mirrored blade and sparkled on its finely tempered edges that bore marks like the ripple shadows of pure water. This was my lifetime's work: this single sword, unique from the tip of its blade to the scalloped pommel, a sword fit for a king to wield, a king whose day would come long after I was forgotten dust. Whoever he might be, he would have a sword to reckon with, and as long as Excalibur existed, I would never really be forgotten. I hefted it, admiring the play of light on its great cross-guard and loving the textured firmness of the hilt, bound in the belly skin of a giant shark. Caius Britannicus had never had the opportunity to admire the wonder that his Lady of the Lake had provided. But he had swung it once, before it was gripped with shark skin, and it had not slipped in his bloodied hand. I placed it gently in its case, into the doeskin-lined depression shaped so carefully to its size, and closed the lid.

Ullic's great ceremonial helmet still lay on the bench, and I picked it up and held it at eye-level, looking into the still-fierce, golden eyes of the eagle's head that fronted it above the massive, predatory beak. My professional interest was stirred briefly as I wondered how the artist who made this thing had kept the giant bird so lifelike, but then the eyes dissolved and I saw Caius staring into my face that day, almost fifty years before, when he had found me paralysed among a pile of corpses. A lump swelled in my throat and I grunted and jammed the helmet onto my head. I hoisted the case containing Excalibur up to my shoulder and set out to walk back to my house—to my beloved wife, who might or might not be there, dependent upon her ever-expanding timetable of meetings of the Women's Council—and to the rest of my family and the inheritors of our dream, the grandsons of my best friend and myself.

I wondered which of the two boys would wield the sword in years to come? Would it be Uther, already a brawler at six months and bold with his mother's magpie beauty, or would it be his gentler cousin, Merlyn, the golden-haired Britannicus? The debate gave me pleasure and I found myself whistling for the first time in months as I walked through the summer sunshine.

Equus was coming towards me, deep in conversation with Joseph, the young apprentice who was now our best craftsman. I saw what I had not noticed before—that Joseph was now a full-grown man—and I smiled, accepting the knowledge, once and for all, that the world belonged to the young people now growing, and that my own tasks had almost been completed.

AUTHOR'S NOTE

RANKS AND TITLES

In the Author's Note to *The Skystone*, the first book of the four-volume cycle *A Dream of Eagles*, I included some notes on the composition of the Roman army, the legions of ancient Rome. I have not reproduced them all here, because by the time the events in this book took place the influence of the legions had declined, and they play no significant role in the story that follows. A few terms remain, however, from that root, and they are easily explained.

The *cohort* was a legion's major operating formation, as today's Company is a regiment's, and the senior Warrant Officer of each cohort was known as the *pilus prior*—the front spear. The title of Lead Spear—*primus pilus*—was held by the senior Warrant Officer of the entire legion, the regiment to which the cohort belonged. The Commanding Officer of a legion was a Legate, and I have used that term interchangeably with the title "General," since that is what it means. Occasionally, a triumphant and popular general would be hailed in the field as *"Imperator"* by his victorious troops. *Imperator* literally means "Emperor," and by the end of the fourth century A.D., when Rome's day was almost over, many an emperor—most of them short-lived—was proclaimed in this manner.

The modern titles "Count" and "Duke" descend directly form the Roman titles and leadership roles of *comes* and *dux*, both popular in the late days of the Empire, but the best-known Roman rank today, thanks to Hollywood epics, is probably that of Tribune. Each legion had six tribunes, and they were the equivalent of today's Staff Officers: Colonels and Majors. The Roman court martial, with its jury of assembled tribunes, has given us the word tribunal.

ROMAN CAVALRY

By the end of the second century A.D., cavalry was playing an important role in Roman legionary tactics and represented up to one-fifth of overall forces in many military actions. Nevertheless, until the turn of the fifth century, the cavalry was the army's weakest link.

The Romans themselves were never great horsemen, and Roman cavalry was seldom truly Roman. They preferred to leave the cavalry to their allies and subject nations, so that history tells us of the magnificent German mixed cavalry that Julius Caesar admired, and which gave rise to the *cohortes equitates*, the mixed cohorts of infantry and cavalry used in the first, second and third centuries A.D. Roman writers also mention with admiration the wonderful light horsemen of North Africa, who rode without bridles.

Fundamentally, with very few exceptions, cavalry were used as light skirmishing troops, mainly mounted archers whose job was patrol, reconnaissance and the provision of a mobile defensive screen while the legion was massing in battle array.

Roman cavalry of the early and middle Empire was organized in *alae*, units of 500 to 1,000 men divided into squadrons, or *turmae*, of 30 or 40 horsemen under the command of decurions. We know that the Romans used a kind of saddle, with four saddle horns for anchoring baggage, but they had no knowledge of stirrups, although they did use spurs. They also used horseshoes and snaffle bits, and some of their horses wore armoured *cataphractus* blankets of bronze scales, although there is little evidence that this form of armour, or armoured cavalry, was ever widely used.

Until the fifth century, and the aftermath of the Battle of Adrianople, it would seem that almost no attempt had been made to study the heavy cavalry techniques used in the second century B.C. by Philip of Macedon and his son Alexander the Great. It was that renaissance, allied with the arrival of stirrups in Europe somewhere in the first half of the fifth century, that changed warfare forever. In terms of military impact, the significance of the addition of stirrups to the saddle was probably greater than that of the invention of the tank.

THE EARLY CHRISTIANS AND THEIR CHRIST

We use the name Jesus Christ today as though the two words were first name and surname, but that is a relatively modern usage. To the Christians of the

Roman Empire in the fourth and fifth centuries, Jesus was "Jesus, Christus"—Jesus *the* Christ—because *Christus* means *the* Saviour, *the* Redeemer. The definite article is built into the name. For that reason, the device shown on the left, known to us as the *Chi-Rho* monogram, was in widespread use at that time as the Christians' symbol of belonging.

The Greek letters *Chi* and *Rho*, joined in the monogram exactly as they are today in Christian liturgical vestments, were the first two letters of the written word *Christus*, and the *Chi-Rho* had long since replaced the sign of the fish, which had been the password of the earliest persecuted Christians.

PROPER AND PLACE NAMES

Most of the names used for characters in this novel would have been common in Roman times. The following is a guide to phonetic pronunciation:

Caesarius	Cee-zary-us
Caius	Kay-us
Claudius	Klawdy-us
Flavius	Flavey-us
Gaius	Guy-us
Luceiia	Loo-chee-ya
Plautus	Plough-tus
Quintus	Kwin-tus
Seneca	Sen-nic-a
Stilicho	Stil-itch-o
Tertius	Tershy-us
Theodosius	Theo-dozy-us
Valentinian	Valen-tinny-an
Vegetius	Ve-jeeshy-us